ROMULUS BUCKLE
& THE
CITY OF THE FOUNDERS

THE CHRONICLES OF THE PNEUMATIC ZEPPELIN

ROMULUS BUCKLE
& THE
CITY OF THE FOUNDERS

THE CHRONICLES OF THE PNEUMATIC ZEPPELIN

RICHARD ELLIS PRESTON, JR.

47NORTH

Text copyright © 2013 Richard Ellis Preston, Jr.

Published by 47North
PO Box 400818
Las Vegas, NV 89140

Cover illustration by Eamon O'Donoghue

ISBN-13: 9781611099188
ISBN-10: 1611099188
Library of Congress Control Number: 2012951771

For my parents, Richard and Janet.
For my wife, Shelley.
And for Kellie.

PART ONE:

FIRE, STEAM, AND HYDROGEN

–I–

THE MAGNIFICENT ROMULUS BUCKLE

ROMULUS BUCKLE WAS AN AIRMAN, a zeppelin pilot, to be exact, or, to be less exact, in the local slang, a gasbag gremlin, a dirigible driver, a balloon goose, an air dog, or whatever moniker any lazybrat might cook up in his gin-stewed cerebellum. Cap'n Buckle, as most of his crew called him, was a tree-tall fellow, six feet and a couple of caterpillar lengths more if he was an inch, his cheeks and chin scruffed with whiskers the color of sand dunes, in ample quantities for a man of the ripe old age of eighteen. He was shot bolt-through with aviator dash, that legendary, heart-stirring *dash*: he laughed heartily and often, and his eyes, deep and glacier-water blue, made women swoon (all except for the beautiful Martian named Max, of course, who found him far too droll).

One might think Buckle was young to be in command of a sky vessel as dauntingly impressive as the *Pneumatic Zeppelin*— and he was—but he led a crew whose average age did not exceed twenty years by much, except for Max, of course. Nobody knew how old Max was, and she was never in the mood for telling. But then, there was no "getting old" around the Snow World—the old California—in those days, not in the time of the Noxious Mustard (also referred to as stinkum if you were using gutter talk) and the Carbuncle Plague, with the nasty beasties a-lurkin', Bloodfreezer storms, and the high-percentage risk of one's blackbang musket exploding in one's face every time one pulled the trigger. Politically, everything was complicated by the little wars, the "skirmishes," with each clan almost always at odds with every other, their fears stoked by the shady trader guilds, which played them all against each other for a halfpenny's profit. Toss in roaming wolf packs of pirates and privateers to stir up the pot, and the entire situation became quite aggravated.

But, ah, the sky. The sky was the place to be as far as Buckle was concerned. It was no matter to him that zeppelineers were sitting ducks in their fragile steam clunkers that flew far too low, were notoriously difficult to bail out of, and were frighteningly susceptible to the catastrophic "pop" (steam engines, with their red-hot furnaces and boilers, did not really belong up in the sky inside giant fabric bags of flammable hydrogen, constantly battered and rattled around and shot at, not really).

Zeppelin pilots had a life expectancy of six months in a skirmish zone, one year in peacetime. But the second statistic was meaningless because all of the Snow World was a skirmish zone, always had been, at least since the day of The Storming (and nobody knew where that statistic had come from, anyway).

Buckle and his crew, members of the Crankshaft clan, had already lasted a year: a whole year since they had stolen the *Pneumatic Zeppelin* from the one-eyed Katzenjammer Smelt of the Imperial clan and made the spectacular airborne contraption their own. And like all the storied but doomed zeppelin captains and their crews, they took on a swaggering mythos that earthbound citizens would whisper about in awe, long after their heroes had been incinerated in midair somewhere over the Big Green Soup.

Zeppelineer swagger always started with the topper. Buckle's hat was a masterpiece, a black felt John Bull swimming with moving parts, a mechanical menagerie of steam tubes, brass gears, gauges, and a mercury-filled barometer. He liked to tuck the brim low over his eyes and tap it when he was thinking.

Buckle's long leather coat was lined with gray wolf fur, tanned a brown so dark it was nearly black, double-breasted with two rows of shining brass buttons on the chest. The coat was satisfyingly weathered, with a fur-tufted rip across the upper left shoulder, where a privateer's musket ball had punched through the cockpit glass and grazed him five months before.

Leather belts, in their fashion and width, were measures of an aviator's soul, and Buckle's belt was wide and intentionally plain, tucking the coat in at the waist and providing a holster for his pistol. He also wore the common airman's black trousers with a red stripe—though one rarely glimpsed them between the knee-length coat and his high leather boots.

The leather scabbard of Buckle's saber hung from two gargoyle-headed pegs at his left shoulder, the two gold tassels on its hilt swinging with the gentle vibration of the airship. Swordsmanship was a necessary skill for all zeppelineers, for the scarceness of steam-powered weapons and the unreliability of all blackbang-powder firearms, single-shot as they were anyway, was such that combat often fell to hand-to-hand, and the well-weighted sabers were the Crankshaft gentleman's (and gentle-woman's) bonecutters of choice.

Thus appropriately clothed and furnished, Buckle loved standing at his post two paces before the helm. He often shunned his captain's chair to plant his feet on the deck, and occasionally he would take the helm wheel himself, his hands resting on the brass sheathing burnished to a soft gleam by the hands of every pilot before. His spirit felt more alive when he was "plugged in," his top hat connected to the pressurized steam system of the *Pneumatic Zeppelin* so its gears crawled, tubes hissed, and barometer gurgled.

The *Pneumatic Zeppelin*'s bridge was a fantastic hive: within easy reach of each station loomed panel after panel of ornate levers, cranks, and knobs that spread out like a gigantic church organ, an elegant riot of vacuum tubes, steam switches, quicksilver instruments, brass gauges, and copper dials. The nose of the gondola was encased in a geometrically pleasing bubble of lead-glass panels framed by wrought iron, which provided the flight crew an expansive, if murky—the quality of glass was very poor at that time—view of the sky ahead. The glass was in fact so muddled that the crew often preferred to do sightings over the flank gunwales, which were open to the icy wind.

The forward section of the piloting gondola contained seven stations, for the captain, navigator, assistant navigator, ballast operator, engineer, helmsman, and elevatorman. The chief navigator was Sabrina Serafim. Her assistant, Wellington "Welly" Bratt, sat on her immediate right. Beside Welly was Nero Coulton, the ballast officer who operated the water and hydrogen boards (at the ripe old age of twenty, Nero was already monk-bald on the top of his pate). The engineering station, where Chief Engineer Max usually resided, was located aft of Nero. Immediately behind Buckle loomed the helm wheel, manned by Marcus De Quincey. At the portside window stood the equally impressive elevator wheel, and that station belonged to Lieutenant Ignatius Dunn. The last bridge post was located in the aft signals cabin, the little kingdom of Ensign Jacob Fitzroy.

The most colorful member of the bridge crew perched on a wooden stool alongside Buckle: the mutt Kellie (short for Kellie of Kells), a wirehaired mishmash of many dogs from which a terrier ancestor had emerged primarily victorious, was enthusiasm itself packaged in blacksilver fur with blazes of white on the paws, chest, and muzzle. Her large, fox-like ears, pink on the interiors, stuck straight up through the little leather pilot helmet she wore, and her leather harness sported a few mechanical gizmos of her own.

As the proud mascot of the airship, Kellie resided in Buckle's lap on long voyages, the two of them sharing an easy silence as the Snow World with its sky of never-ending clouds drifted past, while Buckle—on the surface an adventurer-soldier who exulted in action—relished periods of meditative quiet. Still, those moments were few and far between. His crew surely loved him because he treated them fairly and well, but even more so because when Lady Fortune frowned, when the fastmilk had suddenly soured or the ship was on fire and the hydrogen threatened to explode and the enemy threatened to board, all eyes turned to Captain Buckle—and he always found a way out of the fix.

Like the fix they were heading hell-bent for leather into now.

Buckle shifted his weight back and forth to get the circulation in his feet flowing. The *Pneumatic Zeppelin* was approaching her destination, and he was moments from shouting the order to perform a crash dive ("crash dive" was something of a misnomer where a lumbering zeppelin was concerned, but the term stuck nonetheless). They were descending into dangerous territory, and Buckle wanted to give any undesirables lurking below as little advance warning of their arrival as possible. A zeppelin was a big, fat, slow target to start with—no point in giving someone extra time to aim at it.

Buckle sucked in a breath of cold air to calm the flutter of nerves that always rose inside his chest just before they went into harm's way, and he liked the hawk-like sharpening of his senses that followed. Time slowed for him. Things became almost painfully clear. He felt every tiny shift in the airship's altitude and direction, knew every groan in the spars and decking, and was father to every shudder and shift in the propellers: his body was as much a part of the *Pneumatic Zeppelin* as her keel, and he knew her every ache and worry.

And he *knew* her. Yes, the *Pneumatic Zeppelin* was a rigid airship socked full of hydrogen cells, but she was such a magnificent machine that Buckle often could not escape the feeling that she was, somewhere deep inside, somehow alive. He spoke to her often, when they were alone. He felt that there was as much life in her as there was in a giant tree in the forest, a vibrant, hidden, ancient kind of life. He loved his ship, yes, his gargantuan dragon-daughter, who could be described as awesome, but not as beautiful. And, as the girlfriends—all lovely damsels of the Crankshaft clan—who had come and gone through Buckle's life could attest, no flesh-and-blood female stood to do better than second best against the beloved airship that occupied his every thought and attention.

Such things were not unusual. This was the way of most zeppelin captains. But Romulus Buckle, who could be described as a sort of kind, unintentionally effective rake, left a particularly catastrophic romantic wake, because girls fell in love with him at first sight, only to be ousted from his affections by the air machine, which would never, could never, do him wrong.

Buckle cleared his throat. "Ahead two-thirds," he shouted into the chattertube, grabbing the brass handle of the chadburn, the engine-order telegraph, cranking it forward on its dial to ring the bell and set the pointer to *Ahead Two-Thirds*. The chadburn emitted its normal puff of steam as the second identical pointer, controlled by the engineers in the engine gondola, swung into position parallel with the first.

"Ahead two-thirds, aye!" An engineer's voice rang high and tinny from a chattertube hood, the ship's voice-communication system.

"Fifteen degrees, down bubble," Buckle ordered. "Down ship. Crash dive."

"Crash dive, aye!" the elevatorman Dunn shouted, whirling the elevator wheel.

"Down ship. Fifteen degrees, down bubble, aye," Chief Navigator Sabrina Serafim repeated. "Crash dive."

"Vent hydrogen," Buckle said. "Twenty percent across the board."

"Venting twenty percent," Nero replied, cranking over the copper wheels on his instrument panel.

"Ahoy! Ahoy! You greasy cloud rats!" Buckle shouted into the chattertube mouthpiece at his left elbow, his voice loud enough to overcome the howl of the wind passing the gondola and the hum of the maneuvering propellers behind. "Eleven o'clock low! Target in sight! Man your battle stations! I repeat—though don't make me repeat it again—man your battle stations!"

They were about to embark on the most important mission of Buckle's career.

And the most dangerous.

But first, they had to pick up some cargo.

–II–

THE PNEUMATIC ZEPPELIN

BUCKLE TOOK HOLD OF THE wooden handles on the forward gyroscope housing as the *Pneumatic Zeppelin* plunged into her stomach-lifting drop. In his mind's eye he saw his huge airship swing down from the clouds, a razor-backed, torpedo-shaped monstrosity nine hundred feet long and one hundred and sixty feet in height, its fabric flanks fourteen stories high.

The sudden descent placed considerable stress on the airframe, but as always, Buckle's airship handled it well: her thousands of yards of canvas skin rippled in thunderous snaps over the circular metal airframes, every girder groaning in its flexible joint. Everything was pinned to the keel, which shuddered, sending a dull vibration into the decks of her three streamlined gondolas, piloting, gunnery, and engineering, all tucked tightly in line underneath, nestled inside endless miles of rope rigging and antiboarding nets.

From below, Buckle's ship looked like something of a shark, with the entire length of her underbelly encased in bronze and copper plates bolted and screwed together into a tight Frankenstein skin. Weight was always a concern for airships, so the metal plates were quite thin, but they provided an excellent defense from ground-fire "pottings." The piloting gondola under the bow looked like a long, gold-copper pod, its glass-domed nose reflecting the weak orb of the sun now forever locked behind a permanent overcast. Under its belly was slung the pneumatic turret and the long barrel of its cannon.

The air vessel's main cannons, housed in the gunnery gondola amidships, would have their muzzles showing, run out and ready to fire: ten firing ports lined the gun deck, five on each side, an ambitious number for a time when blackbang cannons—good ones that did not threaten to blow up both you and your entire tea party when you fired them—were rare and expensive. The *Pneumatic Zeppelin* carried five cannons—four twelve-pounders on the gun deck, plus a long brass four-pounder in the bow—still a quite respectable set of artillery for any clan airship.

Between the backside of the gunnery gondola and the nose of the engineering gondola, the 150-foot-long hull of the *Arabella*, the launch, would be visible, tucked up inside the belly of the *Pneumatic Zeppelin* and slightly offset from the main keel.

At the stern of the sky vessel, under the shadows of the cruciform fins and rudder, the four main driving propellers whirled, four colossal razors slicing the sky, churning against the whistling updraft of the wind as they thrust the behemoth forward. Dozens of exhaust vents, tubes, and scuppers—the "Devil's factory"—thrust straight out from the rear of the engineering gondola, snapping upward above the propellers like the legs of upturned spiders, spewing white steam, belching black smoke, and hissing water.

The *Pneumatic Zeppelin* was a machine of fire in a cold, cold world.

Slowly, evenly, Romulus Buckle descended, one with the *Pneumatic Zeppelin*, his mechanical monstrosity, a feather-light colossus, and as it came down it rotated slowly to port, casting a huge, equally rotating shadow on the blasted white landscape below.

-III-

SABRINA SERAFIM

CHIEF NAVIGATOR AND FIRST MATE Lieutenant Sabrina Serafim kept a careful eye on her instruments, measuring the *Pneumatic Zeppelin*'s altitude, pitch, and rate of descent. She occupied the forward portside chair in the nose of the cockpit, with Romulus Buckle's station at her back and Assistant Navigator Wellington Bratt seated on her immediate right. Sabrina was a perfectly slender version of a full-grown wood nymph, with a graceful, narrow, elfin face, its tendency toward Asian angles softened by hints of baby fat, and nothing less than pretty. Her skin was pale with a yellow hint to the pigment, clear except for a light smattering of freckles on her nose, but the constant flow of cold air through the gondola always pinked her face—the exposed cheeks between her goggles and silk neck scarf—into a pleasant glow.

What was most striking about Sabrina in the physical sense was her bright red hair, which she kept long but wore pinned up under her derby hat, with the exception of two flaming locks that always escaped above each temple and dropped down to brush her cheekbones. Her jade-green eyes inside her goggles brimmed with perceptiveness—a sort of sixth or seventh sense if you like—that could be disarming at times. Her derby, like Buckle's top hat, housed a stupendous contraption of gears, winder-cranks, and steam tubes, which puffed and rattled when she was plugged into the airship, which she was at the moment.

Sabrina dressed with drawing-room style, normally wearing leather gloves and a long, tapering leather coat lined with mink fur and sporting cuffed sleeves ringed with silver buttons; she loved fine details and had commissioned the best Crankshaft seamstress to embroider fine silver fleur-de-lis into the high collar and lapels. Under the coat she wore a white blouse with lace bunched at the throat. Her breeches were black with a red stripe like Buckle's, though hers were jodhpurs, which flared at the hips and narrowed at the knees, where they disappeared into midcalf boots in a fashionable tuck.

The stylish accoutrements notwithstanding, it was a bad idea to cross Sabrina Serafim.

Her nickname was not "Sabertooth" for nothing.

But no one called her that to her face: she didn't like it.

Sabrina also owned a sword, a red-tasseled saber she kept slung across two old horse-head pegs above her head, and she knew how to use it—in spades. She was left-handed and that was an advantage in a battle of blades, for it tended to confuse an opponent.

A light crosswind kissed the *Pneumatic Zeppelin* with the bump of a butterfly's wing; the titanic airship shuddered ever so slightly, so imperceptibly that no one aboard except the captain and chief navigator sensed the innocent tug of drag.

"Crosswind from the northwest, starboardside, Captain," Sabrina said as she reached for a wooden-handled lever, slowly sweeping it sideways as she watched her drift-measuring dial, as intricate as an Austrian grandfather clock, wavering in front of her. "Adjusting for horizontal drift, helm. Two degrees to port."

"Two degrees port, aye," De Quincey repeated, nudging the rudder wheel a tock or two. He was a big man and taciturn, rarely speaking of his own accord. His black hair swept about his long, stern face where his deep-set eyes and chestnut-brown skin offered a somewhat sinister countenance until one recognized his gentle nature. Sabrina liked him.

Buckle kept his eyes locked upon the rapidly approaching earth through the round observation window at his feet. Kellie circled the decking around the window, sniffing, tail wagging, anticipating high activity. "Keep your eyes peeled," Buckle said.

"Aye, aye, Captain," Sabrina replied, familiar with Buckle's thousand-yard stare, the intense functioning of his mind's eye just before the call to action. The maneuvering propellers responded to the drift controls and she felt the shift in their vibration ripple through her body.

"Descending, ninety-eight feet per minute," announced Welly.

Sabrina eyed Welly as he leaned over the drift telescope, calculating their rate of drift, his pencil scratching furiously across his navigational maps, pinned to the dashboard. The kid could have easily rounded up, described the rate of descent as one hundred feet per minute, but he was striving to impress and that was fine.

"Maintain dive," Buckle said, sounding almost annoyed.

"Boards steady, Cap'n. Aye," Nero said. It was Nero's job to bleed the hydrogen out of the cells at the correct rate to maintain the steady descent.

Sabrina mumbled the words she often mumbled, even though afterward she always regretted mumbling them, but she was by nature something of a cynic. "We're sitting ducks."

"Piece of cake," Buckle responded absentmindedly, as he had many times before.

"Sure, a real peach," Sabrina answered. She peered down at the shattered landscape and then leaned over her navigation table to check her map. She tapped her derby at the brim, where a little copper arm with a magnifying glass swung out of its nest among the valves and tubes, its miniature gears whirring with steam power, and dropped in front of her right eye. The map was old and blurred, stained yellowish by exposure to the mustard, as many things that had survived The Storming were; enlargement was required to make out the smudged small print.

Sabrina peered into the drift-telescope eyepiece affixed on the instrument panel in front of her. "Magnolia Boulevard intersection with Hollywood Way. One Three Four Freeway running east-west, due south. Right on target," she announced, with more than a smidgeon of pride in her voice. "Welcome to the Boneyard."

–IV–

THE BONEYARD

THE *PNEUMATIC ZEPPELIN* DESCENDED INTO the heart of the sprawling valley once known as the San Fernando. Low brown foothills loomed to the south and east, their rough backs striped with rivers of snow and ice. Buckle sniffed. Despite hundreds of years, the place still stank of ash. He did not like this—going to ground when a cunning enemy like the Founders might be on the move. There was no easier target than an earthbound zeppelin. It was little more than a bounce, yes—Buckle would have his feet in the snow for only a minute or two—and the likelihood of the reclusive Founders being anywhere near the Boneyard was almost nonexistent, but a little needle of anxiety stabbed him nonetheless.

Pluteus and his grunts had better be on time, on target, and ready for evacuation.

Buckle clamped his teeth. Once Pluteus and his soldiers were aboard, they would be on their way to the City of the Founders, the most powerful clan's fortified citadel, considered impenetrable to attack, on a desperate expedition to save their leader, Admiral Balthazar Crankshaft, from the clutches of the Founders, who had abducted him.

It was also of no small matter that Balthazar was Buckle's father by adoption, and really the only father Buckle had ever known.

"Airship sighted!" the aft lookout's voice rattled down the chattertube. "North northwest, five miles off the stern!"

Buckle leapt to the stretch of open sky at the starboard gunwale, pulling his telescope from his hat and whipping it out to its maximum length. Looking back, he caught the tiny black dot over the mountains with his bare eyes and trained the scope on it. The slipstream of passing wind dragged at the glass, making it difficult to see, but the bulky form of the magnified sky vessel suggested that she was a tramp, a trader guild steamer, and no threat to Buckle and his airship.

"Tramp!" Sabrina shouted, peering through the powerful main telescope affixed in the nose dome. "Heading east."

"Aye!" Buckle shouted back into the gondola. Due east meant the tramp was probably on her way to sell her goods in Gallowglass territory. And judging from how she lumbered, her holds were packed, probably full of ivory, fish, and whale oil from the coast.

Still, Buckle hated having a foreign airship of any kind at his back.

Pluteus and his grunts had better be on time.

Buckle looked down. As the *Pneumatic Zeppelin* descended to the earth, the blasted corpse of the Valley came into sudden, wince-inducing focus. The ground was a mess, a crumbled catastrophe of architectural ruin: endless miles of gutted buildings and abandoned suburbs collapsed down around themselves in a porcupine's back of naked girders, walls, and chimneys. The street grid was still visible under the debris, making aerial navigation easy.

But what made the place ghostly beyond description were the endless bones. The sea of bones. Ice-rimed skulls and rib cages, femurs and spines. Human bones, mostly, with surely some dog bones, cat bones, horse bones, bird bones, rat bones, possum bones, and squirrel bones mixed in.

They called it the Boneyard.

Unimaginative, but accurate.

Scouts reported that skeletons still sat inside the caved-in cars, bony fingers still clutching the steering wheels. Frozen bones snapped under one's boots with each step, the scouts said—an ocean of skeletons under the snow. Exposed bones were a pearly color, picked clean by crows, hawks, and vermin, the tattered remnants of their clothes long since carried off to line nests and burrows. An endless glut of rusted cars still lay locked in a traffic jam on both sides of the freeway, all heading northward; the tires had been an excellent source of salvaged rubber until exhausted only a few years before.

No official clan lived in the valley now, even three hundred years later. There were still pools of heavy stinkum gas lurking about, squirting out of unused pipes or suddenly surging up from toilets and sewers. But that was not the real reason: it was simply too spooky to live in that snowy swamp of bones. Some people did live there. People who didn't mind the horrors. People who stripped the cars and skeletons of valuables and traded the goods, all of them stained telltale yellow, with their fingers stained yellow, in the markets to the south.

Scavengers. Yellow-fingered Scavengers.

And Scavengers didn't like visitors unless they were coming to buy.

–V–

MAX THE MARTIAN

MAX, THE CHIEF ENGINEER, HURRIED down the main keel corridor of the *Pneumatic Zeppelin*. She had just come from the boiler room, where furnace number two, affectionately known as Smoky, had "spit" a seven-inch iron rivet (launched by the sudden snap of an overheated metal plate, the rivet was fired like a bullet out of a gun, leaving a little round hole in the outer skin), and the boilermen had been forced to shut it down. It wasn't a huge deal—the other five boilers could generate enough superheated steam to maintain the airship's systems at their highest efficiency—but Max hated going into action with malfunctioning equipment. And that happened far too often for her tastes, she had to admit.

Zeppelineering was not an exact science, by any stretch of the imagination.

It was more of a juggling act.

Max walked in the silent, gliding fashion of Martians, effortlessly, as if her hips were oiled, as if she were carried along by a friendly current of air. But she was not nearly as smooth as a regular Martian, because she was only half Martian. Her father had been a Martian, actually a descendant of Martian rebels, and her mother, bless her soul, was human. Humans and Martians found each other attractive and could mix if they wanted to, but this was rare, because there were only a few Martians. Since the time the aliens had arrived, the people of earth had called them Martians, even though it was clear they had come from much farther away than that. The aliens had never given up any information about themselves or where they had come from, and the few descendants of the survivors did not seem to know or remember.

Max knew nothing of her Martian ancestors. Her mother and father were long dead. She was another one of Balthazar's orphans, and as an alien she was fated to a lonely existence in the world. She had a brother, Tyro, who had been severely wounded in the Imperial Raid—he now lay in a coma, lost to her, perhaps forever.

Max wasn't Max's real name. But the alien name her father gave her was so unpronounceable by humans that something else had to be used to refer to her. Her Martian name contained many sounds that a human voicebox could not reproduce, but went something like *Kaa-speethththlojogga-rantan-(unintelligible)-skee-(unintelligible)-grtzama-klofgurt-(unintelligible) pivkthth-max.* When the name was actually pronounced by a Martian, about the only thing any human heard clearly was the last bit, "max," so everybody called her Max, including her mother.

Martians were a beautiful, rare species, tallish and slender and graceful, but their appearance took a little getting used to if you had not grown up around one of them. The stripes on every Martian face, which tapered to points about the temples, cheeks, and throat, were always unique to the individual. Max was only half Martian, but the Martian genes dominated her appearance: her white skin and black stripes were quite pronounced, and she wore the aqueous-humor-filled goggles that the Martians always wore because their sensitive eyes were irritated by the dryness of the earth's atmosphere. The clear, soothing water completely filled the goggles and made her hypnotically black eyes look bigger than they actually were.

Max wore a black leather flying helmet of the old style; it lacked the excessive cog and valve trappings of the pilot's, but its brass-tubing system for her goggles' aqueous-humor reservoir gave it a streamlined flash, and lining the crest of the helmet were a series of oval metal lockets that housed the sensitive devices she used to tinker with the most delicate parts of the *Pneumatic Zeppelin*'s vital systems.

From underneath the helmet flowed the long black locks of Max's hair, always unruly but sheer as silk, dropping to swirl about her shoulders. She wore a black turtleneck sweater under a knee-length, raven-black leather coat lined with ebony bear fur, black pants, and slim black boots that cupped just under her knees. All of the blackness in Max's clothes accentuated the white quality of her face and the swirling black stripes at the edges of it. In a way, it made her more alien than she needed to be.

But perhaps that was the point.

The *Pneumatic Zeppelin* was about to land in the Boneyard. Max wanted to be on the bridge, but she could not help trying to scrutinize every inch of girder, wire, pipe, bolt, and baggy-wrinkle along the long keel corridor that was the spine of the entire sky vessel, running nine hundred feet and nine inches from bow to stern. The huge hydrogen cells, twenty-eight of them in all, in fifteen compartments, loomed overhead, fabric cathedrals fourteen stories high, each strapped into position within a spider's nest of girders, wires, catwalks, ladders, and blast panels, always groaning and grinding under the stresses placed on such a city-sized contraption in flight.

Max's sharp eye caught a tiny jet of steam issuing from under the Axial catwalk over her head. A small feeder pipe had burst, probably under the stress of the crash dive. Stress. Managing structural stress was a big part of the chief engineer's job. Max was the master of a surgeon's array of tools designed to measure the amounts of force being applied to every inch of wire, rope, fabric, and metal inside the *Pneumatic Zeppelin*. Countering the effects of altitude, windstorms, and temperature fluctuations was an intellectual battle. She constantly assessed hydrogen flows and steam and water pressures in miles upon miles of pipes and tubes: there was always a leak springing up somewhere as the rigid but supple airship frame constantly shifted against the wind.

And the engines. The engines! The *Pneumatic Zeppelin's* six immense coal-black furnaces and boilers had been well built— her compliments to the Imperial clan's shipbuilders—but there was always a fine line between stoking them up to maximum efficiency and actually blowing them up.

As much as it pained the chief engineer, the feeder pipe would have to wait.

Max arrived at the forward circular staircase that wheeled down into the piloting gondola. Descending two steps at a time, she was in a rush to jump into the revolving turret of the hammergun—a pneumatic cannon—slung under the gondola's waist. The hammergun was not the chief engineer's official battle station, but Max had claimed the honor early on and Buckle had not been inclined to fight her on it.

Max alighted on the gondola deck behind Buckle, and with one smooth motion swung her body down into the hammergun turret. She attached her safety harness, plugged her headgear into the chattertube line, and wound the canister crank that opened up the hammergun's operating valves. The cocoon of bronze pipes around her hissed and creaked with the rising pressure of the superheated air.

"Nice you could make it for the show, Max," Buckle said without looking back. She could hear the usual smile in his voice. "We have a skirmish looming, you know."

"I would like to chat with the hack who bought us a box of substandard boiler rivets," Max replied, pressing forward the hammergun's priming levers with a satisfying metal-on-metal *chunk ka-chunk.*

"That would be Ivan," Sabrina said.

Max made a tiny, unconscious grimace. She didn't care much for Chief Mechanic Ivan Gorky. But it would be amusing to watch him fuss when she chewed him out.

"Any damage?" Buckle asked.

"Just a skin tear," Max replied. "Number two is shut down."

"Good old Smoky," Buckle grumbled.

Max pressed her gun-maneuvering lever up, pitching her and the turret forward so that the long barrel of the hammergun pointed almost straight down. Once the turret rotated into firing position, it was exposed to the outside air: the freezing wind battered her seat in its unkind but familiar fashion. She peered down the aiming sight, scrutinizing the snowbound landscape below. The cannon barrel was fully retracted, so it wasn't much of a sighting. She would not be able to extend it out to operating length until after they landed and then ascended again.

Her spine tingled. She loved operating the cannon, firing it, stalking any prey she could find. Martians were predators. The visceral charge of the hunt burned so hot in Max's half-Martian veins, she wondered how a full-blooded Martian could stand it.

–VI–

THE ART OF THE BOUNCE

SABRINA SAW MAX SWING INTO the hammergun turret and grinned inwardly. She always felt safer with Max on the gun. Max was deadly. And Max loved it, even if she would never admit to loving anything.

An odd pang struck Sabrina's gut, the sort of random emotion—rare for her—that came out of nowhere when one was completely occupied with some other task. This was a weird sort of sadness. Max was Sabrina's sister—in name only, for they were both adopted by Balthazar—but they had never been close. They had shared books and taken classes at the Academy together, but they had never sat together at the dinner table. They had never shared a secret.

"Fifty feet," Sabrina said. "Landing zone directly below. Magnolia and Hollywood Way. Rate of descent thirty feet per minute. Attitude zero degrees. Drift at one degree port bubble."

"Helm compensating," De Quincey said.

"Dead slow," Buckle ordered, ringing the chadburn device as he cranked its handle.

"Dead slow, aye!" engineering responded, along with the ring of the chadburn bell.

The roar of the propellers steadily decreased.

The piloting gondola hummed with the silence of expectation. The rudder and elevator wheels creaked ever so slightly as De Quincey and Dunn nudged them back and forth. A cloud of steam passed beneath the glass under Sabrina's feet, driven by a light tailwind from the exhaust vents at the rear of the gondola. Sabrina eyed the array of intricate metal gauges, cranks, dials, and levers around her, observing the static-inertia meter, a palm-sized glass orb of clear liquid encased in copper, where two large bubbles measured the *Pneumatic Zeppelin*'s horizontal and vertical level. The liquid was seawater "boil," a solution of distilled phosphorus algae. The boil would glow at night if one pressed the button to tap the agitation hammers within, thus disturbing the algae and making it generate bright, eerie bioluminescent swirls of greenish illumination. All of the vital cockpit instruments contained boil.

Sabrina heard Max cooing in the chattertube. Martian females had soothing voices, and cooed when they were pleased with themselves: it was a pleasant sound, a sort of a mix of a cat purring and a dove warbling. Max was a master of the coo because she was usually amused by herself and annoyed by everyone else. It was also her version of laughter, unless one could really get her splitting her sides. Sabrina could remember seeing Max laugh like that only once, when Sabrina was seventeen.

"Pleased with ourselves, are we, Max?" Buckle said, also aware of the cooing.

The cooing stopped. "Just be careful with my airship, Captain," Max replied, her voice hollow but loud over the chattertube connection. As far as any crew member was concerned, the *Pneumatic Zeppelin* was "my airship." "Another hole would surely ruin my day."

Buckle leaned in to his chattertube mouthpiece and shouted, "Eyes up! Wait for the signal!" He pulled his saber down from its gargoyle pegs and clipped it to his belt.

A signal flare rocketed up into the sky directly in front of the zeppelin's cockpit dome, leaving a curling trail of black smoke until it popped, its burning magnesium casting an intense white arc as it floated down and disappeared into the bones below.

"Signal flare sighted," Sabrina commented dryly. "Thirty feet to ground."

Welly spun a hand crank. "Lowering static lines," he said.

"Pluteus sighted!" Max's voice rang in the chattertube from her position in the belly turret. "Ten o'clock low."

Kellie barked, her tail wagging, ears bolt upright.

"Right on time," Sabrina said, nodding her approval as she eyed the copper-winged clock at her station. And sure enough, here came Pluteus B. B. Brassballs and his twenty-man company, filing through the snowdrifts, rubble, and bones. They were close, but Pluteus and his Crankshaft clan troopers, referred to as the "Ballblasters," were never easy to see: the soldiers wore dun brown and white to match the dirty snow, and dulled the brass on their rifles to prevent them from gleaming in the diffused sunlight.

Pluteus and his men were the closest thing the Crankshaft clan had to an army, an uneven collection of brawny ne'er-do-wells who excelled at the art of war, infantrymen who traveled light and struck hard at any target Admiral Balthazar Crankshaft ordered them to hit.

Pluteus and his Ballblasters had been hunting for a Gallowglass clan airship that had reportedly crashed in the Boneyard a week before. The troopers carried pressurized tanks, hoping that they could locate the wreck and tap whatever precious hydrogen might be left in the reservoir tanks before the yellow-fingered Scavengers tore everything to shreds. Hydrogen was lighter than air, but in the Snow World it carried more weight than gold.

And now, with great suddenness, both the Ballblasters and the *Pneumatic Zeppelin* had been called upon to embark on a mission that verged on suicide.

"Prepare to take the passengers aboard with all good speed," Buckle ordered.

"Ten feet to ground," Sabrina announced.

Buckle ducked back inside the gondola, snapping his telescope shut and tucking it back into his hat. "All stop," he ordered, leveraging the chadburn dial to its vertical slot.

"All stop, aye," engineering repeated, ringing the chadburn bell as their sister dial matched the first.

Sabrina heard the whirling propellers go silent as they wound down to a lazy roll. Low as an earthworm's balls and just as slow. Her stomach felt like there was a rock in it.

"Be ready to bounce," Buckle told Nero through clenched teeth. "I'll want air and I'll want it precipitously."

Buckle hated being on the ground like this. So, for that matter, did Sabrina.

"Ready to bounce. Aye, Captain," Nero replied.

"We stop for nothing after this," Buckle grumbled.

"Airspeed zero. Hull at ground," Sabrina said.

Kellie started barking. It wasn't a good bark. The hair jumped on the back of Sabrina's neck.

They were at their most vulnerable position. Stalled, with the gondola hulls floating a mere three feet off the ground.

And then the shooting started.

–VII–

BLACKBANG MUSKETS
AND HARPOONS

BUCKLE, HEART RACING, JUMPED TO the port gunwale and looked out. Scattered puffs of black smoke erupted from the blasted ruins surrounding them, bursting from rubble piles, burned-out vehicles, and doorways. Blackbang musket balls left long, sparkling tails of burning phosphorus and corkscrewed as the projectiles lost speed, and they looked to Buckle like a swarm of burning bees. Sharp *plinks* and *tonks* snapped against the gondola as musket balls bounced off its bronze-plated flanks. A kerosene lamp hooked to the gondola prow shattered with the high crash of breaking glass, its kerosene falling loose of the fuel canister in a wobbling pancake of liquid.

And there was another sound, a far worse sound for the soul of a zeppelin captain—the rip of puncturing fabric. Bullets punching through the envelope overhead. Bullets coated with burning phosphorus.

Buckle ducked back into the gondola. "Ambush! Port and starboard! Gunners let them have it!" he shouted into the chattertube mouthpiece.

Buckle did not actually have to say the last bit—the *Pneumatic Zeppelin* crew, weapons at the ready, were already returning fire, aiming at the sources of the telltale smoke puffs and phosphorus streaks. He heard the low, burping *bumpf* of his crew's muskets replying to the attackers, combined with the sound of the Ballblasters triggering their firearms in a measured response outside.

"Lower the nets!" Buckle ordered, his hand instinctively reaching to the polished brass butt of the pistol in his belt. This was the perilous window of opportunity for the Scavengers, who could attempt to board and seize the earthbound air machine. That is, if the Scavengers had any desire to charge the ship rather than take potshots at it.

"Lowering nets! Aye, Captain!" Sabrina shouted, reaching over her head to pull down a lapis-lazuli-handled lever.

Reels of chain-mail netting rattled as they unrolled down both flanks of the gondola, driven along slender rails by metal pulleys spewing steam. Within thirty seconds, the antiboarding netting would seal the underside of the airship, making a ground breach rather difficult.

It would also strand any of Pluteus's men outside if they had not made it aboard yet.

"Ivan! Thirty seconds!" Buckle shouted into the chatter-tube. His chief mechanic and brother, Ivan Gorky, another one of Balthazar's orphans, would be manning the open rear hatch of the engine gondola at that very moment, a blackbang pistol in one hand, his other yanking Pluteus and his troopers aboard into the narrow gangway corridor.

"Ten seconds, Cap'n!" Ivan's voice, tinged with a Russian-throated grumble, returned in the chattertube. "Ten seconds and you're good to go!"

"Ten seconds!" Buckle repeated, his voice suddenly sounding loud in his ears—the racket of the gunfight had quieted: muskets were being hastily reloaded on both sides. His nose stinging with the punch of gunpowder, his blood a cavalry charge of adrenaline, Buckle paced the deck. He needed to get his zeppelin up and off the damned ground. He glanced over the port gunwale, his view partially obscured by drifts of black-bang-powder haze. Not a Scavenger could be seen, but there had to be at least fifty of them.

Buckle didn't want any more of the Scavenger's muskets.

But the thunder of the firearms started up again. Buckle heard another ball zip through the fabric skin somewhere above his head, *chink* against something metal, and drop at his boots, a deformed and smoldering lead orb.

Ivan's voice rattled in the chattertube: "Everyone aboard!"

"About time," Buckle muttered. "All ahead flank!" He snatched the chadburn handle and slammed it back and forward three times, ringing the bell three times. "Now, Nero! Up ship! Emergency ascent. Increase hydro twenty percent across the board. Jettison ballast five and six."

"Bouncing, aye!" Nero shouted, rapidly flipping levers on the hydrogen and water-ballast boards.

Dunn grunted as he wound the elevator wheel to maximum lift.

Buckle braced his feet as the deck lurched to a steep angle. The engines and propellers, now throttled up all the way, rose to an eardrum-throbbing roar. He heard a deep *whoosh* as rivers of water thundered from the amidships ballast tanks, their scupper hatches wide open, cascading to the earth below. Released from the water weight, straining with acceleration, and given a vertical punch with extra hydrogen in its gas cells, the *Pneumatic Zeppelin* lunged upward.

Buckle heard the heavy, metallic *chunk, chunk, chunk* of the compressed-steam hammergun belting away as Max, now elevated enough to use the cannon from the belly turret, rained razor-sharp harpoons down upon the attackers. The hammergun had a limited range, but it employed a long, expensive belt of ammunition and was blessed with a near-continuous rate of fire, unlike the blackball muskets that took even an experienced shooter more than half a minute to reload. As for range, well, this skirmish—like most skirmishes—was almost point-blank.

"Forty feet and rising!" Sabrina shouted over the noise. "Emergency ascent in progress."

A Scavenger's musket ball, perhaps the last shot fired in the melee, struck a glass panel in the cockpit dome, leaving a spiderwebbed crack.

"Scurrilous derelicts!" Romulus Buckle shouted in disgust.

–VIII–

UMBILICAL

WITH THE *PNEUMATIC ZEPPELIN* AIRBORNE, Buckle felt much better. "Serafim. You have the bridge," he ordered, unplugging his top hat from the mainline.

"Aye, Captain," Sabrina said. Welly slid into the chief navigator's chair, as was the protocol.

Buckle refastened his scabbard on its gargoyle pegs. "At three hundred, raise boarding nets and reduce to all ahead full. I will be in engineering. I must speak with Pluteus immediately."

Sabrina nodded. "Aye, Captain. Give my regards."

"I'll keep your name out of it. He's not going to like the news," Buckle said.

"Aye," Sabrina replied.

Buckle turned between the staircase and the hammergun turret and entered the narrow passageway at the back of the piloting gondola. On his right was the door to the map room, currently unoccupied, and on his left was the door to the signals room where the signals officer, Jacob Fitzroy, a skinny, territorial kid of sixteen years, sat amidst codebooks, signal flares, message scrolls, mirrors, and pigeon cages.

"How are your crazy birds, Fitzroy?" Buckle ducked his head in and asked.

"Regurgitating and crapping all over everything, sir," Fitzroy replied. "They don't like the muskets."

"Very good. Carry on," Buckle said, and strode to the end of the passageway, turning the crank on the round umbilical hatch until the main latch released. He swung the hatch open and Kellie bounded out between his legs. Buckle swung the hatch shut and turned. He paused, blinking. It took the brain a moment to process the void after he'd been cooped up in the narrow gondola for hours on end. The forward umbilical ramp was a flexible metal footbridge, rocking back and forth over the chasm of open sky between the piloting and gunnery gondolas. The ramp was now at a considerable angle due to the steep climb of the airship, and Buckle had to plant both hands on the rails to steady himself. Great rushes of icy wind passed him on both sides as they swept around the gondola and blustered along the length of the ramp, making every one of its thousands of metal hinges rattle and creak. The massive ellipsoidal belly of the envelope dwarfed everything from overhead, while the high rumble of her forward maneuvering propellers vibrated the air from their nacelles on both sides.

It would have been easier to climb the piloting gondola staircase up to the main keel corridor and stroll through the warm, enclosed interior of the zeppelin to the engineering gondola staircase at the stern. It would have been easier. But from the umbilical, Buckle could better inspect whatever damage the Scavengers might have done to his airship. And it was faster.

Buckle dropped a quick glance at the Boneyard, now two hundred feet below: the occasional puff of blackbang smoke popped here and there against the white landscape, but the range now rendered the shots ineffective. He scrutinized the underside of the zeppelin envelope as it loomed above him: the metal-plated skin was designed to be open in many places on the bottom, and he could often catch glimpses of the fourteen-story-high interior. From here, the *Pneumatic Zeppelin* always seemed to him to be some kind of hoax planet, pulled down from the sky and discovered to be actually a huge, complicated construction of fabric, girders, gasbags, catwalks, pulleys, rigging, and wires—a colossal feat of otherworldly engineering. Sweeping banks of gleaming bronze steam tubes, whistling copper vents, and dripping water-ballast scuppers running above the umbilical ramp made the impression even more fantastic.

Mostly, though, he was relieved that the only visible damage to his sky vessel seemed to be a few scattered musket ball holes.

The *Pneumatic Zeppelin* leveled out at three hundred feet, and the last few steps of Buckle's ramp journey got much easier. He reached the umbilical hatch in the nose of the amidships gunnery gondola, flipped the latch, and entered as Kellie darted in between his legs.

Stepping over breeching ropes and pulleys, Buckle hurried down the middle of the gunnery gondola to reach the aft umbilical hatch in its tail. The forty-foot-long gondola was teardrop shaped and streamlined, but shorter and broader than the piloting gondola, housing the four twelve-pounder blackbang cannons—two on each side, their brass muzzles nosed back from the open firing ports—and a host of firing hatches and slots. The chamber stank with the acrid sulfur of ignited blackbang powder. The crew within, eighteen stalwarts, both male and female, were busy cleaning their recently fired muskets and delicately unloading the cannons: the skirmish had not required the expenditure of the expensive cannonballs—a good judgment call by the experienced master gunner, Tyler Considine, and a husbanding of resources appreciated by his captain.

The gun-team members were all regular airship crewmen—hydros, riggers, skinners, and more—trained in gunnery as their post when the call to battle stations came. Buckle traded a quick salute with the chief skinner and captain of gun crew number three, Ensign Marian Boyd, a petite twenty-two-year-old spitfire with cropped brown hair and pale cheeks roughened by freezing wind. She had a touch of a snarl in her smile that reflected her ability to rappel across the cliff-like flank of a diving zeppelin or stare down a brawny boilerman with cool, daredevil ease.

Skinners, the crewmen tasked with maintaining the mountainous fabric envelope that was the hide of the entire airship, usually possessed colorful personalities, and their propensity for calculated gambles reflected the dangerous nature of their business. It was normal for a skinner to be good at his or her job— lousy skinners usually, and quickly, ended up as pockmarks on the Snow World landscape below.

"Gun number three secure, Captain," Boyd said as Buckle strode past.

"Very good," Buckle replied. He always forgot how small she was—her personality being so big—until he was right next to her. "Where is Mister Considine?"

"Up in the magazine, sir," Boyd answered. "Was the package picked up successfully, sir?"

"Yes. Excellent work. Carry on," Buckle said as he passed through the main gunnery deck and into the aft umbilical access corridor, where Kellie was waiting at the hatch.

Buckle popped the hatch and stepped out onto the aft umbilical ramp. The *Pneumatic Zeppelin* had leveled out and a lack of crosswinds left the ramp steady and flat. Kellie took off at a run. Buckle followed, passing under the long keel of the *Arabella* launch.

Heading toward the stern beyond the *Arabella*, the umbilical ramp passed between the two big blurs of the aft maneuvering propellers, both identical to the forward maneuvering propellers. Seventy-five feet ahead, Kellie was already waiting at the nose hatch of the engineering gondola.

Buckle did not need to glance back toward the bow to know that the *Pneumatic Zeppelin* was climbing to clear the Santa Monica Mountains. His view to the rear, past the engineering gondola and the smoking, steaming Devil's Factory at the stern, was of the sprawling, snowbound San Fernando Valley and the San Gabriel Mountains to the north; many miles beyond that, to the northeast, the Crankshaft clan's stronghold stood secure in the rocky citadel of the Devil's Punchbowl.

Home.

Odds were he and his crew would never see home again.

–IX–

CRAZY IVAN

As Buckle swung into the engineering gondola through the nose umbilical hatch, Kellie jumping in through his legs, he heard shouting over the din of the driving machines.

"I oughtta skewer you, you mudlarking Russian berserker!" Pluteus Brassballs bellowed in his gruff baritone.

"Try it! You should be thanking me! You should!" was Ivan Gorky's response, his voice shriller but defiant.

"You nearly blew my head clean off!" Pluteus charged.

"Ungrateful wretch, ah, General, sir!" Ivan cried.

Exactly what Buckle had been afraid of...

The access corridor in the nose of the engineering gondola was very short—not more than five feet—a narrow hallway lined with metal tubes: Buckle cleared it in one stride.

Please don't spit on him, Ivan, Buckle was thinking. Please don't spit on Pluteus.

Buckle emerged onto the main propulsion deck, ducking under the teeth of a rotating cog wheel as the skunk-reek of hot oil, both whale and synthetic, slapped him, encouraging his nostrils and eyes to close of their own accord. The chamber was blazing hot, despite four ventilation ports in the nose that admitted a constant stream of freezing wind—the engineers and mechanics alternately broiled and froze, but they were used to it.

The press of heavy machinery at every angle, much of it moving, made the large gondola feel claustrophobic. But despite its cluttered nature, it was a beautifully designed art deco cavern, where the gigantic propeller shafts whirred in a sea of metal interlocking gears, accompanied by hammering banks of giant pistons whose whir and concussion assaulted the ears; legions of copper tubes rattled with pressurized steam as hundreds of levers and wheels routed it into different systems of the airship. This gondola could be more accurately described as the propulsion-control room, for the actual engine room, with its boilers and furnaces, was installed inside the body of the zeppelin on the main deck above.

Buckle strode down the shaft alley to find Ivan, chief mechanic and ship's inventor, his eyes wild, toe-to-toe with an angry General Pluteus Brassballs and his twenty angry troopers. The Ballblasters were big fellows, wrapped in heavy fur-lined coats of the same white-tan color and gripping blackbang muskets. Several of them had a pigeon or a hawk, heads hooded and bobbing, tethered on their shoulders.

The six members of the *Pneumatic Zeppelin's* engineering and mechanic crew present had sidled up beside Ivan, their grimy fists balling up for a fight.

Buckle jumped between Ivan and Pluteus. "Ho, there!" he said. "I thought we were all on the same side!"

"So did I, Romulus!" Pluteus snarled. "But your man here, this lazybrat Russian of yours, he fired his pistol so close to my head that if I hadn't veered I'd be earless on one side! I'm dang near deaf now as it is!"

Buckle saw that Pluteus, big, stocky, and muscled to wrestle a bear, was rubbing his left ear and cheek, which were stained black by gunpowder.

RICHARD ELLIS PRESTON, JR.

"I saved you!" Ivan shouted, waving his arms, "I thwacked a Scav who was about to blast you in the backside! You should kiss my feet!"

Ivan had a little pet wugglebat, one of the few Martian beasties that was harmless, and the only one that was downright cute. Ivan had named his chattering pet Pushkin, and the loyal creature was always poking its furry head out of the left breast pocket of his jumpsuit. Pushkin, disturbed by his owner's shouting, had now popped out of the pocket and clambered up onto Ivan's shoulder, chattering like a chipmunk—which it did resemble, its six legs and bat-like wings notwithstanding.

Colonies of wugglebats often lived inside the cavernous envelopes of zeppelins. The *Pneumatic Zeppelin* had its own colony, and Ivan was gruffly protective of them.

"All right! All right!" Buckle said, turning his attention to the highly agitated Ivan Gorky. "Ivan, you have got to cool down."

Ivan, a man of average height, with a lanky frame and narrow face, stopped waving his arms and froze, his dark-blue eyes locked on to Buckle's. One could never tell how Crazy Ivan might react to anything. Ivan's mouth began to work, his thin lips screwing over his teeth until his beet-red face faded back to its normal pallor. He jammed his hands into the hip pockets of his oil-stained leather jumpsuit, which sported pockets everywhere: pockets full of hammers, wrenches, tweezers, and countless other devices. His pistol was now tucked into a bandolier strapped across his chest. On top of his head he wore an ushanka, a Russian winter hat, with the earflaps always dangling. His ushanka was bare of instruments except for two pairs of goggles, one for regular protection and one for magnification, though it was strange when he wore the magnifiers, because they tripled the size of his eyes and made him look like an owl. Ivan wore the magnifier goggles often, far more than was necessary. Buckle was certain he did this to annoy people who were bothering him, and it worked for the most part.

Ivan now yanked down his magnifier goggles, so his enlarged blue eyes loomed unsettlingly huge on his face. If he thought that his bug eyes were going to dismay Pluteus Brassballs, he was dead wrong. "If this earthworm wants to duel me, Cap'n, I'll meet him on the roof," Ivan snapped.

Buckle rolled his eyes. The roof was the very top of an airship, and, under churning skies, the precarious ice-slicked fabric was the setting for many famous duels. Buckle grabbed Ivan by the shoulders. "That is it, Ivan. No roof. Get out of here. Go to your cabin and cool off, you got me? There will be no duels today."

"Aye, Cap'n," Ivan grumbled, scratching Pushkin's head with his finger. Pushkin stretched his neck and hopped from paw to paw to paw, which is what wugglebats do when you rub them. The Ballblaster troopers and the engineers melted away from the scene: chances of the confrontation escalating had dropped to zero once the ship's captain arrived on deck. Ivan turned and headed for the circular staircase, firing a sullen glare at Pluteus before climbing up and out of sight.

-X-

PLUTEUS BRASSBALLS
AND HIS BALLBLASTERS

"LUCKILY FOR THAT SURLY GALLINIPPER he is a decent mechanic,"
Pluteus grumbled, "or he would not be worth an ounce of his
ballast."

Buckle grinned, shaking Pluteus's hand. "Good to see you,
Pluteus."

"Good to see you, kid," Pluteus replied warmly, slapping
Buckle on the shoulder with such a smack that it stung the
skin beneath the leather. "Talk loudly. Gorky blew out my ear!"
Pluteus stuck his finger in his right ear and cranked his lantern jaw open in an attempt to silence the bells jangling in the
battered eardrum. He had a rectangular face, like a bull, with
small, piercing eyes made even smaller in appearance by his
high forehead and a scalp nearly devoid of hair. A long, thick
white scar ran up his neck like a tree branch, forking out in
several directions under his right eye.

"Sounds to me like he saved your worthless hide," Buckle
replied.

"By accident!" Pluteus said with a wave of his hand. "When
that gangway ramp came down, he was swinging that pea-
shooter of his real wild, his legs jimmying around like somebody

put a tangler in his pants. I am lucky he didn't blow my head clean off."

"He is a tad excitable," Buckle said, noticing that his engineers were still tense, their eyes darting up from their stations and casting daggers at the troopers, who, having removed their bulky gas-collection cylinders from their backs, had immediately found various ways to relax in the busy atmosphere of the gondola; they stretched and lounged as they stuffed pipes with tobacco and fed strips of meat to the reconnaissance hawks and packets of grain to the messenger pigeons.

"Why were you not wearing your gas masks?" Buckle asked Pluteus. In stinkum zones the troopers usually wore iron helmets equipped with built-in gas masks. Today, with the exception of their metal breastplates, they looked like light-cavalrymen, in long sheepskin coats crisscrossed with leather bandoliers packed with blackbang cartridges, fabric-covered pith helmets, jodhpurs, and knee-high leather boots that laced from toe to top.

"What?" Pluteus shouted, pointing at his ear.

"Why weren't you wearing your gas masks?" Buckle shouted.

"Heavy armor is not worth the weight when your life depends on moving fast," Pluteus answered, removing his thick leather gloves. "As for stinkum in the San Fernando Valley, bah. You're not going to find any now unless you fall into a well." Pluteus tamped tobacco into a large pipe he drew from one of his shoulder pockets, and then shot Buckle a serious look.

"Follow me, please. This way," Buckle said, leading Pluteus down a short ladder into the underside observer's nacelle, a bullet-shaped compartment under the engineering gondola with a glass section in the floor. Buckle and Pluteus each took a seat in a padded observer's chair as snow-streaked, softly undulating foothills swept past beneath them. The zeppelin, heading southwest, was rapidly gaining height to pass over the Santa Monica Mountains.

Kellie carefully climbed down the ladder. There was hardly a place on the entire airship that the dog hadn't figured out how to get into.

"That's one crazy dog," Pluteus commented as Kellie hopped down from the last rung of the ladder and hopped up into Buckle's lap.

"Not as crazy as my mechanics," Buckle said, patting Kellie's head.

Pluteus's gray eyes shifted into seriousness. "Tell me that we are on our way to rescue Balthazar," he said, scratching a match on his boot sole, then puffing at his pipe with it. The smoke was instantly sucked away by cold streams of air passing through the flank observation slots.

"We are," Buckle said.

"Or we die trying," Pluteus said, puffing at his pipe again.

"Or we die trying."

Pluteus's narrow eyes narrowed even more—he was by nature quite a suspicious sort. "Who aboard knows about the mission?"

"My entire crew."

Pluteus's eyes narrowed to the point of disappearing. "Loose lips sink airships, my boy."

"Not in my crew," Buckle answered evenly. "You know that."

After a brow furrowing, Pluteus's eyes opened up a bit. "Where is Balthazar?"

"In the City of the Founders."

Pluteus's eyes sprang wide open. He stopped working on his pipe for a moment, then clamped the stem between his teeth and took a deep pull. "Treacherous fogsuckers," he whispered.

That was it. Admiral Balthazar Crankshaft, the leader of the Crankshaft clan, a man whose beard was shot through with white, who had made it into his fifties in a world where few ever reached their thirties, had been brazenly kidnapped by the Founders clan three days before.

It had been a real coup, a real piece of work, a real plot of skullduggery.

For many years the clan ambassadors had been working toward the Palisades Truce, a ceasefire agreement between the Crankshafts, Spartaks, Gallowglasses, Tinskins, Imperials, Alchemists, and secretive Founders, who had been the holdout until the last round of negotiations. With the Founders on board, the thrilled ambassadors called a meeting of all the clan leaders at the abandoned Palladium Stronghold in the mountains of the Pacific Palisades. Balthazar Crankshaft and the other clan leaders arrived to discover the Founders negotiators, led by a figure known only as the Vicar, cloaked in red hoods, which they refused to remove. The first round of talks went nowhere. In the late hours of the second night, after a hard fight with the small contingents of bodyguards who had accompanied the leaders, an unknown group of assailants abducted Balthazar and several other clan chiefs. No one knew who had carried out this diabolical act, for the Vicar had apparently been kidnapped as well.

At dawn, the messenger pigeons filled the gray skies. The remaining clan lieutenants gripped their swords and remained tight-lipped, violently suspicious of each other, unwilling to break the news to their own people until they had figured out how to proceed.

Spies were everywhere.

Loose lips sink airships.

Clans needed strong leaders to survive, leaders who often held many secrets—and when a clan leader fell, it was assumed that clan was now vulnerable.

As a victim of treachery, and without Balthazar, the Crankshaft clan council moved quickly, bunkering their airship fleet and recalling Pluteus Ballblaster from the field. Balthazar's brother, Horatio, temporarily took the reins of power.

They were at war. But who had abducted Balthazar? The Crankshaft clan did not know who the enemy was.

Until, on the next evening, the message from Aphrodite arrived.

–XI–

A MESSAGE FROM APHRODITE
(by Messenger Pigeon, of Course)

APHRODITE WAS A CODE NAME. No one knew his or her identity. He or she was a spy inside the City of the Founders who supplied information to Balthazar Crankshaft and Balthazar Crankshaft only. Balthazar had never told anyone about Aphrodite. The Crankshaft clan council only learned of Aphrodite's existence through a carrier pigeon message Aphrodite sent to them two days after Balthazar was kidnapped.

The message, once unwrapped from the pigeon's bony leg, read as follows:

> *Founders abducted BZar. Rescue possible if*
> *immediate, before BZar murdered or relocated.*
> *Inside City. La Brea Prison Warren.*
> *Underground. East wing. Main Corridor. Cell 24.*
> *Aphrodite*

Buckle had seen the actual letter, scribbled on a scrap of stinkum-yellowed parchment that had once been a cover page for a novel entitled *Moby-Dick*, shown to him by Balthazar's near-frantic lieutenants, hands shaking, at the clan stronghold in the Devil's Punchbowl. A rescue plan was rapidly formulated, a near suicidal mission: an assault on the City of the Founders itself.

Buckle instantly volunteered himself and the *Pneumatic Zeppelin*, prepared to die in order to rescue Balthazar Crankshaft, his adopted father and the greatest hero of the Crankshaft clan.

"We're going in hot as fire pokers, then," Pluteus said, with a little charge in his voice.

"They won't be expecting it," Buckle replied. He felt a little strange as he started to explain the council's attack plan to Pluteus, who was the clan's undisputed master of infantry strategy and tactics. Pluteus was Balthazar's cousin by blood, and the two men, along with Balthazar's brother, Horatio, were the old lions of the Crankshaft clan. "We plan to drop the assault team outside the perimeter walls," Buckle continued. "We know a way in from there, following old sewers straight in to the back door of their subterranean prison."

Buckle saw Pluteus's eyes flash, though his face remained calm. "*Who* knows the way in?" he asked pointedly.

Buckle set his jaw. Pluteus had every right to wonder who amongst the Crankshafts might possess such intimate knowledge of the Founders' city and its underground. "I cannot say."

Pluteus narrowed his eyes at Buckle. "I do not trust this Aphrodite," he snapped.

"It is not Aphrodite."

Pluteus took a deep breath, moving on. "We'll need our heavy gear," he said. Buckle saw Pluteus's mind racing behind his eyes, tackling the logistics of the brazen attack plan.

"All of your equipment is on board. Phoebe made sure everything was in order before we left." Pheobe was Pluteus's supply officer.

Pluteus nodded, staring straight at Buckle without looking at him.

"The *Pneumatic Zeppelin* will come over the wall to evacuate the team once we have Balthazar," Buckle said, feeling a tiny shiver crackle up his spine. Flying his airship over the fortified City of the Founders at rooftop height was so insane it might just work. "The fog should provide sufficient cover."

"The Founders," Pluteus grumbled, puffing his pipe, watching the snowcapped peaks drift under the floor window. "Of course it was them."

"And they were supposed to be the most virtuous of us all," Buckle said quietly.

"Ha! Perhaps in the beginning—but not anymore, lad," Pluteus said with a cynical chuckle that sounded like it stung his throat. "The original three might have been visionaries, but they're long gone, moldering in the grave. What we are stuck with now is their inbred, watered-down descendants, all lazy-brats, skulkers, and blackhearted defectives. The good blood has gone rancid and their empire is lost. Treachery is their milk and honey, and they're obsessed with conquering us all."

Pluteus paused, taking another pull from his pipe. Buckle listened to the drone of the engines at full power, the *whup-whupping* of the propellers not far behind the gondola, the grind of the huge turbine shafts spinning a few feet over their heads. His stomach tightened: he felt unsettled, as if he had just eaten a bad apple. If Aphrodite was proved correct and the Founders had abducted Balthazar, then the Founders had committed an act of war. And the Crankshaft clan was already weary of such tensions, having been on the brink of war with the Imperials for the last year. "It was not supposed to be this way," Buckle said, and sighed. "This is not the world the three Founders intended."

"Nothing is ever the way it was supposed to be, Romulus," Pluteus replied. Then he was lost in his thousand-yard stare again.

A tiny hitch vibrated in the metal beneath Buckle's boots. He raised an eyebrow in alarm. The *Pneumatic Zeppelin* was slowing down.

In the next moment there was a commotion at the ladder above; Pluteus's infantry sergeant, a weathered pugilist named Scully, ducked his head down the hatch. "Airbanger—you've got a hole in yer gasbag!"

A hole in the bag. A hole in the bag meant the possibility of a breached hydrogen cell. Loose hydrogen inside a zeppelin was an impending catastrophe.

Buckle, with Kellie bounding at his heels, shot up out of the hatch so fast that Sergeant Scully had to jump aside.

–XII–

"AIRBANGER—YOU'VE GOT A HOLE IN YER GASBAG!"

EVEN IF THE HYDROGEN CELL had not been compromised, a hole in the skin envelope of a zeppelin was never a good thing. Immediate repair of any significant breach was a necessity. At high speed—and the *Pneumatic Zeppelin* was running at all ahead full—the constant battering of the wind would snatch at the loose skin and make the hole larger and larger. The airship had a rigid iron superstructure set in flex joints that made it supple as a whole, but a current of air roaring like a locomotive into the interior would place horrific stresses upon the gigantic gas-cell balloons and the elements that secured them. Airships taking massive damage to their outer-skin envelopes had been known to tear themselves apart internally, even in moderate winds.

Max, sporting both pistol and sword at her belt, hurried in from the umbilical hatch and joined Buckle as he strode toward the circular staircase. Pluteus's Ballblasters eyed "Balthazar's zebe" with suspicious leers, as they always did.

"Where's the rip?" Buckle demanded.

"Topside, over cell thirteen in compartment seven," Max said. She did not look worried. She rarely ever looked worried.

"From above?"

"It would appear so, Captain. The breach is reported to be sizable. Lieutenant Serafim gave the order to reduce speed. Skinners have initiated repairs."

Buckle started up the circular staircase to the main deck with Max at his flank, their boots ringing on the cast iron steps. The hot stink of smoke, steam, and lubricant oil hit them as they rose into the engine room.

"Do we have a hydrogen breach?" Buckle asked.

"Damage assessment is ongoing," Max replied. "No reports of cell compromises yet."

"Well, we shall know soon, one way or the other," Buckle said as they emerged inside the cavernous envelope, which housed the twelve-story-high hydrogen cells and steambags, all floating like monstrous gray elephants, each secured in a colossal web of girders, ladders, catwalks, wires, ropes, tubes, climbing shafts, ventilation shafts, and pipes. High above, the outer skin rippled.

A punctured hydrogen cell would flood the zeppelin, a huge bottle containing furnaces, boilers, steam engines, and kerosene lanterns, with explosive gas. The *Pneumatic Zeppelin* was designed with twenty-eight gasbag cells, set in horizontal pairs in fifteen compartments across the ship's main axis. Normally, about one-tenth of the cells were filled with superheated air to supplement lift—the much-preferred hydrogen was expensive and scarce—and when a cell contained hot air it was referred to as a steambag. The massive cell balloons were constructed from overlapping sheets of goldbeater's skin, which was made from the intestines of cows. The *Pneumatic Zeppelin* had required 825,000 sheets of goldbeater's skin for her gasbags.

That was a dang lot of cows.

Buckle, Max, and Kellie strode past the six gigantic boilers, which looked like black-steel locomotives perched on both sides of the aisle. The firebox furnaces—all except number two—glowed yellow and roared. The pressurized boilers gurgled in an eardrum-pummeling cacophony, fed fuel heartily by the stokers, the "sky dogs," stripped to the waist, their muscles shining under the perspiration that flowed in runnels down skin blackened by coal dust and fire.

Buckle hurried through the blast doors at the main valve-switching station and leapt up the forward staircase, moving so fast that Kellie, and even Max, with her long legs, had to strive to keep up with him. He led them up to the Hydro deck where the catwalk, lined with hydrogen tanks, heaved between the gray flanks of the massive gas cells. The ship's belligerent goat, Victoria, was tethered to a chattertube pipe outside the ship's zoo, where the chickens clucked, the pigeon coops stank, and fireflies swirled behind glass; she barely gave any of them a second glance as they passed her in their rush to the next companionway, her split-pupilled eyes looking bored as she chewing something that she always chewed, even if there was apparently nothing there to chew.

Buckle's lungs started to labor as he ascended to the Axial deck, the main catwalk that ran down the centerline of the airship from the nose to stern, but he kept up his speed, launching his legs up the small staircase, which carried him up to the Castle deck and the upper reaches of compartment seven.

Buckle glanced up in an attempt to catch a glimpse of any damage to gasbag number thirteen overhead. It always felt like he was in the bottom of a well whenever he looked up into the hydrogen-cell city from below: it was a narrow view between the looming, gray hydrogen cells and the copper blast walls on the sides opposite. Although he still could not view the hole directly because it was above the gasbag, he could see the kaleidoscopic effects of the muted sunlight pouring through the hole and bouncing around in the interior, the light fluttering as the torn fabric skin flapped sharply against a whistle of twisting wind. Then Buckle saw Ivan peering down between the bags, grimacing as he patted the shaft of a primitive harpoon, its point sunk into a wooden support beam.

"Hydrogen?" Buckle shouted.

Ivan shook his head. "Nope. Not a trace. How the hell did those yellow-fingered Scavs get their hands on a shooter as big as this, anyway?"

Buckle eyed the harpoon—it was big, but ramshackle, the bole poorly smoothed, and cut from uneven wood, the impressive iron point ill-fitting at the base, as if it had been designed to fit on something else. Judging from the angle of the harpoon in its resting place, it appeared to have plunged down on the *Pneumatic Zeppelin* from above. Probably fired from a massive crossbow of some sort, positioned atop a hill, Buckle decided, its trajectory arcing high in the sky before it came down on the vulnerable zeppelin. Either way, it was a lucky shot for a Scavenger's near-useless equipment. But it was also a lucky shot for the *Pneumatic Zeppelin*: yes, the harpoon had damaged the envelope skin, but that was eminently repairable; the real treasure, the fragile cell number thirteen and its exorbitantly-priced, explosive hydrogen, had been spared any damage at all, and that was real luck.

"Precious little souvenir, eh?" Buckle shouted back to Max.

"Not the way I would describe it," Max answered.

Buckle's boots clanged on the catwalk as he raced to the small set of stairs leading up to the top Eagle deck. Deck four was called the Castle deck because when all of the blast-shield portals were open along its length—as they were now—it resembled the grand hall of a castle, lined with the waists of the rubber stockings that sheathed the gas cells in towering curtains of mottled gray. The stocking skins were laced with complex mechanical latticeworks that resembled a million metal spiders joined together at the legs, glittering as they quivered at high tension. And the curving arches of rigging, backstays, and piping high overhead under the Eagle deck catwalk gave the ceiling a vaulted look, as architecturally pleasing as the roof of a church.

It only took a few more moments for Buckle, Max, and the dog to climb up the cast iron stairwell to reach the Eagle deck at the top of compartment seven, a narrow catwalk running just beneath the roof of the *Pneumatic Zeppelin*'s envelope. Here, one could almost reach up and touch the underside of the fabric skin rippling along the airship's back, and if one took a look down over the rail of the catwalk, one was rewarded with a vertigo-inducing view of the vertical gas-cell city, which plunged straight down to the keel corridor one hundred and forty feet below.

Hit by a torrent of fresh, freezing air, Buckle lowered his goggles and focused his eyes on the hole in the skin just above the catwalk over cell thirteen: it was an irregular gash about four feet in diameter, with a center of slate-gray sky. Its edges of ragged fabric lashed about like an enraged octopus. The harpoon itself had probably created a much smaller puncture, but the force of the passing air—the sound of it was deafening— had already greatly increased the size of the breach. Ivan and the chief skinner, Marian Boyd, were already working underneath the hole. Two more skinners, Rudyard Tuck and Amanda

Ambrose—both of diminutive size, which was handy in their line of work—hunched low, clutching clockwork hydrogen meters with their chemical sticks, and puttering in repair boxes flipped open at their knees, handing up nine-inch needles, dense hemp thread, and rolls of fabric. Both Ivan and Boyd wore safety goggles and thick leather gloves as they fought to grasp the fluttering shreds of fabric, their hands constantly jerking back, stung despite the padded leather. The left lens of Ivan's goggles was cracked.

In-flight skin repair on a zeppelin running full speed was no easy business.

"This one is a real stinker, Cap'n!" Ivan shouted, finally managing to pin down the biggest flap of loose canvas amidst the cataract of air. "We should slow down!"

"No chance!" Buckle replied, peering up at the hole.

The interior repair was mere damage control: pinning down the ripped fringes of the breach so they would not further aggravate the opening. But somebody had to go outside and stitch a patch over the leading edge of the hole so the wind could not get underneath it, pluck it up, and continue to tear the envelope apart.

And that somebody was going to be Buckle.

"Tuck! Gear me up!" Buckle ordered.

Tuck pulled a heavy safety harness out of a chest and swung it onto Buckle's back, assisting him as he slipped his arms and legs through the straps.

"Captain, sir," Boyd, already suited up in her safety harness and skinwalking boots, yelled. "With all due respect: I volunteer. It is my job, Captain."

"Captain's prerogative, Miss Boyd," Buckle said. Skinwalking was a part of the skinners' pedigree, he knew, but if he could take a crew member's place in a perilous situation, he intended to do so without hesitation.

Tuck clicked Buckle's harness clasps together across his chest, checking and double-checking them, then handed him a white pith helmet with goggles, Havelock flap, and red puggaree, all fur-lined—the traditional Crankshaft headgear—and took his elegant topper for safekeeping.

Boyd shook her head with dismay. "It is my responsibility, sir. You always go out. It is not correct." She shot a look at Max. "Am I mistaken, Lieutenant Max?"

"I disapprove of his risk taking, but the captain does not answer to me. You are on your own if you wish to argue with him," Max shouted. Her black eyes flickered pink inside her goggles, the Martian color of frustration; Martians had eyes like mood rings.

Buckle felt the hollow thump of the heavy parachute cylinder hit his back as Tuck snapped it into place. Ambrose finished securing a special harness and leather helmet on Kellie, who sat with great anticipation, her brown eyes shining through the goggles.

Buckle pulled his goggles down over his eyes and winked at the dog. "You ready, girl?"

Kellie barked.

"I am ready to assist, Captain!" Boyd shouted from his shoulder, her voice sharp with a snap of bitterness.

Tuck handed Max a loaded blackbang musket, and she checked the primer.

"At least it is directly on top," Max shouted. "You will not have to rappel, or hook up to the jackline."

"See! Lucky!" Buckle said to Max. "Thirteen is my lucky number!"

Ambrose snapped safety lines onto the harness-belt hooks of Buckle, Boyd, and Kellie. The leather-wrapped cables were cumbersome, as were the bulky bronze canisters containing their silk parachutes, but eminently necessary.

"A ten-foot square should do the trick!" Boyd yelled, folding a large fabric patch into the tool pocket on the chest of her harness. Her small eyes looked even smaller inside her thick safety goggles, but her full lips, freshened by the brisk air, looked bright red.

"Keep your head up, Cap'n!" Ivan said.

"Aye!" Buckle replied, lifting Kellie into his arms.

Ambrose pushed a stepladder under the flapping hole. A depthless void of gray sky gaped above, pale as death.

–XIII–

KELLIE OF KELLS

THE SENSATION OF EMERGING FROM a hole on the top of a flying airship was something that Buckle had experienced many times before, but that made the new trial no less daunting. Pushing up from the narrow confines of the Eagle deck into the mind-blowing vastness of the sky would put the whackwillies on any-one's head for a moment or two. Fear was a thing Buckle had taught himself to swallow and never regurgitate. But it did take a specific moment to swallow it. And in that moment he held still on all fours, his gloved hands clutching a sea of canvas that surged and rippled under his knees as if he rode the back of some colossal whale. The empty gray sky was blinding, despite his polarized goggles. The freezing wind sucked at every inch of him, biting at his cheeks, threatening to snatch him, snap his safety line, and hurl him into oblivion.

And then the moment was over.

All was familiar. He was firmly planted on the back of his great airship. The heavily doped canvas skin fluttered against the long spineboard. The grappling cannons and pepper guns, bundled in oilskin wrappings, stood erect and unbending in the gale.

Buckle clambered around the breach so that the wind was at his back. The howling air buffeted him, but could not penetrate his heavy leather coat and the fur-lined helmet flap covering his neck. He would have the hole stitched up in no time.

And the view was fabulous. Sabrina, heading due south now, had lifted the airship to nearly three thousand feet altitude to clear the rolling white crests of the small Santa Monica Mountains. Under the stern of the *Pneumatic Zeppelin* receded the broad plain of the San Fernando Valley and the shadow of the San Gabriel Mountains to the north. To his left, the Big Green Soup twinkled dark blue under a distant haze. In every direction he could see the purplish Martian obelisks, dropped on the day of The Storming, looming over the landscape: the Catalina obelisk in the channel to the south, the Piru obelisk in the mountains to the northwest, and the Redlands obelisk in the haze to the east, the tops of their monstrous columns soaring higher than the *Pneumatic Zeppelin* was designed to fly.

Ivan popped up from the hole with Kellie in his arms, pressing Buckle's safety line to one side to make sure it did not foul. He set the dog down facing Buckle and she crouched low, the slipstream pressing her fur pancake flat. She released a happy yip, tail valiantly trying to wag.

Buckle patted the top of Kellie's flying helmet. The dog was a veteran of such adventures at the ripe old age of three, and as dauntless as her master. But the mascot was not on top of the airship to provide companionship—she was there to sound a warning if tanglers approached. Dogs hated the flying beasties, the massive former pets of the Martian invaders: a mad scientist's fusion of pterodactyl, vulture, and cassowary, which could zip through the earth's atmosphere like bullets. Tanglers attacked in a crash dive from a high altitude—a deadly tactic when a man was exposed outside a moving zeppelin. The nefarious tanglers possessed unearthly animal smarts and regularly shadowed airships at a distance, patiently waiting for the opportunity to steal a meal.

Kellie was positioned to watch the sky at Buckle's back.

Tanglers always struck from behind.

Marian Boyd climbed up onto the roof and clamped down at Buckle's left shoulder. She was so small that Buckle half expected the wind to snatch her up and sail her like a kite at the end of her safety line. She opened the repair satchel attached to the chest of her safety harness and handed Buckle an envelope needle, a nine-inch, razor-tipped awl designed to punch through the dope-stiffened fabric of the airship skin. The needle was already threaded with heavy hemp rope. Buckle attached the needle's leather strap to his wrist so the wind could not yank it away from him.

Max rose up in the hole gripping the blackbang musket—packing a nice little punch in the arse for any irritating tangler.

"Let's get cracking!" Buckle shouted at Boyd, feeling his bravado kick into gear. Having removed the skin patch from her harness satchel, Boyd battled the torrent of air as she pressed it down on the undamaged fabric at the leading edge of the breach. Buckle punched the needle through both the patch and the taut skin beneath, yanking the thick hemp thread through and reaching under to draw the needle up again. Each stitch could be no more than three inches apart. He punched the needle through for a second stitch and then a third and a fourth.

Kellie whimpered at Max, who was blocking her view, and pulled herself forward so her paws hung over the opening, cocking her head up at the sky.

Buckle grinned at Kellie as he stitched. When he had found her, more a starved ball of fur than a lost puppy, her appearance in the house had not thrilled Balthazar, who threatened to let the mongrel sort-of-terrier go. But Balthazar's bluster was often ineffective when it came to his children; nine youngsters—one born by natural process to Calypso, the other eight adopted from far and wide—raised to be independent and headstrong, who had no qualms about clashing with the will of their father.

Balthazar and Calypso were the only parents Buckle and his sister Elizabeth had ever really known. Their real parents had been killed when Buckle was six years old, and his treasured memories of them were fragmented and cloudy.

Buckle, fifteen years old at the time, claimed the lost dog as his ship's mascot, even though Buckle was only an apprentice navigator and lacked an airship of his own. There was nothing Balthazar could do. Every captain—or future captain, Buckle argued—was allowed a mascot. Balthazar's dog, a bulldog named Agamemnon, had the run of Balthazar's zeppelin, the flagship *Khartoum*. It was even rumored that Balthazar fed Agamemnon buttered bread on occasion, although he would never admit to spoiling his beloved canine in such a fashion.

"I know what to name her," Buckle had said as Balthazar threw up his hands and wandered off into the sitting room to smoke his pipe.

"Kellie of Kells!" Buckle shouted again, the puppy squirming in his hands, her hot tongue working hard under his chin. The Book of Kells was an illustrated Irish manuscript of considerable age, and Buckle's mother had inherited a copy that had somehow survived The Storming. She loved the book. Buckle did not have many memories of his mother, but he did remember her saying once, as she tucked him into bed after a nightmare, that she often dreamt in its colors.

For a short time, there had been no response from the sitting room, except a lazy puff of smoke drifting in through the doorway. "Kellie it is, then," Balthazar finally grumbled.

"You'd better dunk that mangy hound in vinegar and scrub it until its fur falls off," Balthazar had shouted with false gruffness. "It is lousy with fleas! And it's not sleeping in the house. Not over my dead body!"

Of course Kellie slept in Buckle's bed that night (both of them ended up having to take a bath in vinegar) and nearly every night since, wherever Buckle laid his head.

And, on the roof of a zeppelin three years later, it was the bark of this once flea-bitten dog that saved Buckle's life.

–XIV–

TANGLERS

KELLIE'S BARK WAS A HIGH-PITCHED squeal of warning. Buckle knew he was in trouble. A dog could sense a tangler coming. But a tangler came so fast the warning usually only amounted to a second or two.

But it was enough.

"Tanglers!" Max shouted.

Buckle grabbed Boyd by the collar of her work coat and threw both himself and her flat. The skin fabric bounced and snapped back under his weight, and for an instant he feared he might have impaled himself on the repair needle, but it was still clenched in his hand.

A huge shadow slashed over Buckle, its wings blocking out the sky, the claws snapping like giant scissors. He had an impression of a feathered riot of blue, crimson, green, Roman purple, white, and yellowy orange, the velociraptor body beneath ripped with scaly muscle, the arms and legs tipped with talons as big as butcher's knives.

The huge beastie missed and then it was gone, diving over the starboard side.

Max's blackbang musket boomed. Buckle jerked his head up to see the wind snatch away a big puff of black smoke as a second tangler dove down upon them.

The second tangler spun wildly, dead, gut shot. Max's musket had done its work. But it was plummeting toward them, the great wings blocking out the sky.

The nightmare head flopped back and forth atop its sinew-wrapped neck, the kookaburra beak and sweeping skull crest dominated by big amber eyes that were bottomless and ancient.

Even when a tangler was dead, the yellow eyes still glowed for weeks.

The tangler slammed down with the resounding wet *thump* of a flesh-bound locomotive.

Part of the tangler—probably a wing—walloped Buckle, hurling him across the roof, knocking the air out of him. He heard the tangler bounce off the canvas, and caught a glimpse of its spinning corpse disappearing over the starboard side.

Buckle lay stunned and gasping. It was as if he were staring up at the gray sky from the bottom of a well dancing with white sparkles. The sounds of ripping fabric and snapping tangler bones echoed in his brain. Was Marian Boyd still in his arms? He could not tell.

Buckle heard shouting. Kellie was barking up a storm. He shook his head to rattle his senses back into order, and he suddenly became aware that he was sliding, the torrent of wind pushing him through something slick. He dug his gloved fingers into the slippery skin until he found the line of a superstructure girder and stopped his movement. Another shake of his head failed to knock the blur out of his vision. Panic surged inside him. One tangler was still out there. And that one had surely zeroed in on him.

Somewhere in the foggy distance he heard Max shout the order: "Reload!"

-XV-

RELOAD!

MAX KNEW THINGS WERE BAD. Very bad. Hunching back down the stepladder in the breach hole, she grunted as she lowered the stunned Boyd, splattered with blue-green tangler guts, into the waiting arms of Tuck. Boyd had been within easy reach after the tangler strike. Buckle and Kellie, however, had been knocked flying, their safety lines twisting and squeaking at the lip of the hole.

Ivan and Ambrose frantically reloaded the musket on the catwalk: it took more than thirty seconds to reload a blackbang musket, and they didn't have thirty seconds. The surviving tangler would have already looped under the zeppelin, climbed high into the sky, and set its angle to dive again.

They should have prepared two muskets.

Max drew her pistol and planted her boot on the stepladder, launching her lithe body up onto the roof. She hunched low in the whipping wind. The area around the breach was a mess—the tangler collision had pocked the envelope with five or more jagged sinkholes; wobbling gobs of blue-green guts slimed everything.

Max couldn't see Kellie but she could hear her—the dead tangler's bounce must have knocked the dog into the air and over the side, and left her dangling by her safety cable along the flank of the airship.

But Kellie, although her situation was probably unpleasant, was not the one in absolute jeopardy. Tanglers had tunnel vision as hunters: once a tangler chose a victim it would continue to attack that one target repeatedly until it made a meal of it or the tangler was dead.

And the target was Captain Buckle.

Buckle was about thirty feet aft of Max's position at the breach. He was obviously discombobulated, head down, crumpled on his stomach with one hand clutching his safety cable and the fingers of the other sunk into the skin, straining for a grip amidst wind-blasted streams of blue-green tangler guts. He might be badly hurt. She couldn't tell. But one thing was certain—he was a sitting duck.

Max immediately moved toward her captain in a crouch, the wind causing her to slip and slide along the skin. There was no hesitation in her action: the overwhelming desire to protect Buckle consumed every inch of her being, to the detriment of everything else. She was his protector, the shield on his arm, the body between him and the bullet.

But she still had to be careful.

In her haste, she had not hooked up to a safety line.

She reached Buckle and grabbed the collar of his coat, lifting him up onto all fours. He felt heavy and unsteady. She shot a quick glance at the featureless pale sky and saw nothing. But she could feel the tangler coming. She could feel it in the skin on her back.

"Captain!" she yelled.

Buckle raised his head. Splatters of tangler blood, exposed to the wind, skittered across his face in rivers. Max realized that he was looking at her without focusing his eyes. He mumbled something she couldn't make out. It wasn't time for conversation anyway. She planted both hands on the scruff of his jacket collar and dragged him back toward the breach.

She heard Kellie barking. The tangler was back.

Max released Buckle and spun, whipping out her pistol and pointing it at the sky.

She caught the tangler fluttering above her barrel sight, hurtling down on them like a meteor.

Max pulled the trigger. The blackbang pistol erupted with a dull thud, the puff of smoke instantly sucked away by the wind.

The tangler swerved and dodged her shot. It veered and vanished down the starboard side. Moments later Max heard a smattering of musket shots from below. The alerted crew was firing at the tangler. But only a lucky shot would take the elusive creature down.

Max had thirty seconds before the tangler came back again. She jammed her pistol in her holster, took hold of Buckle's safety line, and tried to pull him, but her boots kept slipping in the loose, gooey mire; she couldn't throw her weight into it, not with the wind brutally straight-arming her, constantly knocking her off balance, threatening to throw her over the side.

She wasn't going to get the captain back inside this way. Not in thirty seconds, she wasn't.

"Ivan!" Max screamed. She knew that he could not hear her down inside the Eagle deck.

Kellie howled with fury. Max pushed Buckle flat and stood over him, her eyes on the sky. She drew her sword.

Come on, Buckle, stay lucky.

~XVI~

A CERULEAN SLIP

TEN SECONDS LATER, MAX REALIZED something wasn't right.
With her head tilted up, the blade of her saber gleaming under
her eyes, she saw that the sky above her was empty. She spun
around. But she already knew she wasn't going to make it. She
glimpsed a flapping shadow coming at her with only an instant
before the impact. The clever beastie had made its third attack
low and level and straight at Max's back.

An instinctive gasp of terror sucked freezing air into her
lungs. Adrenaline and muscle fired, seeking to aid survival, but
she didn't even have time to raise her sword.

From the corner of her eye she saw a blackbang musket flash
at the lip of the hole.

The tangler swerved and careened to the left, its huge talons, outstretched to their farthest extent, tearing the air as they
sliced past. But the monstrous left wing slammed into Max,
knocking her over the starboard side of the *Pneumatic Zeppelin*.

For a heartbeat Max plummeted in a whirlpool of confusion. She knew she was falling. The dreaded "Cerulean slip."
Her brain shook itself loose of the concussion. She blinked and
saw the massive tan flank of the *Pneumatic Zeppelin*'s envelope
rushing upward in front of her. She had one instant left to save
herself or there would be nothing between her and her grave but

three thousand feet of air. She raised her saber with both hands and drove it into the blurry wall of fabric rushing past her. The blade cut the skin like paper, leaving a long rip down the side of the envelope without slowing her down.

For a moment Max thought it wasn't going to work. What a nice fix. Not only would she fail in her attempt to save the captain, but she would cut the airship nearly in half before falling to her own doom.

In the next moment the sword handle yanked and bit in her hands, slowing down as the blade lost its cutting momentum against the stiffened fabric; it bumped through a set of heavy stitches before jerking to a stop that nearly separated her arms from her shoulder sockets. Max was dangling now, battered about in the slipstream, only ten feet above the drop off where the envelope veered inward to the belly of the balloon. She couldn't hold on there for long. She looked up: the four-story-high vertical rent slashed by her saber flapped ominously above. It was her only way back in. Leveraging her body up with both of her hands on her sword hilt, she desperately kicked and pulled, but could not reach the gap.

–XVII–

BUCKLE CAN'T FLY

ROMULUS BUCKLE SNAPPED OUT OF his haze, assisted by a cold slap of wind. His back hurt. His legs hurt. It hurt when he breathed. His eyes focused on the depthless chasm of the sky and the vast hump of the zeppelin's back, the gap between him and the breach a rippling swamp of blue-green guts and blood.

He saw Ivan's head and shoulders pop up in the breach. He was heaving hand over hand on Buckle's safety line, yanking Buckle forward in jerks as his hands plowed through the muck. Ivan shouted at him, but the wind stole the sound before he could make it out.

He heard Kellie, somewhere nearby, barking furiously.

Buckle's brain flashed. The tangler.

His heart leapt in his chest. He scrambled into a crouch, stumbling as his taut safety line yanked him forward.

He was only ten feet from Ivan and the Eagle's Walk.

But once again he was too late.

He clawed at the pistol in his belt, but his fingers were slick and numb.

This time the tangler came in unhindered. It swooped into the gap between Buckle and Ivan—so low that the ends of its talons slashed the envelope in long, serrated rips—and snipped the safety line between them as if it were a piece of string. And, having learned a trick from the last pass, the tangler dragged its right wing, catching Buckle flush across the back, catapulting him into the air and over the side.

Romulus Buckle sailed out into the empty sky. Everything seemed nonsensical. He felt like a horse had just kicked him in the back. He watched his pistol wobbling as it fell, and it was falling much faster than he was for some particular reason.

In the next moment, as the buffeting air thundered around him, Captain Buckle realized that he was in a world of trouble.

He saw the *Pneumatic Zeppelin* above, his gigantic air machine trailing streams of white vapor and black smoke as it churned across the high heavens. And even though the *Pneumatic Zeppelin* was very big, it was rapidly getting smaller and smaller and smaller.

The severed end of Buckle's safety line lashed back and forth above him and he unhooked it from his harness. It slithered away in the air as he fell beyond it. He looked to the earth, where the white-brown Santa Monica Mountains slowly, inexorably rose up to bury him in their bosom with one tremendous *slap*.

Buckle had two parachutes—a main and a reserve—ready to deploy from the brass canister on the back of his harness. But if he pulled the rip cord and opened the parachute, he was doomed: suspended in a lazy float, he'd be cut to shreds by the tangler. He searched the sky for any sign of the flying carnivore. There was another attack coming, he was certain of that, and it would be from behind.

Buckle took a firm grip on his saber and slowly drew it, the vertical force of the air making his arm wobble.

He twisted around.

The tangler was there, right on top of him, hurtling in, wings swept out, coming straight at his back.

Buckle swung his sword in an arc, aiming to lop off the tangler's head. The beastie flung its head aside. The saber caught nothing but air. The tangler's talons snapped, snatching the sword out of Buckle's grasp before chopping the blade in half. The two pieces of sword fell in glittering spirals toward the snowy ground below, chasing after the lost pistol.

Buckle glanced around. The tangler, of course, had vanished. He considered pulling his rip cord. He only had a few seconds before it was too late to do so. But a parachute just guaranteed a gruesome death by tangler.

Buckle realized that something was pattering rapidly against his forearm: it was the nine-inch repair needle fluttering alongside his wrist, still attached by its leather strap. A desperate plan bubbled, half-formed but urgent, in his mind. With his cold-numbed hands, he grabbed the needle and buried the base of it in his fist.

He had one last chance.

Back and forth his eyes searched the gray sky, seeking the little black dot that would explode into the five-hundred-pound tangler coming at him at the speed of nightmares. If the tangler swooped in with its barbed talons leading the way, Buckle's plan had a chance. If it didn't, well, maybe he could take the stinking beastie down with him anyway.

What a damned pill, a captain falling off his airship. Falling into the sky. Actually he had been knocked off, so maybe that didn't count.

Buckle kept whipping his head around, trying to catch a glimpse of the tangler. It was there in a moment, a dark shadow in the upper corner of his right eye, diving down upon him from above. Buckle angled his body so the rushing air spun him around to face his attacker.

The tangler was coming too fast. It was almost on top of him, its wings spread wide, neck arched, head high, the talons aquiver, coiled to split him wide open.

Buckle yanked the main chute ripcord. The parachute burst out of its canister and mushroomed open, hitting the tangler with a brutal, buttery wallop. The furious tangler's beak split though the silk that had swallowed it, followed by the massive head, while the talons shredded their way through beneath. Buckle jerked at the end of his harness and jackknifed upward, crashing into the sprawling mass of tangler and parachute. The force of the collision knocked the wind out of him, but he clamped his arms and legs around the throat of the thrashing beastie.

The ruptured folds of the parachute pounded Buckle's body. He saw a splatter of his own bright red blood on the silk flapping against his head. But in that instant, he was immortal, overwhelmed by being so close to the alien monster, the cobblestoned scales of its neck hot against his cheek, the surge of the gigantic heart pumping just beneath, the overripe vegetable smell of it, the eternal depths of the huge left eye, yellow as all the history of the world, glaring down at him.

The tangler released a guttural scream that vibrated so violently it stung every inch of Buckle's skin.

He had hitched a ride on a tornado.

The outraged tangler, its wings still largely pinned by the parachute, twisted back and forth as it sought to shake Buckle loose. It whacked him with the length of its beak, each blow threatening to cave in Buckle's rib cage. The talons whirled beneath, seeking a hold on a boot or calf.

Buckle only had one chance. He swung his arm back and, with all the force every sinew, muscle, and tendon in his body could muster, plunged the repair needle into the tangler's left eye. The needle sank its entire length into the socket, soft as a bag of jelly, until it jammed into something hard. A geyser of amber liquid spewed from the gashed orb and was snatched away by the rushing air.

The tangler released a deafening bellow and wrenched its body violently, throwing Buckle loose before it went limp.

Buckle didn't go far. He was now falling alongside the dead tangler, anchored to it in a swirling morass of tattered silk and knotted parachute lines.

His situation had not markedly improved.

–XVIII–

HOLLYWOOD LAND

THIRTY SECONDS. THAT WAS IT. Thirty seconds of free fall before his death created a home for a groundhog in the Santa Monica Mountains. Buckle clicked open the safety latch on the main-chute emergency-release switch on his harness. Flipping the emergency switch would fire an explosive bolt inside his main-chute canister, ejecting the main parachute anchor so the reserve chute could be deployed safely without fouling. Buckle hit the switch. The bolt fired—another solid kick in the back—and the parachute lines waffling all around him suddenly went slack, joining in the battering delivered by the loose folds of the parachute.

Buckle shoved himself away from the snake's-nest mass of tangler, parachute, and ropes. Something jerked him back. He reached down and found a rope wrapped around his ankle. He swung the razor edge of the repair needle to slash the line, kicked free, and pulled the reserve ripcord.

The reserve parachute popped out perfectly, whiplashing Buckle back into a much slower descent. Stunned and adrift, he felt like he was floating as light as a bubble, after plummeting three thousand feet. The mountain loomed a hundred feet below. Beyond that, to the south, lay the massive Los Angeles basin, its dense clusters of tall buildings the only things visible above a great sea of yellow-brown fog.

Beneath his boots Buckle saw the tangler, its body somersaulting end over end, until it slammed into the crest of the mountain ridge, disturbing the pristine snow with a whopping *sploosh* of blue-green innards.

The mountain rose up at Buckle too quickly. The reserve chute had been deployed too low and late to give him much of a cushion: he was coming in far too fast for a decent landing. This was going to hurt. He tugged on the control lines waffling next to his ears, aiming to land on the open ridge where the thwacked tangler had plopped. He took deep breaths to rein in his pounding heart. He concentrated on the calm, reassuring sound of the air rippling across the parachute silk…rocking him like a baby. No need for concern. He'd find a big fat snowdrift to land on.

Buckle peered up and caught a glimpse of the *Pneumatic Zeppelin* in the sky, high, high above. Sabrina, as first mate, would have taken command now. The airship was on course, southbound. She had not turned around. The mission was too critical to turn back for a dead man, even if it was the captain.

Buckle glared at his boots as they swayed beneath him. It was his mission. He was supposed to rescue Balthazar. Now he was out of the picture, perhaps permanently, if luck didn't go his way.

The mountain crest rushed up to meet him in a dirty white wave of frozen bushes and snow. He swung past the towering letters of the HOLLYWOOD sign, each one stained a weird gray yellow, propped up with timbers, and pied with a patchworks of rusty metals. Actually, they now read as HOLL WOOD, because the tangler's body had crashed down upon the

Y, smashing it asunder in a blast of splinters, green copper tiles, and intestines.

A shame, Buckle thought. He didn't know what the sign was ever meant to be, but it was a grand navigational landmark. And it wasn't so bad, coming down here in Hollywood Land. At least he knew where he was. Alchemist territory. Yes, the Crankshaft and Alchemist clans weren't on the best of terms, but the animosity was fueled more by suspicion than any actual nose-to-nose conflict. The isolated and xenophobic clans rarely had much contact with each other, and most everyone was locked in a state of uneasy truce or on the verge of conflict with everyone else—except for the Crankshafts and Imperials, who were engaged in an off-and-on skirmish war. But the Gentleman's Rules would apply to Buckle and the Alchemists, meaning the Alchemists would be required to feed a downed airman some soup and return him to his home clan unharmed.

Ice-sheathed branches crackled at the soles of Buckle's boots as he raised his knees to clear a bush-covered ridge. A huge snowdrift loomed in the ravine below. He yanked hard on his control line to reduce the parachute's lift, and it ducked down. He stretched out his legs to catch the crest of the big, soft snow pile. He missed.

Not so lucky today, Buckle thought—just before he slammed into the trunk of a tree.

Everything went black.

A gentle breeze whispered in Buckle's ear. His eyelids fluttered, stung by the weak sunlight. His whole body ached, but he ignored that. He knew that he was lying on his back in the snow. He knew that he was lying on a mountain in Hollywood

Land. He knew that the Alchemists had not found him yet. He knew that the *Pneumatic Zeppelin* was continuing on its mission without him.

Buckle squinted until his eyes adjusted to the light, and focused them painfully on the cold gray sky. He pulled himself upright, his leather jacket squeaking against the dry snow, and sat motionless. The quiet stillness of the mountain was so absolute it seemed to demand that he make no sound of his own. His breath swirled around his face in vaporous puffs, but despite its coldness, the air seemed much warmer here than it was thousands of feet up on the roof of the *Pneumatic Zeppelin*.

Something thrashed back and forth under the HOLL WOOD letters, which were only fifty feet away. Buckle reached for a pistol that was no longer there. The movement was coming from the tangler corpse: one leg convulsed erratically, churning up the sea of jade-colored guts steaming in the snow around it.

The one amber eye glowed. The tangler's massive head was broken—split wide open—and still the surviving orb held its devilish light. Buckle dragged himself to his feet. Every sinew and muscle felt bruised and weak. He whacked the release button at his sternum and the safety harness dropped away into the snow with a *chunk*, taking the reserve chute and its lines with it. Something dripped down his face and he wiped at it, the glove coming back streaked with slushy blue-green tangler blood; he realized that he must be coated with the noxious-smelling stuff from head to toe. Whatever.

He needed a plan. Someplace to go. Lifting his goggles onto the top of his pith helmet, he stared up at the ruins of the Observatory, which were not more than a half mile away on the crest of the mountain: a large dome—said to house a magnificent telescope, and which served as the main stronghold of the Alchemist clan—towered at the center of the fortress-like structure.

Considering that Buckle had landed smack dab in the middle of Alchemist territory, he was surprised that they hadn't jumped all over him yet. He decided to make for the Observatory and let the Alchemists take him in according to the Gentlemen's Rules. What else was he going to do? Walk home? After all, stranded zeppelineers were not uncommon. It should be easy, if awkward—unless he was labeled a spy. Then it could take a forever of negotiations and ransoms to get him home.

Buckle set off at a brisk walk, gritting his teeth against the stringy pains running up and down the length of his body. He didn't have far to go, and the Alchemist patrols would surely intercept him before he reached the Observatory, anyway. He drew his pocket watch out of his coat—thankful it was still ticking after all of the hits he had taken—and flipped the brass cover open to check the time. He turned the winder round and round between his thumb and forefinger, as he always did when he was nervous about something.

~XIX~

THE OBSERVATORY

It took Buckle about twenty minutes to slog his way across the snowbound slopes to the approaches to the Observatory. Soon he was crossing a wide-open field in front of the building. There were no signs of activity, no footprints in the snow, no sentries to challenge him. But several times he thought he heard a breech hammer *snick*, perhaps cocked by Alchemist musketeers with trigger fingers poised, hidden in the ruined outbuildings at the edges of the park.

His heart skipped a beat, but he kept on slogging.

Showing fear would get him nowhere. The Alchemists were a mysterious bunch who bolted together hulking machines in their work bays under the mountains, and they didn't like strangers. Buckle knew that much about them.

As Buckle neared the Observatory, a cream-colored art deco castle capped with a telescope dome, he saw something he had never noticed from the air: a six-pointed spire, perhaps forty feet in height, with a bronze astrolabe perched at its zenith, thrusting skyward from the center of the lawn. The hexagonal spire was battered and chipped—its original white surface stained a mottled yellow—but its basic form had survived remarkably well. Three towering figures in long cloaks, each nine feet tall, were sculpted into the vertical recesses of the spire's angles.

At first Buckle assumed that the impressive block was one of the old monuments from the time when the Founders clan was master of all of the stronghold colonies. The figures would represent the Three Founders, two men and one woman, brilliant scientist-engineers, who had been the architects of the new civilization and Founders' city. Legend had it that a *fourth* Founder, aghast at the rise of the steam machines, had wandered off into the wilderness and never returned. The fourth Founder was mostly forgotten, if he had ever truly existed, though he did pop up as the Old Hermit Monk, a rather nasty character in a fairy tale Buckle's mother occasionally read to him. But was this truly an old Founder's statue? It was unthinkable that the Alchemists—who had never been a proper colony clan anyway, much like the Crankshafts—would allow such a thing to remain standing in their own front yard.

Buckle answered his own question as he circled the spire. A total of six human figures had been chiseled into the sides of the monument. This was not a Founders statue. It was something else. But the six stone men whose names were inscribed at their statue's feet—Kepler, Galileo, Copernicus, Hipparchus, Herschel, Newton—had been lost to history, at least any history Romulus Buckle was aware of.

Buckle gazed at the spire, folding his hands behind his back in a casual fashion, even though his shoulders ached. He didn't feel like pausing and gazing, but he knew he was being watched. He could smell horses. But still no one had challenged him. Was he going to have to stride up to the front door of the Observatory and rattle the knocker? Apparently so. Well, if that was what the Alchemists wanted, then that was what he was going to do...

Buckle heard something coming up behind him, something wheezing and puffing and winding and grinding, something with footsteps so heavy they split the ice with sharp cracks and shook the ground under his boots.

–XX–

WOLFGANG RAMSTEIN
AND HIS ROBOT

Buckle spun on his heel to see an armored robot stomping toward him. It was nine feet tall, a hulking brute of a machine encased in iron armadillo plates. A breastplate of grinding cogs and gears covered a turbine spinning inside the chest cavity. Oval windows of heavy lead glass lined the sides of the rib cage, revealing compartments churning with steam, boiling water, and fire. The head, a smooth copper dome with two horizontal slits for eyeholes, which glowed a superheated red, had eight brass vent tubes—four on each side—releasing intermittent bursts of hissing steam. The clodhopper legs, thick as tree stumps, swiveled in well-oiled ball sockets at the hips. The right arm had a gigantic metal hand, while the left arm was equipped with a round battery of cannon barrels circling the wrist.

The Alchemists were famous for building robots of fantastic configurations, but Buckle had never seen one before. He could outrun the massive machine but...where would he go?

Surely the Alchemists were familiar with the Gentleman's Rules.

The robot approached more rapidly than Buckle expected, its iron boots belting the earth with *thud, thud, thud*s that bounced the loose snow with each footfall. It halted when it was toe-to-toe with him; great sighs of steam shot out of its vent tubes and then petered out.

Buckle swallowed so hard he almost choked himself. His nostrils and the back of his throat were stinging from the pungent stink of hot metal and sizzling whale-oil lubricant. The motionless robot loomed, its inner turbine still whirring, its eye slits alive with the reflections of the fire and heated air within.

Buckle got the odd impression that the behemoth was trying to hypnotize him.

"You didn't run!" a voice boomed from Buckle's right. "And it was a crackerjack good thing you didn't! Crackerjack!"

Buckle snapped a look to his right. A young, thin man roughly equal to his height and age was approaching. He wore a brown leather motorcycle cap festooned with eyewear, a long white double-breasted coat, and dark-brown boots agleam with rows of polished buckles. Long leather gloves encased his hands nearly up to the elbows, and both forearms were crowded with straps loaded with unusual devices. He held some sort of little-box invention studded with winding handles and gears.

"I suspect I could have outrun your little friend, here," Buckle said, trying to sound calm.

"Ha!" the young Alchemist huffed as he arrived alongside the robot. "You run, you get incinerated. A simple formula with an inevitable result." The young Alchemist's face lit up with a lopsided but enthusiastic smile from beneath his thick mustache. He had ruddy skin that looked scrubbed and healthy, and friendly olive eyes set deep under his bushy eyebrows. His dense russet-colored hair jutted out in every direction from beneath his cap, which accommodated a forest of different goggles and lenses, each and every one designed to swing smoothly into position in front of his eyes with the tap of a lever.

"The proof is always in the proverbial pudding!" the young Alchemist shouted. He twisted a number of switches on the control box he held, and it issued a series of odd noises. "Let's have an exhibition, shall we?"

The robot jerked its shoulders back with a *clank*, its chest turbine accelerating as it heaved out its left arm, which was the one cuffed with the circular ring of small blackbang cannons. The arm straightened, locked, adjusted its aim slightly, and fired a thundering volley in a volcano of black smoke. Buckle instinctively ducked. The echo of the blast boomed across the mountains. He heard a resounding *crack* and turned to see a tall tree fifty yards away collapsing into a fire-ringed hole in its trunk. It toppled in a crash of splintering wood and a shattering of the ice that had long encased it.

The robot swung its smoking arm back to its hip and swiveled its head, attentively watching the young Alchemist.

"Crackerjack!" The young Alchemist chuckled. "Impressive! Am I right? Of course I am right. Eight portable cannons, self-loading, fired singly or in salvo. Explosive rounds. And that's just for starters."

"Impressive," Buckle said. It was what this fellow obviously wanted to hear. And it *was* impressive. He paused, trying to cook up a decent story. He could say he was a Crankshaft ambassador on a diplomatic mission, and needed assistance to return to his home territory. But ambassadors never traveled alone—and not by parachute. And if the Alchemists smelled a lie in his story he would be clapped in irons as a spy.

"Look..." Buckle began, uncertain of what he might say next.

"So," the Alchemist blurted, interrupting, "you're a Cranker, are you?"

"Crankshaft. Yes," Buckle replied.

"And the *Pneumatic Zeppelin* is your gunship," the young Alchemist stated, grinning wickedly.

"It is. Yes," Buckle answered, uncertain.

"That was a colossal scrape you had with that tangler," the young Alchemist continued, affectionately patting the robot's massive iron hip with his gloved hand as he spoke. "Knocked you off your gasbag and still you survived. The odds on squeaking out of that fix still breathing would have to be astronomical, yes?"

Buckle's eyes narrowed. "How do you know that?"

The Alchemist pointed two fingers at his own eyes and then pointed them at the sky. "Always watching, Cranker. Watching. We have big eyes down here: telescopes of tremendous proportions and magnifying capacities. We observe, study patterns, collect information."

"Information on who?" Buckle asked.

The Alchemist's face soured for a moment—a blabbermouth who suddenly realized he was spilling secrets—and then the grin reappeared. "Hummingbirds and butterflies, of course. I've said too much, really. I always talk too much. All nonsense. Such a bore, I am. My goodness, you are quite sticky."

Buckle was beginning to think that the truth was the best chance to extricate himself from this mess. "Look, I desperately need to get back aboard my airship."

"Ah, that may be a problem," the Alchemist said. "They seem to have sailed away without you."

Buckle looked up at the sky. The *Pneumatic Zeppelin* was now a tiny silver dot high above the ruins of Los Angeles. "If they knew I was alive they would come back. I could order them to come back. Do you have any way to signal them? You must have a way."

"*Order* them back?" The young Alchemist asked, cocking his head.

"I am Romulus Buckle, captain of the *Pneumatic Zeppelin*, and I must speak with your clan leaders on a matter of utmost importance, which affects us all."

The young Alchemist's eyes lit up and he smiled like the cat who caught the mouse. "Captain!" the young Alchemist repeated. "Well, I'll be carbuncled. A Crankshaft airship captain plunked down here among us. And I was supposed to let my robot squash you, as if you were just some cast-off ballast rat!" He laughed and thrust out his hand, and when Buckle took it, he shook vigorously. "Captain Romulus Buckle, let me properly introduce myself—I am Wolfgang Copernicus Ramstein, and this is my robot, Newton. Welcome to Hollywood."

–XXI–

THE ALCHEMISTS
ARE FRIENDLY?

IF THE ALCHEMISTS WERE A friendly bunch, the only one who
showed it was Wolfgang. Buckle stood before Altair Pollux,
an altogether pudgy little lemon of a fellow who, pacing
back and forth with his hands folded behind his back, his
round belly thrusting out of his long white coat, frowned
a hundred different ways as he pondered his visitor's fate.
Altair had become the temporary leader of the Alchemists
since the disappearance of his aunt, Andromeda Pollux, who
had been abducted along with Balthazar and the Imperial
clan leader, Katzenjammer Smelt, at the Palisades Truce. As
far as first impressions went, Altair struck one as very bald,
very bitter, very egotistical, very untrustworthy, and very
stupid.

Altair stopped and glared at Buckle for the fifteenth time.
"And what am I supposed to do with you?" he asked for the
fifteenth time.

Buckle gave Altair his easy smile to hide his annoyance with
the pompous little lazybrat. "I propose that you believe what I
have told you, because it is the truth," he said, removing his pith
helmet and tucking it under his arm. "And the circumstances of
our situation are both dire and immediate."

Altair rolled his vapid blue eyes up to the ceiling and sighed in an oh-it's-so-bothersome way.

Buckle followed Altair's gaze up to the dome, its plaster riddled with patched cracks. Wolfgang had referred to the grand hall as the Alchemist's Sky Temple. A gigantic telescope, a beautiful, monolithic tube polished to a gleaming bronze, loomed over all the proceedings, poking up at the sky through a long vertical slot in the roof. The entire floor was a rotating device, the walls encircled with steam-driven shafts ready to propel the entire chamber around in a circle to allow the telescope access to all 360 degrees of the horizon. An Alchemist female was perched in a seat high on the telescope, her eyes pressed to the viewfinder. When her hands intermittently adjusted the control levers, the steam shafts fired, driving a complex system of gears, wheels, and levers, which emitted a heavy but smooth *whir* as the chamber swung around.

Buckle wondered if she was still watching the *Pneumatic Zeppelin*.

The room swung around. To Buckle's senses it seemed as if the walls were rotating around the floor, but his brain knew the reality was the opposite. He eyed the large oval table where the Alchemist Council had assembled in haste, evident in the disheveled appearance of a few of the ten leaders. The table itself was a grand sample of engineering art, roughly forty feet in diameter and inlaid with interlocking gears of bronze, copper, brass, and iron. This metal decoration had been present on every wall and door that he had seen when Wolfgang and Newton had escorted him inside the narrow corridors of the Observatory. It gave the surfaces a geometric depth, and was not unpleasing to the eye.

And as they entered the interior of the Observatory, Buckle had become aware of profound vibrations rising from beneath his feet, the rumblings of gigantic furnaces, crucibles of molten metal and fire, deep in the labyrinth of forges and laboratories below. The Alchemists were master inventors, hammer-swinging metalworkers addicted to the steam and bolt. But even more intriguing was their near-magical ability to animate their creatures of metal—Newton, for example—so the machines seemed to be able to think for themselves on a basic level. In that very moment, what phantasmagorical constructions were secretly being birthed, eyes blinking with fire, in the depths of the mountain under Buckle's feet?

"This is so flabbergastingly ridiculous," Altair whined, scuffing the floor with the toe of his boot. "How do you say you can you help us, again, Cranker?"

"He's already told us how, Altair," a soot-stained Alchemist woman said, the patience in her voice wavering. Her eyes, like those of the other ten Alchemist leaders around the table, measured Buckle with suspicion, but he had noticed that their glances toward Altair were unkind, even embarrassed. The council was made up of seven men and three women; all but one looked to be in their early thirties, older than the twenty-something Altair, all dripping with the gravitas he lacked. They all wore the long white, double-breasted coats of the Alchemist clan. The one older man was obviously the military chief, perhaps forty-five years of age, with dark-brown skin and hefty gray patches in his black beard, and over his white coat he wore an iron breastplate embossed with a copper astrolabe.

"Well, I want to hear his story again, Capella, if you don't mind!" Altair snapped, his eyes bulging, a line of spittle dangling from his protruding lower lip. "And if I don't buy this slime-coated Cranker's fabrication this time, I'm going to toss him into the furnace and have done with this once and for all."

The assembled Alchemist leaders angrily bit down on their silence. Apparently Capella was the only one willing to openly disagree with the blustering Altair.

"Sir, I repeat," Buckle said, raising his voice, suddenly afraid to be at the mercy of this dimwit. It was very hot in the chamber, and he was sweating uncomfortably inside his coat. "I am telling you the truth. Yes, I fell from the *Pneumatic Zeppelin* after being attacked by tanglers and so, yes, I never intended to drop in on you the way that I have. But perhaps events have conspired to assist us all."

"We saw what happened. We saw everything. It is obvious that you are not a spy." Altair sniffed, wiping the spittle from his lower lip with his sleeve, leaving a damp streak at the wrist. "If you were a spy you'd already be in the furnace."

"I understand," Buckle said. "But listen to me—I was on the roof of my airship and vulnerable to the tanglers because I was patching a skin breach midflight, something that is done only in the most desperate of circumstances."

"Yes, yes," Altair interrupted. "You say, you claim, that you were on your way to free your Admiral Balthazar Crankshaft from the clutches of the Founders, who are keeping him prisoner in the city."

"Yes, and every second counts," Buckle said.

"How do you know the secrets of the Founders? How do you know it is they who have taken him?" Altair asked, his eyes narrowing at Buckle.

"We have a spy inside the city."

"Ha! Spies do not survive inside the city!" Altair bawled, slapping his hand flat on the table. "We know. We've tried. Trick! Furnace!"

Buckle's temper, not the longest-fused around, almost got the better of him. He swallowed hard, cooled his anger, and played his ace. "Help us. Your Andromeda Pollux is surely imprisoned alongside Balthazar. This may be your only chance to get her back."

Altair's eyes bulged with such rage that, for an instant, Buckle thought he was going to jump across the table. "What do you—*you*—know of the situation regarding Andromeda Pollux? And how do we know this isn't a trap, Cranker? And who says it was the Founders who kidnapped our leaders? For all we know it could have been you. It could have been you, and now you are trying to convince us to raid the Founders' city to fulfill your own bloody agenda!"

"A single airship with twenty-one troopers attacking the Founder's City is hardly an agenda," Buckle answered. "It is a rescue attempt whose very audacity mitigates the low odds of success."

Altair popped a smirk and banged his fist on the table in triumph. "Your tale of woe suffers from a fatal flaw, Cranker. The ambassador of the Founders was also kidnapped at the Palisades. They are victims and just as leaderless as we, you, and the Imperials are."

"The Founders did announce their ambassador had disappeared along with the others," Buckle said evenly, "but I am convinced that was just to throw us off. I am certain that the Founders clan is preparing to invade us all, to recover the territories they lost. And what better way to crack and scramble us than to eliminate our leaders and set us against one another? They'll have a field day once we've torn each other to pieces."

"Furnace!" Altair bawled.

"Altair! That is enough," Capella announced, with considerable authority. She was a tall, slender person, slightly gawky because her arms and legs were almost too long to match her torso, but she possessed a strange beauty. Her forest-green eyes dominated her face, bordered at the temples by two strands of her black hair beaded with tiny copper bolts and washers.

Altair whipped his head around, flinging spit. "You stay out of this, Capella!" he snapped.

Capella cocked her head and peered down her long nose at Altair with the posture of a schoolmistress disciplining a child. "I believe the Cranker. And while I don't trust him, I trust the Founders even less."

All of the other Alchemists on the Council nodded, except for the older general, who looked quite upset.

"We must do whatever we can to get Andromeda home safe and sound," Capella added.

"Help me call my airship back," Buckle interjected, stepping forward. The argument was turning in his favor, and he wanted to add to the momentum. "I beg you to join us. Together we can assault the prison and save our people. But it has to happen now."

"Shut up!" Altair snarled. "Furnace!"

Capella took a step forward. It was a small step up to the edge of the table, but it was enough to make Altair wince. There was no doubt that she was now taking control of the proceedings. "It is time to act. Those in favor of assisting the Crankshafts raise their hand," she said.

Everyone on the Alchemist Council raised their hand except Altair.

"What? I am in charge when my aunt isn't here! You all know that!" Altair bawled, almost in tears.

"Yes, you are, Altair," Capella replied. "But majority rules every council decision. We are going to assist the Crankshaft expedition if there is even a remote possibility of recovering our Andromeda."

"I object!" Altair howled, launching himself away from the table. "I object with the utmost vigor, and when my aunt gets back she is going to hear all about this! And he also ruined our Hollywood sign, if you remember!"

Altair stormed toward two huge doors set in the north wall of the dome. Newton stood motionless there, his eyes glowing mildly, with Wolfgang lounging at his hip. Altair looked as if he might try to shove Newton as he passed, but he thought better of it and waddled furiously out of sight.

For a moment the room stood quiet. Faint vibrations from the heavy equipment below tickled the soles of Buckle's feet. "Capella—you have done the right thing," he said.

Capella shot Buckle a less-than-welcoming glance. "We are in a state of emergency, Captain Buckle. I have made a decision based upon a desperate hope; a decision that conflicts with my better judgment." Capella turned to the old soldier. "General Scorpius, you shall accompany the Crankshafts. Select an elite detachment to complement their force."

"As the Council requests, it shall be done," Scorpius muttered with a respectful nod, his voice low and gravelly.

Wolfgang thrust out his arm. "Newton and I, with extreme enthusiasm, volunteer to join the expedition!" Newton lifted one of its massive arms, as if copying Wolfgang in an afterthought.

Scorpius shook his head. "Adventure, lad? You surely are cracked."

"He is young, Scorpius," Capella whispered, almost sadly.

Buckle stepped forward. "The Crankshaft clan expresses its heartfelt thanks to all members of the Alchemist Council. With your assistance I am certain that we shall accomplish the mission at hand."

Capella turned to Buckle with a piercing stare. Altair may have been a buffoon, but there was not an ounce of ignorance in this woman. "I am willing to take you at your word, Captain Buckle," she said. "But if you are misleading us—if Andromeda is not rescued—I shall make you rue the day you were born. So...we have an understanding, yes?"

–XXII–

ONE MARTIAN SAVED,
ONE CAPTAIN LOST

THE BONE-CHILLING WIND BUFFETED IVAN as he rappelled down the starboard flank of the *Pneumatic Zeppelin*'s main envelope. His right hand swung his safety line while his boots fought for toeholds against the superstructure girders beneath the rippling fabric. He felt no physical discomfort.

But he cursed the pain in his heart.

Ivan had been helpless, no more than a howling spectator, when the tanglers knocked Kellie, Max, and Buckle over the side. In an instant they were gone, and then he was left alone, halfway out of the hole in the roof, alone in an ocean of blue-green guts under a gray sky, with the chopped end of Buckle's safety line limp in his hands.

His eyes foggy with shock, Ivan had focused on the last safety line as it creaked back and forth at the edge of the breach in front of him. It took a few moments for him to realize that it was taut with weight.

The dog.

I'm not losing anybody else today, even if it is just the damned dog, Ivan thought. He grabbed the line and hauled the light animal back up. Kellie's wind-blasted head popped up over the side, ears flapping on top of her helmet, and once Ivan got her up on the roof, she belly-crawled her way back to him. As he pulled her in and cradled her body, he was surprised at how precious her life felt in his arms, how healing it was to save at least one soul from disaster.

Ivan detached the safety line from Kellie's harness and lowered her to the catwalk below. The dog shook her body as if she were wet, then glanced around with alarm. She yelped, a plaintive cry of despair, and took off running, searching for a master she knew on some level was already gone.

Ivan let her go. Ambrose and Tuck had lifted Marian Boyd, her head bleeding, to her feet on the catwalk; all three of them looked at him, their faces pale. He shook his head and they stared at him dumbly.

"The captain," Ambrose had muttered plaintively. "Please, sir, what of the captain?"

"He..." Ivan said, but he did not have any words to continue. Buckle was his brother by adoption and his closest friend in the world—at least, the closest friend Ivan allowed himself to have. But the world took everything away. That was what the world did.

"Ivan! Come in, Ivan!" Sabrina's voice rattled from the chattertube hood on the catwalk, barely audible in the great rush of air through the breach. "This is the bridge! Did we lose someone? Ivan, do you read me?"

Ivan flipped open the chattertube-mouthpiece cover. "Man overboard! We lost both Captain Buckle and Max!" he shouted. "Both Captain Buckle and Max went over the side!"

There had been no response. Sabrina had probably gasped, then ordered the observers to search the sky for parachutes. Ivan slammed the chattertube cover back with such force its metal clasp broke and the cover fell, banging and rattling down through the wires and catwalks below.

It was then that Ivan realized the *Pneumatic Zeppelin* was yawing to starboard—battling a tremendous drag—and felt the starboard engines rumble up their revolutions to counter the yaw. He jumped to the catwalk rail, and when he looked down his heart sank: the starboard sides of the towering gasbags beneath him were wobbling violently, battered by a massive wind current ripping through the airship's insides.

There was now another hole in the envelope, somewhere along the right flank. A big one. He could fix it as long as the superstructure girders, wrenching in their sockets as the wind torrent battered the gasbags like giant sails, didn't come crashing down in the meantime, folding the whole airship up like an accordion.

That would be bad.

"Finish the patch from the inside!" Ivan yelled at Tuck and Ambrose, as he launched himself down the stairwell. "Do the best you can!"

Ivan fought an awful sense of foreboding as he scrambled headlong through the maze of the airship's ladders and stairwells, leaping from platform to platform over forty-foot chasms between hydrogen cells, hurdling rails and dropping to catwalks beneath at a breakneck speed that only one who knew every inch of the complex decking could achieve without falling to a near-certain doom. And as he neared the site of the damage, the rogue air currents screaming through the wires sought to suck the oxygen out of his burning lungs, but still he ran.

When Ivan rushed down the main keel corridor outside the crew quarters in compartment seven, he immediately saw the looming vertical slash in the envelope, a lightning-bolt-shaped gash at least four stories high. Tall flaps of loose skin jerked violently around the breach, offering a wide-open view of the gray sky. Several skinners and crew members were already scrambling to initiate interior repairs from the upper decks. But this thing was going to have to be fixed from the outside.

Two bracing wires supporting the base of compartment seven's superstructure ring snapped, slicing away like razors with a wiry *zing*. Ivan's heart, already pounding, began to pound harder. He shouted—not words, really, but more a guttural howl of dismay.

The *Pneumatic Zeppelin* was coming apart.

From the corner of his eye, Ivan caught sight of something strange, a silver flash where nothing silver should have been. It was the blade of a sword, jammed into the joint between two girders at the base of the breach. He vaulted the rail and swung down onto the joint, ducking the torn fabric edges as they whipped in the whirlwind. He saw Max dangling outside, the slipstream pounding her body. She had one hand on the sword grip, the other clutching a flap of ragged fabric, which had cut through her glove; streams of blood (Martian blood is red, even redder than human blood) frothed pink around her fingers as it churned in the wind.

Max was still alive. But she wouldn't last very long.

She was frozen and exhausted. Her head was down. Her hands were slipping.

Ivan lunged, hooking his right arm around a girder as he crouched and leaned into the fluttering breach. The wind snatched at him—for an instant he thought he was about to be sucked out into the sky—as he grabbed Max's wrist and jerked her clenched hand away from the envelope skin. She lifted her head and looked up at him, her black hair swirling everywhere, her teeth chattering, her eyes glimmering white inside her ice-coated goggles.

Ivan lifted the weight of her against the airflow. She released her grip from the sword and grasped his other hand. The muscles in his arms threatened to cramp, so he yanked her up with one big wrench of his body. She came up so quickly it surprised him, and he bear-hugged her. They toppled backward, landing hard on the corridor grating. The wind knocked out of him, his back shooting with pain, Ivan gasped, sucking in deep draughts of air as Max lay sprawled on his chest, shivering violently. Her body felt light on his, much lighter than he would have imagined for her size, as if she were hollow-boned like a bird. He realized that he had never even touched Max before. The two of them had never gotten along. It was not a Martian thing—Ivan did not have a problem with Martians—it was because she was always trying to mess with his engines.

Ivan had saved her. He could feel her Martian heart—the Martian heart located in the left side of the chest, like a human heart—beating against him.

And he was glad that he had saved her.

Max's body stiffened and jerked as if she had just awoken from a bad dream. She jumped up, her black hair swirling in the air currents.

"On your feet, Chief Mechanic!" Max shouted in a hoarse voice. "You must see to any systems damage." She braced her boot against the intersection joint and wrenched her sword loose, returning it to her scabbard in one smooth motion.

"Aye!" Ivan had replied, having difficulty as he tried to rise from the catwalk. Max offered her hand; Ivan took it, and he was surprised how much strength she had when she pulled him to his feet.

"Check the hydrogen lines first," Max shouted, then clambered up to the walkway. "Move!"

A simple "thank you" would have been nice, Ivan thought.

Half an hour later, out on the windblown exterior of the *Pneumatic Zeppelin*, Ivan's back still hurt. The airship was running at less than maximum speed, but sixty knots still packed a wallop. He skimmed down his safety line as he arrived at the monstrous, forty-foot-high tear in the envelope skin.

Max was there, along with three teams of skinners that included Rudyard, Amanda, and Marian Boyd, who had bloodstained bandages jutting out of her flying helmet. There were also four of Pluteus's Ballblasters, well tethered and perched at the perimeter with their muskets ready, eyes peeled and turned toward the sky, even though it was unheard of to run into a second hunting pair of tanglers in one day.

Max, Marian, and the skinners sewed emergency patches, battling to keep the wind from whipping loose fabric into their faces, a real hazard with jagged, doped edges and nine-inch needles in the mix. Ivan slid into position to assist Marian. He was anxious to do something. He wanted to be busy. He did not want to think about Buckle being dead.

Max waved Ivan off. "What are you doing, Ivan?" she shouted. "There is no need for a mechanic out here! Get back inside!"

"A simple 'thank you' would have been nice," Ivan grumbled.

-XXIII-

SECOND-IN-COMMAND

SABRINA SERAFIM GRIPPED THE RUDDER wheel, the solid swing of its smooth brass handles reassuring against her hands. She had taken the rudder wheel from De Quincey, needing an anchor for her soul. Half an hour earlier, she had seen Buckle fall. She shuddered, not wanting to remember. The gondola cockpit was silent, and the winding and hissing of the instruments on her bowler hat seemed unusually loud.

"We shall maintain all ahead standard until repairs are completed," she told Welly, who was now seated in the chief navigator's chair. "Adjust for drift. Keep us on course."

"Aye, Captain," Welly replied, his voice quavering.

Captain. Sabrina took a deep breath. Romulus Buckle was gone. Her captain. Her brother. Her friend. It was impossible. She had always been certain that Buckle was bulletproof, untouchable. What an awful way to die: cut to shreds by a tangler as he plummeted to earth. It wasn't the way he should go. It was improper.

Kellie stood at Sabrina's feet, tail tucked between her legs, panting, foam coating her tongue after she had run miles of airship passageways and catwalks in a vain search for her master. Sabrina had tried to pick her up, but she squirmed away, inconsolable. Perhaps Kellie would have preferred to jump overboard with Buckle to join him in his end.

The dog's quivering misery made Sabrina feel even worse. Here she was—the acting captain—and her insides were knotted with anger at the unfairness of the world.

At least the *Pneumatic Zeppelin* was holding its course more easily now. Sabrina had had to compensate for the starboard-side drag less and less. This was good. With three skinner teams on the repairs, the job should almost be done—as long as no more beasties showed up—and she could get the airship back under full power again. She was in command now; standing at the helm where Buckle should have been, she felt alone.

"The sea breeze is stiffening from the west with the onset of evening, Captain," Welly reported. "Recalculating drift corrections."

"Aye," Sabrina replied.

Other than the sounds of her commands and Welly's acknowledgments, the gondola had been running silent since the tangler attack. Welly's pencil scratched loudly now and again as he worked his navigational math, his usual smile missing from his face as he leaned over his station. Poor Welly. He bore as much affection for Buckle as anyone. Well, Welly, you'd better get used to the chief navigator's chair, Sabrina thought, because it is yours now. And get ready to be nitpicked, because no navigator ever wants to have a captain who used to be a navigator, because they're always leaning over your shoulder, telling you how you're doing everything wrong. She smiled a little, surprising herself.

Sabrina was always a little hard on Welly because of that, because of the annoying twinge of embarrassment she felt at having her pimply apprentice, who was a full three years her junior, wearing her hat and telling everyone who would listen of his adolescent devotion to her. She would upon occasion refer to him as "the kid," even though she knew he hated it. But deep underneath, Sabrina quite liked Welly (in a big-sister sort of way), with his earnestness and honesty, and she often caught a glimpse of the handsome man who was struggling to grow up and out of the gawky, awkward "kid."

Sabrina was no stranger to loss. There would be no wet-eyed sadness from the acting captain. Not with a crew devastated by Buckle's death at exactly the moment when they needed him the most, mere hours before the *Pneumatic Zeppelin* was to plunge down into the poison mists of the Founders' city, charging headlong into the unknown, into a fortified bastion where they would be outnumbered and outgunned.

Buckle's loss was painful, but it changed nothing. Balthazar Crankshaft had to be saved. Even if the *Pneumatic Zeppelin* and her entire crew perished in the effort, no one doubted that the sacrifice would be worth it. Don't miss Buckle too much just yet, Serafim, she mused to herself, for you may be joining him soon.

And for just one instant, Sabrina allowed herself a twinge of hope, the tiny comfort that somehow, somewhere, Romulus Buckle might still be alive. He had escaped the clutches of certain death before. But as the little hope grew, it only further illuminated the reality of Buckle's death. She buried it.

Pluteus arrived in the gondola, his boots clomping down the iron stairwell and across the gondola's teakwood deck. He stank of sweat and gunpowder, so Sabrina could smell him coming as well as hear him. "I've been informed that we are currently drifting along at half speed, Serafim," he said, frustration coloring his voice. "How long is that going to last?"

Sabrina winced. She did not want Pluteus on the bridge. She adored him, but he was overbearing. "Not much longer, I'd wager, Pluteus. But our repair is a big job. We were ripped wide open at the kidney."

Pluteus placed his hand on Sabrina's shoulder; it was heavy, cloaked in a long leather glove with an armored plate stitched into the forearm. His hand had always felt reassuring. Pluteus was a big, gruff infantryman, but as Balthazar Crankshaft's cousin, he was like an uncle to most of the *Pneumatic Zeppelin*'s crew. "We are all sorry about Romulus, my dear," Pluteus said. "I know how close-knit you and he were."

Sabrina patted Pluteus's hand and tried to smile. "Thanks, Pluteus. But right now all I want to do is get Balthazar back. We owe it to Romulus to pull this one off."

Pluteus nodded and took a long, deep breath. "He won't be the only Crankshafter to die today, I am afraid," he said.

"Think lucky. Buckle always thought lucky," Sabrina said.

Pluteus grinned. "All right, well, my troopers are getting geared up," he said as he turned to leave. "Give me a signal five minutes prior to disembarkation, please."

"Pluteus, I, wait..." Sabrina blurted.

Pluteus stepped back. "Yes, Lieutenant?"

Sabrina's nerves twisted inside her stomach. She hadn't wanted to have this conversation with Pluteus. But now she had no choice. "I am going with you."

"Going with me *where?*" Pluteus asked.

"Down there. Into the mustard."

Pluteus blinked. Then he looked angry. "No. No you are not, Serafim," he replied.

Sabrina stepped away from the helm, motioning for De Quincey to return to his station at the wheel. "I was already slated to accompany Romulus. I can help you," Sabrina whispered, glancing at Welly, De Quincey, and the others, bodies

ROMULUS BUCKLE & THE CITY OF THE FOUNDERS

only a few feet away at every hand, all able to hear every word they were saying.

Pluteus sighed through his nose. "You are the acting captain now, Serafim. Your place is here."

"Pluteus, I…I am the only one who knows the way into the city."

She saw surprise flash in Pluteus's eyes. "You? You are the one? And how in blue blazes do you know that?"

"It is not important."

"Is not important? Answer me, Serafim," Pluteus demanded, stepping forward to face her directly. "How do you of all people have firsthand knowledge of secret passageways in and out of the City of the Founders?"

"Balthazar knows how."

Pluteus leaned very close. "I need to know *how*."

Sabrina had always looked up to Pluteus, even emulated him, and now she had just seen the shock in his eyes shift to angry suspicion. It angered her. "Not here, General Brassballs, and not now."

Shock registered in Pluteus's expression. He looked as if he wanted to slap her. "Balthazar may allow you the privilege of hiding your history, and so be it. But when it affects the here and now, I demand to know the facts."

"Step aside, General," Sabrina said, encouraged by the baritone authority brimming in her voice. "With all due respect—*I* am the captain here."

For a moment Pluteus did not move, his eyes hard and mean, the veins in his neck popping. Then, like a lion thwarted, he lurched aside.

Max's voice rang from the chattertube hood. "Chief Engineer to the bridge," she said.

Sabrina leaned in to her chattertube mouthpiece. "Aye, Chief Engineer."

"Emergency skin repairs are complete, Captain," Max announced. "But no more than all ahead standard recommended."

"Aye, Max. Good work," Sabrina said. She stiffened up, feeling a surge of energy. Her spine suddenly felt as it if it were injected with iron. She grabbed the engine telegraph lever and cocked it forward to all ahead full, sounding the bell. "All ahead full!" she shouted into the engine-room chattertube.

"All ahead full!" an engineer answered. The second dial on the engine-room telegraph swung to match the first, and the bell rang again.

"Your chief engineer recommended no more than standard, Captain Serafim," Pluteus commented dryly, glowering.

"I am going to make up your lost time for you, General," Sabrina answered, feeling the *Pneumatic Zeppelin* surge under her feet, the propellers winding up to a thundering hum. Kellie raised her head as she always did when the ship accelerated... but dropped it and fell to whimpering.

Sabrina nudged the rudder wheel, and as the weak light of the afternoon sun drifted its shadows across the cockpit, the glass nose of the gondola swung down toward the yellow miasma below, toward the Los Angeles basin, fogged with poison, and toward the fabled, wicked city within it.

–XXIV–

THE CROW WHO
COULD NOT CAW

MAX PAUSED ON THE MAIN keel corridor just a few feet from the piloting gondola stairwell. She had felt the *Pneumatic Zeppelin* rev up to all ahead full with little concern: she knew that the captain—whether it was Buckle or Sabrina—would push the engines to their fullest regardless of her recommendations. The situation demanded such risks. And she was certain that the patching would hold.

She was staring at her hands. She could not make them stop shaking.

She clamped them behind her back.

Captain Buckle was lost, and it was her fault.

No one would blame her, of course, not after she'd killed one tangler and nearly lost her life to the second while trying to drag her captain to safety. But that made no difference at all. Buckle was dead. She had failed him.

Snap out of it, Max! she thought. Things would be harder now, with Buckle gone. But she had to truly be the first mate and help Sabrina as best she could.

If only her hands would stop shaking.

Max hurried down the circular staircase with her hands still clasped behind her back. When she stepped onto the gondola deck, she scanned the gauges and dials at the engineering station, making sure that the zeppelin's systems were in good shape. She also immediately smelled the tension simmering between Sabrina and Pluteus. Sabrina looked calm, but Pluteus's face was flushed; he was shifting his weight almost imperceptibly forward onto the balls of his feet.

Sabrina turned her head and smiled sadly at Max. "Good work, Max. Aerodynamics are acceptable."

Max rubbed her ice-rimed goggles with the sleeve of her coat, doing so more to keep her hands busy than to actually defrost the lenses. "She will hold together as long as we do not run into any weather."

"I trust you have recovered sufficiently from your fall?" Sabrina asked.

"Yes," Max replied. It was almost a mumble. Max did not feel like talking.

"I was told that you did everything you could on the roof," Sabrina said. "No one could have done more."

Max nodded, unable to look Sabrina in the eyes. Kind words, but each one stabbed Max in the heart.

"We all know—" Sabrina started.

Something burst in Max's head. "What are your orders now, Captain Serafim?" Max asked, cutting Sabrina off, daring her to continue with her ineffective sympathies, her unintentional tortures.

"All right, Max," Sabrina said softly. "All right."

"There is no point in dwelling upon tragedy, Captain Serafim," Pluteus said gravely. "Time is a-wasting, and you have not answered my question. How do you know the way into the City of the Founders?"

Despite the ratcheting up of the tension, Max was grateful for the distraction.

"I haven't time for explanations now, General Pluteus," Sabrina replied with an authority in her voice that Max had never heard before. "See that your troopers are prepared. I shall be joining you presently."

"I am a general and a council elder—" Pluteus started.

"And I am the captain," Sabrina replied evenly. "See to your men."

Pluteus glared.

Max glanced back at Sabrina. Sabrina was correct that the airship captain was the commander on the airship. But what was this she had just overheard? Sabrina knew about a passageway leading into the City of the Founders? In a world where no one on the outside knew anything about the mysterious city, it was a considerable revelation. Pluteus was reasonable in his request for her to explain how she knew such a thing.

But Balthazar always allowed his adopted children to keep their secrets.

Something big and birdlike swooped up and landed on the gondola's starboard gunwale rail, where it was open to the sky.

Tangler. That was Max's first thought. A tangler zipping in to snatch a meal. She grabbed for her pistol.

"Tangler!" both Sabrina and Pluteus shouted, both drawing their pistols. Nero, unarmed, threw himself to the deck.

The dog—the thought flashed in Max's mind—the dog was too distraught to even bark.

It was not a tangler.

So the dog did not bark.

The bird-thing perched on the gondola rail was a machine, a bizarre metal construction that resembled a huge crow. Gears and cogs hummed across the length of its body, and glass portals roiled with steam and boiling water within; polished copper feathers lined the wings, glimmering in the gray light, while the eyes glowed red over a jet black beak on the metal skull.

Max and her shipmates stared over their pistols at the mechanical apparition. Neither she nor they had ever seen anything like this before.

The crow looked back at them with its red eyes. It released a jet of steam from a valve on its back and then seemed to relax, as if conserving its energy.

Uttering a small yip, Kellie jumped to her feet, hurried up to the mechanical crow and carefully sniffed one of the brass claws clutching the rail.

Max slowly lowered her pistol. The others did the same. Nero rose to his feet, looking a bit sheepish.

"Well, keep my powder dry," Pluteus stammered. "What wizards construct such wondrous contraptions as this?"

"Alchemists," Sabrina whispered.

The crow lifted its left leg, causing Kellie to jump back an inch, and there, clutched in its brass talons, was a leather-bound scroll.

Welly cautiously stepped forward and took a hold of the scroll, which the crow's talons released with a convulsive jerk as soon as he touched it. He rolled the scroll open, its parchment paper crackling as it was stretched out.

Welly read the note and then read it again. "I…" he started, and stopped, as if his eyes could not make out the elegant handwriting.

"Out with it, man," Pluteus huffed.

Welly looked up from the scroll, blinking, stunned. "It's from Captain Buckle. He's with the Alchemists. He wants us to come retrieve him."

"What?" Sabrina asked, incredulous.

Max was afraid to believe her ears; she felt as if she had suddenly forgotten how to breathe. Kellie, on the other hand, somehow understood, leaping up and chasing her tail as she did when a particular excitement was too much for her.

Welly waved the scroll, overcome with joy. "He is at the Observatory. The captain! Captain Buckle's alive!"

PART TWO:

SUBTERRANEAN

-XXV-

NINETY-NINE SOULS

CAPTAIN ROMULUS BUCKLE SMILED THE way he smiled when he had some air under him. He stood shoulder to shoulder with General Scorpius, Wolfgang, Wolfgang's assistant Luckmoor Zwicky, six Alchemist soldiers, and two robots inside the cramped and creaking main hold of the *Arabella*, the *Pneumatic Zeppelin*'s launch. The *Arabella* was not flying on this trip—she had been lowered by cables to pick up her passengers near the Alchemist Observatory, and now she was being ratcheted back up into her berth inside the belly of the hovering mother zeppelin—but it was close enough to flying for Buckle.

Scorpius cleared his throat and scratched his hoary gray-black beard. He obviously was not comfortable off the ground, and neither were the tall Alchemist soldiers with him. Wolfgang looked quite pleased, however, as did Zwicky, a scrawny, book-wormish type. Wolfgang and Zwicky ran the two robots Scorpius had chosen to accompany his platoon: Newton, with all of his firepower, and a strange machine they called the Owl, because it looked like one, or at least its face did, while the rest of its body more resembled that of a metal ostrich. Ten Alchemists and two robots did not an army make, but from the looks of their equipment and the three massive trunks packed with gear they carried with them, they would add needed punch to the Crankshaft rescue mission.

The Alchemists were expecting to find Andromeda Pollux in the Founder's prison. Why? Because Buckle had told them she would be there. He did not know if she would be there, but... surely Andromeda would be sitting in a cell next to Balthazar's.

Buckle did not want to anger the Alchemists. He did not want to be squashed by Newton.

And there was another fly in the ointment, as far as Buckle's potential predicament went: looming at his shoulder was a hulking Alchemist soldier named Caliban Kepler. Kepler was a bear of a fellow, his bulk straining at the seams of his long white coat, his face so beefy that his leather cap and goggles seemed almost swallowed up by the fleshiness around them.

Capella De Vega had assigned Kepler to Buckle as his "bodyguard," although Buckle figured the man was actually an assassin ordered to exact revenge if Buckle attempted a double cross, or failed to secure the release of Andromeda Pollux.

The Alchemists did not fool around.

Still, Buckle felt he had struck a good deal. Once the Alchemists agreed to assist the Crankshaft expedition, they had activated some strange mechanical crow to deliver his hand-written message to the *Pneumatic Zeppelin*. And Capella De Vega had invited Buckle to peer through one of their gigantic tele-scopes to watch his airship rotate on her heel and steam full speed back in his direction. Perhaps two hundred Alchemists, every one of them begrimed in some way with soot or oil, had come outside to the monument park to view the zeppelin as it arrived. They seemed to approve of the massive airship, nodding as she came to a hover fifty feet above the Observatory dome and dropped her static lines.

Buckle found his pocket watch and spun the winder back and forth between his fingers. The *Arabella* shuddered and made a distinct *bump* as she arrived in her berth in the belly of the *Pneumatic Zeppelin*. Copper-encased anchor bars slid into position with scraping *clank*s. Crew members in the launch bay shouted orders back and forth as they secured the *Arabella* in her hangar.

Buckle moved forward. The drawbridge ramp in the *Arabella's* nose cranked down, admitting gray light into the launch's dark interior. He strode out onto the loading platform where Max, Kellie, Pluteus, two Ballblasters, and the ship's surgeon, Harrison Fogg, waited to greet him. Their faces were both alight at the sight of him and tight as they scrutinized the Alchemists coming behind, especially the hulking Newton. Buckle chuckled under his breath.

Kellie raced forward with a happy yip and wheeled around Buckle's feet, her tail a blurry hurricane. He reached down to pat her head and she jumped into his arms, licking his face with such a fury it felt like her tongue was scraping the beard off his chin.

"Welcome aboard, Captain," Max said. Her voice was emotionless, but her eyes glimmered blue inside her goggles. Martian blue reflected happiness.

"Thanks, Max," Buckle replied. "It appears that you and I are tanglerproof."

"Just barely, Captain," Max responded dryly.

Buckle smiled, his gaze lingering a moment on the dazzling blue shimmers lurking in Max's goggles—he saw joy in her eyes only rarely, and when he did he always felt a great surge of encouragement, though to what purpose or effect he was not sure. And the presence of the Alchemists did not perturb Max as it did the others, not even in the slightest. Buckle knew such surprises never ruffled her feathers.

General Pluteus, on the other hand, stepped forward with his hand on his pistol holster and a storm of suspicion in his face. "Captain Buckle," he growled, "what is the meaning of this armed Alchemist force? Are you under arrest? Have they made you a prisoner?"

Buckle set Kellie on the platform and slapped his hand on Pluteus's shoulder. "Stand down, Pluteus," he said with a reassuring smile. "They are here as friends."

"Friends? Friends?" Pluteus stammered.

"They are joining us in our assault on the City of the Founders," Buckle said.

Pluteus went quiet, but his jaw was working. He looked like he had just bitten down on a bugbear turd as he eyed the Alchemists.

"Status report, Max," Buckle said.

"The ship suffered damage to the exterior envelope, but temporary repairs have been completed to my satisfaction, Captain," Max said, taking a half step forward. "All systems are functioning at maximum efficiency. Crew is at regular complement of sixty-eight. With the addition of twenty-one Crankshaft infantry, and now ten Alchemists, not counting the two robots, there are a total of ninety-nine souls aboard, sir."

"Very good, Max," Buckle echoed. "Ninety-nine souls."

"Captain Buckle, are you unhurt?" the ship's surgeon, Harrison Fogg, asked. At the ripe old age of thirty-six, he was by far the oldest member of the airship crew. Fogg was a tall, slender fellow with a rambunctious face and the bedside manner of a comedian, although at the moment he was rather serious. "We have been quite concerned."

Buckle smiled. He had great affection for the lighthearted Fogg. "Just a few bumps and bruises, my good surgeon," he said. "I'm afraid I've got nothing for you to chop off today."

Fogg's clear green eyes danced. "Well, and I was all ready to slice you open."

Buckle could not wipe the smile off his face. He was elated to be back aboard the *Pneumatic Zeppelin*, and now, with the launch secure, he felt the mighty airship swinging around, her motors and propellers winding up to full speed.

But there was much to do.

Buckle turned to face the Alchemists waiting patiently on the ramp. He almost bumped into the brute Kepler, who had inched up behind him. The Alchemist soldiers lugged their heavy equipment lockers in pairs; Newton carried one by himself as Wolfgang supervised. Zwicky stood at the flank of the giant-eyed Owl. General Scorpius towered at the front of the group, stiff as a board, his unkindly gaze locked on Max.

"General Scorpius, welcome aboard the *Pneumatic Zeppelin*," Buckle said.

"We are honored and most impressed," Scorpius replied, his eyes scanning the length of the massive launch bay before returning to squint at Max.

"General Scorpius, my chief engineer, Max, will see to your men if you will come forward with General Pluteus and me to my quarters."

Scorpius did not move. "Captain Buckle, I..." he started, and Buckle was aware of considerable disapproval in his voice.

"What is it, General?" Buckle asked, although he suspected he already knew the answer.

"We are not in the habit of trusting Martians, Captain Buckle," Scorpius announced flatly.

Buckle's interior flashed with anger. He suddenly did not like General Scorpius at all. He wanted to berate him for his small-minded bigotry. But where would that get him? There wasn't time. "As you wish, General," Buckle answered evenly, preventing himself from glaring, although there was no hiding the disapproval in his voice. "General Pluteus, have one of your men see to the Alchemists' accommodations."

"Sergeant Scully! Take our guests to the ready room!" Pluteus ordered.

Sergeant Scully stepped forward with a click of his boot heels. "Aye!" he shouted.

Buckle motioned for Scorpius to follow him. "This way, if you please, General," he said, forcing the words out pleasantly. He knew that Kepler would follow him whether invited or not.

Buckle turned to lead the way down the main corridor. Pluteus grabbed him by the arm, his fingers so tight they pinched his skin, and pulled him forward a few steps as he swung his mouth close to his ear. "With all due respect, Captain Buckle, have you lost your mind?" Pluteus hissed. "Bringing these nefarious ironmongers aboard our zeppelin?"

"It was necessary, General," Buckle whispered back. "We need all the help we can get, and you know it."

"Necessary? Firstly, they insult our chief engineer. Secondly, they'll cut our throats at the first opportunity!"

"Do you forget, Pluteus, that they lost Andromeda Pollux on the same day we lost Balthazar? They are searching for her. I proposed an alliance, and now the contract is signed and the ink is dry. Now we are all in this mess together, whether we like it or not."

"Bah!" Pluteus said under his breath. "I vote that we jettison them at two thousand feet and have done with this," he muttered. But there was nothing he could do for it.

~XXVI~

CAPTAIN'S QUARTERS

BUCKLE MARCHED QUICKLY ALONG THE main keel corridor with Kellie, Pluteus, Scorpius, and Kepler hard on his heels. There wasn't much time. The *Pneumatic Zeppelin* would arrive at the disembarkation point in twenty minutes. They strode toward his cabin in the bow, moving through the crew quarters, infirmary, mess, and galley before the corridor angled upward into the elevated nose section of the zeppelin; they passed the officers' quarters and the library, and then arrived at the big wooden door etched with the word *Captain*.

Buckle looked at Kepler, who stared back with his dark, uninterested eyes. "You wait here. I won't be going anywhere," Buckle said.

Kepler shook his head and took a small step forward, as if threatening to kick the door in.

Buckle looked at Scorpius. "No offense to your man, here, General Carbon, but this is where Crankshaft secrets reside."

"Makes you nervous, does he?" Scorpius said as he turned to Kepler. "Wait here."

Kepler nodded and stepped to one side. His eyes never left Buckle, however.

Buckle swung the door open and walked into his cabin, Kellie bolted in. The two generals followed. Once inside, Buckle swung the door shut, stranding Kepler on the landing.

"Impressive," Scorpius said as he looked around. "I daresay we have few chambers more grand than this sky palace."

The captain's cabin aboard the *Pneumatic Zeppelin* was remarkable, Buckle knew: the forward wall was a towering semicircle of glass, being the bottom half of the huge window dome set in the airship's nose. It provided an expansive view of the sky and clouds skimming past, casting everything within in a mild silhouette. The wooden walls and ceiling were built around the superstructure girders and the base of the Axial corridor, which ran into the center of the nose dome overhead. The chamber was big in comparison to the cramped living spaces of the airship, and it encompassed a bedchamber area, a towering steam-valve organ, and the large "Lion's Table" where officer meetings and chart mapping took place.

The captain's quarters was both the captain's sanctuary and a communal space, the platform in front of the window being employed as a stage for the crew to put on small concerts, poetry readings, and plays. Buckle and his officers often took their dinner at the Lion's Table, smoking pipes over their grog ration as they gazed out at the sky afterward.

"The Imperials know how to build fancy airships, I'll give them that," Buckle said, walking to his chart rack and drawing a large map out of a brass tube. Kellie bounded up onto his bed, her bat-like ears perking up as she panted happily.

"This is an Imperial-built airship, is it?" Scorpius inquired.

"Yes," Buckle replied as he unrolled the map and laid it out on the Lion's Table, weighing down the corners with copper paperweights of sculpted lions that wept and clutched a shield with a cross. Buckle looked at Pluteus and Scorpius: they were standing shoulder to shoulder, ramrod straight, their helmets tucked under their arms, as rigid as men might be if they were teetering at the edge of a cliff. "I presume the two of you have never met before?" Buckle asked.

"No, Captain Buckle," Scorpius answered. "We have not."

"I've never had the pleasure," Pluteus said, but his words were thick with venom.

Buckle folded his hands behind his back and sighed. He wanted to change his clothes—they were crunchy under their coating of dried tangler guts—but there were more pressing matters to attend to. "Gentlemen, while we wait for my navigator to arrive, let us have a formal introduction. General Pluteus Brassballs of the Crankshafts, this is General Scorpius Carbon of the Alchemists."

Pluteus and Scorpius turned to face one another.

"General Carbon," Pluteus said.

"General Brassballs," Scorpius said.

They exchanged a formal shaking of hands with all the warmth of two snakes, and turned back to face Buckle.

Buckle glared at the generals. "We all want our people back, gentlemen, and once we hit the ground there will be no time for squabbling. Necessity has made us allies, if only for the moment. Trust must be absolute. Our survival will depend upon it."

"Of course, Captain Buckle," Pluteus said. "I am an old soldier. You need not explain such things to me."

"Nor I," Scorpius chimed in, his voice indignant.

"Very good," Buckle said with a nod. At least he had the two old salts agreeing on something.

There was a knock on the heavy wooden door of the cabin.

"Enter!" Buckle shouted, pacing behind the table, hoping that Sabrina had arrived so he could brief the generals and then release them to ready their men.

The door swung open, pushed by one of Kepler's tree-trunk arms, and Howard Hampton hurried in with a tray of steaming tea.

"Cookie thought you'd like some tea, sir," Howard announced, huffing, obviously having come at a considerable pace from the galley. "Almond, sir. Your favorite, sir."

The two generals looked at Howard askance, but Buckle couldn't help but grin. The boy was so happy to see him that his smile was shaking as he offered his tray. "Very nice," Buckle said, taking a cup and pouring a shot of fastmilk into the brown tea. He looked to the generals. "Anyone for a cup?" he asked.

Pluteus and Scorpius scowled and shook their heads.

"Thank you very much, Howard," Buckle said. "Now off you go."

"Yes, sir. Glad to have you back, Captain," Howard cheered breathlessly as he scurried back to the door.

"Nice to be back, Howard," Buckle said. "And offer the fellow outside the door a cup on your way out, please."

"Yes, Captain," Howard grunted, as he leveraged his weight to open the door, while balancing the tea tray with one hand. Kepler swung the door completely open and the boy exited with a wary smile for the big man. Kepler left the door open for a brief pause, scrutinizing the room with his small eyes.

Outside on the landing, Howard Hampton said, "Would you like a cup of tea, Mister Alchemist?"

Kepler grunted, then stepped back and let the door drift shut of its own accord.

Buckle didn't know whether Kepler's grunt was an affirmative or not. He sipped the hot almond tea, sweet with goat's milk fresh from Victoria's teats. Female goats were kept on board airships as a source of fresh milk, called fastmilk, which was a necessity with tea. Goats were good-luck charms, and aircrew were a superstitious lot, often clipping off a lock of the goat's beard to store in a locket or pocket or whatnot. Aboard airships, the goats were always beardless.

The tea was quite pleasing with the milk. Kepler should try some.

Scorpius cleared his throat rudely, stepping up to the Lion's Table. "Captain, I hate to interrupt your tea party, but there is little time to discuss strategy and prepare my men."

"We shall begin in a moment," Buckle said. He, too, was impatient. But getting frustrated would not help him with the generals, who glowered at him like bulldogs. "Please, sit down if you wish."

Neither general moved.

No tea. No chairs. Damned bootjacked infantrymen, Buckle thought.

Another knock on the door.

"Enter!" Buckle shouted.

Kepler opened the door. He didn't have any tea, and Howard Hampton was gone. Buckle hoped that Kepler hadn't eaten Howard. Sabrina entered with her map case, casting an uncertain glance at Kepler as she stepped in.

"Navigator reporting as requested, Captain." Sabrina said, her green eyes shining. Kepler slammed the door shut behind her.

"Navigator?" Scorpius grumbled, eying Sabrina's red hair with obvious suspicion. "I thought this was a commanders' meeting, Captain Buckle."

"My navigator's presence is essential, General," Buckle replied. "For she is the only one who knows the way into the City of the Founders."

–XXVII–

THE NAVIGATOR'S SECRET

NEXT CAME THE TENSE SILENCE that Sabrina had expected. Scorpius screwed up his eyes and glared at her as if she were the one who had kidnapped Andromeda Pollux. Pluteus's stare was only a few degrees less scalding. Buckle, on the other hand, looked slightly bemused, although she was the only one who knew him well enough to see it. She walked up and placed her map case on the Lion's Table, nicknamed thus by the crew because the legs were carved to resemble the forelegs and paws of lions. Sabrina had spent many hours sitting there with Buckle and her fellow officers, often listening to one of Max's violin concertos before dinner on special occasions.

Sabrina laid out her map of the Founders' city—the map she had drawn up for Buckle—on top of an old road map on the table.

"How is it that a member of the Crankshaft clan does possess such an intimate knowledge of the City of the Founders?" Scorpius questioned, never taking his eyes off her. "A fortress no one enters and no one leaves?"

"I got out," Sabrina stated flatly.

Scorpius flicked his eyes to Buckle and then back to her. "You got out," he repeated in a fashion that made obvious his distrust of her words.

"Yes," Sabrina replied.

Scorpius had every reason to be incredulous. It was said that no one had ever met anyone from the City of the Founders, beyond their crimson-cloaked ambassadors. It was a place of phantasms, obscured behind dark fables. Stories were told about an elite clan of near immortals sequestered in a grand citadel, feasting on beef and cherries while they masterminded an empire guarded by invincible zeppelins, locomotives, and soldiers that could fly. The city itself, sealed up behind massive walls and an ocean of Martian mustard gas, was rumored to be a filthy metropolis existing mostly underground, its thousands of citizens locked in scab-riddled poverty as they slaved inside factories and foundries of unimaginable size and scope. And no downtrodden citizen, no matter how resourceful, intelligent, or desperate, ever, *ever* escaped.

"And just how did you get out?" Scorpius demanded.

"I was carried out, as a child," Sabrina said.

Scorpius leaned forward. "Carried out by who?"

"General, we do not have time for this," Buckle said sharply.

Scorpius glared at Buckle, then turned a cold eye to Sabrina. "It is said that Isambard Fawkes has hair as red as fire, and that each member of his family does possess hair more scarlet than the next."

Sabrina met Scorpius's gaze with cool detachment. She had expected the interrogation.

"That is enough, General Scorpius," Buckle said. "We can discuss fairy tales and myths at a later date. Proceed, Lieutenant."

Sabrina slid her finger across the map of Los Angeles. "We disembark at the landing point: Melrose and La Brea Avenue. From here we travel due south on La Brea for about a mile, crossing the moon moat, a wide ditch apparently created by a big explosion on the day of The Storming. The Founders patrol this ditch with forgewalkers in sealed armor suits, and it would be best to avoid them. Once inside the ditch, we enter the sewer system here. We work our way through the old channel pipes to a large sewage-holding tank—long since abandoned—but which takes us under the walls of the city and one hatch away from the underground prison warren. I will be able to locate Balthazar and Andromeda's cells once we are in there."

"Locate the cells? How? How do you know this?" Scorpius spluttered.

Sabrina glanced at Buckle.

"How she knows it is not important," Buckle said.

"It is important to me," Scorpius shot back. "I have to trust this woman with my life and the lives of my men, not to mention the life of Andromeda Pollux, which is worth more than all of us put together."

"I'm no spy, damn it!" Sabrina blurted, then clamped her lips together. Her heart was pounding.

"With all due respect, General Scorpius, that is enough," Pluteus interjected. "The young officer remembers nothing more. She is the adopted child of Balthazar and we all trust her absolutely. That will have to be good enough for you."

Pluteus's defense of her honor surprised Sabrina, though she concluded that it was due to his distaste for an Alchemist interrogating one of his own more than to his standing up for her and her mysteries, which also confounded him.

Scorpius took a step back. "I and only I, Scorpius Carbon of the Alchemists, shall determine what is good enough for me."

"Sabrina, continue with the briefing," Buckle ordered.

Sabrina took a deep breath and ran her finger across her map. "Okay. Once we secure our people, we will move above ground and into the city. It is only a short distance to the main plaza, a big open area where the *Pneumatic Zeppelin* will lower the launch and evacuate us."

"March straight into the heart of the City of the Founders?" Scorpius sputtered. "This is your escape plan?"

"Surprise is our main weapon, General," Buckle said, tapping his hand on the table. "We shall be in and out before they know we are there."

"Bah!" Scorpius huffed, but he did not argue.

"We have run out of time, gentlemen," Buckle said. "Scorpius, you have been briefed on the battle plan, and you are either with us or you are not."

"The Alchemist Council has commanded me to assist you," Scorpius replied. "I have no intention of failing to follow my orders."

"Good," Buckle said. "Generals, see to your preparations. We shall join you presently."

Scorpius made a little bow. "Captain," he said respectfully, then avoided Sabrina with his eyes as he turned and strode for the door. Pluteus gave Buckle a quick nod and followed Scorpius.

"Chief Navigator, stay a moment, please," Buckle said.

"Of course, Captain," Sabrina said, folding her map back into its case. She knew he had many questions for her, questions he could never ask.

Buckle returned to his teacup and took a long sip. "It is strange," he said. "We are only a few moments from our assault on the Founders' city...but I feel quite subdued, as relaxed as a man about to slip into a warm bath. Perhaps after falling three thousand feet with a tangler nipping at my heels, running the gauntlet of the city doesn't seem so dangerous in comparison."

"Perhaps," Sabrina answered as she watched Buckle drink his tea and ruffle the silvery fur on the top of Kellie's head with his free hand. She still could not quite get over her amazement that he was there, standing right in front of her, unhurt and in the flesh, after she and everyone else had given him up for dead not more than an hour before. She also noticed that his forehead was wrinkled in an uncharacteristically serious way.

Buckle stepped to the dome window and looked out, folding his hands behind his back. The late afternoon clouds glowed, variously bright and dark. "Ours is a mysterious world," Buckle said quietly. "Under every shadow lies a secret."

"Yes," Sabrina said.

Buckle turned to face her. "But there are a thousand secrets inside every soul."

Sabrina did not reply. She felt nervous. Had Buckle decided that she was untrustworthy? No one knew anything about her history, except Balthazar—and he didn't know everything. And now that it was obvious she had a connection to the City of the Founders, would Buckle and the crew spurn her as a turncoat? She looked into Buckle's blue eyes and found them soft and calm. She suddenly felt safe.

"I have seen into your soul, Sabrina Serafim," Buckle said. "And I shall always trust you."

–XXVIII–

DEAD RECKONING
AND OBELISKS

MAX WATCHED DE QUINCEY AS he rocked the rudder wheel back and forth in his hands, guiding the *Pneumatic Zeppelin* as she descended, countering a weak crosswind flowing in from the sea to the west, pushing at the airship's starboard flank. He inched the rudder wheel to starboard, to press the *Pneumatic Zeppelin*'s nose back into line over old Hollywood. The huge zeppelin groaned comfortably as it leaned its colossal mass into the crosswind.

De Quincey was a very good helmsman.

"Light crosswind to starboard, evening sea breeze," Welly announced. He was at the chief navigator's station now. "Recalculating rate of drift."

"Aye," Max replied. Welly looked like a hunchback, with his big brass oxygen cylinder strapped to his back, its bulky, glass-plated helmet pushed up on his head and its flexible tubes loose about his shoulders. Everyone in the gondola was wearing their oxygen equipment, including Max; she found the heavy gear quite cumbersome.

Max took a slow, deep breath as she observed the ground through the glass nose dome of the gondola. The cityscape below was hidden beneath a gray fog that blanketed the entire

Los Angeles basin. Ruins of office buildings and skyscrapers jutted above the fog bank's surface in jagged clusters of rusting girders and crumbling masonry. One could not see the deadly layer of mustard gas from above. The alien mustard was dense, and it hugged the ground beneath the fog bank, rising to no more than thirty feet at the most, while the harmless sea fog swirled up to fifty feet higher above it.

The fog bank came closer and closer as the *Pneumatic Zeppelin* descended. Their plunge into the misty depths and the City of the Founders was, by her calculation, no more than ten minutes away.

No defenders had come up to meet them, nor had a shot been fired. No one had noticed them, as far as she could tell. The deadly fog bank surrounding the City of the Founders may have kept everyone and everything away—but perhaps it also made it nearly impossible to see anything coming.

"Make sure you account for the added weight, navigator," Max said. "And watch her trim. With thirty-one extra troopers and two robots aboard, we are notching up power for altitude and sluggish on the turn."

"Aye, Lieutenant," Welly replied, checking two pocket watches clamped to a panel. Darius Banerji, the apprentice navigator, was now in the cockpit at the assistant's station. Both Welly and Banerji bent low over their instruments and charts, constantly checking and updating their calculations as they proceeded to position the *Pneumatic Zeppelin* over the exact point—one they could not see—that Sabrina Serafim had dotted on their maps.

Welly peered into the leather-cushioned eyepiece of the binocular-shaped drift scope, which was built into the instrument panel, pointing straight down through the floor of the gondola. The drift scope's magnification was set to match the ship's altitude, and its lens, etched with a set of parallel black lines, allowed the navigator to measure the sideways motion of objects passing beneath the airship, and thus calculate the current rate of drift.

"Fifteen seconds," Welly said without looking up. "Fifteen seconds starboard, south by southwest."

"Fifteen seconds starboard," Banerji repeated, his eyes on the daughter compass and a timing hourglass streaming with golden sand. "South by southwest. Aye." He made fractional adjustments to the drift indicator by tweaking a series of small wooden knobs.

Welly lifted his head up from the drift scope, his forehead pink from being pressed into the leather headrest. "Taking obelisk sextant reading," he announced, lifting a complicated metal telescope seated in a maze of gears and dials to his eye. Other than the Big Green Soup of the Pacific to the west, and the snow-locked peak of Mount Wilson to the east, the only permanent landmarks the navigators had to work with were the gigantic Martian obelisks that loomed at many points on the horizon.

Max watched Welly taking his obelisk reading. She felt a twinge of despair. It was the Martians who had dropped the obelisks, mountain-sized rectangular slabs of purplish stone that towered in the sky, many of them tall enough to split low-lying clouds as they passed overhead. Up close, they were uneven and craggy, hoary with ice, the unknown stone they were cut from more blue than purple. No man had ever been able to chisel, blast, or melt even the tiniest chip off one. It was said, in the *Histories of Charlie W.*, that in the time before the obelisks, there was a wonderful, magical source of power called

ROMULUS BUCKLE & THE CITY OF THE FOUNDERS

electricity, but the obelisks suffocated it. It was even said that, oddly, the obelisks were responsible for milk souring almost immediately after being drawn from a cow or goat, and this was the reason people now called it *fastmilk*, because you had to drink it right away.

The obelisks made mankind hate the Martians, so Max hated the obelisks.

Max watched Welly bring his obelisk sextant to bear on the Catalina Obelisk, looming very close to the south, triangulating its position against the Redlands Obelisk to the east and the Piru Obelisk to the northwest. Welly could take accurate sightings, pinpointing his position down to just a few meters.

Max was upset—the fact that Martians were never supposed to get upset made her even more upset—and the fact that anyone who looked at her would see it made her angry. She knew her eyes were pulsing with a faint scarlet—she could see the liquid color reflecting in her goggles. She hated her eyes, her Martian eyes. She was a hybrid, and in the genetic milkshake she had inherited her father's black alien eyes, which betrayed every passionate feeling with sudden parades of color. Her eyes had forced her to live a stoic life, an emotionally tepid existence, where she kept all others at arm's length in order to keep her private feelings private. But now she could not find a way to stuff her anger down, not all the way down, at least.

Max was indignant because Sabrina Serafim was joining Buckle on the Crankshaft rescue expedition. Max wasn't jealous of Sabrina personally—the chief navigator was as capable as anyone to accompany Buckle—but she was piqued by Buckle's complete, even careless, disregard for the regulations governing zeppelineers and ground operations. The captain of a Crankshaft

airship was never to get involved in dangerous ground operations. The captain's place was aboard the airship. And if the
situation on the ground demanded the captain's presence, then
his second-in-command was required to take the helm. Never,
ever, were both the captain and his first mate to be exposed off
the ship in a hostile environment.

Never.

Max adored the rules and regulations of the sky-vessel tradition. One could even say that she was obsessed with them.
Yet she understood that sometimes the rules had to be bent,
depending upon circumstances. But what Buckle was doing was
wrong. It endangered the ship. Sure, Max was an excellent pilot,
but she wasn't the best. Not like Romulus Buckle. Not like
Sabrina Serafim.

And right now, as the *Pneumatic Zeppelin* descended into the
dense fog bank above the City of the Founders, they needed
their best.

Max saw the reddish glow in her goggles getting a shade
brighter.

The engine-order telegraph dinged with a puff of steam as
Max swung the dial handle. "Ahead one-third," she shouted
into the chattertube.

"Ahead one-third!" came the response from the engine
room, along with the sister dial dinging into the identical
position.

Ahead one-third was slow. Very slow. Docking speed. But
they were about to dip down into the fog bank and, safe from
the eyes of any Founders' sentinels, proceed the last two thousand yards hidden but flying blind. The navigators' only refer-
ence to their position would be calculations according to their
watches, maps, compass, and last known rate of drift.

"Vent steambags, thirty percent, across the board," Max ordered.

"Venting steambags, thirty percent, slam bang, aye!" Nero Coulton answered, flipping master switches on the hydrogen board, which controlled both the gas cells and the steambags. Lift was first reduced by venting hot air, rather than bleeding off the hydrogen.

Max felt the *Pneumatic Zeppelin* lose a hint of her lightness. She removed her sword from its hooks overhead and buckled the scabbard to her belt. The air cylinder on her back annoyed her. She peered down through the floor observation window: the gray mass of fog came closer and closer, its wavy undulations becoming less distinct as the character of the surface, a misty cloud, emerged, looking vaporous, ethereal, and damp. The tops of tall palm trees, frozen as fuzzy icicles, poked out of the miasma in irregular lines, still in place along the unseen boulevards below.

"Thirty seconds to immersion!" Welly shouted in the chattertube.

"Oxygen masks on!" Max shouted into her chattertube hood. "Oxygen masks on! Make sure you plug back into the chattertube line!" She double-checked her crew, making sure that De Quincey, Dunn, Welly, Banerji, Nero, and the assistant engineer, Geneva Bolling, pulled on their masks. She heard the rattle of the mask clasps as they were snapped, the squeak of the leather straps as they were tightened under chins, followed by the *clink* of the cylinder knobs being cranked open, hissing with compressed air.

"Signals! Verify mask on!" Max said, twisting backward to look past the staircase into the rear corridor, where the door to the signals room was located. She saw the signals officer, Jacob

Fitzroy, lean out of the signals room, his oxygen mask oddly large on his small face and head. He gave her an annoying thumbs up.

"Verbal confirmation, if you please, Mister Fitzroy," Max said.

"Mask on, Lieutenant Max," Fitzroy answered, his high voice soft inside his helmet.

"Eyes up for floating mines!" Max shouted. She pulled her heavy oxygen mask over her head and tightened the straps before she plugged herself back into the power and chattertube lines.

"Entering fog bank!" Welly yelled from inside his mask, his voice muffled, his breath misting the interior of the glass.

"Engage boil," Max ordered, her words dropping hollowly inside her helmet.

"Boil engaged, aye," Geneva Bolling responded at the engineering station, flipping the levers to activate the pressurized agitation rods inside the cockpit's liquid-filled instruments, causing the bioluminescent creatures within to emit their soft green illumination.

The vast ocean of fog rose up and swallowed the *Pneumatic Zeppelin*. To Max it seemed as if they had been sucked into a shadow, a swirling gray vault of nothingness. Her skin was suddenly damp and warmer, her goggles speckled with pinhead droplets of condensation. She could hear her heartbeat drumming in her ears; the oxygen mask and fog absorbed sound so efficiently that for a moment, she was concerned that the engines had stopped, so complete was the sudden silencing of the familiar drones of the propeller nacelles.

Max's eyes swung to the instrument panels where, in the eerie half darkness, the bioluminescent boil glowed moon green inside the chadburn dial, inclinometers, floating gyros, drift and deflection pointers, thermometers, thermohygrometers, winding clocks, compasses, barometers, and a vast array of tubes and cylinders.

"Flying blind now," Welly stated, a compass in one hand and a watch in the other.

Max kept a close watch on her compass. "Maintaining course. Ballast, maintain forty-five feet altitude. We want to keep our feet out of the mustard."

"Forty-five feet and steady as she goes, aye," Nero repeated.

"Keep your eyes peeled for mines," Max said. It was a useless order, she knew. The pea-soup fog would hide any floating mines until they were almost upon them, and the zeppelin was far too big and slow to avoid them even at docking speed. It would be up to the men positioned outside on the bow and flanks to deflect any mines. She started laboring to breathe—as if her air was becoming too thick—until she realized that she had not opened the oxygen lines to her helmet from her air canister on her back. She cranked the cylinder knob open, filling her mask with musty oxygen that smelled as old and dead as dinosaurs.

–XXIX–

A MINEFIELD CHAINED
TO THE SKY

"ALWAYS OUTSIDE THE AIRSHIP THESE days," Ivan grumbled as he hooked his safety line to the bow-pulpit railing at the nose of the *Pneumatic Zeppelin*. The world was a gaping wall of gray mist that fell away into the void ahead of him. Mechanics were supposed to work inside the machine most of the time, weren't they? Oh, well. He was warm enough, bundled up in his fur-lined coat, boots, and gloves, and the oxygen mask, designed for high altitudes, was insulated with dog fur. Besides, the ocean fog was warm. Warm but wet. The good thing was that tanglers weren't supposed to like the fog. The bad thing was that nobody really knew what other sorts of unknown beasties might lurk in the permanent mists.

Ivan preferred not to think about that.

He was perched on the nose of the great zeppelin, a dot on its sheer, rounded face, standing on the iron frame of the black bowsprit, from which the jibboom extended forward nearly fifty feet in a tapering V shape, festooned with the tacks of jibs, stays, long rolls of antiboarding netting, and the furled spinnaker sail, leading the ship like a hollow arrowhead. He screwed his boots down on the narrow bowsprit in an attempt to secure his footing. The *Pneumatic Zeppelin* was moving so slowly that

139

the slipstream wasn't a problem, and he was well anchored with two safety lines—one hooked to the bow pulpit and the other hooked into the small rail along the port side of the gun turret—but he was holding a twenty-foot wooden fending pike, and if floating mines appeared, he would be leveraging himself into a variety of precarious positions.

Ivan wasn't the only one on the exterior—the airship's entire complement of skinners and riggers were also stationed evenly on both flanks of the ship's axis, all armed with fending pikes, their numbers supplemented by a Ballblaster here and there. He could see none of them in the dense mist, however, not even Chief Skinner Marian Boyd, who was only a few yards to his right on the other side of the bowsprit, so for all intents and purposes, he was alone.

Ivan peered into the vaporous nothingness that pressed him with its gentle, invisible current. He could only make out fifteen feet of the jibboom before it vanished, plunging into the obscurity of the mists. He cursed the condensation distorting his goggle lenses; his constant wiping resulted in muddy streaks that were only slightly better in terms of clarity. But his main discomfort was an itch on the end of his nose. He considered lifting the oxygen helmet up so he could quickly scratch the offending skin, holding his breath until he clamped the mask back down—he was certain that the airship had not yet descended to the level of the yellow-colored mustard gas—but he thought better of it. He gripped his fending pike tightly, hoping that the painful clutch of his fingers would distract him from the itching that was rapidly threatening to drive him mad. The fending pike had a copper grasper attached to the tip of its pole, and Ivan could open and close the grasper by manipulating a control wire that ran alongside the shaft. The fending pike was light, made of hollow wood and thin metal, but the awkward tug and pull of it was taxing his muscles already. Ivan wasn't a big fellow; the thin rails he had for arms possessed a wiry strength good for twisting wrenches, but not for manhandling jousting lances.

Eyes up. Watch the sky. Or at least the gray wall, which is all the sky you'll get, Ivan thought. If there actually was a floating minefield within the fog bank surrounding the City of the Founders, and such things were not merely the inspired imaginings of storytellers beefing up their myths around the campfires, then he'd better be ready. He peered into the roiling mist. Once a mine came at him, either straight on or skidding along the leading edge of the bowsprit, he would only have a few seconds to bring the fending pike to bear, grasp the chain, and pass it along to the next crewman twenty feet behind him, who was ready to pass the bomb to his fellows along the flank from bow to stern.

Ivan sighed inside his mask. It was as if he was aboard a ghost ship. He could see very little except his side of the bow pulpit, and the bowsprit plunging into oblivion, along with its bracing wires and tack. The constant *whoosh* of the passing wind outside the helmet and the low *ping* of the air cylinder valve left him alone with his own thoughts, thoughts that were amplified along with the rasps of his own breathing.

His own thoughts. His own thoughts usually frustrated him. Trying to figure out people and politics was as tangled and unrewarding as philosophy. He liked math. Practical problems. A Gordian knot of malfunctioning machinery allowed him to immerse his mind in the complicated calculations of a perfect grease-lubricated solution. That was the crackerjack life. Sitting in a garden and ruminating on the world was as limp and useless as pap. And being here, alone in the mist with one's own thoughts, despite the possibility of sky mines, was sort of equivalent to sitting in a garden. Pap.

And of course there might not even be any sky mines. No one knew. He could be out here half an hour, maybe more, and never see anything but vapor. That would be a good thing, yes, but unlikely. Not uncommon in the Snow World, sky mines were the favored defense of fixed positions against airship raids: tethered to the ground by chains, they were small hydrogen balloons that piggybacked loads of blackbang explosives porcupined with pressure triggers. Sky mines were expensive and unreliable, and often duds, but it only took one good bump—a brutal blast of shrapnel and flame—to incinerate a hydrogen airship.

Ivan's imagination took off. If they struck a sky mine he would feel the airship shudder—if he wasn't instantly vaporized by the first detonation—and then drop violently as the hydrogen gasbags exploded in rapid sequence. He could unhook his safety harnesses and jump free of the fireball. But he wasn't high enough above the ground to deploy his parachute. He'd rather jump than burn. He had seen friends die by fire in airships. He didn't want to go that way.

What was all this thinking? Pap.

His eyeballs quivered, straining from his intense peering into the void. He placed his hand on his mask and worked it around in small circles so the padding massaged his head, hoping to ease some of the stress on the muscles in his forehead and cheeks.

He heard a screeching, a weird, assaulting sound, both metallic and animal, and for a moment it unnerved him. Was it something alive? Some sort of horrible beastie that lived in the fog?

The screech came closer and closer, and when Ivan saw dull yellow flashes in the murk ahead, he realized what it was. A metal chain was skidding along his side of the jibboom, casting sparks and catching here and there on the tack. He swung the fending pole forward and pulled the grasper wide open. The sparks grew brighter and brighter and the screeching increased with such intensity he thought it might shatter the faceplate of his helmet.

"Let's have at it, you bastard sticker!" Ivan shouted, more to try to clear the pressure on his eardrums than anything else. The vertical chain popped out of the fog, a wreath of fiery sparks swirling at the point of contact between its rusty links and the bowsprit, and fifteen feet up, at the end of the line, bobbled the black, spiky ball of the sky mine.

-XXX-

BALTHAZAR'S ORPHANS

CAPTAIN BUCKLE STOOD IN HIS cabin, looking up through the huge nose-dome window, hands folded behind his back, watching the sky mine skid and jerk along the port side of the jibboom of the *Pneumatic Zeppelin*. The mine had materialized from the undulating mist as if a ghost, but there was nothing ghostly about it: its chain was smothered in coppery green rust; its black balloon, shining with condensation, was packed with waterproofed-oilskin explosive packets, each spiked like cactus with tap-headed pressure triggers.

Buckle saw Ivan extend his fending pike from the left side of the bow pulpit and capture the chain with the clamp of his grasper, smoothly swinging the sky mine out and away from the ship. The sky mine slipped out of sight to the port side as Ivan passed it over to the next crew member waiting behind; on and on the bomb would be transferred along the length of the great airship, until the last person freed it beyond the fins at the stern.

Somewhat relieved, Buckle stepped to the washbasin beside his bunk and flipped open the hot water tap to scrub the last crusts of tangler guts off his hands. He had also managed a fresh change of clothes, and had scraped his leather coat and boots relatively clean of the tangler goo as well. Now, with his sword and pistol belts comfortably snug against his waist, his metal breastplate clasped tight around his rib cage, his heavy air cylinder and its helmet riding easily on the tough sinews of his shoulders, he felt strong.

It was Buckle's last tranquil moment away from the accelerating preparations for the attack. Kellie chewed at her paw on his bed. He smelled cinnamon: the cook, Perriman Salisbury, had sprinkled cinnamon on his potato pancakes at breakfast, which he had eaten at the Lion's Table with Max, Sabrina, Ivan, and Surgeon Fogg. Salisbury, or Cookie, as everyone called him, only uncorked the cinnamon jar when dangerous missions lay ahead. Cinnamon on your pancake meant that Cookie thought you were in for it.

And the tough part of the day had not even begun.

Buckle had returned to his quarters to pick up Balthazar's medicine. Sabrina had brought the vials from home, and the ones she had given to Buckle were secured inside a metal tin, which was tucked into a small leather chemist's pouch. The medicine was an amber-colored elixir mixed up by the Crankshaft clan apothecary, to help alleviate the shaking fits from which Balthazar had begun to suffer in his mature years. Balthazar's infirmity was a well-kept secret. Only those closest to him were aware of his condition. He still appeared to be quite healthy and hale, so when a seizure came on, his children whisked him out of the public eye before anyone could witness his affliction. Unfortunately, the convulsing attacks were becoming more frequent, and the physicians had nothing more for it.

Balthazar had been without his medicine for three days now.

Buckle tucked the pouch into his coat pocket. He worried that if Balthazar fell ill while in captivity, the Founders would try to exploit his infirmity. If the Founders even had him. If Aphrodite wasn't double-crossing them and setting up the *Pneumatic Zeppelin* for an ambush. Buckle shook his head. If Balthazar trusted Aphrodite, then he would trust Aphrodite.

Balthazar. Buckle shivered at the thought of losing Balthazar. Buckle was six years old when his parents died, and he had been raised as one of Balthazar's sons, educated and trained to become a clan leader so, when the time came, he would be ready when called upon.

And the time had come.

Buckle loved Balthazar and Calypso dearly—as did the other seven orphans the strict but loving couple had adopted into their family. Most had been brought into the fold as infants or small children, such as Buckle and his sister Elizabeth, Max and Tyro, and Ivan. Sabrina had been adopted later in life, at the age of thirteen. The two youngest adoptees were a pair of twins named James and Jasmine, both rescued from the wreck of a downed privateer airship ten years before, at the age of three.

There was one more son, the eldest, and the only natural child of Balthazar and Calypso, the twenty-four-year-old Ryder, who was the heir apparent to Balthazar's command. Ryder had been wounded defending his father on the night of his abduction at the Palisades Stronghold, and his injuries had landed him in the infirmary at the Devil's Punchbowl, much to his great personal chagrin. Ryder had wanted desperately to take part in the rescue mission.

Buckle removed his top hat and placed it on the Lion's Table before he turned and strode for the door. Kepler was waiting faithfully outside on the landing, he was sure.

It was his time. Romulus Buckle knew that he would rescue Balthazar and bring both him and the *Pneumatic Zeppelin* safely home. Of that he had no doubt. No doubt at all.

~XXXI~

WHEN THE SKY FELL
AT TEHACHAPI

THE *PNEUMATIC ZEPPELIN* HAD BEEN the jewel of the Imperial
fleet until Buckle took her.

Up until that time nearly a year ago, Buckle had never considered trying to steal another clan's airship; Crankshafts were
not in the business of sky raiding—boarding an enemy ship
usually meant heavy casualties—and while on the ground, the
zeppelins were always well guarded at anchor in the heart of the
clan strongholds. It would be perilous and costly to attempt to
snatch one.

That was, until the nefarious and cowardly Imperials,
without declaration of war and without warning, attacked the
Crankshaft garrison at Tehachapi.

That was the night his sister, Elizabeth, was killed.

Buckle remembered the blitz the way one remembers a
dream: vivid and clear in some parts, while vague and cloudy
in others. It had been quiet as he walked from the council hall
back to his quarters in the Crankshaft family compound. The
moon glowed dully behind the clouds as always, and the cold air
amplified every sound: the hiss of the torches and street lamps;
the slow, rhythmic *chunk, chunk* of someone unseen but close

by chopping firewood with an axe; the crunch of his own boots across the frozen crusts that lined the ruts in the street.

The compound was located beside the airfield, where five Crankshaft airships and a dozen independent tramps and traders floated at night anchor, very low, their gondolas no more than twenty feet above the ground, their whale-like bodies illuminated by legions of swirling lanterns dangling from the mooring towers and docking ropes. On the towering flank of each Crankshaft sky vessel loomed the red lion rampant, the symbol of the Crankshaft clan.

Buckle had been in a mood as foul as Martian mustard—he had just been outvoted by the clan treasurer and the majority of the council; they had dismissed his proposal to purchase another war zeppelin from the Steamweavers. The Crankshafts were merchants by nature, the council had said, and needed more small, long-distance trader vessels for the rubber trade, not ponderous gunships.

As Buckle walked past a small rock lodged in a frozen rut, he took a listless kick at it—he remembered the sharp whack at the toe of his boot quite clearly. It was then that he realized that huge objects were drifting silently under the dark clouds overhead.

Zeppelins.

Buckle's logic told him a Crankshaft zeppelin was returning home. Many of the Crankshaft clan's airships were deployed; Balthazar was away, with his flagship *Khartoum*, and so was his brother Horatio, captain of the gunship *Waterloo*, as well as most of the smaller traders and cutters. But none of them were due back any time soon. No messenger pigeons had come in heralding their early arrival. No docking crews had been assembled to mill about the hawsers at the mooring towers, the smoke from their pipes curling about their heads.

Fear caught in Buckle's throat. Something was terribly wrong.

The Crankshafts were not at war with anyone. Balthazar, the great soldier and diplomat, had done his work well.

A sledgehammer wall of air, spitting particles of dust and ice, nearly knocked Buckle off his feet. The big blackbang bomb—which had fallen in the alley behind the smithy—belched a deep wave of roiling black smoke, swallowing him up, choking him. Buckle ran—his memory of this part was hazy, but he remembered running, sprinting at full speed, though he could not see more than three feet ahead of him, running to get to the airships. He was the chief navigator aboard the *Bromhead*, an armed trader, and he had to get to her. He had to help get her into the air. Explosions rocked the earth and walloped him from side to side. Muted flashes lit up the murk as if he were inside a thunderstorm. Figures scrambled past him in the smoke, but he could not make out who anyone was; their shouts pierced the muffling vapors, sometimes yelling orders, sometimes screaming the names of children.

Buckle wheezed. His smoke-tortured lungs threatened to burst, but he kept on running. He stumbled into a gap of clear air. Brilliant flashes—the bombs and the defenders' phosphorus flares—shocked his eyes. He saw the docked Crankshaft war zeppelin, the *Victory*, a sitting duck tethered to its mooring tower, catch fire. He stopped, staring, gasping: a drowning man. The *Victory*'s hydrogen cells erupted in geysers of flame and it collapsed in upon itself, toppling toward the earth, its superstructure skeleton glowing white-hot as the skin burned away in red-edged ripples.

Move, Buckle thought. *Move!* He set off running, and, just before he plunged into another wave of smoke and airborne

debris in front of him, he saw the awful flash of another exploding Crankshaft airship. It was the *Bromhead*. The fireball lit up
the entire world, and he glimpsed—just for an instant—the
clear outline of an attacking zeppelin above; on its flank he saw
the symbol of the iron cross.

The Imperials.

When dawn broke over the smoking ruins of the Tehachapi
stronghold, four of the five clan airships docked there—the
Victory, Bromhead, Whirling Dervish, and *Albert*—were nothing
more than smoldering heaps of twisted metal fallen to earth.
Only the *Gibraltar*, a big armed trader, had miraculously survived, now a forlorn titan floating over the wrecks of her sisters. Forty-one Crankshaft clanspeople were dead, and 122 were
wounded.

Calypso Crankshaft, wife to Balthazar and mother to his
children, had been killed in the blitz. Buckle's sister, Elizabeth,
her room in the left wing of Balthazar's house incinerated by
an Imperial bomb, was one of a dozen whose bodies were consumed by the explosions. Nothing left to mourn. Nothing left
for the funeral pyre.

Romulus Buckle was consumed by rage.

Pluteus Brassballs, himself seriously wounded, led the
efforts to rescue trapped clansmen and make preparations to
evacuate the now uninhabitable Tehachapi stronghold. Balthazar
and Horatio, aboard the *Khartoum* and *Waterloo*, returned at
best speed and arrived within two days. The eleven remaining
Crankshaft airships, complemented by five hastily hired cargo
tramps owned by the trader guilds—who ratcheted up their
prices when they knew you had an emergency—were loaded,
and the entire clan relocated to the garrison at the Devil's
Punchbowl to the south.

Although he preferred to always negotiate terms of peace and trade, Balthazar was no shrinking violet when it came to battle. The Crankshaft clan now was vulnerable, and every other clan knew it. He was convinced that the best defense was high aggression: he immediately began formulating a counterstrike against the Imperials. Even as the wounded Crankshaft clan was airborne between Tehachapi and the Devil's Punchbowl, the airship infirmaries packed with bleeding wounded, the cold Castle deck of the *Khartoum* a morgue where the wrapped bodies of twenty-nine clanspeople, including Calypso, lay, Balthazar called the surviving council members and commanders into his quarters to discuss an immediate and daring counterstrike.

"Yes, our clan is seriously crippled," Balthazar said. "But this is a moment in which we must show the caliber of our resolve. Because if anyone believes that we can no longer defend ourselves, we shall soon be overrun."

Balthazar's plan called for a small force to raid the Imperial stronghold and destroy as many of their airships as possible. It was not elegant and it was not pretty: it was march or die, to awe with the steel of fearlessness and determination, to bloody the Imperials or perish in the attempt.

Buckle volunteered instantly.

Max volunteered. Tyro volunteered. Sabrina volunteered. Balthazar prevented any more of his family from stepping forward after that. He had just lost Calypso and Elizabeth—sending four of the remaining eight children on a suicidal mission was all the great lion of a man could handle.

The raid on the Imperials, led by Horatio Crankshaft, was a costly success. Two of the Imperials' finest war zeppelins and a number of smaller airships had been blown to pieces at anchor, but nearly a third of the Crankshaft attackers had perished, including Buckle's best friend, Sebastian Mitty, and the entire crew of the armed trader *Zanzibar*. Buckle, with his captain dead and his crew decimated, decided that rather than destroy the Imperial flagship, the *Pneumatic Zeppelin*, he would *steal* it. In this he succeeded, despite losing half of his company, and he brought the *Pneumatic Zeppelin* back to the Devil's Punchbowl to great personal glory. Balthazar was miffed that Buckle had altered his battle orders, but the clan needed the warship desperately.

Buckle was awarded the captaincy of his captured prize, the traditional honor that he vigorously demanded, and he chose the young but experienced Ivan, Sabrina, and Max—his brother and sisters—as his senior officers.

The *Pneumatic Zeppelin* was a family affair.

~XXXII~

THE OWL WHO COULD HOOT

BUCKLE HURRIED ALONG THE KEEL corridor with Kepler—big and out of place as a beached whale at his shoulder—intrusively matching his every step. Kepler was gnawing on a piece of sausage—where he had gotten the sausage from, Buckle didn't know, but the meat stank of garlic. Their boots rang heavily on the gratings, weighted down as they were with their brass oxygen cylinders and breastplate armor, and Kellie zigzagged just ahead, frustrated by their reduced speed.

They swerved around the gunnery gondola's magazine dumbwaiter shaft and entered the ready room, where Pluteus and his Ballblasters, sealed in armored suits from head to toe, were moving aft to assemble on the *Arabella*'s forward loading platform.

Pluteus stepped up to Buckle, grinning widely inside the glass faceplate of his bulky helmet. He thrust a blackbang musket, primed and loaded, into Buckle's hands. "Ready to die, Buckle?" he asked.

"Never and always," Buckle replied.

The Crankshaft armor consisted of iron plates that the blacksmiths rounded off to deflect musket balls. Their full metal helmets looked ancient Greek in style, with cheek guards girding heavy glass faceplates. Pluteus's helmet sported a tall red brush signifying his rank. The troopers were also weighed down with double sets of oxygen cylinders, and impressive arrays of gunnery belts, bandoliers, swords, and daggers. They didn't seem to mind, however, watching the proceedings through the thick glass of their visors as they cradled their heavy blackbang muskets in the crooks of their metal-sheathed arms. Two of the Crankshaft troopers carried a portable pneumatic rifle, a large weapon that required a team to handle it.

Sergeant Scully and Corporal Druxbury had large canvas satchels hooked to their belts; in each of the satchels was one sticky bomb, a heavy chunk of concentrated blackbang gunpowder, coated with a gluey stickum so it could be pressed against door locks and exploded. This was a prison break, after all; they were expecting to blast a few doors.

Scorpius and his Alchemist soldiers were also ready on the platform, grouped closer to the nose of the *Arabella* as she rested at her berth inside the gigantic hangar. The Alchemists were more lightly armored than Pluteus's troopers, but still formidable in elegant bronze breastplates and greaves that crawled with rotating gears. Their oxygen cylinders were far more ornate than those of the Crankshafts, and their helmets were smooth, polished sallets, like Newton's head.

Newton and the Owl stood off to one side as Wolfgang and Zwicky tinkered with them. Robots waiting patiently, Buckle supposed. The Owl was coming along, but it had been decided that Newton, too big, slow, and noisy to accompany the assault force, would remain aboard the *Arabella* and provide cover when they arrived at the evacuation point inside the city, which would probably have developed into a running gunfight, unless they were incredibly lucky.

And luck had not been on Buckle's side so far today. Or had it? Only the Oracle might know.

Wolfgang grinned at Buckle as he approached. "Prepare to be dazzled, Captain," he said as Zwicky handed him a wrench, "when you witness the finest Alchemist robots in action."

"You don't say," Buckle replied, scrutinizing the odd Owl. He could feel Kepler's hot, garlicky-sausage-smelling breath on the back of his neck. He ignored it.

"Quite a mechanical wonder, isn't she? Pure crackerjack," Wolfgang boasted, grinning even wider at Buckle's focused attention. "I'll be running her for the duration of this mission. Zwicky here—my faithful assistant and robotics apprentice extraordinaire—shall be running Newton."

"She?" Buckle asked.

"Of course," Wolfgang chuckled. "She, Captain. My beautiful Owl here, she's got a truly female personality. Very stubborn." He winked.

The Owl was certainly a strange robot: the head resembled an owl's because the face was dominated by two large eyelike saucers, concave bowls of circular canvas rings stitched into thousands of miniature cogs that held them taut. The metal head seemed designed to do little more than hold the eyes in place, though there was a small round opening in the area of the mouth. The Owl's body looked like a mad scientist's merging of a metal cheetah and a metal ostrich, long and lean, built for speed. It had two five-fingered hands that it casually flipped open and shut like a fan when it wasn't occupied, and sometimes tapped at the glass window in its midriff, where steam surged in its belly.

"I admit she takes a little getting used to, Captain," Wolfgang stated emphatically, patting the Owl's head. "But she's a real peach."

Buckle couldn't see any weapons on the Owl. "What's she for?"

"She's a reconnaissance robot," Zwicky said, clicking shut the access panel he'd just been tinkering inside. Zwicky's personality was much more prickly than Wolfgang's, although Buckle sensed it was more a nervous insecurity than true rudeness. "The Owl sees with sound, like a bat. She emits a distinct series of whistles, and when the sound waves bounce back she can 'see' them."

"Shouldn't you call them ears, then?" Buckle asked.

Zwicky screwed up his face as if he'd just bitten into a worm-packed lemon.

Wolfgang laughed. "Well, technically, yes. But since she organizes the different echoes she sees into a map of what's in front of her—she can, in her way, see sound. So we call them eyes."

"I see," Buckle replied.

Wolfgang laughed. "The Owl was developed for night operations. She will prove especially effective inside the fog."

"Robots ain't worth the screws you put into 'em, if you ask me," grumbled one of the Ballblasters, a sour-faced private named Moss, who was coaxing his messenger pigeon into a hermetically sealed canister at his waist.

"Nobody asked you," Zwicky snapped back. Wolfgang simply rolled his eyes.

"Keep it down," Buckle said, moving forward on the platform. Not many people liked the weird robots that the Alchemists were so fond of. As children, they all had been told wild stories of Alchemist machines going haywire and wiping out entire towns and villages, cracking open a hundred skulls before being stopped, and so on. The stories were probably all a bunch of poppycock: just a few of the many dark tales available to scare children with in the Snow World.

"Captain! Up here!" Sabrina shouted, waving from the open loading hatch in the nose of the *Arabella*. She wore armor and oxygen equipment similar to his, and her map case hung at her hip alongside her pistol holster.

Buckle slipped around the Alchemist soldiers and strode up the wooden ramp to Sabrina. Kepler stayed with him step for step.

"Fashionably late, as usual, Captain?" Sabrina asked.

"Just attending to the affairs of state, my dear," Buckle replied.

Sabrina gave Buckle a bemused look before turning and shouting at the assembled crowd. "All aboard, people! And double- and triple-check your gas masks, because you won't find any forgiveness from the mustard!"

~XXXIII~

INTO THE MUSTARD

BUCKLE, SABRINA, AND KEPLER DUCKED into the forward loading hatchway in the bow of the *Arabella* and headed down a wide ramp into the main cargo hold, a cylindrical chamber eighty feet long, twenty feet wide, and fifteen feet high. Once reaching the hold, Sabrina turned back to enter the elevated bridge located in the nose above the forward loading door. Buckle and Kepler followed Sabrina into the bridge, as the Crankshaft and Alchemist troopers streamed down the ramp and into the main hold behind them. There was no need to man the stations—the *Arabella* was going to be lowered thirty feet to the earth by the *Pneumatic Zeppelin's* steam winches—but Sabrina could monitor their position from there.

Buckle stepped up to the glass nose dome, folded his hands behind his back, tucking them under his oxygen cylinder, and peered into the empty wall of fog. He could tell that the *Pneumatic Zeppelin* was slowly descending, not only by the feeling of dampness he had in his bones but because the mist was getting darker and darker by degrees.

The loading door under the cockpit thumped shut with a heavy wallop, followed by the sounds of the lock bolts slamming home. The expeditionary force was all aboard.

Buckle glanced at Sabrina, who was already bent over the drift scope. "See anything?" he asked.

"Vertical visibility is actually pretty good," Sabrina replied. Buckle heard the gears of the drift scope clicking as she moved them back and forth. "Rotten-banana yellow down beneath, but pretty good. Fifty to sixty feet." Heavy fog was impossible to see into horizontally, but fog banks were generally shallow, so the ground could often be glimpsed if you looked straight down into them. "Surface in sight. I have an intersection directly below. I can't make out any road signs, but the street plan's orientation matches Melrose and La Brea. I have no doubt that Max and Welly will plunk us down exactly where we are supposed to be, light as a feather in the drop."

Buckle also had complete faith in the dead reckoning skills of Max and Welly.

Max's cool voice rang down the cockpit chattertube hood, which was connected by umbilicals to the mother airship's chattertube line. "Ready to disengage launch!" she shouted from the cockpit. "Disengage!"

The *Arabella* jerked, making everyone bend at the knees a little—except perhaps the robots—as the launch swung out of its berth in the center of the zeppelin. The *Pneumatic Zeppelin*'s gigantic steam winches started grinding, and the *Arabella*'s control cables unspooled, smoothly lowering the launch.

"Masks on! Air canisters on!" Max's voice rattled through the chattertube, followed by the squeal of a bosun's whistle.

"Masks on! Air canisters on!" Sabrina shouted, sneaking one last glance down the drift scope before she pulled her helmet on.

"Aye!" Buckle replied. He turned and strode into the cargo hold. "Masks on! Oxygen on!" he shouted. "We're descending into the mustard!"

The assault team had assembled amidships, ready to disembark from the main cargo doors, hemmed in by the launch's innards of steam pipes, driving shafts, hydrogen tanks, and water-ballast tanks; the rigid superstructure was folded back like a huge accordion overhead, with the envelope skin and gas cells draped limply between each crease. Everyone turned to face Buckle when he shouted the order, including the Owl, which stared at him with its gigantic eyes. The hold filled with the sounds of dozens of oxygen cylinders hissing to life at once.

Buckle pulled his helmet over his head and secured the leather straps of the gas mask, pulling them snug into their clasps with a few sharp tugs. He rotated the sealing dial on his chin and felt the rubber borders of the mask tighten around his forehead and under his chin. He reached to his left cheek and gave his air-hose knob a twist, filling his ears with the gush of pressurized air. One had to wear an oxygen mask above fifteen thousand feet of altitude, where the oxygen was too thin to breathe, but Buckle did not like the claustrophobic sensation of his head being pinched in a box, or having his vision impaired by the thick, muddled glass of the visor plate. Pilots relied on their eyesight for survival, to see what was coming before it was already upon them, and the murky masks felt unnatural, even dangerous. Goggles, with the clear lenses spit and polished enough to magnify the sky, were the zeppelineer's eye gear of choice.

Sabrina arrived at Buckle's shoulder and they hurried forward to join the group, with Kepler, screwing on his helmet, at their heels. Buckle worked his way along the hull to the loading doors, keeping his musket pointed up as he brushed past the heavily armored Ballblasters and Alchemist soldiers.

"Crackerjack!" Wolfgang gave a muffled shout from inside his helmet as Buckle nudged past him.

Buckle nodded, pressing his shoulder up against the wooden frame of the amidships loading door. Kepler, bulling his way through behind him, jammed his considerable bulk in at his back. The space on the slender deck was tight for thirty-two people, most encased in heavy armor, and all wearing gas cylinders, plus two toe-treading robots.

Buckle took a deep breath of the stale air inside his helmet. His heart raced, but his nerves were calm. His faceplate was fogged, but his mind was clear. The hiss and ping of his oxygen tank, the whooshes of his own breathing, the metallic pump of the cylinder behind, swam in his ears. The mask stank of sour sweat and damp leather. The hold lay in semi-darkness, illuminated only by the shifting gray light seeping in through the skiff's cocooned envelope, and he could not see much, sandwiched the way he was at the edge of the crowd.

An *Arabella* crewman, two pistols stuffed into the bandolier strapped across his chest, his face lost inside the condensation on his faceplate, was perched on a step above the door, one hand on the drawbridge lever. Pluteus was in front of Buckle, sideways and facing the door, his armored shoulder and helmet gleaming a warm copper in the soft light. Wolfgang, crowded in against Buckle's right shoulder with his head down, repeatedly swiped Buckle's elbow as he wound a lever on a small, whirring metal box lined with dials and switches.

Then they plopped into the mustard.

The glowing yellow gas, heavier than air, poured in. It surged over the gunwales and flowed down in dense waterfalls that pooled on the deck and rose with frightening speed. Buckle felt a tiny but significant twinge of anxiety as the gas swamped the hold up to his waist, and then his chest, until it flooded up and over his facemask, submerging him and everything around him in a swirling undersea world of sickly brown-yellow, poison-colored murk.

I hope my oxygen mask works, Buckle thought.

–XXXIV–

FORGEWALKERS

A LIGHT *THUMP* HIT THE bottoms of Buckle's feet. The *Arabella* had landed. Nice work, Max, Buckle thought.

The launch crewman at the loading door threw the latch aside with a dull *whack* and booted the drawbridge; it swung out in a wide flop, revealing a snowbound world of ruins, everything broken and collapsed, the gutted buildings looming like ghosts in the yellow mist. A land of poison.

"Go!" Buckle shouted at the top of his lungs, trying to defeat the heavy, damp muffling effect of his mask. He charged down the ramp. His boots landed on a frozen street whose uneven concrete had been cracked by ice and earthquakes. Rusted-out automobiles with punched-in windshields, stripped down to mere chassis and broken springs, rested in clumps here and there; bones lay scattered in heaps between. Shadows loomed high and low in the mist, abandoned wrecks of the life that once bustled there, fronted by the stair-stepped remains of walls, and rows of frozen jacaranda and palm trees lining the boulevards.

A big, twisted business sign was still barely legible: *Pink's Hot Dogs.*

Buckle stepped forward, his musket at the ready. The fog was thick and absolutely still, obscuring everything beyond twenty feet but the biggest buildings. A set of railway tracks—intact, obviously built since The Storming—ran down the center of the street. There was a weird amber flickering in the mist that seemed to emanate from its depths. The musket felt very heavy. He did not carry a musket very often; he was partial to his pistols.

Kepler came into view at Buckle's side; Kepler's musket looked much smaller in Kepler's huge hands. Buckle looked back to see Sabrina behind him, a pistol ready in one hand as she fished her maps out of their case with the other. Pluteus and Scorpius had disembarked, leading their soldiers down the ramp in good order and fanning out to the south. Wolfgang moved into the lead, the Owl cocking its head back and forth as it walked alongside him.

The wooden hull of the *Arabella* loomed in the mist, resting oddly along the street like a beached sea vessel, her dozens of thick lowering cables stretching upward and disappearing into the fog, where the huge shadow of the *Pneumatic Zeppelin* hovered forty feet overhead. The *Arabella*'s weather deck was lined with gas-masked crewmen—the deck could be employed as a rampart when the envelope was folded down—and Buckle saw the hulking Newton, Zwicky, Chief of the Boat Christopher Glantz, and a handful of musketeers positioned along its length to provide covering fire.

Buckle raised his hand to signal Ensign Glantz. The *Arabella*'s drawbridge ramp cranked up and shut. The winch cables jerked taut and the *Arabella* lifted off, rising upward into the fog with a groan of straining rope and creaking bulkheads.

Buckle peered at his pocket watch through the wet glass of his helmet visor. They had roughly forty minutes of usable oxygen in their cylinder tanks. Forty minutes to get inside the walls of the Founders' city, or all that would be left of the expedition would be a stack of corpses and a somewhat confused robot.

Sabrina stepped alongside Buckle, her map in one gloved hand and her compass in the other. She pointed due south, straight down the middle of the old La Brea Boulevard. Pluteus signaled for the soldiers to advance at the ready; they moved forward in an arc with Scorpius and the Alchemist soldiers on the left flank. To Buckle, the soldiers looked as alien as the Owl, their human flesh locked inside their armored suits, their faces distorted and dark inside their helmet windows, dripping with condensation.

Wolfgang and the Owl took the lead, the Owl strutting in awkward chicken-prances: it started whistling, emitting high-pitched tones that echoed as they bounced back and forth, haunting in the dense fog. Wolfgang followed at the Owl's heels, reading and adjusting dials on his instrument box.

Sabrina bumped into Buckle's shoulder as they advanced in the pocket behind the troopers. She was trying to get her bearings on her map through her fogged and dripping visor, and seemed to be having only partial success. Kepler trailed at Buckle's back, far enough behind that Buckle could only see him if he turned around—if Buckle had given it much thought, it would have made him uneasy.

They slogged across the dirty snow and ice for what seemed like an eternity, but by Buckle's watch was only twenty minutes. Wolfgang and the Owl advanced, barely visible in the murk, flanked by Ballblasters on each side, the Owl rotating its head back and forth as it emitted its eerie little whistle every few seconds. The Crankshaft and Alchemist soldiers swayed as they walked, their musket barrels traversing the ground in front of them. There was so much debris along the sidewalks —the flotsam and jetsam of apocalypse: car hulks, fallen building facades, high snowbanks, and collapsed trees—that the group had to funnel into the middle of the street if the heavily armored troopers were going to move with any speed at all.

And the middle of nearly every street and alley had been cleared, making way for the omnipresent railway tracks that forked off in every direction to vanish into the mists.

A green street sign emerged from the fog, twisted and mangled, still dangling above the intersection: it read *North La Brea*.

"Moon moat ahead!" Sabrina shouted to Pluteus, her voice straining inside her helmet.

Pluteus nodded and peered at a watch strapped to his forearm armor.

The formation continued moving forward. To Buckle it felt as if the atmosphere suddenly got much colder. A low ridge appeared ahead, a frozen ripple in the ground spanning the street and stretching as far as the eye could see in both directions. The earth had been tossed up in a great swell here, the earthquake-like force that caused it having also obliterated the buildings that once spanned the ground. Buckle had heard of the moon moat: it was a mythical place, created by the shockwave of a monstrous Martian shockbomb dropped on downtown Los Angeles on the day of The Storming. Inside the moon moat, the mustard-gas-filled blast crater was a plain of pulverized and melted ruins—that is, until the Founders came.

Wolfgang, the Owl, and the leading Ballblasters easily climbed the low outer slope of the moon moat, and everyone else followed, picking their way around jagged outcroppings of concrete, rebar, and disjoined skeletons. Buckle saw an odd-looking little machine resting on the crest of the rise, out of place in the rubble: faded gold lettering that spelled *Espresso* was stamped on one side, but he had no idea what that word meant.

The inner slope of the ridge was a wash of loose shale, and although the angle was easy for Buckle to descend, it was a bit more of a chore for the heavily armored troopers, who scuffed and slid with considerable difficulty. The interior of the moon moat wasn't very deep—the force of the blast seemed to have been directed horizontally—and from what he could see, it looked as if most everything inside it had been knocked flat and bludgeoned into crumbled heaps, with the exception of the newer railway lines, which ran through it at various angles.

The yellow fog was very thick here, and the dense concentration of toxic alien gas had corroded every surface: the ground, both snow and split concrete, was as pitted and pocked as a drought-stricken streambed. Still dissolving, everything smoldered and smoked. Sinkholes and depressions, both large and small, had formed in spots where the weakened earth had caved in, giving the surface a moonlike appearance—hence the name.

Growing up, Buckle had heard the tales told, the stories of the great moon moat that made the City of the Founders impenetrable, from both without and within. And now, as he strode into it, the place was surely as bizarre as the old stories had described.

Just how his navigator, Sabrina Serafim, had escaped the city, he would like to know.

The expedition advanced due south, although now there was no longer much of a street to follow. A gigantic black sphere—four stories high if it was a foot—emerged from the mist ahead. It was a Martian mustard sphere—a gigantic gas bomb. It was said that on the day of The Storming, the Martians had dropped fifty of the huge spheres in a ring around the downtown, rendering the city uninhabitable. The terrible mustard gas spewed in continuous streams from hundreds of taps lining the exterior of the spheres, which, like the one directly ahead, were still emitting the poison after more than three hundred years—still maintaining what had become the City of the Founders' most effective defense.

Pluteus signaled for the unit to swing to the right of the sphere. Buckle eyed it as he passed. The thing was huge, even with the bottom fifth of it buried in the crater it had created when it hit the ground. The black metal skin had a sickly silvery sheen to it, perhaps from weathering, perhaps corroded by its own poison, but the metal was still smooth except where it was punctuated by the spigot funnels.

Buckle kept checking his watch as the group advanced. Twenty minutes of oxygen left. Eighteen minutes of oxygen left. He could see Sabrina and Pluteus, and the handful of troopers immediately in front of him, but all the others were no more than shadows moving in the murk, shadows that occasionally passed under vague hints of girders and walls. The Owl whistled again and again, its metallic cries making the place seem even more desolate. Buckle's soul felt cold. If ever there was a land of the dead, he thought, this was it.

The members of the group instinctively pressed closer together. Buckle stayed glued to Sabrina, who had her head down, focused on her map almost every step of the way, and he sensed that Kepler had crept up closer to his back.

The Owl suddenly stopped and made a whirring sound. Wolfgang thrust his arm in the air, hand open. Everyone halted. The Ballblasters dropped to one knee and froze.

Sabrina, looking down at her map and compass, had not noticed Wolfgang's signal. Buckle grasped her by the shoulder and yanked her to a stop. She turned her head and peered at him, her eyes dark inside her dripping visor. Buckle pointed at the Owl. Sabrina lowered her map into its case and slowly drew her pistol.

The silence left by the Owl's sudden muteness was frightening. Buckle gripped his musket but there was nothing but fog to aim at. He pointed it between the backs of the two Ballblasters in front of him anyway, in the direction the Owl seemed to be looking. His faceplate was so sludged with dust and moisture he couldn't see anything more. He could hear his breathing accelerate in his helmet, the sound mixing with the oxygen cylinder's hiss and ping; he could even hear the rapid beating of his own heart. This was no place for an eagle-eyed aviator, damn it.

"All right," Buckle whispered to himself, "don't become completely worthless." He took a deep breath and wiped his glove across the faceplate glass, managing to clear a streak he could see through.

The Owl released two small peeps and cocked its head back and forth as it scanned the mist. Steam puffed from its exhaust vents. It suddenly spun in one small, fast circle before stopping and peering in the same direction again. And then it held very, very still.

They had been stopped for perhaps forty-five seconds—no more than that—but to Buckle it was too long. Bad luck. Bad, bad luck. He held his watch up to the clearer section of his face-mask to read it. Fifteen minutes of air left.

Buckle shared a grim look with Pluteus. They couldn't afford to sit still much longer, no matter what was out there directly ahead of them. Pluteus raised his hand to signal his men.

The Owl shrieked. Buckle nearly jumped out of his skin. The Owl's echo bounced back. The Owl flung out one lanky arm and pointed. Wolfgang raised his head from his instrument box and pointed vigorously in the same direction.

Wolfgang tried to shout something at Pluteus, something that sounded distinctly like "Forgewalkers!"

The Crankshaft and Alchemist troopers raised their muskets and aimed at the wall of mustard-colored fog. The two troopers manning the pneumatic rifle swung it up onto its tripod and charged the breech with a loud snap of the metal bolt.

What cursed bad luck, Buckle thought.

And then everybody started shooting.

~XXXV~

SKIRMISH IN THE MOON MOAT

WHEN THE FIRST BALLBLASTER'S BLACKBANG musket fired, the sound was muted, but the concussion of the shot slapped the side of Sabrina's helmet. Her faceplate glittered as muzzle flashes erupted from the fog very close ahead, peppering the vapors with pops and slashes of swirling light.

How close that first Founders' volley came to killing Sabrina was something she could calculate pretty well.

The musket ball punched a smoking hole through the map she was holding, slashing through the gap between her left arm and waist, taking a strip of her jacket sleeve with it, and slicing a shallow trough across her skin just inside the elbow. It delivered a sharp sting, but as the firefight broke loose she completely forgot about it.

Materializing out of the mist, lumbering into view like three upright rhinos, marched the armored Founders patrol. Aye, there were only three of them—at least that was all that Sabrina could see at the moment—but they were big, each over seven feet tall, encased in black-plated metal, and what little could be glimpsed beneath the armor crawled with spinning cogs and pressurized copper steam tubes so overheated that they glimmered red. At first glance, Sabrina thought the armored patrolmen were pure robots like Newton—the interiors of the helmets inside their large glass faceplates were so dark one could not see any faces—but they moved with a smoothness and intention that proved there were men inside the machines. Forgewalkers.

The forgewalkers advanced in crazy, sparkling haloes of light: their forearms belched fire as they blazed away with sets of blackbang-musket barrels built into the wrist plating. The Crankshaft and Alchemist musket balls, zipping through the mist in brilliant white phosphorous streaks, bounced off their armor in bright but ineffective showers of sparks.

Speaking of slowpoke Newton, they sure could have used him here.

The pneumatic rifle opened up, *chack-a-chak*, its flashing harpoons striking the lead forgewalker with enough force to stagger it. A small metal plate spun off the forgewalker's abdomen in a burst of sparks. At least the pneumatic rifle was big enough to do some damage, Sabrina thought, and she felt a touch relieved.

A Ballblaster standing in front of Sabrina jerked, the visor of his helmet shattering in glittering glass fragments. He dropped like a stone, facedown on the decimated concrete. That was the horror of a battle inside the moon moat: even a grazing shot, if it managed to split open your visor, air cylinder, or any of the tubes in between, let the deadly mustard gas in.

From then on, you would live only as long as you could hold your breath.

Sabrina raised her pistol and aimed at the head of the leading Founders scout. He was close, within thirty feet. It was an easy shot. She pulled the trigger and the weapon responded with its familiar kick and puff of dark smoke. She saw her musket ball ricochet off the helmet with a harmless spurt of light.

Someone suddenly hooked her collar and yanked her from behind. It was Buckle, pulling her back, dragging her to the rear of the line. "Stay back!" Buckle shouted, his words barely reaching her over the din of the battle and the insulation in both of their helmets.

Sabrina didn't want Buckle to save her. Damn it—he was always trying to save everybody. "I can take care of myself!" she screamed inside her helmet.

Buckle knocked his faceplate right up against hers. His face looked distorted through the wet, slurried glass. "Save it, Lieutenant!" Buckle yelled. "No matter what, we can't lose you now!"

Once behind the second firing rank, Sabrina tore free of Buckle's hands and fell, stumbling over an uneven bench of cracked earth, landing hard, the impact punching up her arms and into her shoulders as she caught herself with her hands. With a sideways glance, she glimpsed the ponderous, metal-sheathed boots of the forgewalkers slowly advancing, the weight of their machines pulverizing the crumbled concrete in gray puffs. Out of the corner of her eye she saw another member of the expedition fall—one of the Alchemist troopers.

Buckle had her in an instant, lifting her to her feet. "Are you hit?" he shouted. Even though the storm of noise, she could hear the fear in his voice.

"I'm okay!" Sabrina shouted back, and Buckle let her go.

Wolfgang and the Owl, hurrying back behind the line, joined them. "The old Owl, she sniffed them out, did she not? Of course she did!" Wolfgang enthused.

The riot of gunfire faded away with a few ragged shots, as every blackbang-musket battle did: close-quarter skirmishes opened with the muskets and pistols, which, taking too long to reload, were set aside in favor of swords and other weapons of muscle and steam. It was an eerie transition: to be caught in the middle of a furious musket barrage and then fall into a surging near silence as everyone drew swords and charged.

The forgewalkers kept coming, slowly advancing through the ghostly shrouds of yellow gas and black gunpowder smoke. Their gun cuffs, emptied of ammunition, were ejected to the ground; the armored sleeves snapped open and, in blasts of white steam, flipped up bladed wheels that started spinning like buzz saws.

"Fall back!" Pluteus ordered, with a wave of his arm. "Two firing lines! Reload!"

Fall back? Fall back to where? Sabrina thought. Backing up was no good. There wasn't enough air left in their tanks to retreat. And besides—there was no place to retreat to. The *Pneumatic Zeppelin* was gone, already on her way to the rendezvous point, and the mustard stretched for miles in every direction. But what could Pluteus do? He had to keep his distance from the behemoth forgewalkers, hoping for a lucky shot. There was no way they were going to defeat these things hand to hand.

Sabrina holstered her empty pistol and drew her sword. She didn't know why she did that, really—what use was her saber against the armored scouts? But she would feel better if she went down swinging...if it came to that.

It was so quiet. Why was the pneumatic rifle not firing?

"Blue blazes! Get that gun running!" Sabrina heard Pluteus scream. She whipped her head around to see the big rifle standing silent, its power plant steaming—the two Ballblasters manning the weapon working frantically to unjam the breech.

The pneumatic rifle, with its razor-edged harpoon projectiles, was their only chance. Sabrina raced toward it, sheathing her sword and drawing her knife from her belt as she ran. Buckle shouted something unintelligible at her back. She ignored him.

"Front rank, fire!" Plutcus ordered. The front rank of Ballblasters released a crisp volley.

"Second rank, fire!" Pluteus ordered. The second rank of Ballblasters and Alchemists fired.

A sideways glance confirmed for Sabrina that the musket volleys had failed. The forgewalkers came on, knives spinning. The Crankshaft line faltered.

"Go to the blades and hold 'em, boys!" Pluteus bellowed, charging to the front of the fray. "Hold 'em!"

Pluteus knew—they all knew—they had to buy the pneumatic gunners time to clear the breech. The Ballblasters drew their swords and dug in their heels.

Sabrina arrived alongside the Ballblaster gunner as he struggled at the rifle. Both of his gloves were smoking. She peered into the steaming breech and saw the mangled brass casing of a harpoon jammed inside it, along with the broken blade of the gunner's knife. The man had been clawing at the metal with his hands, scorching and shredding the fingers of his gloves.

"Stand aside!" Sabrina shrieked, her voice deafening inside her helmet, shoving the man away.

To her left, she could see the battle figures surging in the fog, the whirling outlines of the soldiers as they fought for their lives, slashing and jabbing at the seams of the enemy's armor, while ducking the slicing whirl of blades.

Sabrina drove her knife blade into the gap between the cartridge and the breech wall, as far forward in the compartment as she could manage. It was difficult to see—damn the condensation inside her mask! With the tip of her blade wedged in, she began to quickly rock the knife forward and backward parallel to the flanks of the chamber. Pressure fore and aft was the way to clear a serious jam. The gunner had panicked, attempting to wedge his knife under the casing and pop it up, and had snapped the blade.

Sabrina glanced at the battle, just in time to see a forge-walker catch a Ballblaster in its buzz saw. Fragments of equipment and ragged metal slewed in all directions, just before the man's oxygen tank exploded.

Something struck the barrel of the pneumatic rifle just in front of Sabrina's face—maybe a blade fragment, or shrapnel, or a bullet, or a piece of armored-sheathed bone—and the eruption of sparks nearly blinded her, the concussion on the barrel stinging her hands. She gasped, blinking her eyes hard again and again, tasting blood, sucking in so much air that the supply seemed to slow, verging on suffocating her—but she never stopped working the blade.

The forgewalkers were closing in. She could feel the shudder of their footfalls shaking heavier in the ground.

The harpoon cartridge jiggled against the knife. Sabrina dug in deeper, her blade deforming the brass casing, seeking a notch to catch and push.

Sabrina glanced at the forgewalkers again. She saw Pluteus, stepping over the corpse of his dead comrade, wading in to the enemy with his heavy saber. The fury of his attack, the resounding crashes of his blade against the body of the steam-powered iron suit, actually made the man inside it take a few steps backward.

The center forgewalker flung out his monstrous right arm, striking Pluteus full in the chest with a violent blast of sparks. The blow lifted Pluteus off the ground and launched him through the air; spinning, he disappeared into the fog.

–XXXVI–

THWACK 'EM!

BUCKLE KNEW THE SITUATION HAD gone from very bad to desperate in the last five seconds. Pluteus was gone, batted away like a doll and probably dead. Another Ballblaster and an Alchemist had been killed. And still the three forgewalkers came on, bladed arms flailing, scattering the hard-fighting survivors on the line. Buckle had his head down, reloading his musket as Sabrina worked on the jammed breech. His heart leapt into his throat. They needed something big. They needed to bust up the man-machines, or this mission was going to end in tragedy here and now.

They needed grenades. Crankshafts did not use grenades. But Sergeant Scully and Corporal Druxbury both had satchels containing a sticky bomb apiece.

A sticky bomb could blow a forgewalker into orbit.

Buckle searched the mist for Scully and found him only a few yards to his right, having rallied a handful of troopers around the pneumatic rifle. Buckle charged up to Scully, planted his hand on his armored shoulder and shouted into the side of his helmet. "Sergeant! Sticky bombs! *Now!*"

Scully jerked back, startled by Buckle's sudden appearance, but Buckle saw a grim grin rip across his rough face. "Aye!" Scully said. He flipped open the bag on his belt and plunged in his gloved hand, lifting out a rectangular block of explosive with a loose, gluey fabric wrapping. He drew a dope-stiffened hemp fuse from his pocket and screwed it deep into the soft body of the bomb.

Buckle glanced back at Sabrina and saw her eject the offending shell out of the breech with her blade. The glittering brass cartridge twirled in the air and bounced off the barrel. The gunners had the rifle firing before the shell hit the ground.

The rapid punch of the pneumatic rifle rapped against Buckle's helmet as the Ballblaster gunners brought the weapon to bear on the center forgewalker, hammering him with a steady stream of bladed bolts.

"Thwack 'em!" Buckle screamed inside his helmet, spattering spit on the glass. With the rifle and sticky bombs now in the arsenal, he was suddenly berserk with hope.

The gunners knew their business. They aimed their fire at one point on the forgewalker—the already compromised edge of the plating between breastplate and lower abdomen—and the man-machine staggered.

"Musketeers! Wait for it!" Buckle yelled, drawing his pistol and holding his arm out in front of Scully's huddle of Crankshaft troopers. "Wait for the armor to pop and then thwack the bastard!"

The four Ballblasters, along with Kepler—who was still at Buckle's back—raised their muskets as one, aiming at the soon-to-be vulnerable section of the forgewalker's metal skin.

The pneumatic rifle, with its high muzzle velocity and the tempered iron of its whirling harpoon bolts, was a powerful weapon. It only took a matter of seconds before the targeted point in the forgewalker's armor, spewing sparks as it warped under the assault, came loose: a section of plate metal dropped away at the waist, exposing a patch of unprotected, red-hot steam tubes and underpadding.

"Now!" Buckle screamed.

Boom! Buckle, Kepler, and the four Ballblasters fired as one. Five streaks of white phosphorus zipped through the fog. The sixth man, the Ballblaster farthest to the right, had his musket explode in his hands, splitting open his helmet and killing him instantly; poor reloading, done in haste, was a death sentence with the unforgiving blackbang.

The five musket balls and the barrage of pneumatic bolts did their job. They sheared through the exposed innards of the forgewalker's midriff, which erupted in geysers of superheated water and a violent spewing of steam. The force of the blow knocked the man-machine sideways, nearly toppling him over. He stumbled for a few steps before the internal boiler, deprived of its water coolant, burped a bubble of flames and exploded, blowing the entire contraption to bits. Bits of shrapnel ricocheted off Buckle's visor.

The forgewalker, now a smoking birdcage of metal perched on two quivering legs, wobbled and fell over.

"Victory!" screamed Wolfgang from somewhere behind Buckle.

The two remaining forgewalkers converged upon the burning remains of their fallen fellow. Then, turning their faceless heads to the pneumatic rifle, they rushed it with all the speed their ponderous suits could muster. They came on with surprising haste, knocking aside any troopers within reach, advancing with an unrelenting fury on the Crankshaft position.

The forgewalkers were only twenty feet away.

The pneumatic rifle jammed again.

Some victory, Buckle thought.

"Sergeant!" Buckle shouted.

"Aye!" Scully answered. He snapped open a tinderbox attached to his left wrist; the flint on the cap struck and a thin yellow flame danced above the back of his hand. He lit the sticky-bomb fuse, which ignited in a fast-burning skitter of red sparks.

Everyone was backing up. The forgewalkers had covered the distance between them in what seemed like an instant. The Ballblaster gunners abandoned their post at the last second, throwing themselves aside just before one of the forgewalkers crushed the pneumatic rifle in a crunch of metal.

Buckle pulled Sabrina back as Scully stepped forward and hurled the sticky bomb. The sticky bomb was a rare commodity, tricky and unstable at best, coated with a gluten-soaked fiber wrapping that allowed it to adhere to almost any vertical surface. The interiors of the canvas carrying satchels were soaked with their own gluten, and were the only thing sticky bombs couldn't stick to. Legend had it that many a soldier who had tried to throw a sticky bomb discovered it stuck to his own hand, and thus unfortunately blew himself up in the effort.

When Scully threw the sticky bomb, he threw it hard.

The whirling sticky bomb struck one of the forgewalkers on the thigh of his right leg and stuck there, its burning fuse flipping back and forth on the metal. The driver halted and seemed confused, rotating his helmet back and forth as he peered down at his leg, and that hesitation sealed his fate. He plucked the bomb off his thigh armor with his metal glove and looked at it, then flung out his arm, palm down, but the sticky bomb didn't drop. The driver tried to shake it off the hand, but the machine wasn't capable of that kind of thrashing movement, delivering instead a dreadful, useless slow-motion wave.

The other forgewalker had also stopped; seeing his partner's predicament, he started backing away.

"Get down!" Buckle screamed, nearly puncturing his own eardrums inside his helmet, and pulled Sabrina down to the crumbled ground with him.

And then the sticky bomb exploded.

The forgewalker vanished in a white explosion that bludgeoned the whole foggy world. When Buckle lifted his head, all that was left of the forgewalker was a smoking flower of metal, each petal long and jagged and still, burst open on the ground. Sabrina wriggled out from under his arm and started reloading her pistol.

She didn't need to bother. The last forgewalker—having taken a final swing at an Alchemist trooper, who ducked his spinning chopper—had already turned tail and was clomping away into the fog. There was a hitch in his gait; it suggested he had taken some damage from the detonations that had obliterated his fellows.

There was a stunned pause as the Crankshafts and Alchemists, all bleeding from nicks delivered by either shrapnel or blade, caught their collective breath.

"Captain Buckle!" Scorpius shouted.

Buckle spun around and got his hands up just in time to catch the loaded musket Scorpius tossed to him.

"Take the Owl and run that scout down!" Scorpius ordered. "Do whatever it takes to destroy him! Whatever it takes!"

"Aye, General!" Buckle replied, and motioned for Wolfgang to follow him. "Wolfgang, you and the Owl are with me!"

"Aye!" Wolfgang answered, twiddling his instrument box as the Owl fell in beside him.

"Is Corporal Druxbury still standing?" Buckle asked Scully.

"Here, Captain!" Druxbury announced from the near murk, stepping into view.

"You still have that sticky bomb, Corporal?" Buckle asked.

"Aye, sir," Druxbury said.

"You're with us," Buckle said. "Let's go! Go!"

Wolfgang and the Owl were already on the hunt, the Owl uttering eerie chirps as it skittered forward, racing toward the point in the mist where the third Founders forgewalker had just vanished. Buckle caught up to them at a sprint with Druxbury at his heels—and Kepler at Druxbury's heels.

The murk thickened, closing in on Buckle until he seemed to be dashing down a tunnel of swirling mist; he could just make out the outline of Wolfgang's back in the disrupted fog ahead, and he accelerated to keep up with him. The Owl continued to beep somewhere in front of Wolfgang, a bodiless echo in the miasma.

They were running headlong and blind into the enemy's nest.

Who knew what booby traps awaited them in the mustard?

But the job had to be done. And they were the ones to do it.

~XXXVII~

CAPTAIN BUCKLE PULLS
THE TRIGGER

BUCKLE SUCKED AIR AS HE ran, his breath coming in loud gasps inside the jiggling weight of his helmet. The air-canister valve pinged as it pumped harder in response to the demand for oxygen, and with all of the noise, he could barely hear the chittering of the Owl up ahead in the fog.

Buckle did not like the idea of draining his oxygen supply so rapidly, but they had to take down the last forgewalker. If he got away and warned the Founders of the rescue party's existence, they were doomed. Scorpius, very aware of this, had sent his most fleet of foot to run the enemy down. Buckle, Wolfgang, and Kepler were only lightly armored, and the Owl was a gazelle. Corporal Druxbury was the only one burdened by the heavy Ballblaster war armor, and he trailed the group, stomping along, but that was the luck of the draw. Sometimes you just had to sweat it.

Buckle shifted his musket from his left hand to his right. Through his bouncing, smeared visor, now streaming with condensation and spattered with dark spots of soil and blood, Wolfgang and the Owl looked like wraiths, shadows pulsing in the streaming murk. It was getting very dark.

Buckle tripped over an outcropping of rough concrete and lost his balance, stumbling forward. A big hand—Kepler—caught him under the armpit just before he fell, righting him with a powerful yank. It was a friendly action made by a man who, with one wink from Scorpius, would be happy to blow Buckle's head clean off instead.

Scorpius. Scorpius had taken command now that Pluteus was most certainly dead. Was it right for an Alchemist to be in charge of the Crankshaft expedition? Buckle wondered. Should Buckle himself take command? No—he was an airship captain. He was not an infantry man. Scorpius was a no-nonsense old salt like Pluteus. Buckle decided to trust him. Considering the circumstances, he had no choice.

Pluteus. His loss was immeasurable in its impact, beyond the agony it struck in Buckle's heart. If they lost Pluteus in a failed attempt to recover Balthazar, essentially losing two of the Crankshaft clan's three main chieftains in one fell swoop, the result would be crippling, if not ultimately catastrophic.

It didn't take long to catch up with the lumbering forge-walker, perhaps a minute. The Owl homed in on him, beeping with what seemed like excitement. The Owl and Wolfgang slowed their pace, allowing Buckle, Kepler, and Druxbury to pull up next to them. Buckle saw the hulking outline of the forgewalker just ahead, tromping as fast as he could go through the mustard, his iron boots shaking the earth with heavy metal clanks. They could easily stay on pace with the forgewalker now, maintaining a separation of about fifteen yards and still keeping his broad back in view.

If the Founders man inside the robot skin knew they were there, he was ignoring them. He was concentrating on getting to where he needed to go—to sound the alarm. Normally a scout would carry homing pigeons and signal flares, but the mustard was no place for a living bird, and nobody was going to see a flare inside the fog bank. No, the driver had to get somewhere else to raise the alarm, to an outpost with a pneumatic-tube hub or a pigeon-coop tower. Or perhaps he had to make it to the very gates of the city itself. It was the sheer impermeability of the gas, the two-way blindness of the Founders defense, Buckle mused, that was going to save the Crankshaft expedition, even though they had been discovered.

The forgewalker clambered up a low rise of blasted earth— the southern edge of the moon-moat crater.

It was time to take him down, and take him down fast.

Druxbury reached into his sticky-bomb satchel, but Buckle stayed his hand, shouting, "Wait, Corporal!" He did not want to expend their last explosive; it was likely they would need it to free Balthazar from his prison cell.

Besides, Buckle had already seen their opportunity.

The back of the forgewalker's armor was scored black, damaged, popped open like a tin can: the driver had not been able to put enough distance between himself and the forgewalkers who had exploded, and the shrapnel had ripped away sections of his armored plating in an irregular, quilt-like pattern. The back of his helmet had been sheared off, revealing a bank of copper tubes and the dull gleam of glass. The glass was surely part of the shell of the driver's self-contained life support system: all they had to do was crack the glass open.

"Hold!" Buckle shouted inside his mask. Wolfgang heard him and stopped; he flipped a switch on his instrument box and the Owl halted as well. Kepler and Druxbury slowed to a stop and peered at Buckle as they gasped inside their muddied helmet visors.

Buckle dashed a few steps up the slope to close the distance, then raised his musket, lining up his sight before the man-machine melted into the fog. He matched the bouncing jerk of the forgewalker's steps, keeping his sight on the gleam of the glass inside the hole in the back of its metal skull.

Just before he pulled the trigger, Buckle wondered whether he was too close. There was a mere fifteen feet between them. Fifteen feet. If that walking behemoth of steam and fire blew up, it might blow him up with it.

Buckle pulled the trigger.

The musket discharged in a yellow flash, its recoil bucking Buckle in the shoulder. He ducked his head under the smoke and saw the forgewalker stagger to a stop at the crest of the ridge. The driver lifted his metal-clad arms and pawed desperately at his machine's iron skull, where geysers of oxygen and steam vented out into the swirling mist. There was no way for his metal fingers to plug the breach.

The machine convulsed as the driver inside it died. The arms flailed, but each jerk came with less and less energy. The spewing air leaks cut off. The red-hot tubes went pink and then black. The forgewalker froze, one metal hand clawing at the sky, standing as cold and dead as a statue in the Martian mist.

The Owl cocked its ungainly head and released a low, rattlesnake-tail rattle, as if it had just sighed.

"Crackerjack shot, Captain Buckle!" Wolfgang shouted from inside his gas mask as he patted the Owl on the head. "Crackerjack shot!"

Buckle lowered his smoking musket. He realized that his finger was still clamped around the depressed trigger with a pressure that made his knuckle tendons ache. He slowly lifted the finger free.

He did not like having to do such things.

–XXXVIII–

THE HEART OF A
MARTIAN ENGINEER

MAX NUDGED THE RUDDER WHEEL under her fingertips as she watched the sea of gray mist drift slowly beneath the *Pneumatic Zeppelin*. She had taken the helm, not because De Quincey had bungled it—he was quite capable—but because she simply could not stand being idle. She brought the airship back up to one hundred feet, out of reach of both the mustard and the sky mines. She felt a relief at being in open air once again, albeit sandwiched between fog below and clouds above. It was late afternoon now, just after five o'clock, and the angled rays of the sun were brighter behind the thinner currents and edges of the clouds, washing the gray, overcast sky in glowing white rivers.

Max kept one eye on her compass and one eye on Welly, who was bent over the drift scope with Apprentice Navigator Banerji tucked in close at his side. They were staying on course by carefully measuring their drift and direction against their own instrument settings and the shadows of the distant obelisks visible through the telescopes. The *Pneumatic Zeppelin* was barely moving, her chadburn set at dead slow. Countering her tendency to drift when at such a low speed was a complicated job, but the situation did have an advantage: the propeller and engine noise were so reduced that they were almost running silent. Their snail-like progress was timed so that they would arrive over the rendezvous point at the same moment the rescue expedition was scheduled to appear there. And sweet velocity, even the slowest kind, was much preferable to a fully stopped airship; hovering over a fixed position for any length of time was a constant battle, even in the lightest of winds.

Max still wore her breathing mask, as did Welly and Kellie and every member of the zeppelin crew, for the mustard gas was heavy and slow to disperse, and pools of the deadly miasma still lurked in the lower decks of the *Pneumatic Zeppelin*. The gondola crew was fully plugged in, with their helmet breathing hoses screwed into the airship's emergency oxygen lines, and their communication tubes connected to the chattertube system. And everyone aboard had their chattertube lines switched open. Max could hear the faint chorus of everyone breathing; it was as if they were all inside her helmet with her.

"Two degrees starboard," Welly said, his voice distant but distinct as it carried through the chattertube. "Drift correction."

"Two degrees, aye," Max replied, her voice close and low in her own ears. Eyes on her compass, gyroscope, and direction finder, all aglow with frog-colored boil, she rolled the rudder wheel slightly to port and heard it make its familiar *tock* sound once as it turned. She stopped the wheel before the two-degree mark was reached, allowing for the zeppelin's own momentum to carry it another half degree to the desired correction.

It was in times of crisis that Max did not mind spending every waking minute with her crewmates; she liked the communal energy when there was urgent business to be done. But Martians were solitary creatures, and under normal circumstances she preferred to be alone; when off duty, she often abandoned her cabin and her books, and clambered up into the

RICHARD ELLIS PRESTON, JR.

crow's nest to listen to the wind and be alone with her thoughts. The crew had found her there in the morning so often, curled up asleep in her heavy coat, that they had long ago started calling the topside observation nacelle "Max's nest."

Max didn't like it when a grinning crew member tapped her awake and she had to thank them, embarrassed, and slip down the companionway half-asleep and needing a hot, black shot of tea.

"Clouds of gossamer, moonlight mysterious as beryl. Lovely night if it wasn't adrift in cataclysmic peril," came the whispered voice of Nero Coulton, the ballast-board operator.

Max would have rolled her eyes if that was something Martians did. The crew was at battle stations and on survival helmets: talking was restricted to commands only. But Nero, the resident poet, knew exactly how much fluff he could get away with. Max wanted to chide him, but she did not. His little stanzas chipped away at the tension by amusing the crew, and he would only deliver one, carefully and poorly devised, per occasion.

Nero was a short, round fellow whose poetry, although as annoying as a loose and rattling screw, was also comfortingly familiar. Nero believed himself to be a wordsmith; it was his sacred duty to stage poetry readings on the fourteenth day of each month. He held his performances in the captain's quarters, drawn up to his full length in front of the glass nose dome, and the overly dramatic renditions of his epic rhymes could drag on for hours. Anyone who missed a reading without a good excuse inflicted monumental hurt upon the great poet. The result was that the crew made it a game, going to extraordinary lengths to discover new ways to excuse themselves from Nero's events. Ivan once faked his own death, the news of his unexpected expiration

189

ROMULUS BUCKLE & THE CITY OF THE FOUNDERS

after eating a bad sausage being grimly delivered just before the performance. Nero did not cancel the show but rather wallowed in the tragedy of the night, his maudlin soliloquies soaked with tears. The report of Ivan's demise was retracted as an "unfortunate exaggeration of events" after the reading was over.

Ivan appeared regularly in Nero's poetics after that, thinly disguised as a buffoonish character called the Donkey of Moscow.

Max heard crewman Arlington Bright sigh in his mask behind her, in response to Nero's words: he was a rigger, and one of three crew members issued a musket and sword and assigned to the piloting gondola to repel boarders. Once you took into account the banks of instruments and chairs, the gondola only had limited space, so the three crewmen in portable oxygen gear plus Max, Kellie, Welly, Dunn, De Quincey, Banerji, Nero, and Assistant Engineer Geneva Bolling, not to mention Jacob Fitzroy in the cramped aft signals room, made for a full house. It was not a sardine can, but it was crowded.

Kellie, her ears poking up out of her gas mask, was up against Max's legs. The dog always came to her when Buckle and Sabrina were off the ship. The animal was like clockwork when it came to her preferences: Buckle was choice number one, Sabrina choice number two, and, although she had no idea why, Max was choice number three.

The pneumatic tube terminal *cha-thunk*ed at Max's left shoulder, ringing tube number four's bell. Tube number four was the engine room. The pneumatic-tube messaging system aboard the airship operated on compressed air and partial vacuums, allowing messages too complicated for chattertubes to be zipped around the zeppelin at thirty-one feet per second. The four-inch copper pipelines connected every major compartment aboard the *Pneumatic Zeppelin*, their felt-capped copper capsules transporting handwritten messages from station to station.

Max retrieved the capsule from the receiving-chamber hatch and flipped it open to retrieve the message within. It was a standard note from Elliot Yardbird, the engine officer, calculating the increased consumption of coal due to increased drag on the damaged skin of the zeppelin. Fuel consumption and bunkering were not a problem on this short trip, but it was Yardbird's job to acknowledge such issues.

Max checked her watch and compass. They should be passing over the outer walls of the city very soon. She returned her focus to the ocean of undulating mist below, scanning for any sign of the watchtowers that were said to once have existed there. Lore had it that the towers were once high enough for their cupolas to overlook the ceiling of ever-present fog, but that the Founders had decided to tear them down because they gave away the city's location underneath.

It was a good hiding place. Flying over it, one would never suspect that the largest city in the Snow World lay sprawled beneath that canopy of befouled air.

The Founders and their city were a mystery; information about them came in scraps and dribbles from traders. The stories were often so embellished that one had to listen to them with a grain of salt. But professional merchants, the favored ones, were given permission to dock at the port of Del Rey, a walled-in airship and seagoing-vessel harbor where the Founders could trade goods without allowing outsiders access to the main city. Del Rey was rumored to be a rough place, characterized by the black-market villainy of the trader guilds, but it was also a vibrant exchange; it was said that ruthless merchants from every

corner of the known world could make themselves rich there—
if they lived through it.

Still, Max wasn't big on rumors. If the watchtowers existed,
she would see them. And if they did, the *Pneumatic Zeppelin* was
probably doomed. Given warning, the Founders would loose
their infamous air armada, said to be more than a dozen war-
ships led by two behemoth dreadnoughts that dwarfed even the
Pneumatic Zeppelin. The Founders' machines would rise up from
their berths in the fog and reduce Max's sky vessel to a burning
cinder in a matter of minutes, if not less.

But what of the dreadnoughts? Nobody had seen the
Founders' fabled fleet for one hundred years.

Max sighed inside her mask and then became worried
that the others might have heard it. Despite the tension of the
moment, she felt a little tired, which was odd for her; Martians,
even half-breeds, possessed tremendous stamina. Yes, it had
been an exhausting day of fighting Scavengers and tanglers, and
yes, sliding off the side of an airship at three thousand feet without a safety line had been stressful. But what had really knocked
the wind out of her was the thought that Captain Buckle had
been killed. The weight, the sheer, awful weight of despair she
felt when his apparent death was reported, had surprised her.
Was it that she had fought to defend her captain, prepared to
sacrifice her own life in the effort, and still she had failed him?

That was partly the reason. But there was more.

Why Max had always felt so protective toward Buckle both
bedeviled and befuddled her. They had both been adopted
by Balthazar as youngsters, and Buckle had taunted Max and
her younger brother, Tyro, because he didn't like "the stinking zebras," whom he blamed for the death of his parents.
Buckle would come at them with fists swinging at the slightest

provocation, forcing Balthazar and Calypso to separate them
for long periods of time, which was difficult in the enclosed
confines of a clan stronghold. At one point, when Buckle was
eleven years old, he was sent to live with his uncle Horatio at
the Devil's Punchbowl outpost for one year, just to keep the
domestic life in Balthazar's house tolerable.

Old Horatio managed to straighten Buckle out, because when
he returned to the family he never raised his hand against Max or
Tyro again. And as Buckle moved into young adulthood, he outgrew
his anger, slowly developing into a gracious brother whose matur-
ing gentlemanliness would become a hallmark of his character.

And yet, through it all, even from the time when she was a
very young girl, Max knew that she loved Romulus Buckle. Or,
more accurately, she knew that she both loved and hated him.
But she never allowed herself to explore her feelings toward him
further; she was unwilling to accept what she might discover
about herself if she did.

As for Romulus Buckle himself, well, after the terrible
nights of the Tehachapi Blitz and the Imperial Raid, after he
and Max had fought side by side and saved each other's life
in turn, she had sensed that something inside Buckle, something in the way he saw her, had changed. He had suddenly
and intimately softened toward her. Perhaps it was that each of
them had lost so much—Calypso, Elizabeth, Sebastian Mitty,
and most of Tyro—that a profound connection forged through
blood and pain was inevitable.

Max and Buckle. Buckle and Max. The blood between
them could not have been more different. But they were joined
on some mysterious level, nonetheless.

Max glanced at her sprawling instrument panel, where
golden sand streamed through a large, boil-lit hourglass. She

had measured the sand to run forty minutes—roughly the amount of time the Crankshaft expedition would have breathable air in their oxygen cylinders.

The last grains of golden sand were falling.

Buckle and company had better be out of the mustard by now.

~XXXIX~

SPIDER TRAPS AND
SEWER RATS

BUCKLE DROPPED ABOUT SIX FEET down the manhole, out of the luminous yellow mustard and into the pitch black of the sewer tunnel. His boots smacked on wet concrete. The weight of his gear forced him to his knees—which he bruised considerably—and with a sharp grunt he lurched aside to avoid being squashed by Kepler, coming down right behind him.

Buckle steadied himself with one hand against the slimy wall. Sabrina and two Ballblasters had already descended and were striking matches to light kerosene lanterns built into the crests of their helmets. The soft orange light glowed on the water-slicked walls and allowed Buckle to get his bearings. He hurried forward as more troopers dropped down the manhole behind him.

Time was not on their side. The skirmish with the Founders scouts had slowed them down, and their exertions had rapidly drained the reserves in their oxygen tanks. Already Buckle had the impression that he was working harder to breathe—as if his air was already thinning—even though his cylinder gauge still reported two minutes remaining in its supply.

Scorpius and Kepler stepped up beside Buckle; being a subterranean clan, the Alchemists also had lanterns installed in their helmets, but with an ingenious built-in tinderbox that ignited the kerosene wick internally, sparked by the rolling of a cog under the chin.

"I don't see any stinkum," Buckle said to Sabrina. What he could see of the tunnel looked clear, and free of the yellow mist. "Are we good?"

"I wouldn't risk it yet," Sabrina answered, neatly folding up her map with the care of a navigator. "Not if we don't have to. Let's move."

"Wait, Lieutenant. Let's not get too spread out," Scorpius cautioned.

Sabrina halted, staring into the depthless black length of the tunnel ahead. Buckle could tell that she was agitated, itching to advance.

Kepler planted his massive hand on Buckle's shoulder and turned him around to face him. Startled, Buckle squinted; Kepler's lamp was bright and the shadows inside his helmet hid his face. Kepler lit a match, a white sulfur flash that made Buckle squint even more. Kepler flipped open the glass door of Buckle's helmet lamp and lit the wick. Another friendly act from his assassin, Buckle thought. Kepler clicked Buckle's lamp door shut and snuffed the match between his gloved fingers.

"Thanks," Buckle said.

Kepler nodded.

The rest of the surviving Ballblasters—seventeen of the original twenty—had now dropped into the sewer tunnel with heavy armored *clank*s. Lighting their helmet lamps, they joined the seven remaining Alchemists and the Owl, which had leapt down the manhole with the surprising lightness of a bird. The last man to descend was Pluteus—yes, Pluteus—who had miraculously survived the titanic blow delivered to him by the robotic arm of the forgewalker. After the skirmish, the Ballblasters had charged into the fog and fished their beloved Pluteus out of a frozen snowbank. Brittle honeycombs of ice had collapsed sufficiently to break his fall; he was bruised and battered, his glass facemask cracked and sprayed on the inside with blood and snot, but he was very much alive.

"That hurt like hell!" Pluteus announced as he landed inside the tunnel, grimacing with pain. "A good day to be alive!

"We've got to move, people!" Sabrina shouted. "Move!"

Sabrina set off down the sewer pipe with such a severe stride that Buckle, even with his much longer legs, had to work to keep up with her. The old sewer was a straight tube, at least as far as Buckle could see—the ghostly illumination of their helmet lamps melted away about twenty feet ahead. The floor was flat concrete, with water channels cut into the base of each wall, which didn't seem to be very effective at draining away the disgusting slop they were splashing through. The arched ceiling dripped with moisture and dangling gobbets of transparent goo.

They were at a near run. The metal-sheathed boots, armor, and equipment of the troopers, not to mention the Owl's iron claws, rattled, jingled, and clanked. It sounded as if there were a horse and carriage coming down the sewer at Buckle's heels. Well, stealth was not required at the moment, was it?

Here and there Buckle thought he glimpsed translucent swirls of yellow mist fluttering in the air, visible only for an instant. Damned mustard.

Buckle's low-oxygen alarm went off. Inside each Crankshaft air canister was a little spring-mounted hammer, which tapped a bell when the tank's pressure indicated less than one minute of air remaining—but they were notoriously inaccurate. He could have ten seconds worth of breathable air left. He heard Sabrina's alarm go off, and within a few more seconds, the alarms in many of the Crankshaft troopers' tanks started ringing.

Buckle coughed. He found it difficult to catch his breath. He didn't look at his oxygen gauge. He slowed his breathing even though his lungs screamed for more.

"Hold on!" Sabrina shouted, her voice sounding muffled and far away over the jangling of the alarm bells.

Laboring to breathe as he ran, Buckle's vision narrowed—or was it just the fogging of his faceplate glass? The ceiling shimmered silver, fluttering. It was getting harder and harder to run...as if something was pushing him back.

Sabrina suddenly stopped. Buckle bumped into her and nearly knocked her over. The entire group skidded to a halt behind them. Sabrina lifted her hands, jerked her chin straps loose, unclamped the oxygen mask, and yanked her helmet off her head. Her bright red hair flopped loose, bunched and soggy with sweat, the pale skin on her forehead and cheeks discolored with deep, pink depressions from the padding of the mask.

Sabrina took a big breath. "Good for the goose, lads!" she announced, grinning widely, her mask dangling from its strap on her left shoulder.

Buckle snatched at his bulky helmet, now an instrument of suffocation, detaching the leather cinching straps and wrenching it off over his head so hard he feared he might have taken a few strips of flesh with it. He guzzled great lungfuls of air—the atmosphere was wretched and it stunk of decay, but it was the sweetest air Buckle had ever tasted. And instead of being slapped by the cold, still air he expected, the skin on his perspiration-drenched face was met by a stiff lukewarm breeze coming from the tunnel ahead.

Looking up as he gasped, Buckle's eyes focused on a gargantuan cobweb stretching across the entire length of the arched ceiling, its silky mesh billowing back like a sail against the flowing air. The web strands shimmered in the lamplight, shivering with the struggles of a trapped moth beating its dull-brown wings against the ancient trap.

"Is that how you knew there wasn't any mustard here?" Buckle asked Sabrina. "The spiderwebs?"

"I don't know about moths and spiders," Sabrina said. "But..." She pointed to one of the darkly shadowed concrete channels running along the wall. Buckle realized it was streaming haphazardly with something other than water; he stepped forward and peered down into the channel with the illumination of his lamp. It was flowing with naked-tailed vermin.

"Rats," Sabrina muttered loudly, still not accustomed to speaking outside of her helmet. "The place is still filthy with rats."

─XL─

THE CITY OF THE FOUNDERS

"DISCARD ALL GAS EQUIPMENT!" PLUTEUS shouted through the howling wind in the darkness of the sewer tunnel. "There is no reason to lug it from here!"

Buckle watched the Ballblasters and Alchemists unstrap their air cylinders, harnesses, hoses, and masks and drop them into the drainage channels, as hundreds of rats squealed indignantly below. Buckle cast aside his own heavy gear with little regret; although the equipment was expensive and it had kept him alive, they had been running at a jog for the last three minutes, and losing the sixty pounds of metal and rubber was a tremendous relief to his spine.

Needing the lamplight, everyone kept their helmets on, faceplates open. The orange illumination jiggled frenetically as the helmets were buffeted by the fast-moving air.

Sabrina was beside Buckle, her red hair floating about her head in the torrent of wind that had greatly increased in intensity in the last two hundred yards. Its blast was strong enough to make Buckle duck, and it battered his eardrums, which were accustomed to the tight insulation of his gas mask.

The powerful air currents had scoured this section of the tunnel clean; there was no hope for spiderwebs to cling here, and the floor and ceiling were as dry as a desert. The source of the powerful outgoing draft, which carried the seaweed odor of ocean air, was unknown, but Buckle suspected it was a way for the Founders to keep the mustard from flowing in under their city.

Sabrina stopped in front of a large metal hatch sunk into the tunnel wall. Its surface ran with horizontal rivers of flaky orange rust; it had the look of an ancient tomb door that had been sealed shut for eternity. She drew a crowbar from her jacket and rammed it into a lock over the hatch lever. "Give a hand, here!" she shouted.

Buckle and Kepler stepped forward and placed their hands on the crowbar, ready to throw their backs into the yank.

"The lock is already broken!" Sabrina bellowed, planting her mouth as close as she could to Buckle and Kepler's heads. "The hatch door is seated tight, but all we have to do is pry it open! Heave!"

Buckle and Kepler threw all of their might against the crowbar. The cumbersome door creaked in protest and came unstuck, shifting open just a hair, squirting a pop of powdery rust, instantly snatched away by the wind. Buckle groaned, his muscles quivering, but Kepler's brawn was making the real difference. Once the hatch portal was cracked an inch—fortunately it swung with the wind current rather than against it—a crowd of Ballblaster and Alchemist hands grabbed hold of the rim and pulled it open.

The hatchway led into total darkness. Sabrina immediately jumped in.

Buckle followed Sabrina with pistol and musket. In the bouncing light of their helmet lamps he found himself in a narrow cylindrical tank about forty feet long, its rusting walls pulsing with cockroaches. His boots sloshed through an inch-deep slush of old sewage, slime, and floating chunks of what looked like Spam, but the vile appearance of the tank paled in comparison to the vileness of its smell.

"Perhaps we should have kept our gas masks on a little bit longer," Buckle whispered, fighting the urge to retch.

"As you may have guessed, we're in the old sewage system," Sabrina replied, apparently not much affected by the stench. "The Founders built much of their new city underground, including the prison. The sewers and subway tunnels of old Los Angeles passing through here were all sealed off. But somebody cracked this one."

"I'm going to have to burn these boots," Buckle grumbled, but he was musing over Sabrina's spilling of a little inside information. He would bet a bucket of hydrogen she would be willing to tell him everything if he asked, but that would violate Balthazar's sacred code safeguarding his adopted children's pasts. Buckle would never ask.

And what in blue blazes was a subway?

Buckle glanced back. Kepler was behind him and the tank beyond was filling up with headlamp beams as the team filed in, each member experiencing their own private dismay at the putrid soup lapping around their ankles.

When Buckle and Sabrina reached the far end of the tank, Sabrina pressed her boot against the old access hatch and shoved it wide open. Buckle was so close behind her that he bumped her rump with his helmet as she clambered out. He paused, allowing her to get clear, and then swung out the opening to drop a few feet to the floor, his boots leaving rude splatters on the concrete.

Buckle took a deep snort of stale air to clear his nostrils. He scanned the new chamber with his headlamp. It was a small, windowless room, a room of the old kind, a utilitarian cement box. Two identical sewage tanks loomed alongside the one they had just emerged from. Hundreds of pipes of various sizes ribbed every inch of the walls, although some had large sections missing, the victims of Scavengers. A desk with an instrument panel and a computer screen, the weird electric machines long since dead, stood in the middle of the room, buried under dirt and dust. A lone wooden chair, an ugly, prefabricated piece, sat forlornly in a corner. The door was large and metal, and most probably locked from the outside.

Sabrina handed her breastplate, helmet, coat, sword, and map case to Buckle. "Hold on to these for me, please, Captain," she said, retaining only her pistol, tucked into her belt. "I'll be back in a moment."

Sabrina clambered up onto the computer desk and, stretching to her full height, cat-jumped up to a ceiling vent and shoved it aside. She pulled her body up through the hole until her boots disappeared. Tiny avalanches of dust fell onto the computer.

Kepler, freshly escaped from the sewage tank and smelling like it, arrived at Buckle's side; he peered up at the hole and grunted.

The little room filled up rapidly as trooper after trooper, headlamps glowing, climbed out of the tank. Wolfgang appeared and, after some difficulties getting the Owl's large head through the hatchway, managed to get both of them down to the crowded floor.

"Well, I'll be potted! What manner of dead end is this?" Pluteus exclaimed, eyeing the items in Buckle's arms. "And where is Lieutenant Serafim?"

"Bounced up and out, General," Buckle said, pointing at the ceiling.

Pluteus gave him a serious glare.

The chamber echoed with the *ka-chank* of a heavy metal bolt being slid aside outside the door. Two more *chur-kersnick*s rattled and then stopped.

The door swung open with a monumental squeal of rusty hinges, and there stood Sabrina, hands on her hips, her whole body caked with crumbly dust. A soft, weird illumination flowed in around her, a bluish-white, fluttering light accompanied by a buoyant hiss.

"Welcome to the City of the Founders," Sabrina said.

–XLI–

PRISON BY GASLIGHT

SABRINA, HAVING HASTILY DONNED HER coat, armor, and sword belt, led the way out of the old maintenance room with her pistol at the ready. Turning to the right, they emerged into an airy passageway of smooth blue-gray stone reinforced at intervals with timber supports. The air seemed very still after the wooly gale in the sewage tunnel; it was slightly warm with a sweet, earthy smell. But by far the most striking elements were the light fixtures, oval glass lamps affixed to the walls by iron sconces, each hissing quietly as it percolated with a large blue flame.

"I wish we had a moment to investigate these lamps," Wolfgang whispered. "What is this fabulous source of illumination? It seems to be some sort of flammable gas—but it could not be hydrogen, could it? No, hydrogen is far too scarce and expensive. It has to be something else."

"Silence," Scorpius grumped at Wolfgang.

Sabrina knew what the gas was. But she was not about to weather even more suspicious glances by volunteering inside information.

"Lamps off," Pluteus, limping behind Buckle with Kepler, ordered in a low voice. There was no need for the helmet lanterns now.

Sabrina pressed the extinguisher lever on the side of her helmet's lamp casing, hearing a *click* as a pair of caliper dampers stamped out the wick inside. With all of the assault team's orange lamps doused, the corridor took on the bright, ice-blue-edged illumination of the Founders' mysterious gas lamps.

"It isn't far," Sabrina whispered back to Pluteus.

Pluteus nodded. "Eyes up, boys. Eyes up and keep your powder dry," he said. "Advance guard, forward." Two Ballblasters pushed forward to flank Sabrina on each side.

Sabrina cautiously turned left into another well-lit corridor that looked identical to the first. They passed a pair of yellow canaries in a hanging iron cage; the little creatures flitted about, their black eyes wary, and their dismayed chirps made more noise than Sabrina would have liked. At twenty yards she made another right turn, leading them deeper into the labyrinth of empty stone passageways. But now they were passing closed wooden doors—entrances to storage rooms.

Sabrina took a sharp left turn around the next corner and ran straight into a Founders jailer—literally bashing headfirst into the young fellow, knocking a bowl of pasty, gray gruel out of his hands.

Sabrina lunged at the stunned jailer before he could react, sweeping his legs out from under him as he staggered backward with gruel splashed across his black tunic. She dropped on his chest with her knife pressed against his throat.

"Not a sound, you hear me, fogsucker?" Sabrina snarled in a whisper, a splotch of gruel dripping from her cheek. "Or I skewer you like a rat."

The unfortunate jailer—a gangly, pimply kid who could not have been more than sixteen years old—stared up at Sabrina with eyes as big as saucers. He was breathing so hard that Sabrina had to lift her rear from his chest or be uncomfortably bounced.

He nodded his head cautiously, wary of the razor-sharp blade resting against his windpipe.

"Damn our hides!" Pluteus growled under his breath as he turned the corner. "Get him up! Get him up!"

Buckle and Kepler helped Sabrina drag the limp jailer to his feet while Sergeant Scully disarmed him, removing his pistol from its holster. The kid was tall, wearing a black uniform with silver piping on the collar and sleeves. Festooned on his cap was a silver phoenix, the symbol of the Founders clan. Tears of terror pooled in his pale blue eyes as gruel dribbled around the silver buttons on his chest.

Pluteus stepped up to the kid and seemed to loom over him, even though the kid was a good five inches taller than he was. "Balthazar Crankshaft—is he here?"

"Ye-ye-yes, sir," the kid jailer answered, his voice high and shaking as if he only had a pinhole to speak through. "T-t-turn right at the end of this passage...then, the cell blocks, you, ah, you—"

"I know how to get to the cell blocks," Sabrina interrupted, slipping her knife back into its sheath. "Is Balthazar in cell twenty-four?"

"Yes. Twenty-four. It's twenty-four. On the central corridor. Cell twenty-four." The kid jailer gasped.

"Your keys," Pluteus said, and nodded to Scully.

Scully drew his knife. The kid jailer winced; sweat poured down his red-dotted face in rivers and his eyes begged for mercy. Scully waved the blade in the kid's face, then leaned down and sliced open his belt, removing his key ring. The kid looked like he was about to faint.

"Which key?" Pluteus demanded. "Balthazar's cell. Which key is it?"

"I don't have it," the kid jailer stammered quickly, his terror surging. "I don't. Please...only the master of the watch, only the master of the watch has those keys, the keys for the special prisoners. I don't have it. I swear. I swear."

Pluteus looked like he might bash the quivering kid's head in.

But it was Scorpius, barging into the fray, who truly had murder in his eyes. "Where is Andromeda Pollux?" he snapped.

"Who?" the kid jailer answered, blinking with fright.

"Andromeda! Andromeda Pollux!" Scorpius continued, managing to bellow with a whisper. "The Alchemist! What cell is she in?"

"I don't know her! I swear. I swear," the kid jailer mumbled, beginning to cry. "I swear it!" he gasped, swallowing with a loud, gargled choke.

A low rumble rose in Scorpius's throat, his words coming with a slow, fury-dripping menace, his gritted teeth white against his dark skin. "For the last time. Where is Andromeda Pollux?"

"She might be in one of the special cells," the kid jailer said, talking fast, talking for his life. "Those prisoners are handled by officers. I don't know who is in those cells. They're above my pay grade. I'm just a jailer. But I do know that there is somebody in there. They take meals in."

Pluteus carefully placed his hand on Scorpius's shoulder and pulled him back. "We'll find her, Scorpius," Pluteus said. "She is here and we will find her."

Scorpius allowed Pluteus to move him away, but he never took his burning stare off the frightened jailer. Sabrina hoped that Pluteus was right. If it turned out that Andromeda wasn't there—that Buckle had been misleading in his information—the

Alchemists would become infuriated, and there was no telling how that messy situation might play itself out.

"There's another one, another important prisoner!" the kid jailer jabbered, offering up everything he had. "Katzenjammer Smelt. The Imperial. He's in cell twenty-six, just south of Balthazar. I can take you to both of them. I can!"

Sabrina saw Buckle jerk, his blood suddenly up. The mere utterance of the name Katzenjammer Smelt, the Imperial clan chancellor, would have pierced him to the core. Smelt was the man who had engineered the Tehachapi Blitz. Smelt was the man whose treachery had killed Elizabeth and Calypso. Their blood was fresh on his murdering hands.

"I say we leave Smelt to rot," Buckle muttered, nearly choking on his own tongue, so great was the rage he was forced to throttle down.

The Ballblasters crowded in the hallway responded with a soft chorus of "Aye."

"Or we take him home and hang him," Scully said.

"That is enough!" Pluteus barked softly. "Now we need to move!"

Sabrina grabbed the kid jailer by the collar. "Quickly, now—where is the master of the watch?" she asked.

The kid jailer's lips shook. "She should be at the front. In the anteroom. At the main entrance."

"Should be?" Sabrina snapped.

"She's there. I just saw her. She's there!" the kid jailer sobbed, eyes flicking, noticing fearfully that Sergeant Scully had stepped behind him. "She's there...please...I swear. And sh-sh-she has the keys. I swear!"

"Okay," Sabrina said, patting his cheek in a kindly fashion. "Now that wasn't so bad, was it?"

There was a hollow *thunk*, as Sergeant Scully whacked the back of the kid jailer's skull with the butt of his own pistol; the kid's eyes rolled up white and he dropped like a sack of ballast. Scully caught him and propped his unconscious body against the wall.

"They are all here, I am certain," Pluteus said. "All three: Balthazar, Andromeda, and the bastard Smelt. But we have only one heavy explosive left. We are going to need the keys from the master of the watch."

"This little glitch with the jailer may prove fortunate for us, Pluteus," Sabrina said. "I have a plan."

–XLII–

THE RELUCTANT VOLUNTEER

WHY DO I ALWAYS HAVE to be the one to volunteer for these crazy things? Buckle thought as he strode, alone and in plain sight, down the middle of the main prison corridor, heading for the front doors. Well, you tell everyone that you feast on danger, don't you? You're a risk taker, a peril raker, an iron-eyed trouble-maker. You don't just embrace risk, you charge down its throat with a grin. *Shut up*, he told himself.

At least the wretched Kepler could not hound his heels up here.

The main prison corridor was a wide passageway one hundred yards in length, which divided the two central cell blocks. Lit by rows of gas lamps flickering along each wall, it was an oppressive rectangular tunnel of stone and shadows, where canary pairs in the occasional birdcage provided the only touches of color and movement. According to the kid jailer's frantic account, Balthazar and Katzenjammer Smelt were being held in the cells on Buckle's left, which had heavy wooden doors plated with copper, and small windows with iron bars. And Buckle desperately hoped that Andromeda was in one of the special cells on his right. Of these, he could see nothing beyond big iron doors set at regular intervals in the stone wall.

Buckle wanted to look in the cells—no one was visible at the windows—and he suddenly feared that the Founders might have beaten Balthazar so badly he might not be able to stand.

But at least Balthazar was here. Buckle's racing heart leapt with relief. They would free him, no question, and the Crankshaft clan would be saved. It looked like Aphrodite, Balthazar's mysterious spy inside the city, had given them good information.

Buckle's boots pinched. They really pinched. And they were not *his* boots—they belonged to the kid jailer. He was wearing the kid's uniform. It was snug, but it fit him fairly well, with its long black tunic studded with two rows of silver buttons and loose-fitting black trousers. But the kid had tiny feet, and Buckle had been forced to stuff his big paddles into the little boots until it felt like his toes were folded under his heels.

Buckle tucked the kid jailer's hat down as low as he could on his forehead. Don't hobble, he told himself.

This was Sabrina's plan. Dressed as a jailer, Buckle was going to stroll up to the front desk and confiscate the keys from the master of the watch at the point of a pistol. Easy as falling off a zeppelin, right?

But why couldn't the kid jailer have been a short, stocky fellow whose uniform could not fit him?

Buckle's feet hurt all the way up to his shoulders.

At least he had not run into any more guards.

"You! Hold there!" A gravelly voice, driven to a tremulous pitch, pierced the air immediately on Buckle's left.

Buckle stopped, his heart skipping a beat, his hand whipping down to the butt of the pistol in his holster.

"You!" The gravelly voice had a deeper, darker tone this time.

Buckle slowly looked to the left. A long arm, seemingly longer than natural, a gnarled, knobby limb that was no more than skin glued on bone, had been thrust out a cell window, the index finger extended, pointing at him. Beyond the arm, above a sunken clavicle, was a face, buried in shadows and a tangled shock of gray hair and beard. It was the face of an old man, his exact age difficult to tell. His eyes, wild and bright as a crazed animal's, bulged unnaturally large and round inside their sunken sockets.

"Do I know you?" the old man mumbled, his lower lip quivering.

"Be quiet!" Buckle whispered harshly.

"What? No one quiets old Shadrack! The blackguards knocked out half my teeth, and still no one quiets old Shadrack! I sing. I sing!" Shadrack rattled his window bars, getting agitated and getting louder.

"Fine. Sure," Buckle said quickly, soothingly. "Sing. Just stop jabbering."

"The roaches in the mush—they speak and I listen," Shadrack said. "And the clouds speak. Beautiful voices. But if your head is not in it, you lose them. They sink away, whispers in the hurly-burly."

"Whispering is good. How about we whisper?" Buckle glanced down the corridor in the direction of the front anteroom. Sooner or later the guards were going to respond to their prisoner's ravings.

Narrowing his lids over his bulbous eyes, Shadrack shot his arm out and pointed again. "You fear them, too. You do not belong here...you do not belong here!" He began to utter a low, tremulous howl.

"Hush!"

To Buckle's surprise, Shadrack went silent. He slammed his face into the gap between the window bars, framed by his bony hands. "Are you here to save me? Are you here to rescue poor old Shadrack? Are you an angel?"

"Romulus!" Pluteus whispered from the darkness of an adjoining corridor twenty feet behind, where the entire assault team crouched in wait. "Move!"

Buckle looked at Shadrack. The old man's face had gone soft, the eyes innocent and plaintive as a puppy's. "Yes. I came to save you," Buckle whispered. "But you have to be quiet, you hear me?"

Tears flowed down Shadrack's face. His tense hands relaxed, the fingers shaking. "My son. Did my son send you?"

"Yes, Shadrack, he did." Buckle had no choice but to lie. "Now be quiet."

"My son..." Shadrack whispered, his eyes clouding over, suddenly lost in a dream.

Buckle started forward. He still had to cover fifty feet up the gently sloping entrance ramp before reaching the prison anteroom.

"Angels with guns!" Shadrack screamed at the top of his lungs. "You have saved me! You have saved old Shadrack! Angels with guns! I am free! I am free!"

Buckle felt like a sitting duck. He lowered his head and lengthened his stride. Behind him, the old Shadrack, face beet red, released a long, guttural, half-moose howl. Buckle forced himself to continue walking: nothing was wrong if he acted like nothing was wrong. He maintained an easy stride as he ascended the entrance ramp.

Just how had he gotten this job, again? Did not Sabrina simply hand him the kid's hat? Come to think of it, he didn't remember volunteering at all.

The entrance to the anteroom loomed ahead, just twenty paces away. Buckle saw the edges of wooden desks and a row of ornamental columns beyond. The front outer doors were tall, buttressed with metal skirts, and dominated the space.

The master of the watch stepped into view at the top of the ramp. She peered down the corridor with no sense of alarm, her arms crossed in front of her in the easy fashion of someone who stood around guarding things—things that were locked up and stationary. She was in her early thirties, pretty in a rough sort of way, her blonde hair bound up tightly under her black cap. The silver stripes on her uniform sleeves and her air of authority left no doubt that she was the one in charge. A large brass ring loaded with skeleton keys jingled at her belt, right beside a pistol sitting in a thick leather holster.

It was the pistol that concerned Buckle the most.

"Is old Shadrack having at you again, Mister Beck?" the master of the watch asked in a loud, husky, and somewhat amused voice.

Another voice came from the anteroom, from another jailer that Buckle could not see yet. "I say we let him take a stroll in the mustard and be done with his ravings," the other guard shouted, then laughed.

Buckle shrugged, tugged at the brim of his hat and coughed, pressing his fist up to his mouth to hide the lower half of his face. He had to buy a little more time. A few more steps were all he needed to see how many people were in the anteroom. His aching feet started to go numb in the undersized boots, threatening to give out underneath him. His blood circulation was cut off from the knees down.

And old Shadrack, mad as a loon, continued howling.

"Mister Beck?" the master of the watch repeated, her tone turning quizzical and concerned.

Balthazar's life hung in the balance, and everything was going wrong.

"Mister Beck!"

Time was up. Buckle yanked out his pistol and marched into the lair of the master of the watch.

-XLIII-

THE FINAL ACT OF THE MASTER OF THE WATCH

With Buckle's pistol mere inches from her face, the master of the watch backed up into the anteroom. Upon entering, Buckle sensed that the semicircular prison entrance chamber was far more elegant than he might have expected: the curved walls were coated with cream-colored plaster and lined with granite columns, each affixed with a flickering blue gas lamp. The domed ceiling overhead bore a beautiful painting of the red phoenix, while the massive wooden doors, ten feet high, weak gray sunlight spilling in around the edges, were gilded in metal etched with scenes of men toiling on an assembly line.

From a long, dark desk on the right, polished to a gleam under stacks of paper and a little iron cage where two yellow canaries resided, a lazy-faced guard of average height gaped in disbelief.

Buckle had two Crankshaft pistols stuffed into the back of his belt and, keeping his first pistol on the master of the watch, he drew another pistol to cover the second jailer. "Hands up," Buckle ordered with the calmness of a man ready to kill. "On your feet with hands up."

There was a fraction of a pause as the second jailer just stared at him, his dull eyes blinking.

"Do it!" Buckle repeated.

The second jailer's hands flew straight up as he jumped to his feet, his droopy-lidded eyes now bright with fear. Buckle knew that he had nothing to worry about with this fellow. But the master of the watch was a different story. She had lifted her hands only slightly, not even up to her shoulders, and although Buckle had stopped, she was still moving, backing up in a slink, intentionally increasing the distance between them, eyeing him like an angry cat. She was going to be trouble.

"Move together. Quick, now," Buckle ordered, nudging both of his pistols inward. He wanted to push the jailers together because there was too much space between them—he had to cock his head back and forth to watch them properly. He only had to keep them at bay for a few moments. Having seen Buckle pull his pistols, the Ballblasters would surely be hurrying up the ramp behind.

But the master of the watch sensed the nature of her predicament. If she was going to resist, her only opportunity was now. Buckle glared at her over the muzzle of his pistol. She had been warned.

The lazy jailer, hands thrust so high they threatened to pull his arms out of the sockets, sidled to his right as requested, closing the gap between him and the master of the watch. Buckle flicked his eyes at the man, and at that instant, in his peripheral vision, he saw the master of the watch make a sudden movement.

"Hold!" Buckle yelled, snapping his eyes back on her. She paused, still, giving him a defiant grin. Her right hand was on her pistol butt. Her left hand was raised, her fingers a mere inch from the silver tassel of a cord dangling from a hole in the ceiling.

The alarm bell.

"Don't do it," Buckle said. His voice came out raspy—damned weak. He knew that she thought she could see hesitation in his eyes, but she was mistaken: it wasn't hesitation, but empathy. Buckle did not want to shoot her.

"You dare…" the master of the watch said, her voice strong and indignant, straightening her back.

"I dare," Buckle answered. Buckle could read her blue eyes and in what he found, he was not mistaken: the master of the watch was willing to die rather than be taken prisoner in her own prison.

"Mother of mercy," the lazy jailer whimpered, edging away. "Mother of mercy. Oh, no."

A profound calmness flooded the face of the master of the watch. Her fingers moved a hair closer to the alarm cord.

"Don't!" Buckle shouted. He could hear the armored boots of the Ballblasters clanging on the ramp stones, growing louder as they approached. And the master of the watch could hear it, too.

Buckle knew what the master of the watch was going to do.

And in the next heartbeat she did it.

She was fast, grabbing at the alarm cord with one hand and drawing her pistol with the other, both in the same twisting motion.

But she wasn't fast enough.

The pistol kicked his left hand as Buckle fired, the loudness of the concussion deafening in the enclosed chamber, the usual cloud of ponderous black smoke blimping into the air. The body of the master of the watch was flung backward against the doors and collapsed in a heap. Her pistol, half drawn, slid out of her dead fingers and tumbled onto the floor stones with a dull clatter.

The canaries shrieked, frantic yellow whirlwinds rattling their cage.

The alarm cord swung, unpulled, brushed by the master of the watch's fingers in the last act of her life.

"Damn it!" Buckle cursed, feeling his stomach twist in his gut as hard as if he had been punched. Surely the sound of the pistol discharge would bring the Founders officials running just as quickly as the alarm would have. He flicked his eyes to check the lazy jailer: the man had dropped to his knees in terror, his hands quivering.

"Please, please..." the lazy jailer mumbled, trying to duck his head down inside the collar of his tunic to get away from the loaded pistol still pointed at him.

Buckle realized that his own body was shaking.

"Buckle!" Pluteus shouted, emerging from the entrance corridor with Sergeant Scully, three Ballblasters, and Kepler at his heels. "What's the shooting for? Now the whole prison knows we're here!"

"I had no choice," Buckle replied. His stomach wrenched again. The acrid stench of the blackbang-powder haze suddenly made him sick. His mouth started watering.

He tried to focus. He had no time for this. There had to be other jailers scattered about the prison, and they must have heard the blast of Buckle's pistol. They had to be coming. They had to be raising the alarm.

"Aye," Pluteus said with a nod at the body of the master of the watch. "Ran into a real trooper, did you? That's why we never die old in bed." He knelt and cut open her belt to remove her key ring. "Have first platoon hold here, Sergeant Scully," he ordered. "If anybody comes through that door—blast them to smithereens."

"Aye!" Scully responded.

Tossing aside his empty pistol and holstering the unused one, Buckle stepped up to the lazy jailer; a Ballblaster had already disarmed him and was quickly tying up his hands. "In which cell is Andromeda Pollux? Speak up!"

"The Alchemist?" the jailer answered. He was obviously thick in the noggin.

"Spit it out!" Buckle snapped.

"She's in special cell fourteen."

"Sergeant Scully, inform General Scorpius that Andromeda is in special cell fourteen," Buckle said. "Kepler! Bring this lazy-brat with us. If he is lying, we shall skin him alive."

Kepler obeyed instantly, stepping forward to grab the cringing jailer by the scruff of his collar, which somehow surprised Buckle a bit.

Buckle's stomach betrayed him. He bent over against a pillar and threw up, spattering the floor stones with the yellowish-gray remains of his breakfast and a gallon of bile. After a few heaving gags, he wiped his mouth with his sleeve and drew himself up.

"You finished, Captain?" Pluteus asked, tossing him the master of the watch's key ring.

Buckle caught the jangling key ring. It was slippery with bright red blood.

"You found Balthazar," Pluteus said. "Now go and get him."

–XLIV–

BALTHAZAR CRANKSHAFT

EXCITEMENT FLOODED BUCKLE'S VEINS AS he hurried down the entrance ramp, blurring the memory of the body on the floor behind him and dulling the putrid taste of vomit on his tongue, at least for the moment. The bloody skeleton keys clattered in his hands. He could not regret such things. What had to be done was done to recover Balthazar.

Kepler was a few steps behind, armor clanking, dragging the unfortunate Founders jailer, who looked at the massive Alchemist like a man being dragged off by a hungry bear.

Buckle took off at a run down the main corridor, the boots stabbing him every inch of the way, passing scattered pairs of Ballblasters positioned to cover the labyrinth of smaller passageways that merged into it.

He met Sabrina and Corporal Druxbury at the door to cell twenty-four.

Sabrina smiled like a child, her eyes wet. "We found him, Romulus! We found him!" She almost sang the words.

And there, peering through the heavy iron bars of his door window, was Balthazar Crankshaft.

"Hello, boy," Balthazar said, smiling. "You're late."

Balthazar Crankshaft was a brawny wolverine of a man, barrel-chested, with thick legs and arms; his head, with its gray eyes and a prominent nose still jutting grandly, despite being broken several times, was made leonine by his flowing, blond-peppered-with-white hair and beard. Balthazar was an ambassador's mix of aggression and diplomacy, of kindness and cold intelligence; he even poured his tea decisively.

"My apologies, Father," Buckle said, grinning. The thrill he felt to be with Balthazar again, to be rescuing him and taking him home, lifted his heart immeasurably. "I hadn't realized you would be timing us."

"I planned on a rescue before supper." Balthazar sighed, in the playful way he used when he was ribbing his children. "Now I fear I have missed one of Salisbury's exquisite dinners."

Buckle tucked the key ring into Sabrina's hand while grabbing his boots and sword belt from her with his other hand. "Go ahead, Sabrina," he said.

Ignoring the sticky blood on the ring staining her hands, Sabrina stepped to the heavy padlock and started applying one skeleton key after another. Buckle limped to a wooden bench set against the wall, sat down, and yanked at the kid jailer's boots for all he was worth.

"Cookie already started fixing you your mutton stew, Papa," Sabrina said. She had called Balthazar "Papa" from the very first day she had appeared at the Tehachapi stronghold, even though she had been adopted at the ripe old age of thirteen. But her daughterly connection to Balthazar was intense: the spiritual bond between them was so obvious, so undeniable, so utterly instinctive, that none of the other children, not even his own flesh-and-blood son, Ryder, were jealous. It just had to be what it was.

With the torture boots off, Buckle yanked his own boots, thankfully, back on.

"No need for a change of clothes just to rescue me," Balthazar commented wryly from his window. "Or are we off to a ball?"

Buckle stood up, stomping his feet as the blood surged back into the flesh in painful tingles. "Let's go. The dance is about to begin," he said.

"Aye," Balthazar said. "When it starts off with a gunshot, it's likely to be a lively one."

"It could not be helped," Buckle replied.

Pluteus arrived on the scene in a ponderous rattle of armor. "Blue blazes! Have you not unlocked that door yet?"

"There are a hundred of them, Pluteus," Sabrina said, twisting key after key.

"I am just happy looking at all of your grimy faces." Balthazar laughed.

Sabrina shook her head as the key ring jingled in her hands. "I hope they weren't too unkind to you."

Balthazar slipped his hand through the bars and patted Sabrina's cheek. "I hardly saw a soul other than my keeper. But despite the whack to the head they gave me at the Palisades, which they patched up rather nicely, I must say, I have been treated reasonably well. Their odd cucumber gruel has been bland but palatable, the bed lumpy but warm; they even gave me a book to read, which I have decided to take with me as a souvenir."

It was curious, Buckle thought for a passing instant, that the Founders would go to the trouble of kidnapping Balthazar and then leave him alone in his cell for three days.

One of the last keys turned in the lock, clicking the tumblers into position.

"Aha!" Sabrina cried. The padlock clicked apart, and she unhooked it and tossed it aside. The door swung open and Balthazar Crankshaft marched out, pulling on his gray greatcoat.

Sabrina hopped forward, squealing with a pure joy Buckle had never seen her express before. "Papa!" she cheered, throwing her arms around Balthazar's generous middle and giving him a tight hug.

"Good to see you, dear child," Balthazar whispered softly before letting her go.

Pluteus, his snot- and blood-crusted chunky face locked in a grin, shook Balthazar's hand. "Nice to see you in one piece, cousin."

Buckle wanted to shove, to kick everyone in the arse. "It is time to go," he barked.

Pluteus tucked a loaded pistol into Balthazar's hand. "I hope you are up for some action," he said.

"Wait, Pluteus," Balthazar said. "There is another clan leader incarcerated here. The Imperial chancellor, Katzenjammer Smelt."

"He shall make a fine dish for the rats," Buckle snapped. "It is time to take our leave!"

"Actually, the fogsuckers kidnapped three clan leaders," Pluteus said, jerking his thumb toward the front of the main corridor, where Scorpius and the Alchemists were huddled around door number fourteen. "Lady Andromeda Pollux of the Alchemists. They found her, too."

"Then we cannot leave without her, either," Balthazar said.

"Aye," Pluteus replied.

"I don't know how you and the Alchemists joined forces, but that is a story I will want to hear," Balthazar said, impressed.

"Smelt is right here, Admiral," Corporal Druxbury said, having stepped down two cells to the south. "Cell twenty-six. I can shoot him if you'd like."

Balthazar shook his head. "Sabrina, release Smelt from his cell. Quickly. He is coming with us."

ROMULUS BUCKLE & THE CITY OF THE FOUNDERS

Sabrina turned, but Buckle grabbed her by the shoulder. The mere thought of the Crankshafts freeing Katzenjammer Smelt enraged him. He didn't know whether to talk or spit. "I say we leave the Imperial here."

"No," Balthazar said evenly. "We take him with us."

Buckle's veins surged with apprehension. His throat went dry. How could Balthazar even consider helping an Imperial? "Perhaps you have not completely recovered from being hit on the head, Balthazar. Have you forgotten what the Imperials did to us? Four zeppelins burned, dozens of our people dead, all at the order of that filthy spiker in the next cell. He is the one responsible for the murder of Elizabeth! He is the one responsible for the murder of Calypso!"

Balthazar took a half step forward; the move was not menacing, but it squared him up with his son. He took the key ring out of Sabrina's hands and thrust them into Buckle's. "You will see to the release of Katzenjammer Smelt," Balthazar ordered. "And you will do it now."

Buckle hesitated. There was no one in the world, no one in the universe, who Romulus Buckle hated with more vehemence than Katzenjammer Smelt. But there was not enough salt in him to disobey Balthazar on the spot.

"Romulus," Balthazar said urgently, "you must trust me. There is more to this than just us and the Imperials. Your anger and mine are worthless to us right now."

Buckle swallowed hard and nodded. He turned and marched toward cell number twenty-six, clutching the key ring in his hands. He could not believe what he was doing.

Instead of gutting Katzenjammer Smelt, he was going to set him free.

226

–XLV–

KATZENJAMMER SMELT

INFURIATED AT THE FURTHER DELAY—A delay caused by the rescue of Smelt—Buckle snatched a key on the dead master of the watch's key ring and jammed it into the padlock of cell number twenty-six. He did not look inside the window. His skin crawled just being this close to Katzenjammer Smelt.

"I have an extra sticky bomb," Corporal Druxbury muttered in Buckle's ear. "You wouldn't mind if I just lit the thing and threw it inside, would you?"

"I would be elated, Corporal," Buckle said under his breath. The first key—the very first key—opened the padlock, and Buckle wrenched it aside. "Come on out, Imperial," Buckle grumbled as he swung the heavy cell door open. "Or stay here. I do not care which."

Buckle clamped his teeth as Katzenjammer Smelt emerged from the doorway. Smelt was a tall, limber man, long-faced, lantern-jawed, and unfortunately handsome, with gray-brown hair cut close to the skull, and a glass monocle clamped over his left eye. He was dressed in the traditional Imperial uniform: silver and red epaulettes decorated his shoulders, and the high collar of his powder-blue tunic was embroidered on each side with the silver iron cross, the emblem of the Imperial clan; his trousers were dark-blue jodhpurs with thick red stripes tucked into black jackboots below. In the crook of his arm he carried a polished pickelhaube helmet with an iron-cross plate and a large silver spike affixed to the top.

Smelt scrutinized the situation with a detached, critical eye, oozing typical Imperial arrogance in the way he peered down his long nose at the world and everything in it.

Buckle wanted to bash him.

Smelt narrowed his stare at Buckle. "You!" Smelt, with a baritone voice imperious even for an Imperial, barked. "Where is my zeppelin, you thieving little blackheart?"

"We all pay a price, don't we, Smelt?" Buckle replied.

"I shall have your head when the time comes," Smelt said. "I shall have your gremlin head and tack it up on my parlor wall. The *Pneumatic Zeppelin* is mine."

"Finders keepers," Buckle retorted. His head was a riot of fury. His hand crept toward his sword.

Perhaps now was the time to bash him.

As if reading Buckle's mind, Balthazar clamped a beefy hand on his shoulder and stepped between him and Smelt. "Greetings, Katzenjammer," Balthazar said. Balthazar and Smelt knew each other, if only in a small way, from a time when they had both been much younger men.

"Ah, Balthazar. Come to finish me off, have you?" Smelt said with an odd wryness.

"Fear not, Chancellor," Balthazar replied. "My son is your rescuer, and your bodyguard."

"Assassin would be the more accurate term," Smelt huffed.

Buckle swung his mouth close to Balthazar's ear. "For this monster, I am no bodyguard," he whispered.

"It is your responsibility to make sure Smelt gets out of here alive," Balthazar said.

Buckle gritted his teeth. "It is my responsibility to get you out of here alive."

"You have your orders," Balthazar said.

"A rather ragtag rescue, Balthazar, I must say," Smelt said. "I would have been put at much greater ease to see Imperial dragoons here rather than this motley bunch—although I am most appreciative of your efforts, of course."

Oh, Buckle so badly wanted to bash Smelt—but he wanted to get moving even more. "Damn it—I shall kiss the devil himself if we could just lace up our boots and go!"

A chorus of warning shouts suddenly echoed from the four Ballblasters guarding the southern approaches of the main corridor. The *boom-boom-ba-boom* of an uneven volley erupted from their muskets, and was answered by enraged yells and scattered muzzle flashes from adjoining corridors to the south. Bullet trails of white phosphorus streaked through the air, ending in shatters of sparks when the musket balls ricocheted off the stone walls.

"Too late! This party is crashed," Sabrina shouted, aiming her pistol down the corridor and firing a round. "Just peachy!"

"We are not leaving," Balthazar shouted. "Nobody leaves until we free Andromeda Pollux!"

"Of course, Father," Buckle said, ducking as a musket ball whizzed past his head in a bolt of phosphorus. "But may I suggest we hurry."

–XLVI–

ANDROMEDA POLLUX AND THE COPPER CORRIDOR

GENERAL SCORPIUS WRENCHED THE LAST key out of the door of special cell fourteen with such a yank that Buckle feared he might snap it off in the lock. "None of the keys fit!" Scorpius raged—he snapped his head to Buckle. "The explosives! Do you have the explosives?"

"Yes," Buckle said, turning to shout. "Corporal Druxbury! Blow the door!"

Druxbury stepped forward and carefully drew the last sticky bomb out of the satchel riding on his armored hip. He pressed the malleable explosive into place with his thumbs, forcing as much as he could into the keyhole.

Scattered musket shots sent lead balls whizzing past. Buckle and Druxbury cringed, but Scorpius did not notice the near misses, grabbing the lazy guard by the throat and thrusting his face into the guard's. "How close is Lady Andromeda to this door? Will she be in danger if we blast the damned thing open?"

"She's in the back," the lazy guard rasped. "There is a corridor and another door. She isn't close."

The enemy, shadowy figures ducking in and out of the south end of the main corridor about fifty yards away, started shooting again. Judging by the irregular nature of their volleys and their poor aim, Buckle was sure that they were up against no more than a handful of frightened prison guards. But the regulars had to be on their way.

"A pistol!" Katzenjammer Smelt demanded, somewhere in the haze of powder smoke. "I require a pistol!"

"Shut up, spiker!" someone howled back.

A musket ball smacked off the wall above the lazy guard's head, showering both him and Scorpius in a flash of hot sparks. The lazy guard kicked in terror. Scorpius did not flinch. "If you are mistaken, if Andromeda Pollux suffers even a scratch," Scorpius hissed, "I will yank out your guts with my bare hands and strangle you with them."

The lazy guard fainted. Scorpius dropped him, the limp body slumping to the floor.

"Hurry, Corporal," Buckle said.

"Aye!" Druxbury replied. He punched the hard tip of the fuse through the greasy outer wrapping of the sticky bomb, thrusting it deep into the body of the explosive.

"Everybody back!" Sabrina shouted. "Fuse ready!"

"Watch your backs, lads!" Pluteus shouted at the Ballblasters engaged in the firing line, twenty-five yards to the south. "Fuse ready!"

Buckle nodded to Druxbury. Druxbury snapped the tinderbox flint; it sparked into a flame under the fuse, which caught, burning in a bright red flutter of papery embers.

Buckle and Druxbury sprinted to the nearest adjoining hallway, where Balthazar, Sabrina, and Scorpius were crouched. "Ten seconds!" Buckle said. He dropped to one knee with Druxbury crouched at his back. On his left was Balthazar and on his right was Sabrina, her shoulder pressed against his.

Sabrina tucked in close against Buckle, and he felt her warm breath in his ear. "This is rather exciting, isn't it?" she said, her dry humor having returned to her along with Balthazar. Buckle smelled her expensive lemoncherrydrop perfume.

"Just peachy," Buckle replied.

"Zip up!" Balthazar ordered, clapping his hands over his ears and clamping his eyes shut.

Then the world exploded and Buckle was nearly knocked over, Sabrina's body lurching into his chest, his right shoulder slamming into the stone wall. The ringing in his ears was deafening. He tried to stagger to his feet and failed; grasping at the wall, he tried again. In the dense smoke, he glimpsed Sabrina's face and wondered why it was covered in fine white dust. What was she trying to say to him? He couldn't make it out.

Everything snapped back into focus. The door. Andromeda.

Scorpius charged past Buckle, plunging into the swirling haze of smoke and ashes, and Buckle charged after him. Buckle, shaking the jelly out of his head, tried to keep up. For a few moments he could not see anything except the shadow of Scorpius's back. A white flash skittered overhead—a phosphorus musket ball skidding along the stone ceiling.

The door to special cell number fourteen appeared in the murk, ajar and burning, wood splintered, metal sheathing ripped back and splayed, the place where its lock used to be now a smoldering hole—it could barely be described as a door anymore.

"I swear on my life, Founders," Scorpius howled, "if you have harmed Andromeda Pollux, I shall burn both you and your city from the face of the earth!" He kicked the blasted door and it slammed inward with a jerky, hinge-snapping squeal. The hallway beyond was thick with glowing orange haze. Scorpius plunged headlong into it through the flames licking the wooden doorframe, and disappeared.

Buckle plunged in after Scorpius. Behind him, the gunfire in the corridor had picked up again in earnest, though this time there seemed to be more muzzle flashes on the enemy side. Time was running out.

Even before he cleared the worst of the blackbang-blast smoke, Buckle knew by the ring of his boots and the dull glimmer surrounding him that he was in a very different kind of corridor. The light became brilliant, a gleaming amber-brown illumination so intense that Buckle had to throw his arm up to his eyes to shield them. The wide corridor dead-ended no more than twenty feet ahead and *every inch of it, floor to ceiling, was sheathed with copper plating.* The ubiquitous blue light of the Founders gas lamps was missing here, replaced by two oil lanterns that hung on pegs along the right wall. Floor-to-ceiling copper bars lined the left side of the hallway, containing a long cell stacked with wooden kegs and boxes.

Scorpius headed straight to a single cell door, also glistering with copper, located just to the right at the end of the passageway. The cell door had a large, barred window.

And peering from that window was the beautiful face of Andromeda Pollux.

"Lady Andromeda!" Scorpius shouted. "By the fortune of the forgotten sun, we are all saved!"

Buckle caught his breath. Andromeda was older, perhaps in her midthirties, and the stunningly elegant balance of her features suggested that her creation had not been left to the unpredictable eccentricities of nature, but rather that she had been chiseled from marble by a genius sculptor. She was pale-skinned, a blue-blooded alabaster ice queen. Her hair, braided to the back of her slender neck, was blondish, swept through with shades of golden hay and sun-bleached sand.

That was all Buckle could see of Andromeda Pollux through the cell window, although the woman appeared to be tall, judging from her height in relation to Scorpius.

"It is very good to see you, Scorpius," Andromeda said with a small smile. To the smitten Buckle—and only a blind man might not be smitten by Andromeda—her voice sounded as clear as water running along a forest stream. She did turn her eyes—they looked dark, reflecting the yellow gleam of the lamps—to Buckle once, scrutinizing him: dressed in the black Founders jailer uniform, he was a mystery to her.

"Are you unhurt, my lady?" Scorpius asked.

Andromeda nodded, glancing at the smoldering doorway as musket fire thumped and boomed out in the main corridor. "I am well, but I fear there is great injury being inflicted on my account."

"We have taken the prison," Scorpius said, "but we cannot hold it for long." Scorpius rattled the door and grimaced. "Damn my hide! What is this?"

Buckle peered at the door lock. It did not have a padlock or keyhole, but rather an ugly iron plate with what looked like two sundials circled by symbols and numbers.

Wolfgang and Kepler loped in through the smoking doorway, both grinning when they saw Andromeda.

When Andromeda saw her clansmen, her face turned both warm and scolding. "Both my dear Wolfgang and Caliban are here as well? I am not worth such risk."

"I most respectfully disagree, my lady," Wolfgang said.

"Wolfgang!" Scorpius said, pointing to the door lock. "What is this?"

Wolfgang knelt at the door and narrowed his eyes. "It is a combination lock," he muttered. "No key is going to open this thing. We need the exact sequence of numbers it has been set to read."

There was a pause, a tense silence, as everyone stared, uncertain on how to proceed. Outside the door, with more shots and shouts, the gun battle was increasing in intensity.

"Cursed luck!" Scorpius raged. He slapped the master of the watch's key ring in Buckle's hands, drew his pistol, and aimed it at the combination lock. Buckle stared—a musket ball wouldn't even dent an iron lock like that one.

"No!" Wolfgang and Andromeda shouted. But it was too late.

The blackbang pistol discharged with a walloping burst of smoke. The ball bounced off the lock, struck the copper ceiling, and dropped at Scorpius's feet, a deformed, smoldering glob of lead.

"Scorpius! No!" Andromeda scolded. "Look around you!" She thrust her finger at the wooden kegs stacked in the cell across the corridor. "That room is packed with munitions!"

Looking more closely at the stacks of barrels and crates in the opposite cell, Buckle saw that they were tattooed with the phoenix and the word *Gunpowder.* Hence the copper plating, which reduced the possibility of sparks.

"If your hot bullet had penetrated one of those barrels, it would have surely been the end of us all, General," Buckle said.

Scorpius stuffed his smoking pistol back into his belt, looking defeated. "My most sincere apologies, Lady Andromeda. I have not acted well."

Balthazar appeared in the doorway of the copper corridor, his bulky frame nearly as broad as the burning jambs.

"Ho, there! Crack Andromeda free and let us be on our way! We are trapped like rats in a hole and soon to be overrun if we stay down here!" He ducked back into the haze-swirling mayhem beyond.

Buckle saw surprise flash in Andromeda's eyes. "Balthazar... the Crankshafts are here?"

Scorpius nodded. "Yes, my lady."

"Good. You and the council must forge all of the alliances you can with the other clans, Scorpius," Andromeda said.

"Ah, but that is your job, my lady," Scorpius replied.

When Andromeda spoke next, she spoke softly. "Give me a loaded pistol and go, General Scorpius."

"What? Go? Without you? I shall have none of that!" Scorpius retorted.

Kepler growled with bearish displeasure, shaking his head.

"You have done your best, Scorpius, and I am proud of you. But fortune is not with me this day. I cannot be responsible for more casualties to our brave soldiers. Leave me behind. Retreat and cut your losses."

"Never! I shall die here defending you, if necessary!"

"You shall oversee the transfer of power to Capella de Vega on the council," Andromeda said. "Do you understand?"

"But what about Altair, your nephew?" Scorpius asked.

Andromeda's gaze flicked to Buckle. She obviously wanted her clan's succession affairs to be private, but there was nothing for it now. "Altair is not capable," she said. "We are no monarchy. You shall award him a minor portfolio and he shall accept it, and that shall be that."

Scorpius stood still, his jaw working under his skin. "As you wish, Lady Andromeda."

Andromeda held her hand out through the bars, a slender, pale hand with the long fingers of a musician. "I order you to relinquish one of your pistols to me immediately, General."

Looking ashen and sick, Scorpius reached into his gun belt.

"I—I can open the door, Lady Andromeda," Wolfgang blurted as if it hurt him, gripping his metal instrument box so tightly his knuckles had gone white. "I can pop the Owl."

"Pop the Owl?" Scorpius gasped. "In here? Lad—that would most likely kill her."

"Do it," Andromeda said.

-XLVII-

FIFTY-FIFTY

"YOU MEAN BLOW THE ROBOT up?" Buckle asked, incredulous. He did not know much about detonating robots, but from the look on Scorpius's face, it was as drastic a solution as he sensed it to be.

"I must collect the Owl," Wolfgang shouted, dashing out into the glowing smoke of the main corridor.

Scorpius lunged to Andromeda's door. "My lady, the pop would surely open the door. But the intensity of a robot-furnace blast, in here—if it does not kill you, it would set off the munitions."

"Move your people back as far as you can, General Scorpius," Andromeda ordered.

"Yes, my lady," Scorpius nodded, defeated. "May fortune be with you." He holstered his pistol, planted his hand on his sword, spun on the ball of his foot, and strode out, motioning for Kepler to follow at his heel.

"And take those oil lanterns with you," Andromeda added. "No need having them fuel the inferno in here."

"Aye, my lady." Scorpius said. "Kepler!"

Kepler collected the two lanterns from their hooks as he followed Scorpius out.

With the departure of the lanterns with Kepler, the copper corridor fell dark, its hazy atmosphere weakly illuminated by the diffuse blue gaslight issuing from the main hallway. Buckle could see little more than the contours of one side of Andromeda's face, lit silver blue, between the bars of her window. He could sense that she was studying him.

"I must admit that I am surprised to see Crankshafts here, side by side with my Alchemists," Andromeda said. "But it is something I do not find unpleasant, or unhopeful."

"Nor I, ma'am," Buckle said.

A heavy exchange of volleys and the scream of a dying man out in the main corridor left them silent.

More quickly than Buckle would have thought possible, the Owl scrambled into the doorway, a weird, huge-headed, turkey-like apparition, glowing orange and red at the seams. Wolfgang was right behind it, manipulating his instrument box.

"Move aside, Cranker!" Wolfgang ordered, short of breath.

Buckle stepped away from the cell door as the Owl passed him, its body emitting waves of skin-pinching heat and the pungent stink of heated metal.

"Wolfgang, I know this is difficult for you, but you must be gracious," Andromeda said.

Wolfgang wound a device on his instrument box, instructing the Owl to lurch up against Andromeda's door. "My apologies," he muttered, sniffing.

Buckle had not taken offense. Wolfgang was just about to execute a robot that he suspected was one of the best friends he had.

The Owl rotated so that its back was pressed up against the door. Wolfgang tapped a few more controls, and it crouched forward a bit, so its spine angled more toward the ceiling. The considerable orange-red illumination leaking from the joints of its body burst out in a flood when Wolfgang unsnapped an access hatch on the lower half of its back. Inside the Owl, the miniature furnace hummed, red hot, the connecting boilers and steam pipes rattling with insane pressures of steam.

Buckle peered over the Owl's bulky head to make eye contact with Andromeda, who was now visible in the pulsing, pumpkin-colored light. "Cover yourself as best you can, Lady Andromeda," he said.

"I fully intend to escape this scrape with nary a scratch," Andromeda said.

There was a pause, both in their conversation and in the skirmish out in the corridor. Through the cell window Buckle saw Andromeda stride to the rear of her stone-walled cell. She flipped her wooden bunk over near the wall, topped the little cave with the feather mattress, and disappeared beneath it.

Wolfgang moved his hands at a frantic pace inside the overheating innards of the Owl, flipping a set of switches in a series of metal *clicks*. "When a robot self-destructs, it is violent," he whispered to Buckle. "I have made the blast as directional as I can, more upward into the door than anything else, but the impact of the explosion will be immense from all angles. It is hard to say what will happen—I have never actually done this before."

Buckle leaned in close, whispered. "Give me some odds."

Wolfgang looked up. "You mean that she...?" He glanced at Andromeda's cell window.

Buckle nodded.

"Fifty-fifty." Wolfgang barely breathed the uncertain numbers.

"Fifty-fifty?" Buckle replied, chewing on it. "Not bad. Better than I usually get, I can tell you that."

"I might be being a tad overoptimistic," Wolfgang muttered, unscrewing something. "I could bring the entire prison down on top of us with this."

Looking over the Owl and Wolfgang's back, Buckle noticed that the dead-end wall of the copper corridor was etched with a scene of workers marching up a mine shaft toward the surface of an industrial city, faces upturned to a clear, cloudless sky where the sun, a fire-fringed copper disc, was emblazoned with the words *The Gospel of Peace and Work*.

What an odd place for such a piece of art, Buckle thought.

The boiler inside the Owl vibrated with a dangerous rattle, emitting a new level of heat that forced Buckle to step back. Wolfgang also moved back, staring at the Owl as if he had just signed its death sentence, which he had.

"Just a few seconds now, Lady Andromeda," Wolfgang shouted. "Hold your breath and cover your ears!"

The Owl started shaking, forcing every bolt and screw to move in a way it was not designed to move. "So long, old friend," Wolfgang said to the Owl. "Let's go, Captain," he urged, grabbing Buckle by the sleeve. "This is going to happen fast."

Buckle followed Wolfgang out of the copper corridor. With a last glance over his shoulder, Buckle saw the Owl vibrating to a blur, rivets popping, its internal steam valves, pressurized beyond the point of reason, bursting with tiny jets of screaming, superheated air.

Buckle and Wolfgang emerged into the acrid haze of nostril-punching blackbang powder in the main corridor. A musket ball slammed into the wooden doorframe just above Buckle's head, sending down a hail of burning splinters. They scrambled low as white-hot musket balls ripped through the fog around them.

"Fuse is lit!" Buckle shouted—only he did not shout it. His mouth opened; his brain had already ordered the words. But the colossal explosion—a heart-stopping *burp*—concussed his vocal cords into stillness.

A gigantic fist of fire grabbed Buckle and hurled him into the murk.

~XLVIII~

HOPE AMIDST THE RUINS

BUCKLE REGAINED HIS SENSES, FACEDOWN on the floor, as a blistering shockwave of hot smoke roared over him. Then came a weird, fluttering silence.

A stream of pebbles trickled down from the ceiling, tapping on his legs. His mouth felt as if it was full of dry ashes; he coughed, as did everyone, their lungs struggling in the dust-laden air.

"Who the hell set that off on my arse?" Pluteus shouted somewhere in the murk. "You damn well kicked the tar out of my line!"

Buckle leveraged himself up onto his hands and knees, and then to his feet. When he turned around he saw the burning timbers of the copper corridor's doorframe glowing in the smoke. He hurried toward it on unsteady legs—his back felt singed—and Wolfgang appeared beside him, thick with light-colored dust, his hat and goggles blown off, blood running from one nostril.

"Too fast and too much, damn it!" Buckle rasped.

"I have killed her!" Wolfgang wailed. "I have killed Lady Andromeda!"

Buckle and Wolfgang stumbled forward over jagged debris, passing Ballblasters as they fanned out to reestablish their firing line across the main corridor. A loose canary exploded out of the smoke, hurtling past Buckle's face in a furious flutter of yellow wings. After a few more strides, they arrived at the burning entrance of the copper corridor. The door was missing and an upside-down waterfall of black smoke poured up over the top of the doorframe, rising to the higher ceiling of the corridor. They charged inside.

The copper corridor, the bottom half somewhat clear of smoke, seemed to be on fire. The ceiling, walls, and floor glowed with streams of volcanic color as the superheated metal smoldered like lava. Buckle could not see any flames in the munitions chamber, which was a good thing.

"Lady Andromeda!" Scorpius, already back inside, shouted from the interior cell. "Lady Andromeda!"

Buckle heard no response. He and Wolfgang scrambled down the corridor toward the gaping hole in the wall where the door with the combination lock had previously stood. Nothing was left of the Owl but twisted ribbons of metal half-sunk into the etched artwork of the dead-end wall. The cell door, or whatever warped skeleton of wood and copper was left of it, had been blown off its hinges and driven into the shattered stone of the ceiling overhead, dripping molten metal into a sizzling pool on the floor.

Buckle stopped at the doorway. The inside of Andromeda's cell was alive with a hundred splatters of fire, as if she had lit a hundred liquid candles. Irregular pieces of wood, copper, and stone, cut into shrapnel by the force of the blast, protruded from the walls at every angle.

Scorpius and Kepler hunched over Andromeda's hiding place, furiously tearing away the shredded mattress, which was laced in flames. The wooden bed beneath had folded into a mass of splinters, with three of its four legs blown clean off.

"Lady Andromeda!" Scorpius yelled, distraught. "Please, Lady Andromeda!" When he lifted Andromeda from the floor, Buckle thought she was dead. Her body was corpse-limp, her arms and legs dangling, her angelic face paler than bone, making the red blood running from her nostrils and ears look black. Rips across her white tunic and trousers were soaked with blood where bits of shrapnel had bitten into her body.

Scorpius, Kepler, and Wolfgang, racing over the shattered corpse of the Owl to assist, carefully laid Andromeda on a clear section of the floor. Yanking off one of his leather gloves, Scorpius pressed his fingers to the jugular at Andromeda's neck, lowering his head.

Buckle held his breath. The room danced in the wavering light of the burning debris, the flames gently crackling.

Andromeda's eyelids fluttered momentarily. Her right eyeball was startlingly bright red, full of blood in the white; blood ran from her ears, nose, and small shrapnel punctures above the hairline.

Scorpius jerked his head up, his eyes sparkling with a joy spiked with ferocity. "She lives! Lady Andromeda lives!"

–XLIX–

THE ADMIRAL'S SECRET

COUGHING, SABRINA STUMBLED AROUND IN the blinding smoke. Ragged musket shots popped here and there from both directions, the incandescent balls ripping through the heavy air with an odd, bee-buzzing sound.

She was looking for Balthazar. He had been standing right next to her when the blast occurred and now, despite her calls, he did not answer.

She found him. He was lying just inside an adjoining corridor, convulsing, his head arched back.

The blast had aggravated his hidden condition.

Damn it to hell, she thought. Not now, Balthazar. Not now.

Sabrina was on Balthazar in an instant, one hand gripping his right wrist, where the muscles beneath, taut as steel, shook. She dug around in her coat pocket until she found the cold glass vial of his medicine. She snapped off the lid, but every time she tried to bring it to his mouth his thrashings forced her back.

Sergeant Scully barged forward out of the smoke, gripping a musket. "Lieutenant! The general wants to leave—" He saw Balthazar and stopped, staring.

Secret or no secret, Sabrina was glad to see the sergeant. She needed his help. "Pin his arms down, Sergeant. Quickly!"

"Aye!" Scully said, leaping forward to apply his strength to Balthazar's flailing arms, grunting as it took all of his effort to press them down.

"Hold him...hold him," Sabrina said, pouring the gold liquid into Balthazar's locked teeth, clamping her hand on his beard to keep him from twisting his head.

"What happened, Lieutenant?" Scully asked. "Is the Admiral hit?"

"No, he was not hit," Sabrina answered, draining the last of the medicine into Balthazar's mouth. As always, his shaking immediately subsided and he lay still, calm but senseless. "You must tell no one of this, Scully. Do you understand me? Tell no one."

Scully nodded. "Aye, lass. His secret is safe with me."

Sabrina managed a quick smile. She did not know much about Scully, but what she did, she approved of. "Help me get him up. We tell the others the blast knocked him out."

"Aye," Scully said, grunting as he swung Balthazar to his feet. Balthazar was already coming around, rolling his head and muttering.

Sabrina swung her small form under Balthazar's opposite shoulder, and they struggled forward in the smoke. Occasional musket shots were fired, their phosphorous trails streaking through the heaving murk, but nobody could see anything. They stumbled over a body—a Ballblaster—and Sabrina feared they had suffered horrible casualties. But there was no way to tell in the haze. They headed northward, moving along the eastern wall, and found themselves staring down the muzzle of an Alchemist trooper's musket.

"Crankshaft, my dear fellow!" Sabrina shouted. "We are Crankshaft! The Admiral is wounded!"

The Alchemist lowered his musket. They were now in the midst of Pluteus's line as they prepared to back up, firing, taking their wounded with them. Scorpius carried Andromeda in his arms, cradling her as he would a baby, both of them shielded by Kepler. Katzenjammer Smelt stood tall beside them—and some fool had given him a pistol.

"Balthazar!" Pluteus yelled. "Jackson! Reyes! Carry the Admiral with the wounded!"

Two of the big Ballblasters swung their muskets onto their backs and rushed to take the weight of Balthazar off Scully and Sabrina's shoulders.

"Independent fire!" Pluteus shouted, then turned to Sabrina. "Your brother is still in Andromeda's corridor," he said, pointing to the burning doorway. The musketry was getting thicker once again. "Go get him. Tell him we are leaving!"

-L-

WHO SAVES OLD SHADRACK?

OVERHEATED AND SURROUNDED BY THE glow of fire-lit copper, Buckle stepped through a smoke-wreathed opening in the split and blistered bars of the ammunition cache and drew his sword. "Give me a long fuse, Corporal," he said. "On the quick!"

Druxbury dug his hand into a side pocket of the sticky-bomb satchel and produced a braided hemp fuse about two feet long. "Five minutes is the best I have, sir."

"Very good," Buckle said.

Sabrina hurried in, dodging the warped metal and rivers of fire. "Romulus! We are going!"

"Just one more second," Buckle replied, cutting a hole in a barrel with his sword. A steady stream of blackbang powder drained from the gash until Buckle jammed one end of the fuse into it, sinking it as deep as he could.

"Balthazar has been injured," Sabrina said.

Buckle glanced at Sabrina, and she nodded at him, ever so slightly. Balthazar's convulsions had appeared at a bad time. "Is it severe?"

"No. I took care of him. The soldiers have him now."

Buckle cursed under his breath, picked up a burning wood splinter, and set it to the end of the fuse, which instantly caught in a flash, the flame slowly working its way back toward the barrel.

"Now it is really time to go," Buckle said, slapping Druxbury on the shoulder as they turned and ran.

They charged out into the wafting murk of the corridor to find the Ballblasters and Pluteus near at hand. "About time! Stay with us, boy!" Pluteus growled.

"I left a gift for the Founders," Buckle announced, searching for Balthazar and finding him, open-eyed and coherent, but leaning heavily on two Ballblasters.

Pluteus immediately understood. "How long is the fuse?"

"About four minutes, now."

"Then we had better get moving," Pluteus said. "Sergeant Scully! One volley to cool their heels and then double-quick to the front doors."

"Aye, General!" Scully replied. "Company, load!"

"You! You!" The shaking, disembodied voice of old Shadrack pierced the dark haze on Buckle's left. "I ask you: who saves old Shadrack?"

Buckle and Sabrina peered at the wild-haired old man rattling the window bars of his cell, his eyes bugging, somehow even wider than before.

"You there! Ho, angel!" Shadrack screamed, spittle flying. "You have come back for me! I know you have come back for me!"

"Company draw ramrods!" Scully ordered. "Ram!"

Buckle took an unconscious step toward old Shadrack, staring at him as he would a crazed animal in a cage.

"Romulus—be careful," Sabrina said.

Shadrack thrust his arms through the window bars, wringing his skeletal hands. "Do not abandon me! I know! I know where the Moonchild hides! I know! Why? Because I am kindred. I, too, have kissed the iron teat, shot through and addled in the brainpan! I can save the Moonchild! But who saves old Shadrack? You! You! You!"

"Company present!" Scully ordered. "Fire!"

The Ballblasters released a musket volley into the void of smoke.

"Fall back! On the double! Go!" Pluteus shouted.

The Ballblasters and Alchemist troopers backed up around Buckle, then turned to jog toward the entrance ramp.

"Romulus! Come on!" Sabrina shouted.

Buckle tossed the master of the watch's key ring to Shadrack. It was an impulse, but for the most part, Buckle didn't want to be responsible for killing the harmless old jabberwock in the impending munitions blast he had devised.

Sabrina grabbed Buckle by the arm and pulled him away. "What is wrong with you? Do you want to stay here? Let's go!"

The last Buckle saw of Shadrack, before he vanished in the smoky haze, was his toothless grin as he shook the bloodstained key ring in front of his eyes.

"Who saves old Shadrack?" Shadrack howled ecstatically.

-LI-

THE WATCHTOWER

MAX STARED INTO THE MUDDLED gray fog. Through her aqueous-humor-filled goggles, her oxygen-mask goggles, and the nose-dome glass, there was enough condensation and fluid distortion to trick and confound even her sharp eyes.

There was nothing to see. Not yet, anyway. The *Pneumatic Zeppelin* was crawling slowly through the dense miasma, her navigators maintaining course by employing compass, gyroscope, and the art of mathematics. They were on a slow ascent, aiming to breach the surface of the fog bank before they arrived at the walls of the city. A clear view was necessary, for the rescue expedition would be sending up flares and messenger pigeons—and both would be impossible to locate if the airship was locked in the murk.

Max's ears, sealed inside the helmet with her, were full of the sounds of her own breathing and the *whoosh-puff* of the airship's oxygen-pumping system. She could hear the ship's company, too, on the chattertubes, exchanging information on altitude, bearings, and engine status. The farther away in the zeppelin the voices were, the tinnier and more indistinguishable they became.

The large bridge gyroscope, mounted in its wooden frame and agleam with bioluminescent boil—as were the sea of glass-encased instruments surrounding Max—reassured her that the airship was riding perfectly on her keel. De Quincey and Dunn nudged their control wheels back and forth, their eyes on their compasses, pointers, and the bubbles in their inclinometer tubes. Welly and Banerji were hunched over the navigation stations in the nose, pencils scribbling, clutching pocket watches, counting foot and yard through calculations of airspeed and time.

Max made her own calculations in her head—Martians were excellent at math—factoring in the compass heading on the binnacle and the hummingbird's touch of drift she could feel in the decking. The survival of the rescue team and of her adoptive father, Balthazar, depended upon the *Pneumatic Zeppelin* arriving exactly at the pickup point, exactly on time—despite flying blind.

Max noticed that her compass needle had hitched over one point to starboard. She opened her mouth to speak.

"Drift correction, helm," Welly's voice rattled down the chattertube line and into her helmet. "One degree to port, if you please, Mister De Quincey."

"One degree to port, aye," De Quincey replied.

Max folded her arms across her chest, satisfied with the work of her crew. They were a competent bunch, if a bit too rowdy, and they would likely accomplish their mission, plopping the duck in the bucket, without her needing to speak a word.

Max was nervous, but her hands had stopped shaking.

As Max stared into the empty gray void, she became aware of a thought, a question, lurking under her calculations. She wondered if this was what her brother, Tyro, saw—a passing nothingness, always. Wounded in the Imperial Raid nearly a year before, Tyro had since been trapped in a coma, his breathing sustained by an iron lung. Max felt stricken and lonely without him. She knew little of the peculiarities her Martian blood was supposed to impart to her, but she did know that she and Tyro could share thoughts, even when physically separated.

But since Tyro's injury, Max could no longer reach him. She would sit beside his bed for hours, waiting, but no communication ever came. She knew he dreamt, however, and what elements of it she could make out appeared to her as a drifting nothingness, much like the fog around her now.

And if Tyro dreamt, no matter the context, his brain was still alive.

The numbers still clicking in her head, Max eyed her compass. "Five minutes to the evacuation point, Mister Bratt."

"Five minutes, aye," Welly affirmed.

"Object low off the starboard bow!" Banerji shouted, the startle in his voice plain in the chattertube line. "Two o'clock low!"

Max leapt forward to the nose dome—taking care not to foul her oxygen and chattertube lines—and peered along Banerji's arm as he pointed into the fog.

A large cylindrical object was slowly emerging from the mist; it was stationary, coming on only at the snail's pace speed of the zeppelin, and fortunately low enough to pose no threat of collision.

"It is a structure of some kind," Banerji said.

Welly's voice burst into the line, fraught with concern. "It looks like—it is a watchtower, Lieutenant!"

"We shall be seen!" Banerji moaned.

"Silence!" Max said. The stone turret was most certainly a watchtower, part of the city battlements that could be glimpsed farther below, but it was long abandoned, streaming with white and green seabird guano, and near ready to collapse. "The tower is unmanned."

Max saw the tension ease in Welly and Banerji's backs as the watchtower slowly slid away beneath them. She looked into the tall, open windows of the watchtower and saw a large, ribbed glass lens hanging at an angle in the shadows; the tower had served as a lighthouse once, before the Founders had cut themselves off from the outside world.

And now the *Pneumatic Zeppelin*, having just passed over the outer wall of the City of the Founders, was coming to call.

Max shrugged her shoulders, loosening them up under the thick rubber skirt of her helmet. Her belt was heavy with two pistols and her sword attached, the weight of it riding on the tops of her hips. She wanted to be down below with Buckle and Sabrina and Pluteus, on the run, locking swords with the enemy.

She desperately wanted to be in the bloody fray.

But such was not her duty today.

"City of the Founders below," Max said.

-LII-

CUCUMBER PIE

BUCKLE AND SABRINA RACED UP the entrance ramp and into the prison anteroom. The air was clearer here, making it easier to breathe. The puttering gray light of the early evening filtered in around the hinges of the huge double doors, mixing with the cold blues of the gas lamps to make the chamber seem lighter than it actually was. Pluteus stood before the doors, jamming pistols into his belt.

The Ballblasters and Alchemist troopers smoothly reloaded their muskets and pistols. They were all coated in sweat and black powder, and the whites of their eyes stood out against their faces. Scorpius had transferred the still-unconscious Andromeda into Kepler's burly arms. Wolfgang lingered at Kepler's elbow, gently wiping blood away from Andromeda's face. Smelt hovered at the edge of the group, reloading his pistol as he peered at it through his monocle.

Buckle's stomach twisted when he saw Balthazar, his face pale, the lips and eyes an unhealthy purple, his hair cast about his face, propped up by the two Ballblasters supporting him under each arm.

"Last again, Buckle?" Balthazar said weakly, but forcing a grin. "This is getting to be a dangerous habit."

"Such are many of his habits, father," Sabrina whispered, stopping to place her hand gently on Balthazar's chest. Her face was flushed, as it always was when she was in action, the blood rising close to the surface of her cheeks, lending a brightness to her countenance that not even the layer of gray dust could much dampen, and it made Balthazar's face seem even more sickly by comparison.

Buckle strode immediately to Pluteus, who was in a hasty, low conference with Sergeant Scully.

"We suffered three dead down below, General," Scully whispered. "Two of ours and one Alchemist trooper. We have seven walking wounded and two supported, including the admiral, sir."

Pluteus nodded. Sabrina and Scorpius stepped alongside Buckle.

Corporal Druxbury emerged from the crowd. "Loaded and ready, General."

"Good," Pluteus said. He turned and looked at Broussard, a Ballblaster who had his ear pressed to the door.

"It is very quiet outside, sir," Broussard said to Pluteus. "Quiet as a mouse with a loaded cannon, sir."

"It could be a trap," Pluteus replied, shrugging as he hefted his musket. "Either way, we charge straight into it."

A musket ball ripped up the ramp and hit the metal sheathing high on one of the front doors, pinging away and smacking into a granite pillar.

"Time to go!" Pluteus shouted. "Navigator, stay behind me until we re-form up top."

Sabrina stepped behind Pluteus and Scully, their considerable bulk making her look very small in comparison.

As Buckle moved to join the group, he saw the body of the master of the watch lying on the floor stones just to the right of the doorway. She had been dragged to the side like a sack of dirt, her arms still extended over her head, the hole Buckle's pistol ball had made in the center of her tunic ringed with a black gunpowder burn from the point-blank shot. He averted his eyes and then forced them back upon her. Look at her, soldier, he told himself. Do not dare try to save yourself the pain of your own handiwork.

"Now!" Pluteus shouted. He and Scully shoved the doors open as the troopers pointed their thicket of muskets into the widening gap between.

Wreaths of sea fog surged in upon them in an exhilarating cold, damp slap of fresh air.

The City of the Founders. The city of eternal fog.

Buckle did not know what he had expected, but he had not expected this. There was not a soul there to meet them.

Buckle sucked the salty air into his smoke-tortured lungs in gasps, as did the rest of the company, who stood poised, uncertain, their gun barrels wavering. The gray daylight was weak, bleeding away into the evening. Buckle's eyes quickly adjusted to the twilight haze after being buried so long in the shadows of the gas-lit subterranean dark.

Pluteus motioned for the company to move forward and led the way up a cobblestoned ramp; Buckle followed at his shoulder, glancing back and forth. Along with the sea-air salt, he could smell horses, whale oil, and burning coal. This was no ghost town.

Where were the enemy soldiers? Where was anybody?

"Quickly, now," Pluteus hissed, glancing up as a canary sailed out of the prison doorway and flapped up to vanish in the fog.

Sabrina moved ahead of Pluteus and took a sharp right as the group emerged onto a narrow street. The fog thinned and it became easier to see. Buckle gripped his pistol, searching the high, bulky buildings hemming them in on both sides, his gut cringing as he waited for the sharp *crack* of a musket blast that never came.

The fog wrapped the world in near silence, but the jangling of the rescue expedition's gear and their glove-muffled coughing sounded unsettlingly loud.

Buckle's boots padded across the neat cobblestones. The street surface, scattered with relatively fresh horse dung and sliced by a deeply cut set of railroad tracks, glistened wetly in the blue-white light of gas lamps affixed at regular intervals to the stone walls. The buildings, mortared blocks of gray-black granite, loomed along both flanks of the street, studded with doorways and staircases, but no windows. The wooden doors, jambs, and lintels were slightly swollen and split from their constant exposure to moisture, but this decay only added depth to their elegantly carved representations of trees, vines, and flowers. It was difficult to measure how tall the buildings were: their upper floors disappeared into a fog ceiling about twenty-five feet up.

Buckle felt as if he was striding down a tunnel, a tunnel with walls of stone and a ceiling of fog that shifted in density as it drifted, its currents morphing from dark to light and back again, and seemed unearthly.

Could the rescue expedition be running into a trap? Buckle did not think so. The genius of this operation was the sheer audacity of it: the external defenses of the Founders' city were legion, but he suspected they were highly vulnerable to exactly this sort of incursion—from the *inside*. The leaders of the Founders, always looking outward for threats, would have naturally suffered a brief period of confusion, of disbelief, before initiating a response.

But it had been too long. The authorities in the city surely had been warned. Somebody with a musket should have showed up by now.

"Keep the pace up, old salts!" Pluteus whispered.

Pluteus did not need to prod his company; the walking wounded and the unscathed humped along at best speed, carrying Balthazar and the incapacitated Ballblaster with them. Buckle was worried about Balthazar, but he knew the old lion would recover. Buckle was far more concerned about Andromeda Pollux, bloody and limp in Kepler's arms: with the Founders about to embark on a war of domination, a defensive coalition of Snow World clans would be crippled without Andromeda there to help negotiate the alliances. And there was Katzenjammer Smelt, loping along nearby, his giraffe-like frame conspicuous among the squatter, armor-bound Ballblasters. Buckle would have enjoyed tossing the monocled hyena back into the prison, with the magazine with the bomb in it.

Buckle caught up with Sabrina as she advanced at a hurried stride, making a sharp left turn down another misty avenue.

"We are in the Rookeries," Sabrina said in a low voice, then coughed. "The homes of the workers are here. They will be employed in the underground factories until after sundown. The quitting whistle has yet to sound, so we should not run into too many of them between here and the rendezvous point. But we are approaching the market square and that may pose a problem, even if it's not active. The children like to play in the open space. And there are often constables loitering there, attempting to seduce the mothers."

"But where are the soldiers?" Buckle asked.

Sabrina shook her head. "It is confounding. I have no answer for it."

They passed three horses, scrawny nags shivering under wool blankets, tethered to a hitching post, when the street suddenly opened into a courtyard. Empty tables and stalls emerged from the fog. The building faces and walls were near-black, mottled with coal dust and wet dirt, and punctuated with the occasional yellow burst of caged canaries. There was a surprising amount of color overhead—banners, ribbons, and pennons hung limply from every balcony and window sash, all bright with silken crimson, white, and purple, emblazoned with the silver phoenix. In the middle of the square stood a cracked fountain and three statues—two men and one woman—wearing granite robes, all draped in ribbon. At the base of the statues, four young children stood frozen, staring, their wooden swords and dolls clutched in their hands, emerging like ghosts from the mists of the empty city.

Buckle took a deep breath. The sight of the urchins, who looked thin and dirty in patchy oilskin jackets, each wrapped at the waist with a colorful sash, did not alarm him. He was worried about the mothers and grandmothers, huddled in a small group just beyond. The women stood still with shock, watching, slack-jawed, as the expedition of foreign clansmen—a bizarre sight as they swung out of the fog in their blood-splattered, gunpowder-blackened armor, carrying their wounded with them—jogged past.

Once the invaders had clanked and rattled away into the mist, the adults would surely raise the alarm.

Sabrina continued on across the square, ignoring the citizens, and Buckle hurried to keep pace with her.

"The cat is out of the bag, now," Buckle said to Sabrina.

"They will not do anything," Sabrina replied, never taking her eyes off the fog ahead.

"They will not raise the alarm? Why not?" Buckle asked.

"They just *won't*," Sabrina said.

There was a distant *ba-thump*, deep and heavy. A small shockwave shook the earth underfoot, causing the courtyard banners to ripple. The horses stamped and whinnied. The canaries shrieked. Buckle's fuse had just reached the munitions cache and blown up the underground prison.

"Alarm raised anyway," Buckle muttered.

Sabrina pointed to one of the few tables that sported wares—it was lined with pies, green pies whose tops oozed with a whitish glaze. "Do you see those awful-looking things?" Sabrina asked as they passed the table.

"Yes," Buckle answered, glancing back at the mothers and children, who still had not moved, remaining as motionless as the dark statues around them.

"Cucumber pies," Sabrina said. "It's one of the few edible plants they can grow here, cucumbers, and they serve it up so often the people say it will turn your ears green if you live long enough. There is an old Founders nursery rhyme..." Sabrina said with a smile, and to Buckle's surprise, in a low, sweet, breathless whisper, she sang it:

> "Cucumber, cucumber, cucumber pie,
> I'd rather gnaw on a dead rat raw, or fried."

-LIII-

THE TAR PIT GARGOYLES

Buckle inhaled great draughts of cold air as Sabrina led the rescue expedition at a half jog out of the gloomy warrens of the Rookeries and into a wide-open section of the city that contained a railroad yard and huge, circular roundhouses looming in the mist.

Pluteus signaled for the troopers to form a skirmish line, and they fanned out, their equipment rattling on their belts, their boots clomping across oily gravel and railway tracks. Buckle's spine tingled. Again, the place was empty, but furnaces still glowed orange in the near distance, and the air was thick with the smell of burning coke. Huge locomotives, sealed up in glass and iron pods to fend off the mustard, sat on the rails, their boilers cold, furnaces dark—with the exception of one, recently arrived, condensation sizzling on her boiler, loud with the pings of contracting metal.

Canary cages hung everywhere. The little birds were silent, their heads tucked under their shivering wings. Teams of horses, their backs steaming in the wet cold, bobbed their heads in their traces, attached to wagons half unloaded.

Half unloaded. Buckle tapped Sabrina on the shoulder. "You see the wagons?" he asked.

"Aye," Sabrina replied. "Somebody has cleared the road in a hurry."

"We are running straight into it," Pluteus grouched, close at hand.

Buckle gripped his pistol a little tighter. "Well, there is no going back now, is there?"

"We are only a few yards from the pickup point," Sabrina replied.

They cleared the railway yard and followed Sabrina up the ramp of a large causeway that spanned a good fifty feet across and stretched straight ahead, until it vanished into a vast, silent wall of drifting fog. Even though the mists and the diminishing daylight limited his view, the sense of the vast space around him made Buckle feel a bit heady. Beyond the low walls of the causeway, he could see on both sides huge fountains, each more impressive than the next, each flowing with jet-black water, each topped by great granite gargoyles chiseled from dark corners of the imagination. Ghostly shadows of tall structures lurked in the near distance and where the mists thinned: gothic arches, ribbed vaulting, and flying buttresses that ascended into slender spires with copper roofs turned ocean green by oxidation.

"The tar pits!" Sabrina reported.

Buckle knew where they were. The dark swamp of smoldering oil under the causeways, the black water in the fountains—this was the center of the Founders' city, the very heart of its foundation: the La Brea tar pits.

"How much farther to the evacuation point?" Buckle asked Sabrina, who was at his left hip.

"About a quarter mile," Sabrina replied. "Two hundred yards as the crow flies."

"Hold here a moment, Pluteus," Buckle said, raising his hand.

"Halt!" Pluteus ordered softly. "Eyes up!"

The expedition stopped, everyone breathing heavily and coughing. They were looking a bit too ragged; this was a good time to give them thirty seconds to catch their breath.

"Pluteus. Wing the message, 'All is well,' " Buckle said.

Pluteus looked at Moss, the Ballblaster signalman. "You heard the captain, Mossy. Wings up. All is well."

"Yes, General," Moss replied, twisting a lever on the front of his breastplate. The hermetically sealed bird capsule built into the armor opened with a small hiss of air. He reached into the hatch and pulled out a somewhat frazzled-looking homing pigeon, its blue-green head rapidly cocking back and forth. "All is well," Moss repeated, selecting one of several prepared scrolls pegged inside the bird chamber and tucking it into a leather sheath attached to the pigeon's leg. He tossed the pigeon into the air, and after an initial fluttering circle to get its bearings, the bird angled upward and vanished in the mist.

"Let's go," Buckle whispered.

"Forward!" Pluteus urged, and the expedition resumed its advance along the causeway.

"Fifty yards to La Brea Square," Sabrina said, checking her compass.

The rescue expedition advanced along the causeway in good order as La Brea Square, the center of the sprawling plaza and the Founders' city, slowly emerged from the fog. The causeway ran between large spheres of fantastic engineering, their glass domes, some at least thirty-five feet high, stained a beautiful amber color by the noxious gases rising from the tar pits. Towering hoods of burnished metal stood between the domes at regular intervals, housing dozens of large fans that hummed quietly, vibrating the atmosphere as they sucked in streaming columns of fog, forcing fresh air down into the labyrinths of factories, mines, foundries, and smithies below.

Buckle looked up to see a gigantic shadow towering over the center of the square. Emerging from the mist was an immense metal statue of a raptor, constructed of copper now dull with oxidized green, seventy feet high, with its wings flung open in a span at least one hundred feet across. It was the Founders phoenix, the symbol of their master plan for the rebirth of human civilization.

The Founders had almost made it, Buckle knew. But then it had all gone terribly, terribly wrong.

Buckle checked the fog bank overhead. Surely they should be able to see the long shadow of the *Pneumatic Zeppelin* descending to rendezvous with them by now. He saw no sign of the airship. He glanced at a fifteen-foot-high marble sculpture of a snarling gargoyle perched atop one of the blackwater fountains, the cathedral gables of its bat-like wings folded back and held high, as if, tiring of the eternal mist, it was about to take flight. There was a darkly beautiful city hidden in the fog.

Something came clacking, rolling toward him.

He glanced down the causeway and saw a fist-sized black iron ball rolling out of the mist, its stubby neck flashing yellow with a burning fuse, clattering on the marble paving stones as it wobbled.

Grenade.

Buckle shoved Sabrina, sending her sprawling across the causeway stones, away from the grenade. He opened his mouth to shout a warning. The grenade exploded before he could utter a sound.

A bright, violent flash blew up the world.

Blinded by whiteness, Buckle sensed his body hurtling through the air, but the hard landing he expected never came; instead, a floating, velvet darkness swallowed him whole.

–LIV–

THE VELVET DARKNESS
AND THE DUCKLING

"ROMULUS, WATCH YOUR LINE!" A voice came to Romulus Buckle, echoing across time. He was six years old, holding a fishing pole over an icy mountain creek. The fast-flowing water was a liquid transparency, gurgling under and around pancakes of ice that collared frost-rimed rocks and dead vegetation. The creek bed, wavering with the undulating current, was lined with oval stones, all smooth skinned and colored black, gray, and blue, but among them lay the real treasure: chunks of quartz that dazzled in the water, but lost their magic when you took them home and let them dry out in an old glass jar on your bedside table.

Having long forgotten his boring task as a fisherman, little Romulus was peering down at his fur-lined boots—too large for him, making room for a doubling of socks, which was warmer—as the toes pressed down on the rubbery brown strip of earth along the stream bank. He imagined that the imprints might remain there forever, a reminder to all that the great Romulus Buckle had once passed this way.

"Romulus! Son! Your line is getting tangled!" Romulus's father, Alpheus, shouted again, with considerable amusement.

Romulus focused on his fishing line: it had drifted into a clump of dead brush on the stream bank and caught on a low-hanging twig, where it was now jerking against the current. He yanked at the line with his small hand, but he could not work it free.

"Here, Romulus, let me help you," Alpheus said as he arrived, his boots ploshing in the snow, making footprints on the sludgy riverbank much bigger than those of Romulus. Alpheus took the fishing pole from Romulus's hands and gently swept it back and forth, the tip just above the surface of the water, working the line out of the riverbank tangle.

Romulus looked up at the form of his father, silhouetted against the cold, gray sky. Alpheus was a slender man but tall, at least he always seemed very tall to little Romulus, and his heavy wolfskin greatcoat did little to reduce that impression. And when he picked Romulus up and carried him, which was often, the boy was always aware of his father's exceptional physical strength, a strength he witnessed daily, as his father carried immense armloads of wood up the trail for the cabin fireplace, pounded a bent axe back into shape with a hammer, or dragged the horses into their harnesses as they dithered and kicked.

Romulus never saw his father, who seemed to exist in a pool of loving calmness that flowed over the people around him, commit an act of violence or raise his voice in anger, even with the hardships of life in a tiny cabin, alone in the high mountains of a land forever locked in winter.

Ever since he could remember, Romulus knew that his family was in hiding.

"Romulus wasn't paying any attention at all, Daddy," Elizabeth tattled, appearing at Alpheus's waist, bundled in a hat and coat of white rabbit fur. She eyed Romulus with all the disdain and superiority of a sister one year his senior. "He keeps losing hooks, and you said we don't have very many."

"It's all right, Elizabeth," Alpheus said, patting her head and gently pushing her on her way. "I'll take care of it."

"I'm telling Momma, too!" Elizabeth, squealing with delight at any prospect of pillorying her brother, ran off, her boots shedding globs of snow as she skipped up the trail that led to the cabin.

Romulus watched as his father tried to work the line free without losing the hook, and he suddenly felt bad. He sank his cold hands into his pockets and folded his fingers over some odd-shaped twigs he had collected there for safekeeping. He hated Elizabeth, but she was right: fish hooks were difficult to make, and he was letting his father down by constantly losing them in his tangled lines. Romulus crushed the twigs between his fingers, drew his hands out of his pockets, and opened them to watch the broken sticks drop and make little holes in the snow.

Alpheus had taken a step out into the creek, planting a boot on a rock that thrust up from the water, as he concentrated on saving the line and its precious hook. Romulus kicked a clod of snow and wandered away, clomping up a small hillock with some vague idea that, with a little elevation, he might be able to see some of his dozens of lost hooks glittering in the shallows and retrieve them for his father. He reached the crest and stopped, looking down into the bend of the dark creek as he brushed traces of crushed bark from his hands. Pieces of quartz glimmered everywhere along the creek bed, and it was difficult to tell if any of the sparkles might be iron hooks instead.

Romulus took a deep breath and slowly exhaled, watching the white vapor of the warm air curl in front of his eyes. Though all months were winter, it was a nice day for the month of April, and the hidden sun was almost shining through the clouds.

Romulus's attention drifted away from Alpheus, and he peered down into the quiet pool the creek formed as it spread out under the other side of the hillock. The water was deeper here, darker, and a grove of willow trees hid much of it under the curtain of their whip-thin, frozen branches. He noticed a mother duck with three yellow chicks huddling at the edge of the pool; she was acting strangely, waddling back and forth, her honks low and hoarse, as if she were exhausted.

There was something struggling in the pool. It was a duckling, the yellow puff of its body thrashing back and forth in the space where the willow branches touched the water.

Something silver flashed at the duckling's beak. It was a fisherman's hook—one of Romulus's lost hooks—and it had snagged the poor little creature, who was now captured by the line.

The duckling had to be saved. It was his hook and his responsibility. Romulus thought no more on it than that. He skidded down the hillock and jumped into the water. His heart leapt at the icy shock as he plunged in to the waist. He waded slowly, his boots stone heavy, into the dangling branches of the willow tree, his hand reaching for the line. The duckling frantically peeped and slewed around as he approached, its head angled back awkwardly as the hook and line allowed it no more escape than a small circle. The mother duck leapt in from the opposite bank with a splash, honking, wings beating.

"I'm helping! I'm helping!" Romulus shouted, waving off the mother duck, afraid that she might peck an eye out or worse. He heard a slash of fear in his voice, for though he had been certain of the depth of the water in the pool—he had many times poked long sticks into it—he was suddenly afraid that he might have miscalculated. The freezing water was already up to his chest, and he wasn't sure if he was sinking any farther or not. The dark bottom of mud and roots was dangerously soft, and with his heavy winter clothes now waterlogged and impossibly heavy, he felt like he was in quicksand.

Romulus fought off a surge of panic.

His feet found something firm, a sunken log, perhaps. He was not going under—not yet, anyway. If he did, he figured that he could kick off his boots and twist out of his coat, letting them sink down to the black bottom of the pool, and make it back to the riverbank. Of course, his parents would be furious if he lost his fur clothes.

Romulus edged closer and grabbed the duckling, being careful not to close his cold-numbed fingers too tightly around its delicate strugglings. The duckling stilled, its eyes bright. He could feel its tiny heart pounding against the palm of his hand. He took hold of the shaft of the small fishhook, which had impaled the duckling's upper beak, and pulled, but the barb held fast. There was a sudden flurry of wings and a clacking beak behind him, and he froze, squeezing his eyes shut, hunching his shoulders, waiting for an ear to be ripped off. The blow from the frightened mother never came, however, and she retreated to the riverbank to honk plaintively alongside her other three offspring.

Romulus's teeth started to chatter and he could not stop it. It was strange, because the water did not feel cold anymore. He felt terribly numb below his knees. If he was going to save the baby duck, it had to be fast, and more brutal than he would have liked. He pressed his fingers tightly around the hook and drew the barbed end down through the puncture with all the force he dare apply, lest he kill the animal in the attempt. The hook rattled a bit as he worked it loose—unpleasant for both the duckling and Romulus—but it popped out. The duckling, realizing it was free, peeped and kicked wildly. He let it go.

Romulus smiled as the duckling scrambled up the riverbank to its mother. He turned back to head to the shore but staggered, toppling forward, nearly dunking his head in the black water. His waterlogged clothes, ponderous as anchors, threatened to suck him under. His legs and feet were immovable blocks of ice. He tried to scream for his father but he barely wheezed: the vise of cold had squeezed his lungs tight.

He heard a loud splash of water behind him. A wave rippled across the pond, bouncing the ice at the bank; it kissed the underside of his chin as it passed him, but he could not feel it. In the next moment he shot into the air, lifted completely out of the water by Alpheus's strong arms.

A few minutes later, Romulus sat beside a raging fire inside the cabin, stripped naked, rubbed down and wrapped in two of his mother's thickest quilts, sipping harsh tea and still shivering a little.

Romulus's mother, Diana, gave his big toe, which was sticking out of the covers, a good tweak. "That's for being reckless, my reckless little boy," she sighed.

Diana was a small woman—though her plentiful, curly blond hair made her seem a bit bigger—who in every moment worried about her children, and Romulus knew that his adventurous spirit and defective judgment gave her no relief. "Two more cups of tea—you drink every drop—and then off to bed. No discussion," Diana said, wiping her hands on her apron as she turned to tend her kettle on the potbellied stove.

Alpheus appeared from the bedroom, having changed out of his wet clothes. When Alpheus had been carrying him up the hill to the cabin, Romulus thought he had heard his father curse under his breath. If this was true, it would be the only time in his life he would hear his father do so. Now Alpheus looked angry—but only for a moment. He grinned as he took a cup of tea from Diana and settled down into the rocking chair he had made, folding his leg over his knee and leaning in to whisper to his boy.

"Rescue all of the ducklings you wish, my son, but I beg you to be more thoughtful and inventive in your methods," Alpheus said, rubbing Romulus's wet head with his powerful hand. "Become a man of peace, and every act of kindness, no matter how small, no matter what the cost to you, tips the balance of the world in your favor. Promise me that you will always be a man of peace and that you will never, ever, become a man of war."

"I promise, father," Romulus replied.

The flames in the fireplace leapt strangely.

Buckle found himself a grown man again, standing in a long stone corridor lit by the fluttering blue flames of gas lamps. It resembled the architecture he had seen in the Founders' city, but this was no underground prison. The archways were high and vaulted, their columns adorned with grotesque but fancifully chiseled gargoyles and phoenixes, and in every alcove between the arches hung a painting. From each portrait stared a stern face, which, whether male or female, was bordered by varying shades of red hair.

The echoing neigh of a horse and the resounding clatter of horseshoes on stone made Buckle spin around. At the far end of the corridor, he saw a man atop a magnificent white charger, whose hooves threw sparks as it pawed the floor stones.

The rider was hidden beneath a flowing scarlet cloak, the hood drawn down over his face, but it did little to obscure his obvious physical strength, or the menace of his presence.

Buckle grabbed for the weapons at his belt, but they were not there. Fury surged up inside him, fury with the raw unfairness of the nightmare. "Have at it then, specter!" Buckle howled. "But dare not hide your face from me!"

The rider threw back his scarlet hood. The face that emerged, a handsome pale visage with a high forehead and a great mane of crimson hair sweeping to the shoulders, struck Buckle with the hardness of it, of the cliff-like cheekbones, as if the face had been cut from the same rock as the gargoyles in the grand hall. And the green eyes, witch's-cauldron-green eyes, were cold and murderous. The rider drew his sword from its long scabbard with a metallic swish, the cold steel streaming with the blue reflections of the gas lamps, and spurred the white horse forward. The horse charged down the grand hallway, gathering speed at a furious rate.

Buckle heard Elizabeth's voice in his head, distant and urgent. "Wake up, Romulus! Wake up!" she cried. "Wake up!"

Buckle gasped—it was an out-of-body, visceral, stabbing kind of gasp, as if he had just sucked in the ember-filled air over a campfire.

The world crashed back in on Buckle. He choked for breath. He was being dragged by the back of his collar, and it was garroting him. The thunderstorm of a musket battle rolled back and forth against his head. Pain stabbed him from all directions, but he could not tell exactly where in his body it was coming from. He flung his eyes open, looking straight up, and saw nothing but fog.

–LV–

THE WRETCHED AIR ABOVE
LA BREA SQUARE

MAX SAW A PHOSPHORUS-FLARE ROCKET above the fog bank and burst a hundred yards ahead of the *Pneumatic Zeppelin*, exactly where Welly had calculated the evacuation point over La Brea Square should be. The *Pneumatic Zeppelin* was gliding a good fifty feet above the surface of the fog bank, and the Ballblasters' messenger pigeon, popping up from the miasma, had already arrived aboard, scooting into the gondola signals room through the access tubes it was trained to enter. Signalman Fitzroy had confirmed the rescue expedition's location on the ground.

"Signal flare dead ahead. Twelve o'clock low. Directly over the evacuation point," Welly announced matter-of-factly.

"Aye, confirmed," Max replied. Their oxygen masks were stowed now that they had cleared the mustard, and it felt good to talk without the warm but stifling tubed helmet.

The sputtering flare slid away, its dying glow reflected in Max's liquid-filled goggles. She pressed the chadburn handle forward to ahead one-quarter, ringing the bell. The engineers acknowledged and the *Pneumatic Zeppelin* responded smoothly, her propellers humming, the oil lanterns swinging lazily on their posts along the gondola gunwales and the forward spar. The huge airship coasted over an endless sea of greasy fog below and under an endless ceiling of dark gray overcast above: evening was on its way. They slipped through a strange, gloomy slice of the universe.

"Two hundred feet to evacuation point," Welly said.

"All stop," Max ordered as she pulled the chadburn handle back to all stop. The engineering bell responded and the driving propellers went silent, leaving only the sigh of the wind. Applying only the small maneuvering propellers to adjust for drift, she would let the airship glide over the evacuation point, reverse the engines, and set her into a hover to down ship.

Max thought she heard the faint rumble of gunfire below, but she could not be sure. Kellie pressed her ribs against Max's shin, aware, as always, that her master was coming home. Max patted the dog on the head, more out of obligation, she told herself, than sympathy—but when the dog turned her soft brown eyes up to hers, Max turned her head away, lest the creature discover the truth buried inside her goggles.

"One hundred feet to evacuation point," Welly said without looking up, his eyes glued to his map, airspeed indicator, compass, and watch.

"Aye, one hundred," Max confirmed. "Correct for drift, Mister De Quincey."

"Aye," De Quincey responded, ever imperturbable.

Max was going in a little heavy, a little faster than she might have liked, but her crewmates below were likely involved in a running gunfight. Every second would bring more and more of the enemy upon them. She needed to get the *Arabella* lowered, and fast.

The piloting gondola prow skimmed the fog bank, throwing a rolling curl of mist in its wake. To the south, the fog was laced with hundreds of long, wobbling rivers of filthy black smoke, running roughly from west to east, the issue of a sprawling complex of industrial smokestacks. If the stories of the Founders tearing down their highest watchtowers to hide the city under the fog bank were true, it was a wasted effort, Max mused, for the oily spill of their chimneys betrayed its location with gigantic black stripes over a mile long. The reek of the foul pollution assaulted her sensitive Martian nose, and she felt sick. For a moment she considered putting her oxygen mask back on.

"Airspeed five knots. Fifty feet to evacuation point," Welly said.

"Back one-third," Max said, cranking the jangling chadburn handle to that position.

"Back one-third," engineering repeated on the chattertube, ringing the chadburn bell with the daughter dial.

The *Pneumatic Zeppelin*'s engines revved up, the propellers gently whirring in reverse, the vibration jiggling the boil in its tubes.

"Airspeed four knots. Thirty feet to evacuation point," Wellington said. "Twenty feet...airspeed three knots...ten feet...airspeed two knots...five feet...dead stop."

"All stop!" Max ordered into the chattertube as she swung the chadburn lever. "Hover."

"All stop and hover!" came the engineering response.

The *Pneumatic Zeppelin* now hung motionless above the fog bank.

"Directly above evacuation point," Welly said, scratching a line on his map with pencil and ruler.

Max glanced at her watch and leaned in to her chattertube mouthpiece. "Lower the launch."

"Lowering launch! Aye, Captain!" It was Ivan's voice coming to her on the chattertube. Ensign Glantz was chief of the boat on the launch. The chief mechanic was not supposed to be there, but there was no stopping him now.

The great winches and winding gears of the launch's lowering mechanism creaked and groaned behind the piloting gondola.

"Launch descending. Fifty feet of rope. Aye!" Ivan reported through the chattertube.

The *Arabella* was to be lowered fifty feet, and the *Pneumatic Zeppelin* would descend the rest of the way down with it. This would allow the mother airship to provide covering fire for the rescue expedition as they boarded the grounded *Arabella*. The crew were already at their battle stations; the rear hatch of the gondola had been opening and shutting as musket-armed crew members clambered out onto the umbilical bridges.

"Ballast, vent hydrogen five percent for vertical descent," Max said. "Down ship."

"Down ship!" Welly shouted into the chattertube.

"Venting hydrogen, five percent, aye," Nero Coulton repeated, cranking his gas-release wheels on the hydro board.

The *Pneumatic Zeppelin* sank, slow and easy, and the piloting gondola was once again swallowed up in the gray nothingness of the fog bank. The vapors, impregnated with a vile stench of coal smoke, dead fish, sea salt, and rotten onions, made Max gag—it was not the released hydrogen, which was odorless and colorless—and she wondered if the entire city smelled like this.

The fog thickened overhead: it suddenly got much darker inside the gondola. The phosphorescent coating on every dial, register, and control surface glimmered a soft yellow green.

It was quiet. Max could hear the indistinct patter of the tiny mechanical agitators stirring inside the hundreds of boil-filled instrument spheres, vials, and cylinders on the bridge, each one generating its own green bioluminescence.

"Hydrogen five-percent vent complete," Nero said, scrutinizing the instrument gauges on the hydro and ballast boards.

"Aye," Max responded.

Welly had his face pressed into the drift scope. "Rate of descent two feet per second. Estimate launch to make landfall in approximately thirty-five seconds."

Max watched her gyro, compass, and inclinometer.

"Thirty seconds to launch landfall," Welly said. "Zero bubble."

Ivan's voice came rattling down the chattertube. "Launch has cleared the fog ceiling. We are over the landing site. Thirty feet to landfall. Thirty feet."

"Thirty feet, aye," Max repeated back to Ivan though her chattertube hood.

"Rescue team sighted—but we've got a hornet's nest down here!" Ivan yelled.

Max's stomach muscles tightened. The fight they had expected was on. The *Pneumatic Zeppelin*, coming down like a big, fat, slow duck, would not fare well if there was anything down there bigger than muskets. She heard the sounds of blackbang muskets blazing, faint at first, but rapidly gaining in intensity.

"Twenty feet," Welly reported.

"Twenty feet to launch landfall!" Ivan said almost simultaneously on the chattertube, most likely peering down the *Arabella*'s drift scope.

"Twenty feet, aye," Max said, turning to Nero. "Hydro—ready to replenish hydrogen in all sections, five percent."

Nero already had his hands resting on his controls. "Five percent, aye. Hydro ready for the bounce, ma'am."

The fog thinned out and disappeared under the glass observation window at Max's feet. Looking down past the dog, she had a bird's-eye view of La Brea Square below. It was designed as a huge hexagon, with the massive phoenix sculpture at the center, and four causeways leading away from each side. The wide causeways, built to span the massive pool of black tar over which the entire square rested, were bordered near the center by irregular pumping structures capped with amber-stained glass domes.

Directly below, grouped in a defensive circle on the eastern causeway, was the rescue expedition, muskets afire. A considerable force of Founders had the Crankshaft and Alchemist intruders surrounded—and Max could see dozens more racing to the scene from the adjoining streets.

Outnumbered, outgunned, and surrounded, Buckle's expedition was not going to last much longer.

–LVI–

NEWTON AND THE *ARABELLA*

ROMULUS BUCKLE'S EYELIDS FLUTTERED, BATTLING against the acrid cordite that stung his eyes. He caught glimpses of shadows moving in a fog lit up by bright yellow muzzle flashes. He was confused for a moment, until he remembered where he was. He was being carried—or, more descriptively, dragged—as his heels scraped along the ground. Powerful hands laid him down against a wall, and the sudden stillness made his head swim violently. He forced his eyes open, focusing on Corporal Druxbury and Sabrina as they kneeled over him. Druxbury was wrapping Buckle's head with bandages.

"You okay, old salt?" Druxbury shouted, realizing that Buckle had regained consciousness.

Buckle tried to say something—he wasn't sure what—but his mouth would not form the words. A musket ball struck the wall above his head, showering him with sharp bits of granite. Anger flooded through him. He had to get up and fight. He clawed at his pistol holster and tried to pull his body up.

Sabrina shoved Buckle back down, hard enough to bang the back of his head against the wall. "Romulus! For the sake of mercy, stay down!"

Buckle took a deep breath. He tasted blood in his mouth. He could see one of the amber glass domes towering over the opposite wall of the causeway. A line of finely formed letters, corroded with green rust but still quite prominent, were chiseled along the dome's high copper collar: **STEAM POWER FOR OUR BRAVE NEW WORLD OF PEACE AND BROTHERHOOD.**

Buckle turned his head to the left. Andromeda was lying beside him, with Kepler and Wolfgang crouched over her. Her blood-streaked face rested mere inches from Buckle's, her depthless eyes of violet-black staring into his. The white of one eye was soaked by blood, but that ghastly detail now escaped Buckle's notice: the Alchemist leader was not looking at him, but rather *into* him.

The clouds in Buckle's head suddenly melted away, replaced by clarity.

Buckle suddenly knew things. He knew that Andromeda could not speak. But he knew she was urging him to act.

Buckle turned his head to the sky and saw a long, ellipsoidal shadow growing darker and darker in the fog ceiling: it was the *Arabella* making her descent. Grabbing ahold of the low causeway wall, Buckle yanked himself to his feet, drawing his pistol as he rose. Druxbury and Sabrina now had their backs to him, part of the rough circle of Ballblasters and Alchemist troopers who, under the direction of Pluteus, Scorpius, and a somewhat recovered Balthazar, were returning fire at flashes in the gloom that came from every direction. Katzenjammer Smelt stood in the center of the formation, arrogantly heedless of any danger, aiming, firing, and reloading his pistol with the calm ease one might see on a practice range.

Musket balls with their phosphorescent trails whizzed through the miasma, ricocheting off metal, biting into granite with nasty whacks of pulverized rock, smacking holes in the mottled glass of the tar-pit domes.

RICHARD ELLIS PRESTON, JR.

Buckle lifted his pistol, waiting to shoot at a musket muzzle flash. He saw a section of fog burst with a circle of light. He jerked his pistol to the mark and fired. Whether he hit anything or not he would never know.

"Just cannot stay out of the party, can you, Captain?" Sabrina shouted, biting the top off a paper cartridge as she appeared at Buckle's shoulder. "I think they are forming up to the east!"

"Where the hell is that Martian with your airship?" Scorpius bellowed.

"She shall be here," Buckle replied.

"My airship," Smelt howled nearby.

A Ballblaster at Buckle's shoulder cried out and fell backward. It was Reyes. Buckle knelt beside the man to check his pulse. He was dead. The Founders soldiers, Buckle thought as he jammed his ammunition into his pistol barrel and ramrodded it home, were surely more proficient at fighting in the fog than his clansmen were.

A roar of musketry boomed overhead. The slender keel of the *Arabella* had cleared the fog ceiling, and her gunwales, jammed from bow to stern with muskets, had opened up in a barrage of flashes.

"Our transportation has arrived, children!" Balthazar shouted.

The *Arabella* was coming down to land in an excellent position: the length of her hull would roughly straddle the western end of the eastern causeway, placing the airship like a wall between Buckle's force and the Founders soldiers, collected under the huge phoenix statue at the center.

"Good work, Max!" Buckle shouted.

Seeing the arrival of the Crankshaft reinforcements, the Founders on the eastern end of the causeway started pressing.

The vapors rippled with gunfire that was suddenly much closer and heavier in its volume. An Alchemist trooper fell, screaming as he clutched a leg split wide open. His companions dragged him back. Buckle stepped into the breach and discharged his pistol at the shadows in the fog.

The battlefield suddenly fell silent.

Sabrina had been right. The enemy was forming up for an assault.

Buckle drew his sword, the saber blade ringing as it slid out of the scabbard. It was going to be close.

"Form up on me!" Pluteus screamed, striding back and forth. "Double ranks!"

The Ballblasters and Alchemists, hastily reloading their muskets, fell back into two lines.

Buckle hurried into a position at the end of the front line. He stuck his empty pistol into his belt. There would be time for only one volley—and then the fight would be hand-to-hand.

"Fix bayonets!" Pluteus ordered. The troopers drew their bayonets from their belt frogs. "Bayonets!" Bayonets were snapped onto the musket barrels with a resounding *click*.

Buckle heard a gravelly-throated Founders officer shout in the mist ahead, his orders as loud and clear as if he were on parade: "Charge!"

What seemed like a hundred men and women screamed a battle cry, their voices rolling from the fog like an ocean wave.

"Front rank, kneel!" Pluteus yelled. The front rank of troopers dropped to one knee.

"Take aim!" Pluteus shouted.

The troopers lifted their musket stocks tight to their cheeks, barrels unwavering, leveled at the mass of shadows rushing at them through the mist.

RICHARD ELLIS PRESTON, JR.

"Hold!" Pluteus shouted.

The Founders came on, their shadows getting darker and more defined, the pitch of their battle cry growing. There were a lot of them.

"Hold! Wait for it!" Pluteus shouted.

A wall of black-uniformed Founders soldiers, both men and women, burst out of the fog, their muskets spattering yellow with a volley of fire.

"Fire!" Pluteus shouted. The Ballblaster and Alchemist ranks boomed in a solid volley of musketry, blowing up a cloud of dark powder smoke. Buckle saw casualties drop from the Founders line—but they had barely dented their numbers.

"To the bayonet! Have at 'em, old salts!" Pluteus yelled.

Buckle squared his feet and raised his sword. The Founders would surely overrun them. But all they had to do was buy enough time for the leaders to board the *Arabella*.

A rip of musketry and the deep roar of cannon opened up high at Buckle's back. A hail of phosphorus musket-ball traces sliced into the Founders line. He heard the low *chunk, chunk, chunk* of the hammergun, the whirs of its harpoon darts passing over his head. The Founders staggered and slowed. A series of explosive shells rolled across their leading rank from left to right, mowing them down, tearing them to pieces.

Buckle looked overhead: the massive keel of the *Pneumatic Zeppelin* had emerged, as big as a sky city, dwarfing the grand phoenix statue beyond. Her gondolas and umbilical bridges rippled with the flashes and phosphorus flicks of musket fire. The gunnery gondola, cannon hatches flung open, the twelve-pounders drawn back for reloading, was wreathed in rivers of blackbang smoke. The hammergun slung beneath the piloting gondola swung from side to side, barrel bouncing, expending ammunition in violent puffs of superheated steam.

And suspended by dozens of thick ropes and cables fifty feet beneath the *Pneumatic Zeppelin* was the *Arabella*, her descent slowing to a hover, the bottom of her hull mere inches above the causeway. Along with her musket-wielding crewmen on the weather deck stood the hulking form of Newton, the rotating cannon on his arm spinning, spewing currents of black smoke as barrel after barrel discharged blast after blast, raining his explosive shells on the Founders. Zwicky stood at Newton's side, grinning like a madman.

"Fall back and embark!" Pluteus howled through the din.

The troopers backed up toward the *Arabella*, carrying their wounded as they retreated. Scully had a firm grip on Balthazar, making sure he was one of the first in line to board the launch.

Sabrina took ahold of Buckle's arm and pulled him with her. "Let's go, Captain!"

The *Arabella*'s main loading door swung down and slammed on the causeway. Ivan leapt down the ramp, the earflaps of his ushanka askew, waving his pistol. "What are you waiting for? An invitation? Come on!" he shouted.

Kepler was the first up the ramp, carrying Andromeda in his arms, followed closely by Wolfgang, then Scully and Balthazar.

For a moment, as he approached the *Arabella*, Buckle worried about the black Founders uniform he was wearing, his regular gear tucked away in Sabrina's haversack. One of his own crewmen might pot him. Or, more disturbingly, Newton might pot him. He realized that was why Sabrina was holding him by the arm.

"Move!" Pluteus yelled.

Buckle glanced back down the causeway. Musket flashes popped in the mist, but the Founders charge had melted back into the fog, which was still being pummeled by Newton and the Crankshaft guns.

Buckle and Sabrina arrived at the ramp as the troopers embarked in a stream. The air was swimming in gunpowder haze, with sparks and burning wadding streaming down from Newton's hot barrels directly above.

"Let's get it moving!" Ivan shouted. His pet wugglebat, Pushkin, popped its furry head out his breast pocket for an instant, then ducked it back in.

Pluteus followed the last trooper up the ramp, shoving Ivan's pistol out of the way as he passed him. "I told you to watch that thing, Gorky!" he snapped.

"Captain!" Sabrina shouted, halfway up the ramp. "It is time to go!"

Buckle looked back at Smelt, trailing last, taking one last shot into the fog. "Smelt! Get your arse up the ramp!" he yelled.

Smelt spun around. He holstered his pistol and calmly strode toward the ramp.

A Founders soldier, half crazed with bloodlust, his face and uniform spattered with the blood of his massacred fellows, charged out of the fog at Smelt's back. His musket led the way, the bayonet leveled straight at Smelt's spine.

Buckle snapped out his pistol, aiming it just past Smelt's right ear.

Smelt narrowed his eyes in rage. "Assassin!"

Buckle pulled the trigger. The hammer dropped with a useless *click*. Empty. Smelt was one instant away from being skewered. Buckle clenched his fingers around his sword hilt and lunged, shoving Smelt hard to the right. The Founders man howled, adjusting the angle of his bayonet attack to catch Smelt, even as he stumbled.

Buckle slashed his sword across the soldier's musket barrel, knocking the bayonet thrust aside. Then, driving his left forearm up to catch the man under the chin, he stepped into his forward momentum and drove his blade into the man's stomach.

The Founders soldier stopped cold, his face twisting on Buckle's sleeve. Buckle saw the blood-red point of his saber protruding from the man's back—he had run the poor bastard through. The dying soldier gurgled. Buckle felt the wheeze of the man's last breath hot on his cheek, saw the light in his brown eyes extinguish. The man dropped; Buckle yanked his sword free as the body fell.

Buckle turned and saw Smelt staring at him like a man who had just witnessed an unspeakable outrage. Smelt spun on his heel and marched up the ramp.

Sabrina grabbed Buckle, her ringlets of red hair striking as they bounced around her green eyes and pale, sooty face. "Get aboard, Captain! Hurry!" Buckle turned and raced up the ramp with Sabrina.

Ivan, perched in the doorway, yanked at all of them as they passed. "Get lost, Smelt. Nice to see you, Serafim. Nice uniform, Captain—a perfect way to get yourself potted by one of your own!"

Buckle and Sabrina stumbled into the dark hold of the *Arabella*. Buckle sensed the crowd of people within more than saw them. The loading door cranked shut as fast as its steam-powered gears could spin.

Ivan swung to a chattertube and shouted into the hood. "Launch secure! Haul away!"

The *Arabella* jerked, nearly throwing everyone off their feet, the winches high above in the *Pneumatic Zeppelin* being thrown to full power immediately.

Buckle leaned against a bulkhead; he could feel the slaps of Founders bullets thudding against the *Arabella's* wooden hull. He still clenched his saber in his hand; in the weak light he could see the long span of the blade, dull with its wash of blood. He would have to wipe it clean before he returned it to his scabbard—that was all the thought he gave the macabre souvenir.

"Launch ascending!" Ivan shouted into the chattertube. "Fish us out of this mess, will you?"

Buckle strode forward, unsteady on his feet as he bumped through the soldiers across the gently rocking deck. He worked his way forward to the empty bridge. Blackbang bullets smacked the glass nose panels here and there, sometimes cracking the dense glass.

Something drew Buckle to the front starboard side of the nose. He peered down through one of the less rippled sections of glass, observing the waves of fog as they rapidly thickened over La Brea Square below. In the surrounding city he glimpsed the sparkle of glass rooftops, and the dark, hulking roundhouses that served the myriads of railroad tracks that coiled and gleamed in all directions. Directly beneath, he saw the great black lagoon of the tar pits, the amber domes, the scurry of people on the causeways, and the small orange pops of their weapons. For an instant, and only an instant, the fog broke, and he saw a dozen cavalrymen galloping along the causeway. The riders wore black cloaks and rode black horses—all except the leader, scarlet cloak whirling, whose horse, a powerful stallion, was all white.

A dark presence cast a shadow over Buckle's soul. A terrible, untouchable, unreasonable fear whispered to him.

And then the fog closed in. La Brea Square vanished under a gray tide.

A blackbang bullet hit the glass, smack in front of Buckle's face, leaving a bull's-eye crack.

"Romulus! For crying out loud, get your arse away from the windows!" Sabrina snapped as she emerged from the hatchway.

Of no mind to argue with Sabrina, Buckle turned and strode into the safe twilight of the hold. He took a deep breath. The stuffy atmosphere was still. The twisting ratchet of the heavy ropes creaked above. The groans of the wounded men sounded a heartrending chorus. Almost every single man was injured in some way, everyone coughing, grimed with soot, gunpowder, and sweat, bloody and exhausted. But they had saved Balthazar.

Buckle brightened with relief and pride.

They had saved Balthazar.

–LVII–

"WE ARE NOT OUT OF TROUBLE YET, ANDROMEDA, MY DEAR— NOT BY A LONG SHOT."

AS SOON AS BUCKLE'S BOOTS hit the deck of the piloting gondola, he felt rejuvenated. It was exhilarating to be back on board his sky vessel, with the familiar metallic smell of the hot boilers, the oily scent of the engine lubricants, and the chemical odor of the envelope-fabric stiffeners in his nostrils, the ring of the chadburn in his ears, the airy swing of her great mass that rolled through every fiber of his body.

The deck was on a steep rise: the *Pneumatic Zeppelin* was nose up, reaching for altitude, her engines and propellers pitched to full, roaring at maximum power. And now that the rescue expedition was aboard, with Balthazar, Andromeda, and Smelt his precious cargo, it was his responsibility to get them and his crew home alive; with all of his zeppelin-captain arrogance, he knew that he would.

"Captain on deck!" Banerji announced.

Kellie was there, hopping from paw to paw between De Quincey and Dunn, tail wagging a crazy jig, starting into a long, soulful howl of joy. Buckle tapped his chest and she bounded up into his arms. She was not a small dog, perhaps forty pounds, but Buckle did not have time to let her circle his feet and dance, so he opted to carry her. She licked his grimy cheek as he strode forward into the cockpit.

Buckle eyed the sky through the nose dome—the *Pneumatic Zeppelin* had cleared the fog bank, and was now plowing through the clear layer of evening sky sandwiched between the cloud bank above and the sea of fog below. The interiors of the clouds glowed a weak silver white, illuminated from above by the hidden orb of the moon.

Max turned from the bridge and Buckle saw her gaze snap to his bandaged head, the aqueous humor in her goggles glimmering faint green—concerned—even though the rest of her demeanor was pure business. But her eyes, her Martian eyes that he found both so transparent and so unreadable, seemed strangely sad as they scrutinized him. "Welcome aboard, Captain Buckle," she announced. "We are bound north by northwest, all ahead standard at forty knots and accelerating, one hundred feet and climbing. No sign of pursuit."

"Very good, Max," Buckle replied, handing Kellie to her as he strode forward. Kellie licked Max's striped chin. Buckle knew that Max considered dog kisses undignified, and smiled inwardly as she gently lowered the dog to the deck.

"Maintain battle stations," Buckle said, planting his feet as his eyes scanned the sprawling emporium of bioluminescent instruments around him in the gondola. His bridge crew quickly reorganized around him: Max moved to the engineering station on his right, replacing Garcia; Sabrina stepped to the navigator's post as Welly moved aside; Banerji hurried to the rear of the gondola, passing Nero at the ballast station.

The cabin boy, Howard Hampton, stepped forward from alongside the hammergun turret, cradling Buckle's extraordinary top hat. Howard's eyes were wide and worried. "Are you hurt, Captain, sir?" Howard asked.

"I am fine. Thanks, Howard," Buckle answered, collecting his topper. "Let's get the hell out of here, mates! What do we say?"

"Aye!" the crew replied as one.

Buckle tucked his hat on his head and plugged in. "Navigator. Set a course. Helm—north by northeast—straight home," he ordered.

"North by northeast, aye!" De Quincey said, spinning the rudder wheel hard to the right, letting the clattering spokes spin through his hands as the nose of the great airship slowly swung to starboard.

"Aye!" Sabrina said, drawing lines across her map with ruler and pencil. "Setting course for the Devil's Punchbowl."

"Three hundred feet altitude," Buckle ordered.

"Three hundred feet. Aye!" Nero repeated, turning the wheels on his ballast boards.

Buckle watched the water compass on the binnacle. Once the swinging needle pointed north by northeast, De Quincey spun the rudder wheel back to neutral. "All ahead full," Buckle ordered, switching the chadburn dial. He was going to get the *Pneumatic Zeppelin* out of there as fast as he could.

"All ahead full," the engine room answered, switching their dial to match the bridge dial.

"Come starboard four degrees," Sabrina said.

De Quincey thumbed the rudder wheel to the right, until Buckle's water compass slipped four ticks to the east.

A heavy pair of boots rang down the staircase. It was Kepler, still carrying Lady Andromeda.

"Lady Andromeda!" Buckle exclaimed. "You should be in sick bay. Kepler, take her immediately. Howard, show them the way."

Andromeda gathered her wonderful smile. The blood had been cleaned away from her face—though it still hung in coagulated smatterings in her hair—but she still looked frighteningly pale. "I shall place myself in the care of your good surgeon presently, Captain Buckle, but first I must thank all of you for the daring rescue that saved your Balthazar and I. I know you lost good people in the effort."

"Thank you," Buckle said. "But we are not out of trouble yet, Andromeda, my dear—not by a long shot."

"Do not refer to Lady Andromeda as 'my dear,'" Kepler said in a gruff but not unpleasant manner.

Andromeda patted Kepler on the chest as one might pat a beloved horse. "No need to be a stickler, my stalwart Caliban. We are beyond formalities at the moment." She returned her attention to Buckle. "I understand the nature of the situation, Captain, which is why I wished to express my gratitude to all of you now."

"You are quite welcome, Lady Andromeda," Buckle said, with a respectful nod of his head.

"Welcome for nothing!" Katzenjammer Smelt bellowed down the stairwell, marching down in his tall black boots, halting alongside Kepler and Lady Andromeda, where he straightened his tunic with wrist-snapping tucks. "I will have you know, Lady Andromeda, that the *Pneumatic Zeppelin* is mine. It was stolen from me—stolen from me by Captain Buckle."

"All is fair in love and war, is it not, Chancellor?" Andromeda said.

"We were not at war," Smelt answered, glowering at Buckle. "Balthazar had engineered a nonaggression pact with my clan.

Little did I know that it was no more than a smoke screen to obscure their blackhearted treachery."

"We can all argue at a later time. We are at battle stations now," Buckle grumbled, watching the clouds below. "Clear the politicians from the bridge."

Howard jumped alongside Kepler and Andromeda. "Follow me to sick bay, please," he said, climbing the stairwell. The Alchemists departed.

Smelt scrutinized the black stripes on Max's face. "A Martian? You have a *Martian* aboard my zeppelin?"

Max raised one eyebrow. "Katzenjammer Smelt, I presume?" she said dryly.

"Mister Banerji," Buckle said, drawing his pistol from his belt and tossing it to the apprentice navigator. "Take this sidearm and accompany Chancellor Smelt to the library. Remain with him there until you are relieved."

"Aye, Captain," Banerji said, tucking the pistol into his belt as he stepped up to Smelt.

"Library? What library? This is an Imperial ship of war," Smelt grumbled. "This is my flagship!"

"Lead the way, Chancellor," Banerji said, motioning for Smelt to take to the stairs.

"Wait!" Sabrina shouted, stunned, peering down her drift telescope.

"What is it?" Buckle asked.

Sabrina's response was incredulous. "The fog bank...it's opening...a gap just opened directly beneath us. I can see the ground!"

Buckle stared down at the observation window under his feet and, sure enough, he could see black earth appearing under a massive, expanding chasm in the fog bank.

"There are train tracks, a locomotive…" Sabrina said. Suddenly she stiffened with such a jerk that her boots squeaked on the deck. "Cannon flash! A big cannon flash!"

Buckle saw the locomotive: at this height it looked like a black beetle speeding along the tracks, spewing a billowing trail of gray steam. And he saw the huge muzzle flash. "Evasive maneuvers!" he yelled.

De Quincey lunged into the rudder wheel, spinning it to port with all of his might.

The lumbering *Pneumatic Zeppelin* responded well, making a slow bank to port, but she wasn't built for quick maneuvering.

The cannonball came at them with a shriek. Everyone cringed.

"Brace for impact!" Buckle shouted. He saw the cannonball coming, shimmering with white phosphorus that flowed behind it in a sparkling tail; it looked more like a meteor than a huge ball of iron. It struck somewhere amidships with a severe *rip* of canvas, a blast of shattering wood, and the screech of shearing metal.

No explosion followed. All Buckle could hear were the noises of the healthy engines and propellers churning away.

"That was one hell of a cannonball—a hundred-pounder at the very least," Sabrina muttered, leaning into the hard left turn of the airship, her eyes lifted to the gondola roof like everyone else. "If the stockings had not held, I wager we would not be here anymore."

"Well," Welly gasped. "We got lucky as a—"

A massive explosion cut him off.

A hydrogen cell somewhere in the airship exploded, detonating with the apocalyptic, thunderous *whoosh* of burning gas. Buckle saw the fog and clouds light up momentarily illuminated by the fiery geyser that had just erupted out of the port flank of his airship.

The force of the blast rippled along the rigid frame of the *Pneumatic Zeppelin* and threw everyone in the piloting gondola to starboard. Had he not already established a firm grip on the binnacle, Buckle would have been dashed to the deck like nearly everyone else. Two pressure meters on the hydrogen board burst in fiery pops of splintering glass.

Nero lunged back to his station. "Compartment nine no reading! Hydrogen cells sixteen and seventeen pressures at zero! Fire teams responding!"

"Seal all feeder valves to compartment nine," Buckle ordered. He could see De Quincey and Dunn straining as they fought their shuddering rudder and elevator wheels. The *Pneumatic Zeppelin* groaned along the length of her great body and pitched over dangerously to her port side.

The whole world rolled to the left.

Buckle, clambering to keep his balance on the tilting deck, leaned into his chattertube mouthpiece. "All hands! Emergency stations! All hands! Emergency stations!" he yelled. Welly wound up the crank on the klaxon siren.

Buckle jumped beside De Quincey, throwing his strength into the rudder wheel. "Max!" Buckle yelled.

Max jumped across the deck to lend her strength, as they tried to force the wheel to the right.

Buckle pulled his left hand free and slammed the chadburn handle forward. "All ahead flank!" he yelled into the chatter- tube. He heard no response, but he knew from the vibrations of the deck that the engineers had followed his order, firing the engines up to dangerously high, and unsustainable, levels of power.

The ship still continued to roll to port. Why could he not compensate? Why could they not swing the elevators and rudder around to counter the drag and bring the airship level again? The *Pneumatic Zeppelin* was foundering, starting to fall—the blow to her left flank must have been catastrophic enough to cripple both her equilibrium and positive lift; Buckle needed lift and he needed it now.

"Blow odd water tanks one through twenty-seven!" Buckle ordered.

"Blowing water ballast, odds one through twenty-seven!" Nero shouted, whirling control wheels on the ballast board.

The ballast scuppers roared with waterfalls outside. Buckle felt the airship lighten, start to rise. "Damage report!"

It was then that the *Pneumatic Zeppelin* shook with a mighty groan, shivering so hard it rattled Buckle's teeth, and plunged toward the fogbound earth with such a violent spin that Buckle was suspended in a weightless state.

Buckle knew that he only had a few seconds to act.

PART THREE:

THE ISLAND

-LVIII-

THE LOCOMOTIVE CANNON

THE UNIVERSE CAME UNHINGED IN the dark. Buckle planted his boots against the bulkhead as Max clenched the rudder wheel with him, her lithe body pressed hard against his side. The *Pneumatic Zeppelin* spun, blurring the eyes under a cacophony of noise, her superstructure groaning, spars screeching, wires snapping asunder and switching through the girders and firewalls, ropes parting with violent pops, lanterns lurching at oil-splashing angles, their flames staggering. The bridge crew, pulling themselves back to their instrument panels, hung on for dear life.

Buckle fought off vertigo, his muscles screaming, as he, De Quincey, and Max strained as one mass, trying to steer the ship in the direction of the spin—it was prudent to recover by turning with the zeppelin's own momentum and catapult out of it, rather than tear the fragile airship to pieces by forcing it back against its own spiral.

"Uncontrolled spin!" Sabrina shouted. "Two hundred feet and falling! one hundred and fifty!"

"Null out the turn!" Buckle howled, shaking off a sense of blacking out.

"Helm is not responding!" De Quincey shouted back.

"We may have lost a stabilizer!" Max yelled the words in Buckle's ear, but now they barely registered over the roar of the falling zeppelin. Max jumped to assist Dunn on the elevator wheel.

"She shall not come around in time!" Buckle answered. They had no altitude. It would only be a few seconds before the airship crashed to the fogbound earth or, more likely, tore itself apart on the way down. Buckle was surprised that the hydrogen cell explosion had not already blown them all to bits.

The fog bank rushed up to meet them. With his engines near to bursting and his propellers spinning beyond maximum revolutions, Buckle had no more power to apply. But he had to regain lift or nothing else would matter. "Jettison all ballast!" he shouted. "Blow all tanks!"

"Blow all tanks, aye!" Nero replied, yanking down a series of levers on the ballast board. "Blowing all ballast across the board!"

"One hundred feet!" Sabrina shouted.

The *Pneumatic Zeppelin* plunged into the fog bank. The world outside went gray and blank. Buckle, his stomach rolling, saw little more than a vibrating whirl of bright green boil. He heard the surging roar of the ballast water pouring out of the scuppers, and felt their spray soak the air. The water smelled like metal. Relieved of the weight of her water reserves, the zeppelin's descent was arrested; the hard yank of gravity nearly drove Buckle to his knees.

"All ballast tanks, main and emergency, empty, Captain!" Nero shouted.

"Eighty feet!" Sabrina reported.

All water-ballast tanks dumped, and their fall had slowed— but they were still falling.

"All crew engage oxygen gear! I repeat: all crew engage oxygen gear!" Sabrina shouted into the chattertube.

The crew would be fumbling with their gas masks and oxygen lines now. The bridge crew did not have time.

"Nero—flood to maximum hydro across the board," Buckle shouted. The order could prove fatal—flooding all of the gas cells to their highest pressure while he had a fire on board was asking for it—but he had no choice: going down to shipwreck in the mustard promised certain death.

"Emergency hydrogen flood!" Nero said, manhandling the master levers as he opened the feeder valves. "Across the board, aye!"

"Sixty feet," Sabrina reported. "Descent is slowing."

Buckle leaned into his chattertube hood. "Kill all lamps! Kill all lamps!" If he was going to pump hydrogen into compromised gas cells and burning decks, at the very least he would have all of the lantern flames aboard extinguished. The fires in the overworked furnaces were another matter altogether.

"Killing lamps, aye!" Welly said. He spun a copper-handled hand-crank mechanism that lowered snuffers inside the piloting gondola's lanterns, smothering the flames, leaving the crew in a muted darkness where the boil glowed a wild, primordial green.

Her water ballast dumped and gas cells bloated to near bursting, the now buoyant *Pneumatic Zeppelin* came out of her dive only inches above the mustard. The shuddering pressure in the steering wheels ceased, and Buckle and De Quincey eased the *Pneumatic Zeppelin* around, leveling out of her spin as she hurtled through the depthless fog.

"Altitude recovering. Leveling out, Captain. Forty feet altitude. Airspeed ninety-two knots." Sabrina said. "Current heading is roughly southeast."

The terrible pressure on the helm and elevators eased off. Max leapt back to her engineering station while Buckle stepped forward. De Quincey still had to lean on the rudder, pressing hard to starboard to counter a serious drag on the port flank. The *Pneumatic Zeppelin* was flying almost level, but she was flying blind and at breakneck speed, barreling through a void of fog, where the jagged remains of skyscrapers and transmission towers still lurked.

And she was heading away from home.

The *Pneumatic Zeppelin* trembled with an unnerving slackness. Buckle scanned his instruments. He had lost an unknown number of hydrogen cells on his port flank, and the *Pneumatic Zeppelin* was dangerously out of equilibrium. Too much drag to port, too much lift to starboard. Max was already on it, manipulating her systems controls.

"Altitude seventy feet and rising fast, Captain," Sabrina announced.

"Get her level, Mister Dunn! Zero bubble, if you please," Buckle said.

"Even out your hydrogen dispersal, Captain!" Smelt shouted.

Buckle realized that Smelt was still on the deck; he glanced back at the chancellor at the bottom of the companionway stairwell. Smelt straightened his uniform tunic with a stiff tug at the hem.

"Regain your equilibrium properly, damn it!" Smelt snapped.

"Mister Banerji! Get the chancellor off my bridge," Buckle shouted.

"Aye, Captain!" Banerji replied.

Smelt obeyed, turning to climb the circular staircase with Banerji at his heels. "Captain? You, Romulus Buckle, are *captain* of nothing," he said. "You are the king of thieves, but you are the *captain* of nothing."

Banerji and Smelt disappeared up the stairs.

"Well, you did steal his airship, after all," Sabrina commented dryly.

The *Pneumatic Zeppelin* trembled. She felt loose, wobbling, unstable.

"And today I may very well sink it," Buckle replied.

All of a sudden, the fog disappeared, or at least pulled back from the piloting gondola, to leave them stranded in the midst of a gaping hole in the fog bank. They were floating in the center of a large opening, like the eye of a hurricane, the walls of streaming fog whirlpooling around them. From the ground up to thirty feet, the mist was a band of dark yellow mustard; above that, the upper layer of gray sea fog soared another seventy feet.

"We are in another hole!" Sabrina shouted as she peered down her drift scope. "They are controlling the fog! The Founders can open the fog up at will somehow!"

"They have some sort of weather machine," Max stated.

"Impossible," Buckle said, but his response lacked certainty.

A *boom* resounded from below, followed by a high-pitched, shuddering *rip* that caterwauled past them very close to starboard.

"Aw, criminy!" Welly cried.

Buckle looked through the observation window at his feet, past Kellie—who had tucked herself into her cubbyhole under the instrument panel—and saw the dark, jumbled ruins of the old city below. And there, running directly beneath them, the huge black iron locomotive rocketed along the train tracks, the length of it lit up by lines of lanterns. The abandoned streets were crisscrossed with gleaming railway lines—the train could rapidly change course in any direction—and it had to be moving at least eighty miles an hour. The locomotive pulled a coal bunker and a long flatbed car, where, under the stream of white smokestack smoke, a dozen men in gas suits worked on an immense iron scaffold to reload the biggest cannon Buckle had ever seen. The cannon was a beast, no less than three feet across at the mouth of the smoldering muzzle, which was pointed straight up at them.

"Enemy below!" Buckle shouted into the chattertube. "Directly below!"

The Founders gunners had just missed the *Pneumatic Zeppelin* at point-blank range. They had probably taken a quick shot as soon as the fog gap opened, and the zeppelin, skidding along at ninety knots from its crash dive, may have crossed the sky faster than they could traverse their cannon barrel.

"Helm, get us back in the fog! Elevators, emergency ascent! Up ship," Buckle shouted.

"Aye," both De Quincey and Dunn replied.

Altitude was the best defense against the cannon, but the *Pneumatic Zeppelin* was in no condition to make a fast ascent. Dunn spun the elevator wheel and the nose of the *Pneumatic Zeppelin* rose, but she was frighteningly sluggish.

Buckle had to disappear back into the fog before the Founders could get off another shot.

The hammergun uttered its familiar *chunk-chunk-chunk*, the turret vibrating the deck under Buckle's feet. He looked down at the locomotive and saw the gunners ducking, as the cannon's spinning darts ricocheted off the gun in violent staccatos of sparks.

Keep their heads down, Geneva, Buckle thought. Good shooting.

There was a last car on the Founders train, another flatbed with a fantastic device perched atop it, a large metal dish pointing up at the sky, its interior made up of interlocking rings of thick glass lenses, all glowing with a weird mother-of-pearl whiteness.

The opening in the fog bank collapsed, the walls of mist surging back in like a tidal wave, instantly swallowing the *Pneumatic Zeppelin* in gray murk.

"Ninety feet and rising," Sabrina reported.

A cannon shot ripped through the mist. Another near miss. At least the Founders gunners could not see them anymore.

Buckle eyed his altimeter. The airship was ascending—with her ballast dumped, her hydrogen cells swollen, and her boilers roaring far beyond their safe capacity. She was nearly out of control—at least on the vertical plane—but nothing else mattered, as long as she was ascending.

A voice crackled on the chattertube. "Captain! Engines are overheating, sir!"

"Maintain speed," Buckle responded. "Just a few seconds more."

The *Pneumatic Zeppelin* burst out of the top of the fog bank, nose high, like a whale breaching out of the ocean.

"Hard to starboard and due west!" Buckle shouted, relieved to be in the open sky.

De Quincey and Dunn spun the rudder and elevator wheels, whirling Buckle's water compass to the west. The *Pneumatic Zeppelin* slowly leveled out and banked to the left, the night horizon now anchored by the floor of fog and ceiling of cloud. There was no telling how far the Founders defensive complex might extend northward under the fog bank, and Buckle did not want to run that gauntlet. Wheeling westward would take them out over the ocean and, hopefully, out of the reach of the Founders weapon systems.

Max leaned into her chattertube hood. "Damage report, by sections," she said. Voices responded, listing one emergency after another.

Buckle scanned the fog, half expecting to see the behemoth crest of one of the legendary Founders dreadnoughts rising up to engage them, seeking to pop and burn their piddling zeppelin like a gnat, leaving nothing behind but a footnote in Founders history, and a forgotten wreck in the mustard.

Bring it on, Buckle boasted to himself, planting his boots hard on the deck.

The deck of the *Pneumatic Zeppelin* shuddered ominously.

On second thought, perhaps not.

–LIX–

WHIRLPOOLS IN THE SKY

MAX'S DAMAGE REPORTS SOUNDED LIKE the eulogy for a zeppelin already gone down. "Gas cells sixteen and seventeen have exploded and compartment nine is on fire," she said. "The firewalls prevented any explosions in the adjoining sections, but the stockingmen report cell eighteen in compartment ten is damaged and possibly venting. Ten's primary valves have been sealed at the primary switching station. Fire teams are responding on buglight. All decks have switched to buglight."

Buckle nodded. At least three of the *Pneumatic Zeppelin*'s twenty-eight gas cells were out of commission: two destroyed and one venting. Buglight meant that the oil lanterns were doused shipwide, and the zookeeper was loading up special glass lanterns with fireflies—whose bioluminescence burned cold, and thus posed no threat in the presence of hydrogen leaks—and passing them out. The wounded, plowing airship, dragging, crippled in her lift, rammed forward by her overdriven propellers, was trying to roll to her left; De Quincey had to keep the rudder angled to maintain an even keel.

Buckle watched the unbroken, wavy surface of the fog bank 250 feet below. It seemed so tranquil now, in the minute since they had broken the surface, but he had kicked the Founders' bee's nest beneath, and something more might well be coming up out of the fog after them.

Buckle figured all he had to do was make it to the sea: once off the coast and out of range of the Founders cannons, he could turn north and make the long run for home.

An area of the fog bank, perhaps two hundred yards in diameter, suddenly shimmered a weird blue, as if every one of the billions of moisture droplets inside it lit a tiny candle and set to dancing. The sparkling fog opened into a whirlpool, exposing the circular patch of earth at the bottom of its throat. And on the ground was a locomotive—the same one as before, or perhaps another, Buckle could not tell—its lanterns vibrating with speed, the smokestack belching smoke. The strange dish machine on the last car shimmered madly with its mother-of-pearl glow.

And the huge cannon was pointing straight up at the *Pneumatic Zeppelin*.

"Evasive maneuvers!" Buckle shouted.

De Quincey spun the rudder wheel to the left, letting the damaged airship slide into the yaw to port as it wanted to, allowing a faster maneuver than the flying machine could normally make.

The walls of the whirlpool shaft flashed.

"They're firing!" Sabrina yelled.

Buckle gritted his teeth. "Dive!"

Dunn whipped the elevator wheel around toward its full-dive position.

The *Pneumatic Zeppelin* trembled, trying to descend, but without her water ballast, she could not defeat the lighter-than-air hydrogen.

"Emergency vent, forty percent," Buckle said. "Crash dive."

"Crash dive, aye!" Nero shouted. "Emergency vent! Forty percent!" He frantically wound wheel after wheel on his hydrogen board, dumping 40 percent of the hydrogen from every gas cell on the airship.

"Crash dive! All hands prepare for crash dive!" Max shouted into the chattertube. "Hang on!"

The whistling Founders cannonball went wide, passing through the air where the nose of the *Pneumatic Zeppelin* had been not five seconds before, but close enough for its shockwave to buffet the envelope with a spattering rattle.

Jettisoning hydrogen at a stupendous rate, the *Pneumatic Zeppelin*'s nose swung down as she slumped into an accelerating descent. This was what Buckle wanted. The higher he was, the easier he was to spot from the Founders' tubular spyholes; if he was down low, just skimming the surface of the fog bank, then the Founders would have to open a hole right under him in order to see the ship. The rate of dive increased as more hydrogen was released; the superstructure, already compromised by holes, explosions, and fires, began to groan under the stresses of the vertical drop.

The fog whirlpool sucked inward and disappeared in the usual blanket of gray.

"The hole collapsed again," Sabrina noted. "Looks like whatever they're doing to part the fog, they can't maintain it for long."

"Captain! Engine room!" The chattertube squawked with the voice of Elliot Yardbird, the *Pneumatic Zeppelin*'s engine officer. "Boilers are overheating, Captain!"

Buckle had expected the message. "Maintain all ahead flank, Yardbird!" he replied. "Maintain speed!"

"Aye, Captain!" came the response.

"One hundred and thirty feet!" Sabrina reported.

"Level out at one hundred feet," Buckle said.

Dunn wound the elevator wheel back to neutral.

"Leveling out at one hundred, aye!" Nero responded, cranking valve wheels, slowly transferring hydrogen from the reserve tanks into the cells to arrest their descent.

The *Pneumatic Zeppelin*'s nose lifted as she came out of the dive and barreled along the ceiling of the fog bank, hurtling along at eighty-five knots, the prow of the piloting gondola nipping the upper tendrils of mist.

"Ballast, what is the status of our hydrogen reserves?" Max asked.

"Forty-five percent, all tanks, across the board, ma'am." Nero replied.

"Very well," Max said.

"Here we go!" Buckle shouted as he saw the fog swirl open about three hundred feet ahead. "Helm, hard to port!"

"Hard to port, aye!" De Quincey swung the rudder wheel to port and the *Pneumatic Zeppelin* responded quickly enough to glide past the northern fringe of the whirlpool, which vanished after they passed.

"Take us due south, Mister De Quincey," Buckle said, watching the boil-lit water compass in the binnacle.

Two firefly-filled lanterns were lowered from the keel above, the buglights slipping down their chains in silence, swinging in the slipstream, alive with the fluttering white-orange light cast from the abdomens of the fireflies swarming within.

Buckle took ahold of the chadburn handle and dialed it back to all ahead full, ringing the bell. "Engineering, all ahead full," he said into the chattertube.

The chadburn bell rang as the sister dial swung to match the bridge dial. "All ahead full, Captain," Elliot Yardbird's concerned voice responded. "The boilers are severely overheating, sir. And our water coolant reserves are near empty."

Buckle understood the note of concern. They had dumped the blue-water ballast tanks, which were also used as the reserves to draw upon for boiler coolant. Overheated boilers could easily explode, and the engine crews, caught in eruptions of iron and superheated steam, rarely fared well.

"Ensign Yardbird, shut down boilers one and three, and transfer their coolant to the remaining three," Buckle ordered. "I repeat, shut down one and three. Reroute coolant to remaining three boilers."

"Shutting down engines one and three. Rerouting coolant. Aye, Cap'n," Yardbird answered.

Buckle cursed under his breath. Having to shut down boiler number two, Old Smoky, earlier now loomed large in their predicament.

Welly glanced back at Buckle. "Lookouts report a hole opening, Captain," he said. "Eight o'clock low."

Buckle stepped to the port gunwale and peered back toward the stern where the gaping maw of a new whirlpool spun about two hundred yards behind; as he had hoped, the Founders were expecting the *Pneumatic Zeppelin* to run inland for home, and not south to the sea.

"It appears they have lost us, Captain," Sabrina said.

"It appears," Buckle replied.

"Fire control to bridge," Ivan's voice rattled down the chattertube. "My fire teams have no water pressure! We need a white water transfer immediately!"

Buckle glanced at Max. Blue water, used for the fire system, was the designation for water ballast and boiler coolant; white water was clean water for drinking, cooking, and bathing; black water was the noxious stuff, those pipes being used for sewage, chemicals, and refuse flushing. They had dumped all of their blue water ballast, except what had been in the boilers at the time, leaving the overdriven engines dangerously dry after they had evaporated much of what was left in their boiler tanks. The fire system relied on the blue-water tanks as its reserves, but those were gone. White water could be transferred to the fire system but to do so—and maintain pressure with minimum bleed—would require a complicated series of valve deflections at the main switching station.

"Reroute white water to the fire system, Max."

"Yes, Captain," Max replied, already halfway up the companionway.

"We have a lot of hot spots up here!" Ivan shouted on the chattertube. "I need more hands—all the hands I can get!"

Buckle jumped to the chattertube hood. "Reserve fire teams report to compartment nine, on the double!" Lionel Garcia, the apprentice navigator—and reserve fire-team member—dashed up the staircase.

Buckle wanted to punch a bulwark. He may have escaped the locomotive cannon and its fogsucking machine, but now he was limping along on three overheated boilers, holed and burning, low on hydrogen and fifty miles from home. And while the white-water reserves would douse the fires for a while, there was not a lot of it.

They would make it, though. It would not be pretty, but they would make it.

Sabrina glanced back from her station. "Captain, we are approximately ten minutes from the southern coast at current speed."

"First Lieutenant, you have the bridge," Buckle said. "Once you reach Catalina, turn northwest and take us out over the Soup. We shall give the Founders a wide berth on our way home. I am going to lend the midshipmen a hand upstairs."

Sabrina stepped to the captain's station as Welly took over the navigator's chair. "Aye, Captain," she said. "And please do not shut off any more of my boilers, thank you."

"Wouldn't dream of it, my dear Serafim," Buckle replied.

‑LX‑

FIRE AND WHITE WATER

As BUCKLE RACED UP THE iron staircase from the piloting gondola, he dreaded what he was about to find inside the envelope of the *Pneumatic Zeppelin*. The kind of damage they had taken was not the kind you could repair in flight. And draining two of the hot engine boilers of their water coolant—especially after they had been run above the red line for so long—was a good way to end up with a catastrophic explosion.

It did not matter. He had to risk it.

Fire aboard a hydrogen airship was always the first priority. The fire had to be put out. Then he could worry about boilers.

Buckle leapt up into the keel corridor. He was immediately hit by gusts of hot wind, thick with swarms of swirling red embers, that rocked the buglights and whistled through the miles of wires and rigging. Water streamed down from above, weaving jerkily in the wind currents, as if it were raining somewhere up in the vast, vaulted darkness of the superstructure girders and gas cells. Overhead, above it all, the interior of the airship envelope glowed yellow and orange as it fluttered, reflecting the fires still burning within.

It was the storms of embers that worried Buckle the most. Red-hot embers drifting mere inches from the hydrogen gas cells—the thin goldbeater's skins that despite their rubber stockings, were always suspect for leaks.

Buckle sprinted to the nearest companionway and charged up to the Hydro deck. He found three crew members on the Hydro catwalk, having popped the hatch on a ballast tank, their faces drenched with sweat, cranking a hand pump to draw the last few gallons of blue water into a fire-hose line.

"Good work, old salts! Throw in some spit if you can!" Buckle shouted as he passed, hopping onto the next staircase and climbing two steps at a time up to the Axial corridor. He had his head up despite the stinging embers and buffeting wind, watching the awful glow of the fires rise and fall across the ceiling skin of the *Pneumatic Zeppelin*. It was dark in the shafts between the cells, and the illumination of the firefly lamps, wobbling in streams of sparkling water and tornados of churning red embers, was ghostly.

As Buckle climbed through the decks and raced along catwalks he could make out Ivan's voice, both urgent and calm, cursing the world. He heard the goat, Victoria, bleating, along with the sounds of pigeons cooing and hens clucking unhappily. There were the voices of men mixed in, voices shouting back and forth from above.

Buckle clambered up to the Castle deck and raced along the catwalk in compartment eight, ducking through the firewall hatch and into compartment nine. He nearly ran into the backs of two crewmen who, blacked with soot, gripped a fire hose that only dribbled water.

Buckle swerved past the crewmen and his boot plunged off into space, dropping into a fire-laced void where the catwalk grating should have been. Hands snatched Buckle by the collar and yanked him back; he found himself in the burly clutches of the two men manning the fire hose.

"Look out, Cap'n!" the bigger fellow, a boilerman named Nicholas Faraday, shouted over the howling wind. "There ain't no deck there anymore, Cap'n."

"Thanks, Nicholas," Buckle said, regaining his balance.

"We've got no water pressure, Cap'n," Faraday shouted.

"You will in a few seconds. Hold on!" Buckle yelled. He stepped to the catwalk rail and looked down. Both of the gigantic gas cells in section nine were gone: the gaping maw of the blasted compartment, twelve stories of metal catwalks, some of them bent and mangled, poked out of the firewall hatches below; shreds of the goldbeater's cells hung everywhere, burning a translucent purple. The portside envelope was ripped wide open in a towering vertical slash, revealing the clouds beyond.

The damage to the envelope was daunting in its scope: over one hundred and twenty feet high, and thirty feet across at the widest. The edges of the flapping rent glowed orange, burning, brightening as the slipstream sucked wave after wave of embers down into the interior of the airship.

The copper firewalls were still intact, and they had surely saved the *Pneumatic Zeppelin* from oblivion: bolted-in sheets that separated every compartment from ceiling to keel, the firewalls were designed to isolate any hydrogen explosion and funnel the volcanic force of the blast outward and away from the rest of the ship. But there were always openings between the compartments—tube ports and catwalk hatchways—so sometimes the firewalls worked and sometimes they didn't.

It was a miracle that the *Pneumatic Zeppelin* was still there.

"You got some water there for me, Cap'n?" Ivan shouted, hurrying along the catwalk, his goggles and coat encrusted with ash, his ushanka smoking in spots where embers had landed. "We're fresh out and still burning."

"Any second now, Ivan," Buckle said. "Max is on it."

"Never trust a Martian!" Ivan shouted over the wind, though Buckle knew Ivan was glad Max was on it.

"You are truly an arse, Gorky," Buckle replied.

"Are we going to find a place to put in, or try to make it home?" Ivan asked.

"Home," Buckle replied. "I don't want to overnight in a strange port—not with the passengers we have aboard."

Ivan grinned, his white and gold teeth abrupt against his blackened skin. "Good! I have a date, you know."

"Holly?" Buckle asked, knowing full well that the subject of Ivan's affections was Holly Churchill, the winsome daughter of the town mayor, a girl whom Ivan hadn't stopped talking about for days, since she had agreed to attend the Crankshaft Theater's performance of *Golem* with him.

"Ah, who else? Are there any other girls in the world? I don't notice them anymore," Ivan said, then scratched his head under his hat. "I could really use some water."

"In a moment," Buckle said. *Come on, Max.*

A muffled *whoosh* raced down the fire-hose lines as the white water shot along their lengths, plumping them up like fat, wiggling boa constrictors.

"There we go, boys!" Ivan shouted, jumping to assist Faraday and his partner with their hose. "Let's snuff this campfire before it snuffs us!"

Ivan's fire team slapped open the hose nozzle and it erupted with a stream of water that made clouds of smoke blossom below.

"Make it count!" Buckle yelled. "It is not going to last for long!"

"Aye!" Ivan answered, as his fire team and the teams below went to work on the compartment, judiciously dousing long stretches of flames with each pass of the hose, raising a churning fog of steam and sizzling embers.

"This should do it, Cap'n!" Ivan yelled over the thunder of wind and steam.

"It had better," Buckle shouted back. "Or we are going to have to use our pissers on it!"

-LXI-

MORPHINE

MAX STEPPED BACK FROM THE bank of brass-handled valve levers at the main switching station, scrutinizing the selectors she had chosen, making sure that she had found the most effective way to route the white water into the fire-system pipes. A gust of cold air blew past her and vanished down the corridor. She shivered. It was hot here, just forward of the engineering bay and soaked with the heat of it, and the rogue blast of freezing air chilled the sweat slicking her back.

She stepped back, watching the pressure gauges as the rerouted water coursed into the fire system, wiping her hands impatiently—her airship was damaged and needed her attentions.

Ensign Yardbird stepped up to Max's shoulder. He released the deep-throated huffing sound he made when he required attention. He had not had to step far from his station—the boilers and furnaces rumbled in the next compartment no more than twenty feet away—and his hobnailed boots clanging on the gratings announced his approach.

"Yes, Mister Yardbird?" Max asked, without taking her eyes off the switching board. She hoped he had something urgent to discuss—the man was a fount of unnecessary chatter.

"Begging your pardon, Missy Max, but are we going to attempt a scoop?" the rough but polite Yardbird asked.

Max turned and looked at Yardbird. He was a powerful, barrel-chested man; not fat, but doughy. He was stripped to the waist like all of the stokers and boilermen who toiled in the tropical confines of the blazing-hot engine room, and his hairy flesh, glistening with sweat, steamed in the cooler air of the switching station. He had the round face of the Yardbird family, round and big-cheeked, and his cheeks were adorned with brown sideburns that he kept oiled at the edges. Max liked the man, despite his penchant for small talk: he was smart but preferred the simple, laughed often and heartily, spoke the truth as he saw it, and seemed incapable of pettiness. She hated being called "Missy Max," but Yardbird was the only one who addressed her that way, with respectful affection, and so she, against her better judgment, allowed it because he was such a good officer in her section.

"No, Mister Yardbird," Max replied, pressing a valve lever that looked as if it was not cocked all of the way down. The *Pneumatic Zeppelin* had a scoop tube that they could lower into a freshwater lake or river, and pump water aboard to replenish ballast or coolant reserves. It was a bad idea to scoop salt-laden seawater into the airship, unless one was in a dire emergency. "Are one and three shut down yet?"

"One and three are snuffed, ma'am," Yardbird said. "But the boilers are still white-hot, and the others are running very low on coolant. If there's any white water left after the fires, ma'am, I would suggest we pump it back into the boilers lickety-split."

"That is my intention, Mister Yardbird. I assure you that I am not interested in losing a boiler."

"Aye, Missy Max," Yardbird replied. He turned and, boots clanging, strode back into the streaming hot air of the engine room.

Satisfied that she had wrung every last ounce of white water she could into the fire-control system, Max entered the main keel corridor and strode toward the bow with long strides, wanting to make a quick inspection of the ship's damages. Crew members dodged past her along the corridor, some carrying muskets, others lugging water buckets as they searched for ember fires, all hunched against the tunneling wind that still battered them. The firefly lanterns banged against their posts, the gasbags rubbed against their retaining wires with imperious squeals, the superstructure groaned, all informing the chief engineer of the terrible stresses they were being subjected to—terrible stresses they were not designed to take.

If the *Pneumatic Zeppelin* was going to make it home in one piece, she was going to have to make Buckle slow the ship down to a crawl, figure out how to deflect the interior gusts out of the envelope, recalculate fuel consumption, reduce drag, and recalibrate the flying instruments to compensate.

Pluteus stepped out of the sick-bay door as Max approached. She saw exhaustion and sadness in his face in the unguarded moment before he noticed her and tightened his cheeks with his usual steel. "Chief Engineer," he said with a nod.

Max stopped in front of Pluteus. He stank of sweat and gunpowder, and his bronze breastplate was spattered with a dark brown patina of dried blood. Although he had always been the good sort of uncle, she knew that he had never liked her much. She knew he did not like her because she had Martian blood pumping through her veins. She knew that he disliked seeing her black, kaleidoscopic Martian eyes, and the Martian stripes on her pale skin, in Balthazar's house, where Balthazar, his beloved cousin, called her "daughter."

"It is good to see you on your feet, General Pluteus," Max said. "I had been informed that you were injured."

"My bruises are meaningless," Pluteus replied. "I lost eight men today. Eight men. All the rest are wounded in some way or other, as well, though Surgeon Fogg tells me they will all survive."

"I am sorry for your losses. I know that every one of them is a son to you."

The grizzled infantry commander seemed taken aback—he and Max rarely conversed—and there was a sudden softness in his eyes toward her that she had rarely seen before. "I appreciate your concern, Max. We know it is worth every sacrifice to save Balthazar."

Max nodded quickly. She always felt a little unsure of her-self with Pluteus. She had few memories of her parents, but somehow Pluteus profoundly reminded her of her father, who was Martian. That would have burned Pluteus's arse for sure, because he hated Martians. So Max had grown up with a soft spot in her soul for Pluteus, a little Martian girl who forever sought a glimpse of her lost father in a human who despised her. And she had always felt vulnerable in his presence because of it. Even now, as an adult woman, she realized that she was still haunted by a deep-rooted need to engage with Pluteus, make him look at her and listen to her—though in reality she avoided him as best she could.

"Lieutenant, can you go into sick bay and order Lady Andromeda to accept medical attention?" Pluteus asked. "She is refusing, saying she will entertain no doctoring until everyone else has been properly attended to. But she is badly hurt."

Max did not want to deal with a difficult clan leader in the infirmary—not right now. "I am on my way to make a damage inspection. I can—"

"Just order her!" Pluteus growled, the softness disappearing from his eyes, replaced by a distant stare. "It will take ten seconds. You are second mate. She must obey your orders aboard ship." He turned and strode down the corridor toward the bow. "I must make my report to Captain Buckle."

Max stared after Pluteus. She was thankful that his back was turned, that he could not see the pinkish glow her eyes were letting seep into her goggles—not that he would know what it meant if he did anyway. "Very good, General Pluteus," she whispered, and stepped into the sick-bay hatchway.

The sick bay was lit by a great raft of buglights overhead, and they provided a flood of bright, pulsing light. There were more buglights over the ten beds, each one loaded with a wounded Crankshaft or Alchemist trooper. Others, with lighter injuries, sat in chairs or leaned against the bulkheads. Pieces of armor and leather gear, some of it bloody, were strewn on the floor. The room was strangely quiet, the kind of quiet that vibrated the air around people in pain who were gritting their teeth and toughing it out. Surgeon Fogg and Nurse Nightingale rushed about, pulling jags of shrapnel from ripped flesh, wrapping bloody bandages, applying chloroform, and sinking needles of morphine into the muscles of thighs and shoulders.

Andromeda lay on the bed against the forward bulwark, with Scorpius and Kepler hovering over her. She wore a clean infirmary blouse with small white buttons on the cuffs and collar, and blood from her numerous wounds was beginning to seep through spots in the cotton. She looked deathly pale and fragile.

Max removed her pilot helmet and tucked it under her arm as she arrived at Andromeda's bed. "Lady Andromeda, may I please have a word?"

Scorpius stepped to the end of the bed, blocking Andromeda from Max. "What is your business, Martian?" he asked.

Andromeda's weak voice rose from the pillow. "Scorpius, let the officer pass."

Scorpius moved aside.

Max took a step forward. Andromeda looked up at her, one eye bright red with blood. "I am the chief engineer," Max said. "I have been informed that you are refusing treatment, Lady Andromeda."

"Just temporarily, until the others are taken care of." Andromeda sighed, but the way she blinked, the clench of skin at the corners of her eyes, betrayed her true condition to the highly sensitive Max—Andromeda was in considerable pain.

"You are aware that you are the priority," Max said.

"Perhaps, but my discomfort is minimal," Andromeda countered. "I offer you and your crew the most sincere gratitude for your assistance in my rescue along with your Balthazar."

"It is an honor," Max said, ready to depart. "Shall I tell the surgeon you are ready to see him now?"

"What is your name, Chief Engineer?" Andromeda asked.

Max hesitated. She never like pleasantries. "My name is Max."

"Very good. Come, Max, please, sit here beside me," Andromeda said, motioning to a chair beside her bed.

Max did not move. "I only have a moment, Lady Andromeda."

"Of course," Andromeda replied, and patted the chair seat with her hand. The invitation was not going to be withdrawn.

Max reluctantly sat down. "With all due respect, Lady Andromeda, you must allow our medical officers to tend to you."

"That sounds like an order to me," Surgeon Fogg said, stepping past Scorpius and Kepler to stand at the opposite side of the bunk. "Lady Andromeda, you have suffered a severe concussion and multiple shrapnel wounds, and you are quite possibly bleeding internally. I need to start treating you now."

Nurse Shelley Nightingale, a lovely young brunette, arrived at Fogg's shoulder with a large syringe full of yellow fluid.

"Wait! Wait!" Scorpius blustered. "What is *that*?"

"Morphine, to reduce her pain," Fogg answered, getting impatient with Kepler, who had just blocked his way. "Every trooper in here has been tended to. You both risk her life if you delay her treatment any longer."

"I shall submit myself to your care, good surgeon, if Max here will do me a favor," Andromeda said.

"If I can," Max said, hiding her severe annoyance with the game the Alchemist leader seemed to be playing.

"Can you please remove your goggles?" Andromeda asked.

Max blinked. This was an odd request. She could take the goggles off, often for half an hour or more before any irritation set in, but no one, no one had ever asked her to remove them before. Her first instinct was to refuse.

"Please. Just for a moment," Andromeda asked, reading Max's mind.

Max raised her hands halfway to her face and paused. This Alchemist woman, still possessing a profound charismatic radiance, even though she was disheveled and injured, made her want to obey—and she did not like that. But she flipped the switch to drain the aqueous humor into the reserve chamber of her helmet, and removed the goggles anyway.

Max wiped her wet eyes with her sleeve and blinked. The appearance of things was always a bit odd right after she removed her goggles. The world, crisper around the edges and less magnified, also seemed starker. Surgeon Fogg was already bending over Andromeda's bed, sinking the needle into her arm and pushing down the plunger.

If Andromeda noticed the needle, she did not wince, nor take her eyes off Max. "You are half Martian, yes?"

"Yes."

Andromeda raised her hand to touch Max's cheek. Max flinched. No one, especially not a stranger, had touched her face in a very long time.

"May I?" Lady Andromeda asked softly.

Max was arrested by Andromeda's eyes—so violet they were almost black, impossibly iridescent. They reminded her of her brother's eyes. "It is not necessary," Max said. "But if you must."

Andromeda brushed her fingers along Max's cheek; it was a barely perceptible touch, soft as a butterfly's wing beat, the fingertips cool on her skin.

It took a lot to make Max feel embarrassed, but with Scorpius, Fogg, and Nightingale leaning in on top of them, this came close.

Andromeda drew her hand back, folding her long fingers into her palm. "Make me a promise, Lieutenant," she said.

"Lady Andromeda, with all due respect, I need to go," Max replied.

Andromeda's eyes fluttered, the drowse of morphine soaking through her veins. She whispered something. Max leaned forward and turned her sensitive ear toward Andromeda's mouth.

"Never let the world hurt you too much," Andromeda breathed.

Max looked at Andromeda; her eyes were now closed, the lids a shade paler than her cheeks, the skin as fine as porcelain. "I do not," Max whispered, then stood up and replaced her goggles.

"Now if you will excuse me, I have urgent work to do," Fogg announced, motioning for Scorpius, Kepler, and Max to step away from Andromeda's bedside.

Max turned on her heel and strode to the infirmary door, flipping the switch to refill her goggles with their soothing liquid. She was impatient to begin her vital assessment of the *Pneumatic Zeppelin*'s damages. Her short visits with Pluteus and Andromeda had set her back four minutes, by her calculations, and set her insides in a knot.

But somehow she knew that it was not time wasted.

–LXII–

THE ZOOKEEPER

HIGH ON THE EAGLE DECK catwalk, where the roof of the *Pneumatic Zeppelin*'s canvas envelope rippled overhead, and the hulking gray backs of the gas cells loomed at each quarter, Buckle felt a little bit relieved: there were no fires up top, no flames visible along the entire length of the deck.

The pale, swirling yellow light of Buckle's firefly lantern glowed on the copper lattices of the self-sealing stockings that sheathed each and every gasbag aboard the *Pneumatic Zeppelin*. The stockings, formally known as Abraham Sangster's Hydrogen Cell Self-Sealing Apparatus, were massive jackets of thin rubber, designed to instantly close up any hole in the event of a breach, thus preventing the highly volatile mixing of oxygen with the hydrogen gas. The miles of metal latticework spiderwebbing the rubber skins operated on well-oiled gears ratcheted up to high tension, and were so taut that they often emitted a low, vibrating hum.

The stockings had not sealed properly when the Founders cannonball had struck compartment nine, but Buckle was not surprised—the mechanisms had been overwhelmed. The damn ball was the size of a hog, perhaps one hundred pounds, requiring a monster cannon far too heavy for even the biggest zeppelins to carry.

Buckle stepped down the catwalk to the hatchway of the compartment-nine blast shield, slowing as the cold torrent of air pouring in from the sky battered him. He peered into the compartment: the section of the Eagle deck catwalk spanning the chasm was melted, barely more than a skeleton of its original self. Great chimneys of steam ballooned up from the extinguished fires below and vanished when they hit the slipstream. The envelope skin overhead was completely gone, the fluttering edges of the blast hole doused to black, only occasionally gasping out a few handfuls of embers into the night sky with its endless blanket of clouds.

Buckle did not have a good view of the ground. Surely they must be clear of the shoreline and over open water by now. He needed to return to the bridge. He turned from the wind-battered hatch and strode toward the companionway stairwell.

Buckle halted, surprised by the sudden appearance of the zookeeper, Osprey Fowler, on the catwalk; he had not seen Osprey at first. She was thin and lanky beneath a long leather coat loaded with instruments of animal husbandry, and often decorated with white-green splashes of guano. She possessed an olive-skinned, short-nosed beauty, a beguiling loveliness that she hid, lurking under her broad-brimmed hat, goggles, and the cascading tangle of brown hair she allowed to hide much of her face.

"Aye, Captain Buckle," Osprey said as Buckle approached, her goggles glowing with the yellow swirl of Buckle's fireflies, a pink-headed pigeon hopping from one foot to another on her shoulder, scrutinizing Buckle with one eye and then the other. "The animals, Captain, the fire—it frightens them, makes them restless. Did you see that all the wugglebats are gone? They flew away."

"Like rats fleeing a sinking sea vessel, eh?" Buckle said. "I hope they don't know something we don't."

Osprey shook her head. "They are clinging to the outer envelope. The colony will return once they realize the fires are out."

"Do you need something, Osprey?" Buckle asked, both annoyed and intrigued. Osprey rarely spoke at length to anyone, obviously more comfortable with her animals than people. Such was often the hallmark of her strange breed. Every zeppelin had a zookeeper aboard, a crew member who was an expert in homing pigeons and the menagerie of shipboard beasts that the airship carried—fireflies, goats, dogs, cats, chickens, falcons, horses, and so on.

"Oh, no, my Captain," Osprey replied. "I need nothing. What you need is for someone to tell you that you have been lied to."

"Lied to?" Buckle repeated stupidly, glaring at Osprey. He did not have time for her riddles. It struck him as very strange for her to pick such a moment to come to him, to be speaking to him this way at all. But despite her oddness, Buckle had never witnessed a time when either her intelligence or her judgment failed her. "I don't have time for puzzles, Osprey," Buckle announced, preparing to sidestep her.

"Captain..." Osprey said. She stepped in front of Buckle and planted her hand, the small fingers thick with rings of various metals, on his chest. He stopped cold. Osprey had never attempted to block him, or even touch him before. There was one more element to Osprey Fowler that was unnerving: although she would never speak of it, Balthazar was certain that she had once had an audience with the Oracle—the mythical being whom many sought and few ever found—and was told something of the future.

"Who has lied to me, Zookeeper?" Buckle asked. He would give her one quick opportunity to spit out what she wanted to say.

Osprey removed her hand from Buckle's chest and lifted her goggles over the brim of her hat, revealing her startling eyes, the brown irises speckled with gold flecks, luring eyes that always felt eerily like some sort of trap to Buckle, like a diamond resting in the center of a spider's web. Those eyes locked on to his. "Your sister is alive, Captain. Elizabeth lives."

A snake twisted in Buckle's throat. The idea of a false hope made him angry. "How do you know this?" he snapped. "Elizabeth died at Tehachapi."

"Her body was never found."

"She was incinerated like many of the others. In the fires."

Osprey leaned forward, managing to whisper despite the howl of wind between them. "Elizabeth did not die. She was taken." As she spoke she pressed a small object into the palm of Buckle's hand. "And Balthazar knows."

"Balthazar?" Buckle mumbled. He looked down at the cylinder in his hand—it was a pigeon-message scroll—and when he looked up, Osprey was gone. He was alone, the gusting wind pulling at him, rippling the canvas above, swinging the buglight on its creaking handle as he held it.

His sister, Elizabeth, alive? This was not possible. And if she was alive, and Balthazar knew, what reason could Balthazar have for not telling him? And why, of all moments to pick, would the mysteriously oddball Osprey Fowler choose to tell him this secret now? Buckle jammed the scroll into his coat pocket and jumped to the stairwell. He cast the zookeeper's incendiary whispers from his mind; he would disentangle her mystery later. The *Pneumatic Zeppelin* needed his full attention right now.

Buckle arrived on the Castle deck as Ivan, assisted by Faraday, was climbing into a harness to rappel down into the doused compartment vault, now a steaming chimney, with hot smoke and vapors tornadoing up and out of the gusting hole overhead.

"Fires are out as far as we can tell from here, Cap'n!" Ivan yelled. "Fire teams are on patrol. I'm going down to tamp out a few hot spots."

"Good work," Buckle answered. "I shall be on the bridge."

Suddenly the warning klaxon wound up to a wail, hand-cranked into a chattertube hood in the command gondola.

"Battle stations! Battle stations!" Sabrina's voice roared from the chattertube speakers. "Steampipers below! Lower anti-boarding nets! All hands prepare to repel boarders! I repeat. Steampipers below! All hands prepare to repel boarders!"

~LXIII~

STEAMPIPERS

BUCKLE LOOKED UP AT THE sky. Nothing but moonlit clouds loomed beyond the towering rip in the *Pneumatic Zeppelin*'s envelope. He heard the deep rattle of the antiboarding nets being lowered far below.

"Steampipers—I'll be damned," Ivan said, tossing his lowering harness aside and checking on his wugglebat, Pushkin, who had popped his head up from his breast pocket.

"Aye," Buckle said. Steampipers were soldiers with steam-engine contraptions strapped to their backs that made them capable of flight, at least for short periods of time. They were very effective at boarding low-flying airships. The Imperial clan had steampipers; it was not a surprise to Buckle that the Founders had them as well.

"Ivan. Get below and get your men armed," Buckle said.

"Aye. Good luck, Cap'n," Ivan answered, hurrying away with Faraday.

Buckle decided to stay where he was. Steampipers preferred assaulting zeppelins from the top, where there were fewer defenders, gaining a foothold and the advantage of the high ground for their battle with the crew. And once they saw the hole in the side of the *Pneumatic Zeppelin*, they would most surely make it a focal point of their attack.

Buckle reloaded his pistol, ripping the top off a cartridge and pouring the blackbang powder into the barrel, followed by the wadding, ball, and ramrod. The siren continued wailing. He eyed the sky again. He saw nothing. There was commotion on the lower decks as the crew dashed to the armories and took up their battle stations. The *Pneumatic Zeppelin* was not carrying marines, but the Ballblasters and Alchemist troopers—the ones still standing—would be of great assistance in the defense.

Buckle heard the sound of the pneumatic cannon, its familiar *thack thack thack* hammering below. Standard cannons were useless against the highly maneuverable steampipers, but the hammergun, with its high rate of fire and fast barrel traverse, could find its mark.

Pistol ready, Buckle also drew his sword. He edged forward, as far as he dared, to the edge of the mangled catwalk, peering into the fog bank two hundred feet below.

Four streaks of white light rose in the vapors like upside-down falling stars, plummeting up. Four steampipers.

Buckle turned to shout a warning into the chattertube station, but it was gone, blasted away. His call of warning was not required anyway—he could hear the voices of crew members ringing out on the adjacent stations, announcing steampipers sighted at the bow, stern, and both flanks between.

Musket fire blazed across the lower decks as the crew opened up on the attackers. Buckle looked down at the fog bank again. The four steampipers were almost at his altitude, coming on at great speed, zigzagging as they charged, and they were heading straight for him. They had seen the smoldering outline of the compartment-nine breach, a giant red-rimmed doorway into the interior of the airship. Beneath the steampipers, the fog bank glowed with dozens more streaking fire trails.

There was a flash, blue white, in the midst of the four ascending steampipers. One was thrown into a breakneck spin for two seconds before his steampack boiler exploded in a brilliant yellow flash, blowing the flying machine and its pilot to a thousand flaming smithereens that showered down and vanished in the fog bank beneath.

The hammergun had scored a lucky hit.

The three other steampipers throttled up, comet tails brightening, coming on like gangbusters, mere seconds away from the hole where Buckle stood.

Buckle tightened his fingers around the worn, leather-wrapped grip of his sword.

The leading Founders steampiper skidded into the mouth of the envelope gap, feet forward, almost on his back, swinging his steampack around to halt his trajectory. His steampack funnels spewed streams of white flame that forced Buckle to duck or be roasted. The other two steampipers sailed in behind the leader, one angling up and out of sight above the Eagle deck, the other veering inside the envelope and hurtling off in the direction of the bow.

Rolling to his left—Buckle could not roll right, lest he plummet off the sheared end of the catwalk—he jumped to his feet with pistol aimed. The steampiper leader and his spewing contraption hovered over the smoldering compartment vault. The moonlight gleamed on his brass helmet—its rectangular eye slits dark with smoked glass—and on his silver cuirass, emblazoned with the Founders phoenix.

The steampiper snatched a sawed-off musket from his right hip and swung it to bear on Buckle.

Buckle fired his pistol at point-blank range, ignoring the zeppelineers' oath never to discharge a weapon inside a hydrogen airship. Through the burp of powder smoke, he saw a flash at the cheek of the steampiper's helmet as it deflected the ball.

With the steampiper leader's musket muzzle now leveled at him, Buckle tensed to lunge, but there was little he could do to make the fellow miss.

Blam! The steampiper leader jerked sideways, the tunic cloth on his right shoulder erupting with a burst of stuffing and pinkish blood; his musket went off, the flash nearly blinding Buckle, but the shot missed, the ball ringing off the safety rail mere inches from Buckle's waist.

Buckle snapped his head to the left. Sergeant Scully, musket barrel smoking, raced toward him along the catwalk, with four crewmen close at his heels. Scully yanked a pistol from his belt and aimed. "Take that, you fogsucking scum!" he bawled, and fired again. *Blam!*

Ballblasters were no slouches when it came to killing their enemies. Having spun the well-armored steampiper leader with his first shot, Scully sent the second pistol ball into the unprotected armpit hole of the cuirass, drilling the man through the chest. The dead steampiper leader's engines cut out as he went limp and dropped, vanishing into the steaming maw of compartment number nine.

"What's this, Captain?" Scully shouted, his face pink with exertion, as he arrived at Buckle's side. "You gonna take 'em all on by yourself, sir? How about leaving a few for the old salts?"

"I greatly appreciate your shooting ability, Sergeant," Buckle said.

Midshipman Vincent Callas, the apprentice helmsman, came charging down the catwalk with four winded crew members at his heels. Callas looked overly frightened—Buckle did not like that.

"We have at least two steampipers under the roof," Buckle snapped as Callas handed him a loaded pistol. "Take up a defensive position here."

"It's a brawl down below, sir," Scully said, deftly reloading his musket as he spoke. They're crawling in everywhere, sir!"

"Aye, Sergeant. Hold this position no matter what, Mister Callas," Buckle said, hurrying forward to the companionway. "I am going up to Eagle deck."

"Have at 'em, Captain!" Scully shouted. "The fogsuckers won't find a warm welcome here!"

"Mind what you are shooting at!" Buckle yelled back as he charged up the circular stairwell. When he leapt up onto the Eagle deck, he found himself alone, creeping along under the fluttering envelope roof. He saw a steampack and harness cast on the catwalk grating.

Buckle ran toward the bow, covering fifty yards. The enemy had to be close.

A slender steampiper stepped into view in the blast-shield hatchway of compartment four, not more than thirty feet away. The steampiper strode straight at him, helmet and cuirass gleaming, a pistol in each hand.

Buckle raised his pistol. He saw the steampiper, same as he, turn sideways to him, the duelist's method of presenting as small a target as possible for the opponent to hit. They fired their pistols in the same instant.

Buckle missed and so did the steampiper. The inaccuracy of blackbang pistols beyond twenty paces was proven once again.

But the steampiper had another pistol, and Buckle did not.

When the steampiper pulled the trigger on the second pistol, Buckle threw himself to the catwalk grating. The phosphor-laden ball whizzed over his head in a yellow streak, and he heard it ricochet off metal.

Buckle jumped to his feet, tossed his empty pistol aside, and drew his saber. The steampiper, short sword drawn, was already rushing him. Buckle charged: the longer arc of his sword swing would win him the initiative if he was aggressive. It worked. As soon as swords were crossed, the metal blades fracturing sparks as they clashed over and over, the steampiper had to back up or be overwhelmed.

But the steampiper, though considerably smaller than Buckle, clearly female, and wielding a shorter sword, was left-handed and dangerously good. Along with the advantage of hel-met and armor, the female steampiper's counterstrokes were so quick that Buckle barely had time to whip his sword around and parry the stabs away. Yet Buckle slowly won the advantage, forcing the steampiper back on her heels.

Realizing her predicament, the steampiper lunged with a frantic thrust, and when Buckle hopped back, she used the tiny breathing space to vault over the catwalk rail, leaping across a ten-foot gap to grab ahold of a support rope and slide down to the Castle deck thirty-five feet below.

"Are you kidding me?!" Buckle howled. Even he wasn't desperate enough to make a jump like *that*. He raced to a companionway.

Buckle leapt down the last four stairs. His boots landed hard on the Castle deck grating. The female steampiper was on him in an instant, her sword blade waving back and forth, glimmering gold in the yellowish illumination of the firefly lanterns on the railing hooks. Buckle backed up, getting his bearings. From the way she balanced the weight of her blade in her arm and wrist, he knew that he was up against an elite swordswoman. He could hear the battle raging below: muskets blazing, swords clanging, shouts of men and women locked in mortal combat.

The fight for the life of the *Pneumatic Zeppelin* was in full swing.

The female steampiper lunged at Buckle. He backed up, parrying her blows, noticing in the flurry that her sleeves were thick with silver lace—a high-ranking officer.

A sharp vibration hit Buckle's boots along the grating: he realized that someone else had just landed on the catwalk behind him.

Buckle bobbed low, bending at the knees just as an arc of silvery steel sliced the air over his head. Buckle whirled around and kicked the second steampiper, a tall, powerful male, in the stomach, staggering him backward.

Buckle stood up, holding his sword in front of him, sideways to each of the steampipers, who moved in as a pair, like lions, stalking each flank.

Buckle had been suckered into a trap. He would have cursed himself, but there wasn't time.

-LXIV-

BALTHAZAR, RESURRECTED

SABRINA GRIPPED THE FRAME OF the drift scope as she leaned forward, craning her neck to peer over the green glow of her instruments and catch a glimpse of the steampipers swarming under the glass nose of the *Pneumatic Zeppelin*'s piloting gondola. She saw nothing except flashes in the fog bank. Muskets thundered on the umbilical behind, and up the stairwell above. The sounds made her cringe. Many stray bullets, smoking with hot phosphorus, would be puncturing more hydrogen cells, straining the stockings. Even if the zeppelin survived another hydrogen explosion, Sabrina doubted that they could stay aloft for long.

Sabrina itched to grab her saber, to charge up the stairs and join in the fight, but she had her hands full just keeping the damaged zeppelin in the air. Besides, the brawl might well come to her—the piloting gondola was a prime target for any attacker. The gondola was well defended: Geneva Bolling was down in the hammergun turret, while the crew had been issued pistols at their stations; two musket-toting crew members and a Ballblaster had been posted aft, covering the stairwell and the umbilical ramp hatch; even Kellie was primed for action, pacing at Sabrina's calves, ears pinned back, growling.

"How is the rudder, Mister De Quincey?" Sabrina asked.

"As long as she doesn't snap off, we are fine, ma'am," De Quincey replied. Sweat trickled down his face from under his hat, leaving cold trails on his skin as the subzero air froze them in channels of salty ice. It took nearly every ounce of his considerable strength to keep the zeppelin steady.

"Elevators, Mister Dunn?" Sabrina asked.

"Holding, ma'am," Dunn replied, but the strain in his voice was unmistakable.

Every member of the bridge crew was in a battle at his station. Ripped open and dragging hard to port, without bluewater ballast for the trim tanks, and with three of the six main boilers out of action, it was a real balancing act to keep the gigantic hydrogen airship level. Over and over again, the bubbles danced, and time and time again, they fought the air vessel back into line.

The fog bank beneath the gondola disappeared as if they had driven off a cliff, the mist falling away to the endless, black-as-ink Pacific Ocean below. Good, Sabrina thought, eyeing the mammoth Catalina Obelisk that loomed almost dead ahead, a massive pillar of purple-black stone thrusting up from the channel waters and disappearing into the clouds, whose course it cleaved high above.

"Hold course due south, one mile," Sabrina said. "Then we turn due west."

"Aye, south one mile to course change due west," Welly said, working the drift scope and charts.

Sabrina could now clearly see the blue-white comet tails of the steampipers streaking below. She leaned to the open port gunwale and peered down at the ocean.

"Do not expose yourself in such a fashion, Navigator!" Balthazar bellowed, his boots banging down the stairwell, making the crewmen flinch until they realized who it was. "Fly your foundering zeppelin! Let the rest of us put our eyes on the sky! The last thing we need is for you to stick your head out the window and get potted!"

Sabrina ducked her head back from the gunwale as Balthazar stepped up beside her, breathing hard, stinking of blackbang smoke, pistol and sword in his hands.

"Father!" Sabrina said, suddenly angry, wanting to scold him. What was he doing out of bed and fighting steampipers? She bit her tongue. He looked hale, his face flushed, his eyes hard—he usually did recover quickly from his episodes. But she did not like it. "What is the situation up topside?" she asked evenly.

"They have latched on and cut their way in everywhere, but the crew is holding their own," Balthazar said. With the help of the troopers, we have kept the pressure on so they cannot form up and get a foothold. It is down to knives and swords now, for the most part."

"Aye," Sabrina replied. No more pistols. Good.

Balthazar wiped his face with his sleeve. "Watch your hull. They're buzzing under the gondolas, looking to plant grenades. Our sky dogs on the umbilicals are giving them what for, but we've taken casualties, and they have blown some gaps in the antiboarding nets, I'm afraid."

"How of them many are there?" Sabrina asked, her voice squeezing off as she jumped to help De Quincey strong-arm the lurching rudder wheel.

"Thirty, maybe thirty-five, as far as I could tell," Balthazar replied, grabbing a wheel spoke to assist. "And some of the dead ones I have seen—their bandoliers are loaded with bombs."

The skin on the back of Sabrina's neck tingled. If only one steampiper managed to slip away into the vast catacombs of the *Pneumatic Zeppelin* and detonate a bomb in the right place, it would most likely be the end of them all.

-LXV-

SWORDS

ROMULUS BUCKLE WAS A MASTER of the blade, trained from boyhood by the Crankshaft sword mistress Gweneviere Gray. Gweneviere was a tall, lovely woman, not a day over forty years, her youth preserved by outdoorsmanship, but a woman entirely described by the nature of her own name: her hair was silver-gray, her boots were gray, her jackets were gray—even her dog was gray. Her entire person might easily have lifted up and drifted away into the clouds, if it were not for the exceptional green of her eyes, a young ivy color made doubly striking by her own gravity, and the way she anchored anyone to the spot simply by looking at them. She had expected much from Buckle as Balthazar's adopted son, and he had delivered. Endless hours of thrust and parry had evolved into a wickedly easy dance for him.

As a rule, Buckle was always the aggressor, always attacked. Sword combat was a deadly game of the feint and parry, yes, but in the end, the man who kept his opponent back on his heels with the thrust and swing usually won.

Even when he was being threatened from both sides simultaneously, Buckle attacked.

The female steampiper had let Buckle come on, backing up with measured steps, parrying his every blow with expertise.

She was keeping him engaged, setting him up so her comrade could waltz up from behind and skewer him.

Buckle lunged with a powerful overhead stroke that made her stagger backward, buying himself enough space to turn and meet the thrust coming from the second steampiper. The fight had become a blur of slashing swords and deft parries, back and forth, in the semidarkness. The brass faces of the steampipers' helmets gleamed under the whirling yellow buglights; the huge gas cells waffled, and the oceans of ropes hummed in the gusts of wind that still surged through the interior of the airship.

Buckle could not keep this up for long.

Twice Buckle had succeeded in landing killer thrusts on the second steampiper, and twice the man's iron cuirass deflected the blade in a skittering scrape of sparks. And twice Buckle had nearly lost his head—or at least an ear—to the flashing counterstroke.

Buckle, battered by the day's trials, began to tire ever so slightly, and it was then that the momentum of the fight turned against him. The male steampiper's blade sliced the air over Buckle's head as he ducked; it shattered a buglight dangling from a hook, the splinters of glass flashing as they fell, the stunned fireflies holding in a clump for an instant before bursting out in all directions. Buckle whirled to parry the female steampiper's swing, but her blade grazed his sword hilt and slashed across his forearm just above his glove cuff. It bit deep through the cloth and flesh, but did not reach down to tendon or bone. Buckle felt no pain, but he sensed weakness, weakness in his sword arm, and that was worse.

He had to extricate himself from his dilemma or he would be dead within seconds. Slashing violently in each direction, Buckle planted his hand on the catwalk rail and hurdled over the side, dropping into the void below.

ROMULUS BUCKLE & THE CITY OF THE FOUNDERS

Plummeting alongside the dark tower of a gas cell, Buckle slapped his sword into its scabbard. He had made a dangerous move, certainly, diving into a compartment vault from the Castle deck, but it was a calculated one.

And it would be damned hard to follow.

He would surely escape...provided he lived through it.

Buckle knew every inch of the *Pneumatic Zeppelin*—the only advantage he had over his opponents—and after a fifteen-foot plunge, he plopped down on the back of a central airbag, a big, soft cushion with the consistency of a jellyfish. The airbag was filled to bursting with boiling air, and its goldbeater's skin was nearly as hot, so hot that he felt as if he had dropped into a skillet in the instant it took for the balloon to bounce back, launching him forward over its rounded flank. It was exactly the rebound Buckle had hoped for: he was thrown into the guitar-string wall of counterweight ropes above the Axial deck and grabbed hold of one, sliding down it to the catwalk, fifteen feet below.

As soon as Buckle's boots landed on the Axial deck catwalk, he drew his sword again. He heard fighting all around him—shouts and sword clashes, the occasional musket blast—but he was alone where he was.

The female steampiper landed right in front of Buckle, and with a catlike roll to her feet she came at him, her short sword poised and ready. Buckle instantly charged. He swept his sword low, aiming for her knees. She jumped, again with the superb agility of a cat, planting her boots on both rails so she was astride the catwalk. Buckle rolled forward under her, leaping up to take a backhanded slash at her backside. But she had already sprung away.

Buckle turned around, sword steady. She moved toward him, her short sword weaving in front of her, feinting to the left and then to the right.

Swordmaster Gweneviere Gray always told Buckle that he was one of the lucky few who had a sixth sense in mortal combat; once again, it saved his neck. In that moment, he realized that the second steampiper was charging his back, his sword only a few sprinting strides away.

Surrounded. Again.

Buckle drew his dagger and whipped it at the female steampiper. The unexpected projectile caught her off guard, the whirling blade clanging off her helmet, and she jumped back. Buckle spun on his boot heels, turning in to the rush of the second steampiper, who had his sword raised in anticipation of a killing blow. Buckle lunged into him, closing the gap instantly. The steampiper awkwardly thrust his sword down as the space for a swing vanished, and Buckle caught the blade on the hilt of his saber. Buckle drove his shoulder into the steampiper's chest, a bruising collision against the iron cuirass, grabbed him by the collar, and launched him over the catwalk rail.

The second steampiper released a terrified shout inside his helmet as he went over the rail. But Buckle's move was not perfect—the steampiper was big and quick, and he clawed at Buckle's head as he passed over, blunting the force of Buckle's maneuver. Buckle dropped the steampiper more than he hurled him, and the fellow managed to grab ahold of the base of the catwalk with one hand and cling to it, swinging over the vault as his sword fell into the chasm beneath.

Buckle could have finished the male steampiper with a stomp of his boot on the man's fingers, but he was already backing up, off balance and ducking for his life, as the female steampiper attacked.

–LXVI–

KAMIKAZE IN THE COCKPIT

"Keep up the good work, my girl," Balthazar said, turning to head back up the piloting gondola stairwell. "I am going to go up and give my former hosts a few more parting shots."

"Aye," Sabrina said, grunting as she and De Quincey worked the rudder wheel to counter another yaw to port. "Be careful!"

"Steampiper!" Welly shouted, flinging his arm out, his index finger pointing straight out the nose dome. "Twelve o'clock! Dead ahead!"

Sabrina snapped her head around. A steampiper was coming head-on at the gondola, with the velocity of a bullet. A glittering line of hammergun darts swung after him, but could not intersect his line; phosphorous streaks—shots from the crew members on the bow pulpit—missed. The steampiper, his image distorted by the broken nose glass, had one arm raised; in his hand was a grenade bomb, its lit fuse whipping back and forth in the wind with a fluttering red sparkle.

"Grenade!" Sabrina shouted. The steampiper was mere seconds away from being able to lob his bomb in through the open flanks of the gondola, or up into the numberless openings in the bottom of the envelope. "Thwack him!" she screamed.

Welly and Nero lifted their pistols. Balthazar dashed back with his pistol up; the Ballblaster and the two crewmen charged with him, crowding the cockpit around Sabrina with leveled musket barrels. Sabrina ducked her head.

"Fire!" Balthazar yelled.

Sabrina heard a ragged, thunderous clap of gunfire, followed by a shattering of glass in the nose dome. She lifted her head and saw, through the cloud of smoke and the cracked and holed panels of dome glass, a brilliant blue-white flash. At least one ball had hit its mark: the damaged steampack spewed scalding steam and sent the steampiper into a violent spin. A white blossom opened behind him for an instant—a parachute—but the steampack flames instantly burned it away. The steampiper lost his grip on the grenade and it fell harmlessly to the sea. But he yanked his controls to veer his stricken contraption directly into the path of the piloting gondola.

"Kamikaze!" Welly screamed.

That was all the time anybody had before the impact. Enough time for Welly to utter one word, for Sabrina to duck low behind the gyroscope and try to push Kellie under the instrument panels with her, aware that everyone in the gondola was throwing themselves to the deck.

The impact was horrible. The steampiper crashed into the port side of the gondola's nose dome, tearing up instruments as the immense momentum of the steampack carried his body through portside panels of brass, copper, and wood. Sabrina felt the heat of the steampack engine passing above and to her left, followed by a stinging shower of twisted metal, falling brass tubes, bolts, screws, bits of glass, and cold splashes of glowing green boil.

The steampiper and his berserk machine were gone in a flash, deflected in the destruction.

Sabrina opened her eyes and pulled herself to her feet. The port side of the gondola was ripped open horizontally, tunneled through to the middle, the wind slashing through the gap with a sucking roar: the entire portside bulkhead was gone, with nothing left in the breach but wobbling remnants of wood and metal ribs, snapped pipes, and sheared tubes jetting steam or leaking bioluminescent boil that was sucked away in the slipstream.

The elevator-wheel station was gone. Lieutenant Ignatius Dunn, the elevatorman, was gone.

Toward the stern of the ship, over the twisted port gunwale, Sabrina saw the broken body of the steampiper, still attached to his mangled steampack, bounce off the port side of the gunnery gondola and spin straight into stern propeller nacelle number one, four hundred feet beyond. Jammed by the high-velocity bulk of the steampiper and his machine, the propeller's torquing shaft tore itself to pieces. The nacelle split into a million jagged fragments and exploded in a white ball of fire, ejecting the flaming propeller off over the ocean.

"We've lost number one propeller!" Sabrina screamed.

The already unstable *Pneumatic Zeppelin*, now overdriven by the starboard side propellers and bereft of elevator control, immediately lurched to port, threatening to heave completely over onto her side.

"She is going to roll!" De Quincey shouted. Balthazar was now shoulder to shoulder with him at the helm.

"Emergency elevator wheel!" Sabrina screamed as the deck lurched. Both she and Welly threw themselves at the emergency control wheels, which were folded up into the ceiling over the captain's station. Together, they drew the small elevator wheel down.

The gondola creaked as it tipped to the left. Kellie bumped Sabrina's knees, her claws rapidly scraping the wood planks as she scrambled against the rising tilt of the deck.

As soon as the reserve elevator wheel locked into the steering channel, it started to whirl. At the risk of breaking their fingers, Sabrina and Welly snatched the spokes. Sabrina planted one boot on the bulwark and threw her back against the wheel—but her strength, combined with Welly's, could do no more than prevent it from spinning out of control. Half the levers she wanted to reach for were damaged or sheared away.

The zeppelin had lost equilibrium—again. Sabrina needed power, and she needed lift, and both systems were already pushed beyond their limits. "Shut down main starboard propeller number four!" she screamed into the chattertube, its hood now missing. "All ahead flank!"

The *Pneumatic Zeppelin* heaved once more to the port side, hurling Sabrina's stomach into her throat and throwing everyone to the left. The apprentice engineer, Lionel Garcia, lunged to slam the chadburn dial into all ahead flank position, lost his grip, and fell away, crashing hard into Sabrina and Welly, who were now angled below him.

The shattered nose dome swept downward until nothing could be seen but the black sea, three hundred feet below.

Sabrina wrenched at the elevator wheel, the skin on her hands feeling as if it was tearing away under her gloves, but the wheel fought her, heaving back in the opposite direction, threatening to send the airship over onto her back, and every soul aboard to a watery doom.

~LXVII~

NOT DEAD YET

BUCKLE LASHED HIS SABER FROM angle to angle, blocking every one of the female steampiper's blows, as he tried to find an instant to set his feet again. The female steampiper rushed him, not wanting to allow him the luxury of recovering his defensive stance.

An explosion shook the *Pneumatic Zeppelin*, sending a concussive ripple through the superstructure and delivering a violent kick to the support girders and catwalk beneath Buckle and the female steampiper. Losing her footing, the female steampiper stumbled into Buckle and attempted to head-butt him with her helmet. He grabbed her sword arm by the wrist and she grabbed his. They hung there for a heartbeat, the black, polarized-glass eye slits of her helmet pressed to his forehead, the muffled heaves of her breathing mixing with the sound of his own air-sucking in his ears.

And then the world turned upside down.

The *Pneumatic Zeppelin*, and the Axial catwalk with it, suddenly rolled to port so violently that Buckle and the female steampiper, still locked together in battle, were nearly catapulted over the rail. To release a hand to stop one's fall meant leaving one's gut open to a stabbing thrust. So they fell together, twisting against the catwalk rail, and then down onto the ramp grating.

The airship pitched forward with a deafening groan as it rolled even harder to port. The Axial deck catwalk dropped away, tilting and continuing to tilt, the angle becoming so dramatic that it seemed as if the massive zeppelin might end up flat on her side.

Unseen crew members shouted and screamed under the noise, sounding far away.

This is it, Buckle thought, as his boots clawed for purchase on the catwalk that was now slipping under him like a steep wall, his hands locked with those of the female steampiper, their heads and bodies thumping into each other, their legs thrashing, as they clutched the catwalk railing. If the *Pneumatic Zeppelin* locked into a roll, she would collapse and plummet into the sea.

Buckle wrenched his sword arm back and forth, but the female steampiper held on. His back and elbows thumped into the catwalk rail supports, repeatedly knocking the air out of him. Buglights slipped from their hooks and fell in wobbling spirals alongside, bouncing off gas cells and tubes, shattering in exploding stars of escaping fireflies. The screams and groans of the airship's superstructure, deafening in their cacophony, signaled that the entire construction was overburdened and about to fold.

Romulus Buckle did not mind dying. He really did not, especially if he could take a few steampipers with him. He would prefer to live, of course, but what truly agonized him was the realization that he was about to lose his zeppelin and his crew. And he would never save Elizabeth.

Well, they weren't dead yet.

But whatever had happened, it was up to Sabrina to pull their arse out of the fire.

-LXVIII-

A PYRRHIC VICTORY

ONLY A MARTIAN COULD HAVE made it to the piloting gondola with the speed Max did, as the *Pneumatic Zeppelin* heaved over on her side. Max bounded along angled decks and tilting staircases, crouching, leaping, pulling herself along the railings, as she negotiated her way down the keel.

It looked as if the steampiper attack had been driven off, but Max, fresh from the fray, heart pounding, muscles twitching, nose full of the scent of blood, was in a battle frenzy. The calm center of her brain watched the war beast within her with both contempt and awe; the fight had been a near-run thing, yes, but—and here was the rub—the Founders had not attempted to destroy the *Pneumatic Zeppelin*, they had tried to *seize* it.

Max dropped down the angled staircase of the piloting gondola and now, only a few feet from her engineering station, she was witnessing the end of her beloved airship.

The gondola was badly damaged, the port flank partially ripped away and open to the sky, the elevator wheel entirely missing, the port side of the nose dome shattered. And the black, black ocean was looming large below.

The bridge crew, splattered with glowing boil, fought to hold on as they struggled with levers and wheels that refused to respond. Nero and Garcia lay stunned under the ballast station. Sabrina and Welly wrenched at the emergency elevator wheel, and Balthazar, his forehead running with blood, red-faced with effort, was throwing his muscles in with De Quincey's as they attempted to bull the rudder wheel back into line.

Max vaulted the staircase rail and sprang through the air, grabbing hold of the ballast station bulkhead. The *Pneumatic Zeppelin* was almost lying on her side. The airship was not built to withstand the pressures now bending at her every girder and spar. The superstructure would soon collapse under its own weight, if the boilers did not first split loose of their securing rivets and roll to port like burning meteors, igniting the gas cells and blasting all of them to smithereens.

And the black sea gaped below, a gigantic, bottomless coffin.

Max planted her feet on the anchored station chair, avoiding the tilted deck.

"Max!" Sabrina shouted, ducking away from the head-banging current of air roaring through the ruins of the portside bulkhead. "We lost propeller number one!"

Max saw the chadburn shoved to all ahead flank. The engine-room sister dial on the chadburn had not moved in response—it still rested on all ahead full. Hopefully the engine-room crew was simply too busy to make the acknowledging ring on their end of the chadburn, rather than being incapacitated or dead.

Even with all of her damage, with three boilers shut down, and without a main propeller, the *Pneumatic Zeppelin* was responding, inching back toward an even keel, but it was not the quick recovery that was needed to save them all.

Sabrina knew this. "Hydrogen!" she screamed. "Maximum flood! Open all forward hydro tanks from compartments one through ten and all portside tanks! Maximum emergency flood!"

"Aye!" Max shouted, almost hanging sideways from the instrument panel. She slapped up the forward master hydro lever on the hydrogen board, flooding the front ten compartments of the airship and the portside cells with every last cubic inch of hydrogen left in their main supply tanks.

If any of those gas cells were punctured, if any were on fire, if flames somewhere licked a cracked feeder pipe, well, they would pop, vanishing from existence in one stupendous flash. That was the way so many airships disappeared, without a story or a trace for those left behind. They would live on only in the memories of the clan and perhaps in a children's story or two about a ghost zeppelin with a Martian aboard.

Max had never considered her own death. Not even when she had been in life-threatening situations before. The end was the end, was it not? It had simply never seemed to warrant much concern. But now, as she stared doom in the face once again, a painful emptiness surged inside her. An unwelcome yearning. She did not want to die. Not yet. She was not sure how, but something in her life was unfinished, unfulfilled. Max ordered her brain to snap out of it. Such worryings clouded the mind and dulled reaction.

Max gritted her teeth as she helped Welly, unsteady and bloody, to his feet. In the pit of her stomach she could feel the zeppelin rolling upright, her nose beginning to rise. She glanced out the hole and was surprised how much closer the sea was now, its whitecaps visible as it rose up to meet them.

"One hundred feet," Welly shouted, lurching to the altimeter dial.

Her bow flush full of hydrogen, the *Pneumatic Zeppelin* lifted her nose and rolled upright in a spine-crushing swing to the sky.

"Good girl!" Welly cheered.

The zeppelin ascended steadily, though her bank to port was not entirely nulled, and she shook with an unhealthy vibration.

Max took a deep breath of cold sea air that salted her tongue. She could feel the terrible stress on the airframe bleeding away as the airship eased up and approached an even keel.

Sabrina, unclenching her hands one at a time from the emergency elevator wheel to stretch out her cramped fingers, gave Max a worried smile. "We lost Dunn," she said.

"Yes," Max replied. She had not known Ignatius Dunn very well. He had been new, a transfer from the *Khartoum*, and he had proved to be something of a loner. But he was a good elevatorman, and those were rare.

"Nice to see a little sky," Balthazar gasped, eyeing the dark horizon ahead, where the sky and water each filled half of the view. Kellie darted out of her cubby and circled Balthazar's leg; he rubbed her head in an almost absentminded way, his blood-streaked face looking haggard.

"I am having difficulty keeping her on her keel," Sabrina said. "She still wants to roll over. We may have taken stabilizer damage when we lost the portside propeller."

"Rudder is barely responding, Captain," De Quincey said.

Max stepped to the engineering station and scrutinized her boil-lit system controls. Almost every needle and dial quivered on one red line or another. The deck shuddered again and again under her feet.

Sabrina gave Max a glance that Max instantly understood— they both doubted that the *Pneumatic Zeppelin*, in its current condition, would be able to make it home.

–LXIX–

DOPPELGÄNGER

BLOOD WAS RUNNING INTO BUCKLE'S mouth. He was not sure where it was coming from. Perhaps he had bitten his tongue as he and the female steampiper gripped each other's wrists, grunting as they tried to press their sword blades into each other's knuckles, neck, or shoulder.

Even if the catwalk wasn't tilted anymore, things were not going well for Buckle.

And the female steampiper was trying to head-butt him with her helmet, over and over again.

That was where the blood came from, Buckle realized. She had just thumped him on the chin.

"Damn your hide!" Buckle howled. "Quit it with the blasted helmet!" With the yanking of his head, Buckle felt dizzy, and the canted buglights still swinging on their rail hooks blurred and haloed in his eyes. The damned concussion from the explosion that had knocked him senseless earlier had not quite cleared out of his brainpan, and the whackwillies that clouded his senses now were also making him feel weak in the body.

The wound across his sword arm was bleeding severely, drenching his sword hilt with sticky, warm blood, the loss of which was draining his strength.

He spun loose of the female steampiper's grip and shoved her away.

Time was working against Buckle and his zeppelin—so, characteristically, he elected to attack. The voice of Gweneviere Gray marched through his brain: quick to the lunge, quick to the thrust, quick to the lunge. Watch every feint, every preference, know their move before they make it. The female steampiper backed up in front of him, parrying his blows, sparks flying, her sword floating in front of her like a cobra's head. She was damned good, but he had noticed a flaw in her defensive technique, a dropping of her guard just before she went to the thrust, and he waited for it. He eased back, readying for the counterattack he knew would come.

In the moment the female steampiper charged, Buckle saw her hand shift, lowering her guard. He struck, feinting low and whirling his blade upward, over her too-low defensive stroke, and caught her on the helmet, delivering a stunning blow with the pommel of his sword. The female steampiper staggered back, off balance, her sword now gripped vertically in front of her.

Buckle slashed the flat of his blade across her wrist, knocking her sword arm aside. It was a brutal blow, aimed at the main nerve just below the base of the hand, shocking the sinews in her arm and numbing her fingers. He heard her grunt in pain inside her helmet.

Buckle could have chopped her hand off there and then, but he was going for the capture. He wanted a prisoner, a member of the mysterious Founders clan to ask questions of. With a backhanded swing, he whipped his blade across hers, banging her sword out of her hand. The sword spun over the catwalk rail, descending into the gasbag vault in a whirl of silver flashes.

She tried to lunge up into him, to drive that damned helmet into his forehead again. He drove his sword fist into the chest of her cuirass, heaving her sideways against the rail, and with his free hand he grabbed the back of her helmet and yanked it off her head.

When the female steampiper spun around he saw her face, a beautiful, defiant face bordered by a wild, sweat-stuck shock of bright-red hair, a stunningly familiar face with a smattering of freckles about the nose, and pale-green, jade-colored eyes. It was the face of Sabrina Serafim—the same face, the hair just as fire red—a doppelgänger.

Buckle gasped. The helmet dropped from his hand and clanged on the catwalk grating.

The female steampiper bent low, reaching for a dagger in a sheath on her calf with her uninjured hand. Buckle slapped the blade away as she drew it, and it bounced off the catwalk. He brought the handle of his sword up under her chin, knocking her flat on her back.

"Surrender, steampiper," Buckle said as he stepped over her, the point of his sword poised at her throat, "and you shall be given mercy."

The steampiper glared at him. She had a long white scar that ran from under her left ear all the way across her cheek-bone, to end in a curl under the corner of her left eye.

Buckle saw her eyes flick to the near distance behind him. The other steampiper. He spun around.

The male steampiper was there, not fifteen paces back, hav-ing clambered back up onto the catwalk. His helmet was miss-ing, and his hair was also red, though nowhere near as vibrant in saturation as the woman's; a neatly trimmed beard, orange and straw-colored, bedecked his sturdy, green-eyed face. And he had a pistol pointed straight at Buckle's stomach.

Romulus Buckle knew he was a dead man.

A gunshot boomed, loud even over the wail of the wind.

Buckle jerked, stunned that he had not felt the impact of the ball, nor seen the phosphorus streak, nor witnessed the belch of black smoke from the muzzle. He ducked his head down, searching his torso for the bullet hole, his hands held in front of him, fingers splayed.

Buckle glanced up, confused.

The male steampiper fell forward, dead.

Buckle's savior, Katzenjammer Smelt, stepped out of a companionway with a smoking pistol in one hand, another pistol in the other. "Taste some Imperial revenge, you bumptious fogsucker!" Smelt shouted, his monocle flashing over his left eye. He gave Buckle a hard look. "Consider my debt to you paid in full, Captain Romulus Buckle," he said, fairly spitting the word "captain."

The female steampiper pulled herself to her feet beside Buckle. Smelt raised his second pistol and aimed it at her.

"No, Smelt!" Buckle shouted. Too late.

Smelt pulled the trigger. The pistol boomed, phosphorus flashed.

Buckle heard the snap of punctured metal and a gasp of agony. He spun around in despair.

–LXX–

THINGS THAT GO BUMP
IN THE NIGHT

SABRINA STOOD IN THE CENTER of her ruined bridge, trying to figure out another method to get the *Pneumatic Zeppelin* under control again. "All ahead standard. Helm, give me a gentle turn to port."

Max rang the chadburn handle back. "All ahead standard!" she shouted into the chattertube.

The chadburn sister dial swung into the same position, jangling the bell. "All ahead full, aye!" Elliot Yardbird responded from the engine room.

At least the engineers were still alive.

"The rudder is stiff, ma'am—barely responding," De Quincey said, the helm wheel tocking oddly.

"Aye," Sabrina said. "Try a turn to starboard, then."

"I cannot keep the bubble on line; pitch is all out of alignment," Ensign Caspar Wong said—he was the assistant elevatorman, and had just arrived on deck to take his post at the emergency wheel, his face black with gunpowder stains, and still overtalkative. "I cannot recover or maintain equilibrium properly."

"Well, I have no more water ballast, and barely enough hydro reserves remaining to float a frog," Nero, just recovered from his head bump, grumbled.

"Aye," Sabrina said.

"The damage reports shall be coming in momentarily," Max said. "We shall better know what we are dealing with then."

"Two hundred feet and rising," Welly reported, back over his drift scope and altimeter.

"At least we have some altitude," Sabrina said. "We shall have to crawl home, but we shall get there."

"Well done, First Lieutenant!" Balthazar cheered from the back of the gondola, as he helped Ensign Bolling up out of the hammergun turret.

"Obelisk!" Nero shouted. "Obelisk to port! We are on a collision course!"

Swerving into view from the left, and soon to be directly in front of them, loomed the massive pillar of the Catalina Obelisk, thrusting up from the Catalina channel, glowing a black purple across its uneven surface, darker than the clouds. It looked like a column designed to hold up the very heavens themselves.

"Hard a starboard! Hard a starboard!" Sabrina shouted.

De Quincey threw his entire weight into the rudder wheel, which spun once around and abruptly shuddered to a stop. "The rudder is jammed on the starboard swing, Captain!"

The *Pneumatic Zeppelin*, unresponsive to her helm—nose up, barely under control, and locked in an ascent—continued to drift to port, not away from the obelisk, but bearing *into* it with surprising speed.

There was a moment of shock on the bridge as the battered crew stared, unbelieving, as they rode the unresponsive *Pneumatic Zeppelin* on a collision course with the Catalina Obelisk, its monstrous mass swallowing up more and more of the nose-dome window. Welly took an unconscious step backward.

"Damn it! Hard a port! Hard a port!" Sabrina bellowed.

"Hard a port!" De Quincey replied, whirling the rudder wheel.

If the zeppelin could not turn to starboard, then Sabrina would go with the airship's desire to nose to port and swing across the obstacle.

The bow hedged to port, picking up speed as the wall of the obelisk swept past from left to right in front of them. But it looked like it was too late. The obelisk was too wide and too close.

De Quincey pinned the rudder wheel, but there was little more he could do.

"Come on! Come on!" Sabrina shouted. She fought the urge to throw her engines into reverse, to cavitate the propellers. The airship was so damaged and out of balance that such a desperate act would more likely swing them sideways into the obelisk, rather than slowing them enough to maneuver around it.

"Brace for impact!" Max shouted. She leaned into the chattertube: "All hands! Brace for impact!"

There was nothing but a wall of purplish blackness facing them now.

Then, a slice of cloud-filled night, the gray clouds appearing bright compared to the light-sucking darkness of the Martian pillar, emerged on the left, slowly growing in size as the airship swung toward the edge of the obelisk.

It was going to be close.

And for a second, Sabrina thought they were going to make it.

The bow of the *Pneumatic Zeppelin* skimmed past the cliff-like flank of the Catalina Obelisk.

"I think we made it!" Nero shouted.

"No!" Sabrina shouted. "Brace for impact!"

Then came the awful sound, the sound of the airship's starboard-side envelope skidding along the edge of the obelisk, the sound of ripping fabric, snapping ropes, and the weird, awful, rivet-popping screech of superstructure supports wrenching and shearing.

"Collision!" Sabrina yelled.

"If it clips off the stabilizer, we've had it!" Welly cried.

The zeppelin was in contact with the obelisk for only a few moments, in actuality perhaps about three seconds, but to Sabrina it felt like an eternity. For those three seconds, the ship vibrated so violently it rattled her teeth and bones, and she feared it might come to pieces under her very feet.

But the vibrating stopped. The airship had made it past the obelisk, floating free once again. But now she swung hard to port in a wide, unnerving yaw.

Wong wrenched his elevator wheel back and forth, but it barely moved. "We have taken too much stabilizer damage, Captain," he said. "I cannot keep her on an even keel for very long."

Sabrina and Nero tried to assist Wong, but it was no use—the elevator controls were mired in mud.

The water. A cold shiver ran up Sabrina's spine. She did not want to end up in the water.

"Can we keep her airborne long enough to launch the *Arabella*?" Wong asked plaintively.

"No," Sabrina replied. "I am going to try to make for Catalina Island. Otherwise, we ditch in the sea."

–LXXI–

UNFINISHED BUSINESS

THE FEMALE STEAMPIPER HAD STUMBLED back, one hand clutching at the catwalk rail, the other under a smoldering hole low in her cuirass, over her lower rib cage. Blood ran in dark rivulets over her fingers, staining the silver stripe on her black pants below. Pain swam in her green eyes, but did nothing to unsettle the profound disdain he saw for him there.

Buckle had lowered his sword.

"Don't make me finish the job for you, Captain," Smelt had said.

"I am taking her prisoner, Chancellor," Buckle replied.

Smelt holstered his pistol. "She will never talk. Finish her off."

Buckle had turned his back on Smelt and strode after the female steampiper, who was staggering toward the nose of the airship.

"Surrender and I shall give you mercy," Buckle had shouted.

The female steampiper glanced back at him and continued her wounded shamble toward the bow. The *Pneumatic Zeppelin* was making a dramatic bank to port, and this made it difficult to walk along the catwalk if you weren't used to it. Buckle followed her slowly, warily. She was moving toward the nose dome at the end of the Axial catwalk. The interior of the zeppelin was dark—most of the buglights having dropped and smashed in the chaos—and loose fireflies swirled in the black flood of wind currents, their yellow bodies shifting in waves as if it were snowing fire.

The sky in front of the nose dome looked dark and uneven, as if they were flying into a wall. Buckle's eyes blurred and he shook his head. The gray night sky appeared again, and he felt an odd sense of relief.

Suddenly the *Pneumatic Zeppelin* lurched, throwing Buckle forward to his knees. The envelope skin to his right and above him, what he could see of it between the cells, was violently sheared open from fore to aft by some colossal object. It was as if a gigantic knife were slicing its way along the starboard flank of the airship. It sounded like they had flown into a monstrous waterfall: wires snapped, slicing away into the darkness with shrill whips; rivets fired out of their holes like bullets; the superstructure, shaking so violently that it wobbled the catwalk, moaned with the horrible shriek of bending metal.

And then it was over as quickly as it had begun. The *Pneumatic Zeppelin* was loose and floating unhindered again, though Buckle, scrambling to his feet, could feel her drifting into an unhealthy yaw to port.

Buckle peered at the damaged skin beyond the starboard hydrogen cells, where the gray night sky loomed beyond. How much more damage could his zeppelin take? He had to get to the bridge.

"Your prisoner is escaping you, Captain Buckle!" Smelt shouted from behind.

Buckle turned to see the female steampiper limping down the catwalk toward the nose dome, about two compartments ahead of him. He had taken off after her at a sprint, and now he had almost caught her before she reached it.

The female steampiper hunched around the four-pounder bow-chaser cannon to open the round glass hatch and step out onto the bow pulpit. She stood still for a moment, surveying the chasm of sea and sky, before she turned to look at Buckle. Her face was in shadow, her form silhouetted against the gray night sky, her windswept red hair roiling about her head.

"Wait!" Buckle shouted, slowing to a halt ten feet from her. He rammed his sword into its sheath with a leathery swish, hearing the clank of the hilt striking the brass mouth of the scabbard. "Surrender to me! You shall be returned home safely and unharmed! You have my word!"

The steampiper let her gaze linger on Buckle for a moment. For the life of him, Buckle thought he was looking at Sabrina.

The female steampiper turned her back to him.

"Wait!" Buckle screamed, rushing forward.

The woman clambered up the cannon turret, stepped up onto the top of the barbette, and threw herself into the void.

Buckle leapt out into the battering wind of the pulpit in time to see her falling away toward the ocean. At the last moment, just before the *Pneumatic Zeppelin* blocked her from his view, he saw a parachute on the back of her cuirass burst open, a soft puff of white in the darkness.

Buckle gripped the barbette rail as the wind thundered around him. He was overwhelmed by the darkness of sea and sky, and the irregular black mass of Catalina Island looming below. He felt dispirited, as if some desperately needed opportunity had just been lost.

There was also a weird chill in his gut—what doppelgänger theory might explain why he had just battled a near-perfect double of Sabrina Serafim?

The *Pneumatic Zeppelin* yawed to port with a terrifying looseness, fighting to stay under control, but foundering. They were probably going to have to ditch. Buckle ducked back into the nose port: he had to get to the bridge. He saw Smelt peering at him on the catwalk ahead, his monocle swirling with glimmers of the fireflies between them.

"The cat lost his mouse, did he?" Smelt laughed. "Why am I not surprised?"

Buckle did not answer.

"And perhaps you should thank me for how well we Imperials construct our airships," Smelt shouted. "Or we would all be dead by now."

Buckle reached the circular staircase and paused, against his better judgment, to glare at the Imperial chancellor. Why, of all the people in the world, Buckle grumbled in his mind, did it have to be Katzenjammer Smelt who had saved him? Buckle would have rather been chopped up in a propeller than owe anything to this vile blackguard.

"You yellow-fingered thief," Smelt said.

Buckle grabbed the hilt of his sword, drawing it an inch before he stopped himself.

Smelt's impressive, hair-filled nostrils flared. He slid his hand down to the handle of his sword. "The day you draw your sword on me, boy, is the day your shoulders get lonely without your head."

Buckle gritted his teeth. He did not have time for this, this self-absorbed ruffling of feathers with Katzenjammer Smelt.

He forced his blade back down in its scabbard—the click, as he drove it home, was humiliating—and hurried down the companionway.

"The time will come, Romulus Buckle," Smelt shouted after him. "You and I, Cranker, we have unfinished business, and that business shall be resolved at the point of a sword!"

–LXXII–

NO REST FOR THE WICKED

WHEN ROMULUS BUCKLE ENTERED THE piloting gondola, he wondered how the *Pneumatic Zeppelin* could still be controlled given the wreckage he saw. The glass nose dome was shattered, and a strip of the gondola's port side had been torn away in a long, jagged rip, as if a cannonball had raked across it, snapping away instrument panels and rendering banks of once-elegant instruments into grotesque metal spaghetti. The freezing wind howled in through the gap, swinging the buglights overhead, shaking the glowing green boil in its spheres and tubes.

Kellie burst out of her cubby, whirling around Buckle's knees as he hit the bottom of the companionway—she looked to be the only living thing there that wasn't badly worn out. A Ballblaster and a crewmen still guarded the base of the staircase, gripping their muskets, looking exhausted; another crewman, sitting on the deck, his right arm soaked with blood, was being bandaged by Fitzroy; Welly and Nero stood at their stations, their faces slick, their eyes glassy with shock.

Max spun from the engineering station. "Captain on the bridge," she announced, a formality Buckle disliked; even though he had told her so, she still continued to do it.

Balthazar, assisting Wong on the emergency elevator wheel, his face running with blood from a laceration high up on his head, gave Buckle a sour look. "You've got one hell of a mess on your hands here, son. And, by the way, the sky curses captains who don't stay put on their bridge."

Buckle nodded, which was his way of ignoring Balthazar's criticism, and stepped to the helm. Sabrina smiled grimly at his approach, her cheeks damp with perspiration despite the howling, cold air.

"Do we need to relocate to the battle bridge?" Buckle asked. The airship had a secondary emergency bridge, located behind the engine room at the stern, where the crew could transfer control; it was rudimentary and almost blind, and only to be considered as a last option.

"It would not help, Captain," Max answered at his back. "Our flight-control systems and control surfaces are damaged. The *Pneumatic Zeppelin* has simply absorbed too much punishment to maintain equilibrium."

"She is not going to stay in the air much longer, Captain," Sabrina said. "I am making way for Catalina Island, and initiated a slow descent at half full. I recommend an emergency mooring to effect repairs."

"Aye. I'll take her from here, Navigator," Buckle said, as he stepped to the helm wheel. De Quincey immediately released his grip on the spokes when Buckle clamped his hands down on them. Buckle gasped. The amount of effort it instantly took to hold the wheel in place surprised him: it nearly pulled him off balance before he had time to set his feet. "Catalina sounds like a good idea," Buckle said, straining. He glanced back at De Quincey, who was soaked through with sweat.

"You need a hand, Captain?" De Quincey asked.

"Not at the moment, Mister De Quincey," Buckle replied. "But stay close."

Sabrina cast a disapproving glance at the bloody wound on Buckle's arm, as well as the bloodstained bandage wrapped around his head. "You are injured, sir."

"I appreciate your concern, Navigator," Buckle said with a smile. "No rest for the wicked."

"Yes, Captain," Sabrina replied. "Look out—she is extremely heavy to port, constantly wanting to fall out of level, and barely responding to commands." She rubbed her arms as she stepped forward into the navigator's chair, and Welly shifted aside.

"How goes the fight up top?" Balthazar asked.

"It looks like we sent them packing," Buckle replied. He had seen the aftermath of the desperate battle along the keel corridor, the dead bodies of steampipers and his own crewmen scattered on the platforms and gratings, shrouded in drifting gunpowder smoke and mourned by legions of sparkling fireflies. Buckle had observed the carnage with a cold eye. The time for mourning would come later. "Pluteus and Ivan are overseeing deck sweeps in the search for stowaways and bombs. Hopefully we harried them so much they were unable to plant any explosives."

"Nicely done," Balthazar said.

"I hope you killed them all," Nero grumbled. "Serves them right."

"One hundred and fifteen feet and descending," Welly reported.

Buckle watched the sweeping mass of Catalina Island, centered in the broken bull's-eye of the nose dome, looming large in the glittering sea. He scrutinized the topography, looking for a wide slope to make his landing on. The zeppelin struggled to maintain its course, speed, and altitude, and the wheel in his hands, usually light, felt leaden. It was a royal strain just to keep the level bubbles on target as they wobbled in their glass arches.

"Engineering, damage report," Buckle asked.

"We are screwed, aye," Sabrina replied.

"I would appreciate a little more detail than that."

"Almost every major system of the airship has been compromised, Captain," Max said. "The skin is now too irregular to maintain balance or streamlining. Our drag exceeds maximum limits. We are lucky it is a calm night in the air—if we were to fly into even a stiff headwind, I fear the internal pressures would now tear the airship apart. We are running on three boilers with one, two, and three shut down. Water coolant is dangerously low and all water ballast, both the mains and reserves, has been jettisoned. Positive buoyancy is just above the line, and we have only thirty-three percent of hydrogen remaining in the reserve tanks."

"A real peach of a pinch," Sabrina noted grimly.

Buckle nodded. The hydrogen percentage was critical. Anything below 30 percent in the reserve tanks and they would not have enough lift to get off the ground again. And if anything went wrong with the emergency land mooring, a tricky maneuver even with a healthy airship, they might have to vent the existing hydrogen in the gasbags to prevent a crash fire. That would mean that all the hydrogen they'd have left was what was in those reserve tanks.

"One hundred feet," Sabrina said, her eyes buried in the drift scope at the navigator's station.

Max tapped a barometer cylinder and eyed the measurement lines painted on the glass. "We do not have the capacity to recover from our damages in flight. Not enough to make it over the mountains to home."

"In other words, yes, we're screwed. Aye," Buckle said, with a wink to Sabrina.

"Catalina works for me," Balthazar said. "I'll take a hard thump in the arse over a cold bath any day of the week. We shall patch this old lady up and be on our way by morning."

Catalina Island.

Buckle felt his heart sink in his chest. He, for all of his braggadocio, was not going to be able to get his zeppelin home without a perilous stop for repairs. Now he had to make an emergency mooring at night over unfamiliar terrain. Catalina Island was said to be uninhabited—no clan had officially claimed it—but it was known to be a secretive refuge for privateers, pirates, and fugitives, and the Atlanteans were rumored to have outliers operating in the vicinity. And if the Founders clan had decided to be there at some point, they would be there.

"'Have the crew prepare for emergency field anchor," Buckle said, eyeing the dark outline of Catalina against the dully sparkling ocean—it seemed much bigger now than it had just a minute ago.

"Prepare for emergency field anchor!" Max shouted into her chattertube hood.

"Eighty feet altitude," Sabrina reported. "Speed, twenty-two knots. Crosswind of two knots, north by northeast."

Buckle shoved the rudder wheel around. Trying to bring a damaged zeppelin down in a decent hover was one hell of a trick. A flip of bright red caught his eye. It was a tendril of Sabrina's hair, a loose curl dangling against her temple from beneath her bowler hat as she leaned over the drift scope at her station. Buckle fought an unsettled feeling in his stomach. Sabrina was the only person he had ever seen with hair so red as that—until today. How could the Founders steampiper possess scarlet hair equally brilliant? More disturbingly, how could she bear such an uncanny resemblance to Sabrina that it would be difficult to believe them anything less than family, or indeed anything other than twin sisters?

Both of them were even left-handed.

Buckle was bound by oath never to ask another sibling orphan any questions about their past. This was Balthazar's cardinal rule. But the Founders clan was fast becoming the Crankshaft clan's greatest enemy. And it was obvious to Buckle that her nearly identical appearance to an elite officer of their steampiper corps proved that Sabrina's connection to them ran far deeper than an unexplained familiarity with their city and its sewer systems suggested.

The matter had to end here. He had a broken zeppelin to land.

The matter had to end here. For now.

-LXXIII-

FIREFLIES AND BURNING FUSES

"DAMN THIS DISCOMBOBULATION!" IVAN GRUMBLED as he clambered up an access ladder between compartments four and five. His firefly lantern swung from his wrist hook, casting waves of orange illumination back and forth in the near darkness of gigantic rustling gas cells and creaking metal girders. They weren't going make it home for days, his airship was a mess, and to top it all off, he was going to miss his first date with Holly Churchill.

Holly had repeatedly thwarted Ivan's courting, stating emphatically that she was not interested in such dalliances at this time in her life. It had taken him three months to persuade her to accept a date. He was completely taken with her, and in the most gentlemanly way. She wasn't like the other Crankshaft clan girls. She was serious, intense, and did not smile easily—though when she did, she could melt the heart of an ogre. Her sandy-brown hair wasn't the longest, and she wasn't the most beautiful—though there was nothing wrong with her looks—but she possessed an incandescent sultriness, a magnetism that made men climb mountains and write songs, and hate any other poor fellow who might also throw his hat into her wide ring of suitors.

Ivan wanted to impress Holly, to open doors for her, to throw his jacket over puddles for her. He didn't want to be his usual boorish self and screw this one up. In his spare time he had been carving a little present for her. He was an excellent whittler, good enough to be specific about the qualities of the wood he used, and he had spent many long hours sitting on a propeller casing, carving a cardinal for her. The bird was extravagant in its detail, in every feather and dent in its beak, and Ivan could feel the tight little weight of it in snug in the left-arm pocket of his leather jumpsuit.

Tonight they had a date. And he was going to stand her up.

But Holly would understand. Surely. A fellow really should be forgiven when his zeppelin is on fire.

Ivan liked to think about Holly. It made him feel hopeful, and he needed that feeling, especially now, when so many bad things had happened. He snatched the top rung of the ladder and jumped up onto the Axial deck's forward catwalk, sliding the buglight handle off its hook and into his hand. The catwalk grating tilted down toward the nose—they were descending fast. He kept one hand on the railing—things were calm now, but the badly wounded airship could suddenly keel over again without warning, and he did not want to be catapulted off into the superstructure.

Ivan walked slowly toward the bow, peering through the hatchways ahead, swinging the buglight back and forth as he scanned each compartment and access hub, searching for the little black sphere of a steampiper bomb. If the fuse was lit, he would see the glow. He sniffed for the stink of burning hemp. He listened for the sharp hiss and pop of incinerating fibers. Other search teams shouted out, behind and below him, announcing compartments clear: their voices were muffled by the howling wind pouring in from the massive skin rents on both flanks, rippling and rattling every inch of everything inside the *Pneumatic Zeppelin.*

The strategy of the steampiper attack had been clear: some of the steampipers had been pure soldiers, armed with pistol and sword, but others were grenadiers, loaded down with bombs. If the attempt to capture the *Pneumatic Zeppelin* failed, then they were going to destroy it.

It would take only one small incendiary bomb, placed at the proper junction, to blow the entire airship and everyone aboard her into a million burning fragments.

And Ivan was sure that there was still a steampiper or two stowed away aboard the ship. He pursed his lips, his left hand moving to the handle of his pistol in its holster, strapped across his chest. Pushkin stuck his head out of his breast pocket, poking it around. Ivan clicked his tongue, which the wugglebat understood as "Go to sleep," and Pushkin ducked back down. Ivan was not supposed to be on his own; the search teams had been dispersed in pairs, but he and his partner, a rigger named Arlington Bright, had decided to split up, to search more compartments at greater speed. Now he wasn't sure whether he regretted his decision or not.

He should have brought Kellie with him, at least. Zeppelin dogs were trained to sniff out explosives. Some airships used potbellied pigs.

He should have brought the dog with him.

Something rattled on the Castle deck catwalk overhead. Ivan froze. He peered up into the darkness. Clutches of fireflies wheeled in the gaps between the gas cells. On one end of the catwalk, in the bow compartment, he saw a shadow...then he saw the flash of a tiny, flickering light.

It was a flame.

Ivan's heart skipped a beat. No crew person would ever strike a match inside the zeppelin.

Ivan dropped to one knee and held his breath. He drew his pistol, but he had no shot though the grating. Setting the buglight on the catwalk, he crept to the companionway and rushed up the steps, two at a stride, trying to make his boots pat the metal stairs as quietly as possible. He wanted to move slowly, with stealth, but if a bomb fuse was about to be lit, he did not have any time.

Ivan reached the Castle deck catwalk and sprinted, aiming his pistol in front of him. The steampiper was there, ten paces ahead, crouched down. The man had removed his helmet, revealing a swirl of short-cropped strawberry-blond hair, and his back was crisscrossed with bandoliers full of bombs.

Ivan gripped the handle of his pistol. His heart pounded so hard the barrel shook. His shoulder ached, the result of a fall against the corner of a firebox, when the ship had lurched violently before. When he cocked the pistol hammer, the *click* sounded brutally loud in his hears, like somebody had dropped a saucepan.

Ivan saw the match, a tiny waver of white under the glowing pink of the hand cupped around it. The match suddenly burst in a fluttering spew of reddish sparks—a bomb fuse had been lit.

Ivan charged. "Hey! Snuff it, fogsucker!" he screamed.

The steampiper jumped to his feet, the lit match in one hand and the bomb in the other, its sputtering fuse casting a bright illumination onto his face from beneath, making it look ghostly. He was broad shouldered and stalwart, about twenty-five years of age, with pale skin.

"Snuff it!" Ivan howled. He was a mere five paces from the man now.

The steampiper cocked his head with a strange, unnerving smile.

Ivan's finger tightened on the trigger. This fool was going to make him shoot.

The steampiper flicked the match at Ivan. The spinning flame whirled into Ivan's face and he jerked aside, snatching the match out of the air and crushing it in the palm of his glove.

"Damn you!" Ivan yelled.

The steampiper grabbed for the pistol in his belt.

Ivan's pistol boomed with a blast of smoke and muzzle flash.

The steampiper toppled backward, a smoking hole in the chest of his cuirass, landing flat on his back. His limp arms were flung over his head and the burning bomb rolled free, spinning and wobbling down the catwalk in a fishtail of sparks.

"Blue blazes!" Ivan shouted, hurdling over the steampiper as he scrambled after the bomb. The bomb was round, like a little cannonball, except for the fuse stem, and it rolled and clacked along the tilted grating at considerable speed.

A low howl rose in Ivan's throat. He guessed that he might have three, maybe four seconds left on the fuse.

He guessed wrong.

–LXXIV–

THE *PNEUMATIC ZEPPELIN* LOSES HER FIGHT WITH GRAVITY

THE NEW EXPLOSION, A MONUMENTAL gut punch, shook the *Pneumatic Zeppelin*'s piloting gondola as if the airship were riding an earthquake. The night clouds lit up with a brilliant flash of yellow.

Everything shook violently.

Sabrina Serafim knew they were going down. Their chances of survival had gone from rotten to worse. She steadied her weight against her instrument panel, taking a good hold of her drift scope curtain, trying to continue taking altitude readings as the airship lunged, waffled, and then nosed down into another precarious descent.

"De Quincey!" Buckle shouted. De Quincey leapt forward to assist Buckle on the helm.

"Damn the Founders to hell!" Balthazar growled.

"All ahead flank!" Buckle yelled.

Max slammed the chadburn dial forward to all ahead flank. "All ahead flank! I need all the airspeed you have!" she shouted into the chattertube.

"All ahead flank, aye!" Elliot Yardbird's voice returned on the chattertube, joined by the ring of the bell on the chadburn, as the sister needle swung into place.

"All hands! Emergency landing!" Buckle yelled. "Land if we're lucky! Water if we're not! Secure all boilers and brace yourselves!"

"Compartments one and two, all cells now reading zero pressure!" Nero shouted from the ballast station.

"Positive buoyancy can no longer be maintained," Max said. "We are going down."

"Prepare for emergency vent," Buckle said, as the gondola swayed precariously.

Sabrina glanced back at the hydro boards. The hydrogen in the gasbags had to be dumped at the point of impact when you ditched. It was impossible for a hard landing on either earth or sea not to result in snapping superstructure girders, which caused both sparks and punctured gas cells: the perfect recipe for utter incineration.

The thirty-odd percent of hydrogen left in the reserve tanks loomed large now, Sabrina realized. It would be all they had to try to get home with.

"Aye, preparing for emergency hydrogen vent!" Nero replied.

"Eighty feet and falling," Sabrina said. She looked up at the horizon. Catalina was very close. The *Pneumatic Zeppelin* swooped toward the island at too great a rate of speed, but there was nothing for it. The airship was going down, and she had to be driven forward by her propellers for her stabilizers and rudder to function. At least there was no weather but a negligible crosswind. "Seventy feet."

"Secure for emergency ditch!" Max ordered.

Sabrina lowered herself into her chair and buckled into her seat harness. Welly and Nero did the same. She glanced back into the gondola: beyond the greenish banks of boil-lit instruments, it was dark except for two swinging buglights, and one lone firefly making loops in the air over the hammergun turret. The Ballblasters and crewman had retreated into the map room, where they could use the harnesses on the seats; Max was at the engineering station, attaching her safety belt around her waist; Kellie was hidden, curled up in her alcove, as she was trained to do in a ditching drill; Balthazar stood alongside Wong, both of them in their harnesses.

But Buckle and De Quincey were not.

"Get your safeties on, helm!" Sabrina shouted.

De Quincey strapped on his harness.

Buckle did not move, grimacing at the helm, his feet set wide, bent at the knees with the strain of fighting the rudder wheel. "Yawing to port!" Buckle yelled, as he reached up and switched a propeller feathering handle. "Correcting! Landing bumpers down!"

"Landing bumpers down. Aye!" Nero replied, grabbing a large copper handle and cranking it furiously.

"Sixty feet altitude," Welly said. "Two hundred and fifty feet to landfall. We are at thirty knots. Fifteen seconds to landfall."

"We are coming in too fast," Max announced. Leave it to Max to point out the gloomiest details.

"Tell it to gravity!" Buckle answered.

"Aye!" Max replied, though Sabrina could not tell whether she was being serious or not.

"Fifty feet altitude!" Welly reported.

Buckle slapped a set of spoiler levers above his head. "We'll make the island, but it won't be pretty."

Sabrina turned back to her instrument board, the wind pouring in through the nose breach thundering in her ears. Outside she could see the sparkling black sea passing in a blur underneath, the dull-white mass of the large island, encased in snow, coming at them with what seemed like an even greater velocity. She eyed the altimeter needle on her instrument panel. "Forty feet altitude!" she yelled.

"Yawing to port again!" Buckle shouted. "Correcting!"

"Twenty-five knots airspeed!" Welly said. "Five seconds to landfall!"

"Altitude thirty feet!" Sabrina shouted.

"We are coming in too fast," Max repeated stoically.

Max was right. But what was there to do for it now?

"Shut down all engines! Shut down all engines and raise propellers!" Buckle yelled into the chattertube, slapping the chadburn handle to all stop, ringing the bell.

"Shutting down boilers!" Yardbird answered. "Sealing fire-boxes!" The chadburn bell jingled.

The view in Sabrina's drift scope flashed from black to white. "Landfall!" Sabrina shouted. "Altitude twenty feet and the ground is rising fast!"

"Ballast! Emergency vent!" Buckle screamed.

"Emergency hydrogen vent, aye!" Nero responded, cranking open the master venting levers.

It was dangerous to vent when there were fires aboard. Most certainly, whatever had caused the explosion, a steampiper bomb or fiery ember, had left a fresh string of burning debris behind it. But Buckle had no choice at all.

"Fifteen feet!" Sabrina shouted.

"Brace for impact!" Buckle shouted.

Seeing nothing but a white blur through the nose dome, Sabrina buried her head in her arms. But instead of finding blackness under the eyelids, her life flashed before her eyes, sort of. Disjointed childhood memories. Screams in the night, echoing down elegant corridors of gray stone. Flickering blue lamps.

Lifted from her bed by powerful hands and wrapped warmly in her blanket. The sour smell of tobacco and sweat leaking through to her nostrils. The sensation of being carried, carried, carried down corridors and stairwells and streets, and into a cold, damp, unseen unknown.

She had so many plans swimming in her head, so many futures engineered, such a desperate, bloody revenge to take...it would be a shame if it all ended here.

–LXXV–

CATALINA ISLAND

ROMULUS BUCKLE, WITH HIS GONDOLA keel hurtling mere feet above the surface of the island, with hydrogen vented and engines shut down, worried that he may have done his job too well.

They had dropped like a stone.

The slopes of the island rose up toward them: a giant white hand about to strike.

"Ten feet! Twenty knots!" Sabrina shouted.

A hill passed on their right, so close that Buckle could make out the tussocks of dead grass and jumbles of stones on its great white flank. He held the rudder wheel tight, maintaining course down the throat of a shallow valley that ran between the large hill on the right and another on the left.

"Steady...steady, old girl," Buckle whispered, watching his horizontal and vertical level bubbles inside their boil tubes. He had to keep the keel level. Striking the ground at an angle would split the airship to pieces. Even so, since he could no longer maneuver, they were at the mercy of the topography. Digging the nose of the gondola into a hidden hillock would collapse the superstructure like an accordion, and most surely crush the *Arabella* with it. Even if the *Pneumatic Zeppelin* somehow did not explode, the survivors would be stranded far from home, at the mercy of pirates and traders, not to mention any vengeful Founders who found them here.

"Keel is level!" Buckle yelled. "Slide, old girl! Slide!"

The nose wheel of the piloting gondola struck the ground with a brutal *thump*. In the same instant, the broken glass nose dome imploded with a *bang*. A high wall of snow and frozen earth fragments flew up in front of them. The airship bounced back into the air, three or four feet or so, hung for a second, and dropped again.

"All superstructure pneumatic joints maintaining integrity!" Max shouted.

When the gondola slammed down again, it stayed down, locked in an icy slide as the *Pneumatic Zeppelin* became a gigantic, shaking toboggan. A foaming wake of snow rolled out from both sides of the gondola nose. The ground was uneven, delivering tooth-rattling bumps. With the entire weight of the zeppelin perched on its three gondolas, the strains and stresses pushed every metal girder, screw, and bolt to its very limit. The rumbling racket rose immediately into a wall of noise that screwed into the eardrums and mule-kicked the brain.

The rudder wheel shook so violently that Buckle had to release his hands for fear of breaking his fingers. He saw dark blood all over the steering wheel pins, more of it soaking the entire length of the right sleeve of his coat.

The airship started to slow down, and once its forward momentum decreased, it rapidly decelerated to a halt, with a final abrupt jerk.

There was a weird silence. The last surviving buglight swung overhead, its handle creaking as it rubbed on its hook, its yellow light rocking back and forth.

"Are we dead or alive?" Sabrina asked. "I've lost track."

‑LXXVI‑

SHIPWRECK

BUCKLE'S BOOTS CRUNCHED AS HE strode through the snow, big crunches accompanied by a pattering of smaller crunches, as Kellie followed at his heels. Dawn had almost arrived, breathing a warm pink into the lightening darkness. The *Pneumatic Zeppelin* loomed at Buckle's left shoulder, a dark mountain anchored by a hundred hawsers to the frozen earth. Her huge gray envelope, swaths of her skin ripped wide open and gutted, hung listlessly over her superstructure ribs, like the skin of a starved animal. She sat at the end of the half-mile-long channel of brown earth her gondolas had scraped through the snow as she skidded into the valley. She was listing badly to starboard, the huge crimson lion, symbol of the Crankshaft clan, sagging on her flank.

But her back was not broken. They could patch her up enough to at least get them home.

The world was still, almost unnervingly so, after all the raging wind and shuddering decks, but it also gave all sound a wonderful richness and vibrancy. The air resounded with the shouts of engineers and the sounds of hammering, sawing, mallets striking metal, and steam-powered rivet cranks. Skinners and riggers swarmed the wreck from without and within, with needles and long rolls of fabric patching, rapidly stretching, stitching, and gluing. The ship's goat, Victoria, was tethered to the piloting gondola, where she chewed on what looked like a wad of paper; she gave Buckle a disdainful glance and looked away.

Buckle paused for a moment, watching the hydro men tend a line of fires on the far slope, melting snow in mess cauldrons to replenish the water ballast. He despised being grounded in such a fashion, his mighty airship now a beached whale, helpless, hemmed in on both sides by rock-strewn hills. Yes, the ship was snug in her temporary berth, lashed down by Max and her securing teams, and Pluteus's troopers patrolled the perimeter, but he felt terribly exposed nonetheless. He also did not like the buffalo. The island swarmed with herds of the big, shaggy creatures, who apparently cared not one whit about zeppelins, often galumphing right up the hawsers, sniffing and snorting bolts of dense mist from curling nostrils, searching for anything vaguely edible with their dark brown eyes, looking as strange as any Martian beastie.

Snort, grunt, snort, the buffalo would say.

Buckle winced. His arm ached in the sling Nurse Nightingale had tucked it into, after the gentle-fingered Fogg has stitched up the nasty slash across his wrist. "What is it with you line officers?" Fogg had complained. "None of you can stay put. Balthazar and Lady Andromeda are the worst patients a surgeon could ever wish for. Everyone else has to go before them, even if they themselves are shot through and the others are stricken with no more than splinters and hangnails. I have a lot of wounded to attend to, and all of you, once you're not watched, get up and stagger off. I don't have any nursemaids. Frankly, I am considering tying all of you down!"

Fogg and Nightingale had been busy: the shipboard infirmary was full, and they had erected an emergency tent to accommodate the less urgent cases.

RICHARD ELLIS PRESTON, JR.

Buckle felt tired. Damage inspection after damage inspection in the darkness by buglight had strained his wounded body and soul. Weakness flooded his legs. His stamina was shot all to pieces. At least he was well and warmly dressed, wrapped in a soldier's heavy greatcoat lined with sheepskin, its high collar flaps pulled up around his neck. He had replaced his sleek leather pilot boots with foraging boots, their interiors luxurious with wolf fur.

And he had a prisoner.

A steampiper.

A vengeful energy refueled Buckle's legs. He was on his way to interrogate the steampiper in the brig, and he wanted answers. Two Ballblasters had found the man lying semiconscious on the Hydro deck after the boarding skirmish. The young fellow had now had time to recover his senses, all of the time he was going to get, at least. And Buckle was in no mood for defiance or obfuscation. Buckle was not one for torture, but he liked entertaining the idea, where a steampiper was concerned.

Buckle blinked hard. His burst of energy wavered already, but he would mine his marrow for the strength to carry on, reinforced by the rattlesnake juice of spirit. He arrived at the gunnery gondola. Blast marks along the side marked where steampiper grenades had been hurled at the metal plates, denting them with their detonations. He swung into the open rear hatch, immediately encountering the interior darkness and its heavy stink of cordite. He and Kellie swung up the companionway to the keel corridor and strode toward the stern, dodging repair workers and banks of buglights along the way.

A zeppelin on the ground, not sky-moored thirty feet up or dry-docked, but fallen belly down on the earth, each girder in danger of being crushed by its own weight, is, for her captain, a depressing sight. Buckle's guts wrenched as he scrutinized every bent screw, dinged hydrogen tank, popped stitch, and warped hinge, peering up into the bombed-out cathedrals of the blasted compartments, where shredded tapestries of burned goldbeater's skins and imploded stockings hung from deck after deck of melted catwalks.

Dawn clouds soaked in lavender scudded across the gray sky, visible through the great holes in the roof overhead, looking free and clean and bright.

Buckle's grumpiness was rising. The musty aroma of unrolled skin boles and the chemical stink of fabric stiffeners made him slightly nauseous—he was starving—and the constant pounding of the repair hammers and steam-driven metalworking machines antagonized his aching head.

But beyond his headache and empty stomach, he was primarily annoyed at being grounded. The whack of his boots on the catwalk gratings had too much gravity in it—to a neophyte, a well-trimmed airship on the fly seemed as solid and stable as mother earth, but to an experienced aviator, who could feel the float of the platform, feel the slightest degree of tilt, feel the weightlessness of the machine beneath his boots, it was like riding the back of a butterfly. And when the zeppelin lay bound to the earth, so too the magical lightness of its being was lost to the zeppelineer.

It was like walking inside the corpse of a loved one.

Buckle pressed his fingers against the bandages on his wrist and they came back bloody.

Buckle arrived at the brig door, where Sabrina stood beside a crewman cradling a blackbang musket.

"Good morning, Captain," Sabrina said, and smiled grimly, logbook tucked under her arm. She crouched to pat Kellie on the head and looked the pink of health, her skin flushed by the chill of the ocean air, her eyes bright green, her bright-red hair loose under her bowler.

That damned red hair. Hair so red, it was the color of lava. The color of fire. Buckle had never thought that he could be tortured by a color.

"Good morning," Buckle said.

"How is your arm?"

"It stings. I should have that quack sawbones sent before a firing squad."

Sabrina chuckled as she straightened up. "Nice to see your lousy humor is still intact. But you do look a bit pale."

Buckle glared. Sabrina bit her lip. "No more of this dithering over my health," Buckle grunted. "Did you confirm the casualty report?"

"Yes," Sabrina said, flipping open the *Pneumatic Zeppelin*'s large, leather-bound logbook. She took a deep breath before she spoke. "Our expedition has suffered seventeen dead and twenty-six wounded, of which two are in a grave condition. Of bridge officers, Lieutenant Ignatius Dunn was killed in action, and Chief Mechanic Ivan Gorky was seriously injured."

The list of the dead. After every skirmish came the list of the dead. The roll call to the tomb. The casualties had not exceeded his own grim calculations, but the sound of Ivan's name on the list stabbed deep. "What is Ivan's condition?" he asked.

"Fogg says he will live. His situation is classified as serious, but not grave," Sabrina replied, her face belying her own concern over their cantankerous brother. "He was caught in the final bomb blast and thrown into the superstructure."

"Continue."

Sabrina turned a page. The heavy parchment scraped as it rolled over. "The casualties break down as follows: crew of the *Pneumatic Zeppelin*, five dead and thirteen wounded, including yourself; of the Ballblasters, eight dead and eleven wounded; of the Alchemists, four dead and two wounded. Of the clan leaders, Balthazar and Lady Andromeda are both banged up but recuperating. Katzenjammer Smelt seems to have escaped without a scratch."

"Of course. And what of our prisoner?"

Sabrina glanced at the brig door. "I am told he is not being cooperative. I made sure that he has not seen me yet, as you requested."

"Good. Wait here for two minutes, then come in. And remove your bowler."

"Aye," Sabrina replied, her eyes narrowing slightly.

Buckle opened the brig hatch and stepped inside.

–LXXVII–

PRISONER OF WAR

BUCKLE STEPPED INTO THE *PNEUMATIC Zeppelin*'s brig, a small, narrow guardroom with a jailer's desk, and two small, narrow jail cells beyond. Two people occupied the cabin: the guard, an empennage crewwoman named Zara Kenoff, who stood beside the hatch with a loaded pistol in her belt, and the steampiper, who sat at the table, his wrists and ankles in iron shackles.

The steampiper grenadier immediately stood, his chains jangling. He was a tall man, young, perhaps twenty-two and a touch more, muscled despite being narrow shouldered, and his pale-green eyes were bright and quick. He looked a bit underfed. His weapons and armor had been confiscated, and he was dressed in his Founders black uniform with silver piping. His cropped hair was red orange and curly, though nowhere near as impressive in color as Sabrina's.

"You are the captain of this barge, I presume?" the steampiper asked, his voice deep and even, his eyes haughty, his tone annoyed.

"Watch your tongue!" Kenoff snapped.

"It is all right, Miss Kenoff," Buckle said, with a gentle smile. "Please step outside a moment, will you?"

Kenoff nodded, moving to the hatchway. "If you need me, Captain, I'll be right outside the door, sir."

"Thank you," Buckle said, waiting for Kenoff to exit. He turned his gaze to the steampiper, who looked at him and then at Kellie, who peered back. "I am Captain Romulus Buckle of the *Pneumatic Zeppelin*," Buckle announced. "I trust you have been treated well."

"You would release me immediately if you had any sense at all."

Buckle grinned, knowing it would infuriate the Founders man. "You abduct my clan leader and bomb my airship, and you expect clemency from me?"

If the grin bothered the steampiper, he did not let it show. "What happens to me matters not. Your fate is already decided."

"By whom?"

"By those who are fittest to decide."

Someone rapped on the door.

"Enter," Buckle said.

The hatch swung open and Sabrina stepped in, bowler hat in hand, her red hair, brilliant and flowing, on display.

The steampiper gasped, then caught himself, though his eyes shone with confusion.

Sabrina gave the steampiper a wicked grin. "Chief Navigator reporting, sir."

"Commander?" The steampiper sputtered. "What are you doing here?"

"I am not your commander," Sabrina answered.

"Yes, you are," the steampiper snarled, anger rising in his voice. "You are my officer. You are a scarlet. How is it that you now count yourself among the Crankshafts?"

"Because I am a free woman," Sabrina responded.

The steampiper slammed his hand on the table, rattling his chains, his voice quaking as he turned to glare at Buckle.

"What have you done to her, you Cranker scum? What have you done to her mind to make her abandon her family, her blood? To betray the eagles to crawl with the rats?"

Sabrina's green eyes suddenly turned ice cold. "My family is corpses. My blood knows only murder."

The steampiper lunged in Sabrina's direction, only to be jerked back by his chains. "Commander—you have been brainwashed. Think! Tell me your name." He glared at Buckle. "Curse you to hell, Cranker!" He paused, breathing heavily through his nose, then looked sternly at Sabrina. "Tell me your name."

"My name? My name is one of the dead."

The steampiper took a deep breath, turning his eyes to Buckle. "It is you who has done this, this crime. Isambard Fawkes shall hear of this, and your life will be worth nothing."

Sabrina stepped forward. "It is you who is mistaken, sir. I am not the person you think I am." She looked to Buckle. "If we are finished here, Captain?"

"Absolutely. Thank you, Chief Navigator," Buckle said.

Sabrina planted her bowler on her head, turned on her heel, and departed the brig, shutting the door behind her.

"Remember your name!" The steampiper howled after her. "Remember your name and you shall remember everything, Commander!"

Buckle stood quietly, giving the man a moment to compose himself. The steampiper did nothing but stare at the deck.

Whoever Sabrina was, her presence had certainly thrown this otherwise highly composed Founders officer into a fit. "I was hopeful that we might attempt a diplomatic solution to our problems, to whatever grievances you Founders seem to have," Buckle said.

The steampiper raised his green eyes to meet Buckle's. "I don't know how you turned one of our own, Cranker, a steampiper officer, and a scarlet at that, but the day is coming, coming very soon."

"And what day is that?"

"The day the strongest take all that belongs to them."

"And what belongs to them?" Buckle asked.

"Everything," the steampiper replied.

–LXXVIII–

I HAVE SEEN THE STARS
BUT NEVER THE SUN

BUCKLE AND SABRINA WALKED, SIDE by side, under the belly of the *Pneumatic Zeppelin*, the snow swishing around their boots as they approached the stern. It was very quiet—work had stopped for the funeral ceremonies, which were soon to begin. Kellie loped out under the stern and they followed her paw prints, passing under the gigantic driving propellers, which had been folded up to prevent bending in the ground landing; their bronze blades glittered overhead as they hung motionless amidst the hundreds of exhaust, smoke, and heat pipes of the Devil's Factory extending out the back of the airship.

The number one port side propeller was missing, of course—destroyed in the steampiper attack—all that remained of it were its struts. The last fragments of the nacelle had already been cut away by the repair teams.

Buckle saw Newton and a handful of Ballblasters manning a redoubt on the northern rise. He noticed the deep, earth-churned drag marks left by the four cannons as the crew had dragged them up to the top of the hill. Pluteus had sent out compass-point patrols. Pure textbook. There had been no sign of enemy activity. Not a hide nor a hair of anyone.

Beyond the stern of the *Pneumatic Zeppelin* it was a beautiful morning. The low, white slope of the valley descended gently northward, down to the dark-blue sea, cut down the middle by the trough of frosty brown earth created by the zeppelin's gondolas. The sea air was clear, and across the channel Buckle could see the fog bank that hid the coast. Overhead, the white clouds soared high into stupendous vaults, backlit white and pink by the rising sun that found no gap to shine through.

Buckle saw from the corner of his eye that Sabrina was looking at him. The moment had been long and awkward since they had departed the brig. He knew there was much that she wanted to tell him. He also knew that she would not. At least, not for now.

Buckle eyed the fog bank in the far distance. "It is encouraging that there were no further signs of pursuit by the Founders."

"No, nothing," Sabrina said. "No airships, especially no dreadnoughts, and we are too far away for steampipers now."

"What of dreadnoughts?" Buckle interjected. "Fables of gargantuan gunships made up by the Founders to make everyone afraid to resist them? Where were these dreadnoughts when they needed them? Perhaps the Founders rely only on myths."

"Those myths very nearly popped us, though," Sabrina said.

Buckle nodded, though defiantly. "Yes, Serafim. They very nearly did."

"It is a lovely morning," Sabrina said with a sigh. "It feels as if, at any moment, you might see the sun. That would be grand."

Buckle nodded. He almost spoke, but suddenly he felt too weak to do so. He sagged. He felt heavy, weirdly waterlogged... as if he had been dropped down a well.

"Captain," Sabrina asked. "Are you all right?"

Buckle straightened his back, removing his gloves and tucking them into his pocket. The chill of the air did not penetrate the surface of his skin. If he spoke of his discomforts, he would give them too much effect in his mind. He turned his eyes to the sky where the undulating glow of the sun behind the clouds was the greatest. "I have seen the stars, but never the sun."

"You have seen the stars?" Sabrina said, amazed. "I never knew that."

"It is my oldest memory, I think. When I was a little boy—very small, perhaps four or five—there was a terrible storm up in the mountains where our cabin was. It was at night, and after it was over my mother and father woke Elizabeth and me and carried us outside. I remember—I remember that the air smelled funny, like hot metal, and it was absolutely still. And the sky, there was a huge gap in the clouds where you could see the night sky. It was black and full of stars, hundreds and thousands of them, glittering white stars scattered across the heavens. It was as if they had spilled out of eternity." Buckle paused and swallowed, watching Kellie investigate a small animal burrow on the slope. "I don't know if I saw the moon, I don't remember it. The whole thing lasted only a few minutes before the clouds closed again. I watched until the very last star disappeared."

"That is an incredible thing to have witnessed, Romulus," Sabrina said. She was close to him, right at his shoulder, and her green eyes were shining when he turned his head from the sky and looked at her.

"Strange," Buckle mused. "Strange are the things a rap on the head and blood loss bring back to you."

"Not so strange," Sabrina said, with a sad smile. "It is hopeful. No storm lasts forever."

The sounds of boots hurrying through the snow made both Buckle and Sabrina turn. They saw Jacob Fitzroy approaching. "The funeral ceremony is almost ready to begin, Captain."

"I shall come straight away, Fitzroy. Thank you," Buckle replied. He cleared his throat. His fingers felt cold, and he pulled his gloves back on.

–LXXIX–

OLD SALT AND HUMMINGBIRDS

THERE WERE HUMMINGBIRDS ON CATALINA, little flitting creatures with blurred wings that appeared at dawn and danced across the snow in flashes of color, of green and blue and crimson. They were one species that had found a way to flourish after The Storming. Max liked watching them: she was an engineer down to her bones, but there was a naturalist's bird's nest in a corner of her heart.

The hummingbirds darted in and out of the long row of funeral pyres, twenty-two in all, poking at the stacks of wood and dead grass, apparently attracted by the kerosene oil that had been poured across them. Their little flicks of color added something ethereal, something eternally alive, to the dead whose bodies rested atop the pyres, mummy-wrapped in white linen.

"It is said that hummingbirds float free of time," Sabrina said, as she and Buckle arrived at Max's shoulder. "And since they know eternity, they always come to welcome the dead."

"That is a fine thought," Max replied. The funeral and the sadness attached to it were keeping her mind off the *Pneumatic Zeppelin* and her monumental list of repairs. The overnight crews had accomplished everything that had been asked of them, and more, but they were going to be grounded for the rest of the day—at least.

Max coughed, both to clear her cold throat and to force her mind back into the moment. Midmorning was not far off, the overcast bright overhead, but the cold was still deep in the stillness around them. She glanced at Sabrina and Buckle, both standing to her right, and they both looked red eyed and tired. Buckle looked especially pale.

The entire ship's company—with the exception of those on patrol and those too badly injured to move—had been mustered in the ravine. Many of them were walking wounded, swathed in bloodstained bandages. Several had been carried out of the infirmary on stretchers. Even the steampiper prisoner, glowering in his shackles, had been brought forth to attend.

Balthazar was front and center, facing the ranks, with Pluteus and Katzenjammer Smelt at each shoulder. Due to her injuries, Lady Andromeda, who was reportedly not recovering well, was not there, but Scorpius and Kepler were. The Alchemists did not usually cremate their dead as the Crankshafts did, preferring ground burials, but Lady Andromeda had insisted that her people respect the Crankshaft tradition even in death, and honor those who had died helping to save her.

Ivan Gorky was also not present. That was not good. He would have dragged himself out to the ceremony if he could. Max had checked in on him twice in the infirmary, and she was quite worried about his condition, though Surgeon Fogg had repeatedly assured her that the chief mechanic would survive.

It was strange, her newly intense concern for Ivan, for she had always mildly disliked him.

A gentle wind rolled in from the sea, swept across the surface of the snow, and vanished. It was a time of solemn silence in the ceremony. Buffalos lowed in the distance. Twenty-two burning torches fluttered, gripped high in the hands of those who

RICHARD ELLIS PRESTON, JR.

would soon apply them to the pyres where their fallen mates lay in repose.

Twelve of the seventeen pyres were empty, representing the unrecovered bodies of eight Crankshaft and three Alchemist troopers left behind, and one crew person who had disappeared, either incinerated or gone overboard in the battle—not an uncommon occurrence on a sky vessel engaged in war. As far as actual corpses went, there were four *Pneumatic Zeppelin* crew members and one Alchemist atop their respective tombs.

There were also five pyres set off to one side: the corpses of five dead steampipers. They were the enemy, yes, but they were soldiers, and they were being treated with respect. Captain Buckle had asked the steampiper prisoner if there were any special burial rites he wished to have performed for his fellows, but the sullen grenadier had not volunteered any suggestions.

Max cleared her throat again. Buckle would soon deliver his mourning address, and she did not feel quite ready for it. She had to steel herself in a way no one else was aware of. She was half Martian, and Martians lived secret lives: under their cold, imperturbable interiors, they locked down souls driven by primitive emotions, souls capable of immense empathy, of pure love of the highest order, and also capable of the reddest haze of animalistic rage. Such extremes had to be kept in check, every second of every living day.

But Max was highly sensitive to people and their needs, to *who they were*. Even if many of the crew were not much interested in befriending the half-breed zebe, the ice queen—a name she knew some called her—she could not help but be almost supernaturally aware of who they were beneath their own, unstriped skins. Of the dead zeppelineers, she, in the agony of loss, knew them all: Lieutenant Ignatius Dunn, the recently arrived chief elevatorman who was often distant and sullen, but good at his job; Amanda Ambrose, a bow rigger and one of the three excellent violin players on board; Cameron Beddoes, boilerman and a gentle brute, who had once protected Max from two bullies in the schoolyard when they were children; Christopher Glantz, hydro chief and chief of the boat on the *Arabella*, a father of three and a master of checkers. She closed her eyes. She knew them all, knew their dreams, knew their faces and their children, and she could not shake the feeling that she had failed them. She turned her head, but all she saw was the empty pyre of Edward Black, a selfless young daredevil rigger known to all as Blackie, who had disappeared in the fight with the steampipers.

Max noticed a green glow floating in her goggles. She shut her eyes.

She heard the crunch of boots as someone strode across the snow. She opened her eyes to see Buckle step up onto a small platform and pause there, taking a long look at his assembled crew. The hummingbirds flitted about the pyres, delivering their flashes of brilliant color—emerald greens, aquamarine blues, and blood scarlets—amidst the dull grays and whites of the pyres behind him. The flames on the torches rippled high in the stillness.

"My fellow clansmen, crewmates, and soldiers," Buckle began, his voice sounding clear as a bell on the open slope, "we gather here, on this distant island, to honor the fallen. These dead are our brothers and sisters. We remember their lives, we mourn their passing, and we bid them farewell as they embark into the great unknown. And we, the members of the Crankshaft clan, having fought shoulder to shoulder with the Alchemist clan, are honored now to lay our dead shoulder to shoulder alongside yours. May their sacrifice, their blood, show us the way to our own protection and salvation."

Buckle read every Crankshaft name aloud, ending with the traditional funerary words: "They are the bravest of the brave."

Scorpius came to the podium and solemnly read the names of the Alchemist dead. As was their tradition, he said nothing more. But he did give a gracious nod both to Balthazar and Pluteus before he stepped down.

The stork-like Katzenjammer Smelt then took the stage, the silver spike on his helmet polished and gleaming, peering through his monocle at the assembly. Max thought it was odd for Smelt to wish to speak—he had very few friends here. "As the Chancellor of the Imperials," Smelt said, "I wish to express my thanks to all of you for my rescue. I also wish to express my gratitude to your warriors who perished on the field of battle. Their names shall be added to the Imperial List of Heroes." Smelt nodded and stepped back.

Buckle gave Smelt a cold glance as he returned to the podium. "General Pluteus Brassballs, Commander of the Ballblasters, shall now deliver the 'Old Salt's Prayer to the Oracle,'" Buckle announced.

Pluteus stepped forward, scanning the ranks for a moment before he spoke.

"Farewell old salt, my dearest friend,
Your soul returns to whence it came;
But I weep not, for in the end,
You and I shall meet again."

Pluteus lifted his right hand. The torchbearers stepped forward and applied their torches as one. The flames leapt to the kerosene-soaked wood, ripping along the lengths of the pyres in jagged strips before the constructions burst completely into flames.

The torchbearers stepped back. Max bowed her head, as did everyone, observing the minute of silence. The pyres roared in the cold stillness, the yellow flames rising skyward in swirling columns up to twenty feet in height, lighting up the slopes of the island and casting so much heat that everyone's cheeks turned ruddy—with the exception, Max was sure, of her own.

Once the minute was over, Max lifted her head. She glanced back at the dark ellipsoidal mass of the *Pneumatic Zeppelin* two hundred yards to the south—far enough away to avoid any airborne embers—and when she turned her head back, she noticed a figure off by itself, through the wavering mirage of heat around the fires. It was the zookeeper, Osprey Fowler, crouched on a low rise just beyond. She was tending a small fire—a funeral pyre for a dead pigeon, one of hers, somehow killed in the chaos of the previous night. Max did not know how long Osprey had been out there on the periphery, hands clutched and on her knees, with her thick brown hair hanging forward over her face like a veil. Her aloneness in her own act of mourning suited the way she always was.

Buckle stepped down from the podium, signaling the end of the ceremony. The crew relaxed from their state of attention slowly; they were exhausted and sad, and stared into the hypnotic undulations of the bonfires. Sabrina said that one could always see faces in the flames, but Max had never seen one. Perhaps her imagination was lacking.

A musket blast boomed, close by and from behind. Everyone nearly jumped out of their skin, including Max, and it was difficult to startle a Martian. She and the entire assembly spun around as the echo of the gunshot bounced off the hills.

There, holding a smoking musket as he stood atop a low ridge thirty yards away, was the ship's cook, the dauntless

Cookie, Perriman Salisbury. And, forty feet to his left, a buffalo staggered, uttered a wavering sigh, and collapsed. Max felt the thump of its drop in her boots.

Salisbury glared at everybody. "What? The dead are ashes and my tears are ashes now! And the dead aren't hungry anymore, right? But you all will be. And I'm the one who will have to listen to the whining if there's no fresh meat for supper!"

–LXXX–

DAMAGE REPORT

BUCKLE OPENED THE DOOR TO his quarters, and Kellie bounded in. He stopped. He had not seen the blasted remains of his cabin yet. Planks of the wooden ceiling had been ripped away by the explosion over the front compartments, exposing the bare metal supports of the Axial catwalk overhead; the upper section of the glass nose dome was shattered all about the bow pulpit; but the lower half, which formed the leading wall of his chambers, was intact, though cracked here and there. Ribbons of torn skin fabric were draped over the furniture, along with jumbles of blasted wood, shards of glass, and twists of brass and iron. Kellie bounded onto the bed and sat, looking confused by the debris crowding her perch.

Buckle walked in, bits of glass, wood, and metal scraping under his boots. He carried a buglight, but there was not much need for it yet—plenty of late-afternoon light still poured in through the window casements. It was six o'clock, an hour before dusk, and the *Pneumatic Zeppelin*'s repairs had brought her back to flying condition. He plunked the buglight on the pantry, and grabbed a surviving bottle of rum and a shot glass from his liquor cabinet. He carefully wiped a section of the Lion's Table clear and planted the bottle and glass beside a captured steam-piper helmet someone had placed there—probably Howard.

The helmet, its brass plates and dark eye slits gleaming, still seemed to pose a threat. Buckle wondered if there might still be a head in it.

Buckle could hear singing resounding through the zeppelin, the voices of the crew barely harmonious, but enthusiastic. The repair teams had finished their assignments at a feverish rate, and Buckle had given permission for the crew to throw a wake in the mess, their traditional celebration of the lives of the fallen. Extra grog rations were assigned, though not too much—just enough to warm their bellies. The crew still had to be reasonably sharp when they tried to get their wounded flying machine off the ground. But they needed a little cheer, Buckle reasoned, and their exhausted bodies and spirits would be the better for it. And they had good food: greasy steaks filled their plates, liberally sliced from Salisbury's buffalo, skinned and gutted, sizzling over a busy fire as the cook's smokejack rotated it on a spit one hundred paces east of the gunnery gondola.

Buckle's mouth watered—the smells of roasting meat wafted through his cabin, torturing his empty gut. But he had work to do. He ran his fingers across his dust-covered chart rack, selected a meteorological map, and unrolled it on the table—a difficult feat when one arm is in a sling. He plunked the rum bottle on one end, his top hat on the other, and checked the seasonal headwind pattern along the coast. He did not want his damaged airship heading into the wind on the way home, if he could help it.

A rap sounded at his door.

"Come in," Buckle said.

The heavy door opened with the scratch of glass. Max stepped in, holding her engineer's logbook, an ornate tome with flat gears and cogs sunk into its leather cover. "I have the new repair-status reports you requested, Captain," she said.

"Ah, good," Buckle replied.

"It is unfortunate that your quarters have suffered such catastrophe."

"Add it to the damage report, if you must." Buckle chuckled dryly.

Max flipped open her logbook, drew forth the ink pen, and made a small notation on a page. Buckle laughed, but stopped when Max gave him a stern look. It was difficult to tell when she was serious and when she was not. But most of the time she was serious.

Buckle uncorked the rum bottle with his teeth. "Care for a snort?" he asked, then spit the cork onto the pantry counter.

"No, thank you, Captain," Max answered. She rarely drank, though she could be coaxed into it on rare occasions.

"Very well," Buckle replied. He picked up the rum bottle, and the meteorological map, released from the weight, snapped into a tight curl. He poured a healthy two ounces into his glass, nodded to the steampiper helmet, and swallowed the rum. It squeezed down his throat and into his stomach with a harsh but pleasurable heat. Standard's Irish rum. Damn good stuff. "All right, then, let's hear it."

Max ran her finger across her handwritten columns in the logbook. "All major repairs are completed. Airship structure is fundamentally sound. Secondary team work is progressing well. Engines and boilers are intact. Propeller number one was damaged beyond repair, but all other nacelles are functioning. Gas cells one, two, three, sixteen, and seventeen were destroyed. Hydrogen reserves are dangerously low—thirty-one percent, but sufficient to get us airborne again. We can drain hydrogen from the *Arabella*'s reserve tanks if necessary."

"It will not be necessary," Buckle said. Both he and Max knew that they would need the launch in flying shape, in case they could not get the *Pneumatic Zeppelin* off the ground. Once disengaged, the launch could be sent home with a small crew to bring back a properly equipped repair team.

"Understood," Max replied. "The damages to the envelope skin are extensive, both to the flanks and the nose, but the skinners assure me they sealed the breaches sufficiently for transit. I also made a roofwalk personally, and I concur."

"We will launch just after dusk, departing under the cover of night," Buckle said.

Max snapped her logbook shut and nodded. "I can say that we have a very high percentage chance of getting home."

Buckle wanted to fold his hands behind his back, but the sling on his right arm prevented that. "It was a very near thing," he said.

"Razor's edge," Max replied.

Buckle smiled gently, aware of his great affection for his Martian engineer, and the deep empathy he felt for the lonely life she pretended did not affect her. "You and your crew have done a brilliant job. Good work."

"Thank you, Captain." Max's eyes glimmered blue in the aqueous humor: the colors of pride, of happiness.

"I also wanted to thank you for your bravery up on the roof yesterday, when you protected me from the tanglers."

The blue tint faded from Max's goggles. "I failed you, Captain."

Buckle shook his head. "Courage is courage. Courage against long odds is never diminished by the result. So I thank you, my brave, brave friend."

"You are welcome, Captain." The goggles went blue again.

Buckle stepped to his little pantry and collected another shot glass. "Have a drink with me, Lieutenant."

"I appreciate the gesture, Captain. But I should not."

Buckle planted the glass on the table beside his. "I am attempting an appropriate gesture of appreciation here. Well, how about I order you to have a drink with me, then?"

Max cocked her head. "An order?"

"Damned right, it is an order," Buckle announced playfully as he poured. "And a heartfelt request."

Buckle lifted a brimming glass toward Max. She sighed and stepped forward, taking it in her long, white fingers.

"And goggles up, please," Buckle said.

"Another order?" Max asked, almost shyly.

"Another heartfelt request. I should like to see your eyes, Lieutenant. This means a lot to me."

Max reached up to her leather pilot helmet and flipped the lever that retracted the aqueous humor from the space between her eyes and the goggle lenses. She lifted the goggles up to their resting position on the crest of the helmet and wiped her wet eyes with her sleeve. She paused, and then did something that surprised Buckle slightly—she pulled her helmet off, her thick black hair swirling about her face and shoulders. It was an act of casual undress; she rarely did such a thing in his presence.

"Goggles off, Captain, as requested," Max said.

Buckle smiled. Max had caught him off guard, and she knew it: a devious blue haunted her dark eyes. "Very well, then." He raised his glass with his good hand and motioned for Max to step closer. "To the blood."

Max took a confident stride up to him. They hooked arms at the elbow, each drawing their hand back so their glass was poised just below their lips, their faces only inches apart. "To the blood," Max said.

"Aye," Buckle said, his voice emerging in a husky whisper. Two zeppelineers who drank to the blood together were forever bound to sacrifice their lives for each other. Buckle had made this toast with Max before, as he had with several crewmates, but this time it was different—something crackled in the air between them like a swarm of invisible bees. "To the blood."

Buckle threw back his rum, feeling Max's slender elbow rotate in the crux of his arm as she did the same. When the arms came down, he found himself caught in her hypnotic alien eyes. What was this? Buckle could not move. Max's breath, sweet with the rum, warmed his lips. He realized that her Martian heart, pressed up against his forearm, was pounding. Something demanded that he kiss her. He wanted to kiss her. But to do so meant to throw himself off a cliff, and into the depthless chasm of those bottomless black eyes that now danced with purple will-o'-the-wisps. He could not move.

A rapping came from the door as it swung open with a scrape of wood and glass.

Max jerked back. When she yanked her arm away from Buckle, she lost her grip on the shot glass; it spun to the floor and shattered. Buckle's lips suddenly felt cold.

Sabrina stared from the doorway, having shoved the door open for little Howard Hampton, cabin boy and gunner's mate, to enter, proudly striding in with a tray of hot tea. "Howard made you some tea, Captain."

"Very good, lad," Buckle said with a smile, flicking his eyes once to Max. "Place it on the table here, please."

Max pulled her hair back and yanked on her flying helmet. She lowered her goggles, flooding them with the aqueous humor. "I shall see to the next status report, Captain," she announced, and strode for the door.

"Very well, Max," Buckle replied, watching Howard pour him a cup of dark tea.

"This is much better for you than the rum, sir," Howard said. "Especially with such a nasty chill in the air, sir."

"Aye, lad," Buckle said, watching Max disappear out the door. He turned and ruffled the boy's hair. "Aye." There was something different about Howard now...something serious had crept into his blue eyes above the blackbang powder stains on his cheeks. He had witnessed war for the first time. The innocence was gone.

"Cookie cooked up some bangers and eggs for Kellie," Howard continued. Kellie yipped at the word "bangers." Kellie was crazy for bangers. "Cookie said there's nothing like a crash landing to make the hens pop eggs like there's no tomorrow."

Sabrina opened her logbook in her casual, unperturbed fashion. "I have a status report on the piloting-gondola control surfaces, if you wish, Captain."

"Go ahead," Buckle said. As Sabrina began her list of repairs, Buckle could not help but be distracted by the raucous singing resounding from the mess hall. Had they been singing all this time? He could not recall.

~LXXXI~

YE WHO HAVE LOVED AND LOST

IT WAS AN OLD MEMORY—AT least for Sabrina, who was only nineteen, six years distant was an old memory—and it overwhelmed the present moment with such vividness that she actually stopped speaking in midsentence, in order to catch her breath.

She was aboard the airship trader *Condor* once again, a thirteen-year-old whose heart was beating so rapidly she could feel it drumming in her wrists.

"I love you, Sabrina," Gabriel Teague said, his face only inches from hers, speaking loudly over the roar of the steam boilers, just inside the hatchway of the old tramp.

It was a loud, seal-oil-stinking, greasy place—but they could be alone there, away from the laughing eyes of the crew.

Sabrina placed her hand on his chest, halfheartedly pushing him away. "Dear Gabriel," she answered. "It is no good."

His brown eyes never left hers. "I love you."

Sabrina looked away and found the porthole across the passageway to stare at, the gray clouds drifting by. She could say nothing. Yes, she loved him. But she was only thirteen—what did she know? He was two years her senior and brutally handsome, in her opinion, his father the *Condor*'s owner and captain, and she was only a hired hand, a cargo rat one rung above a stowaway, working for bunk and board. "Your father would not approve," she said.

It was such a falsehood. She knew Gabriel's father, and he would not care one whit. But Sabrina feared—she knew—that she would only torture Gabriel with her damaged heart.

"If you do not declare the love I know you harbor for me, I swear I shall throw myself off the airship right now," Gabriel declared, quite defiantly.

Sabrina turned her eyes to his and kept them there. Inside, she was crumbling. Her family was gone. Marter was gone. Helpless to act upon her plots of revenge, she was alone. She *wanted* to love Gabriel.

"I love you then, if saying so will serve to prevent you from jumping over the side," Sabrina blurted, and when Gabriel kissed her, she wept.

"I shall make a fortune for us, you shall see," Gabriel had enthused. "My father has given me shares. Tomorrow morning, after we deliver our rubber shipment, I shall be a wealthy man."

The next morning, Gabriel and his father were dead, along with most of the crew. The *Condor*, stripped of her cargo and hydrogen, was burning.

And Sabrina, the Jonah, bloody and branded with a hot iron, lay in the hold of the slaver pirates, waiting to die.

It was startling what the brain might suddenly choose to offer from its depths, uninvited.

Sabrina inhaled and continued reading her instrument reports out loud. She was unsettled. It was not the memory of poor Gabriel that derailed her. It hurt, certainly, but, no—she was dismayed by what she had just seen.

She did not know what she thought of what she had just glimpsed between Max and Buckle. Seeing them locked

RICHARD ELLIS PRESTON, JR.

together, drinking "to the blood," was not unusual—she had taken that comradely oath with Buckle as well—but the naked moment she witnessed between them, more *sensed* than saw, was startling.

Sabrina and Max were not particularly close, more acquaintances than sisters, but she knew what purple in Martian eyes meant. Max was in love with Romulus Buckle. Max was in love with Romulus Buckle, and he, magnificent, kind, handsome oaf that he was, had no bloody idea.

At first she was just surprised. Now she felt as if she had been kicked in the stomach.

–LXXXII–

BUFFALO STEAK AND A
DUEL FOR DINNER

By THE TIME CAPTAIN BUCKLE, Howard Hampton, and Kellie arrived in the mess hall, the festivities were in full swing. Some of the Ballblasters and Alchemists were also in the thick of it, including Wolfgang and Zwicky, and they appeared to be enjoying themselves. The airship's string quartet fiddled at the back of the chamber. It was not a full quartet, not anymore, not with the fourth chair empty after the death of their second violinist, Amanda Ambrose, the night before, but the remaining three carried on.

"Three cheers for Captain Buckle!" shouted boilerman Nicholas Faraday, shoving through the crowd and thrusting a shot glass of illegally acquired gin into Buckle's hand. "The Cap'n who soars with the tanglers!"

The voices of the assembled crew rose as one. "Hurrah! Hurrah! Hurrah!"

Buckle lifted the glass and threw back the gin, its bite always popping with midshipman memories, most of them fond. He was a gin man no more, however—the juniper berry distillation was coarser to his palate than his much preferred rum.

The men and women cheered, and a chant arose: "Name! Name! Name!"

Buckle raised his hand. The mess went silent. He eyed the empty chair and thought of the name. "Amanda Ambrose," he announced loudly. "The finest skinner I ever saw, the sweetest violinist I ever heard, and the finest ripper I ever met!"

"To Amanda Ambrose!" the chief skinner, Marian Boyd, shouted.

"To Amanda Ambrose!" the crew repeated in unison, then cheered.

The wake party surged on, and Buckle found himself propelled forward by the husky arm of Perriman Salisbury.

"I could cook you up some tangler giblets, Captain," Salisbury joked. "Scraped fresh off the roof. Think of it: the beastie tries to eat you, but you eat the beastie. The irony of it all makes one's mouth water, does it not?"

"Tangler innards are poisonous, are they not?" Buckle asked.

"That is beside the point." Salisbury laughed. He sat Buckle down at a table, and slid a plate of hot buffalo steak, eggs, and bangers in front of him. Another plate, with bangers and a greasy shank bone, was placed on the deck for Kellie.

"Everyone else has been fed, Cookie?" Buckle asked Salisbury.

"Yes, Captain," Salisbury replied. "I always make sure you are the last."

"It looks to be a capital dish," Buckle said, thrusting his fork into the thick cut of venison on the metal plate, swirling it around in its greasy blood and the butter from the eggs, and cutting away a chunk of it with his knife. He jammed the meat into his mouth. It tasted so good he almost fainted.

Katzenjammer Smelt's voice ruined the whole thing.

"Romulus Buckle, I expect you to surrender my airship to me the moment we arrive in Imperial territory," Smelt announced, suddenly appearing across the table. "I will, of course, assure you and your crew safe conduct home."

Buckle, slowly chewing his steak, stared at Smelt. "What is done is done. This is my airship, Chancellor."

"I am honor-bound not to accept such an answer," Smelt said evenly.

The mess hall suddenly fell silent.

"The *Pneumatic Zeppelin* is my airship, and you shall return her to me or suffer the consequences, sir," Smelt pressed.

"Have a drink, Chancellor," Buckle offered.

Nicholas Faraday ambled forward and shoved a glass of gin into Smelt's face. "Aye! Have a drink, Imperial. Take the edge off."

Smelt slapped the gin away, spraying it all over Faraday.

Sergeant Scully lunged forward, hurling his glassful of grog into Smelt's face. "The captain said have a drink, you filthy spiker!"

In a flash, Smelt's sword was free of its scabbard, the flashing tip poised at Scully's throat. "Have at it, Sergeant. Take the last breath you shall ever take."

The mood of the crowd went black. With hissing curses they closed in.

Buckle jumped to his feet. "Enough!"

Everyone stopped. The mess fell silent again.

Smelt lowered his sword and turned to Buckle. "You, sir, are a thief and a blackguard. If you refuse to return to me what is rightfully mine, then I must force your hand as a matter of honor. I invoke the right to challenge you to a Captain's Duel. To the death."

A volcano went off in Buckle's brain. He wanted to lunge at Smelt's throat. He did not.

"Do you accept, sir?" Smelt asked, almost whispering, watching Buckle with the eyes of a cobra waiting to strike. "Or is there not one scrap of honor in you?"

There was nothing in the world at that moment that Buckle wanted more than to run a sword through Katzenjammer Smelt. "By the Code of the Captains, I accept."

"Choose your weapon," Smelt said through gritted teeth.

Swords. That was Buckle's first thought. The blade was his best talent. But his fighting arm was injured. No, if Buckle was going to annihilate Smelt, it would have to be with a firearm. "Pistols," Buckle said, "at ten paces."

"Pistols it is," Smelt replied, his eyes glittering, especially the one behind the monocle.

"Howard!" Buckle yelled. Howard Hampton jumped to his side, eyeing Smelt suspiciously.

"Aye, Captain," Howard said, trying to chew down a mouthful of steak.

Buckle placed his hand on Howard's shoulder. "There is a set of dueling pistols inside the drawer of the Lion's Table up in my quarters. Go get the box and bring it to me up on the roof as fast as you can."

"Yes, Captain." Howard took off at a sprint.

Buckle looked at Smelt and gracefully extended his arm toward the keel corridor. "Shall we, Chancellor?"

Smelt rammed his sword home into its scabbard with a sharp clank and strode out of the mess hall.

Buckle turned to the sea of furious and concerned faces around him. "This will be finished in a matter of minutes. All of you remain here. Remain here!" He spun on his heel and marched after Smelt.

–LXXXIII–

THE ROOF

BUCKLE STOOD ON THE MASSIVE roof of the *Pneumatic Zeppelin*, glaring at Katzenjammer Smelt in the chilly dusk, and wondered just how exactly he had gotten there. Hummingbirds buzzed the skin patches, rushing the hemp stitches and stiffening glue. A mild breeze had come up from the west, tugging at the folds of the zeppelin's skin and driving the long, gray-black sweep of smoke from the funeral fires out over the dark blues of the channel, where the fluttering dots of seabirds wheeled high above.

It had started to snow. The air floated with fat, soft snowflakes that played more than they fell.

Howard Hampton clambered up out of the observer's nacelle access hatch and arrived at Buckle's hip. He flipped open a carved wooden chest to reveal a green felt interior that housed two blackbang dueling pistols, along with balls, powder satchels, and ramrods.

Buckle took the chest and offered it to Smelt. "For your inspection, Chancellor," he said.

Smelt lifted one of the pistols and hefted it in his hand. "Acceptable," he said.

Buckle took the second pistol, and he and Smelt carefully loaded and primed their weapons in silence. Howard Hampton stared at them with wide eyes.

"Ready?" Buckle asked Smelt.

"Yes," Smelt answered, cocking the firing hammer on his pistol with a heavy *click*.

"Howard," Buckle said. "When I give the word you will count to ten."

"Yes, Captain," Howard replied weakly.

"Just count out ten paces, boy," Smelt said to Howard, then turned his gleaming monocle on Buckle. "On ten we turn and fire."

"Pick any distance, Smelt. You are a ghost already," Buckle said.

Smelt smiled. Buckle hadn't expected that. It was a genuine grin, wide and long-toothed across the tight skin of his face, the chin and cheeks smattered with beard stubble. Buckle turned so he faced away from Smelt. He was looking northward: below, he could see the long span of the shoreline; the snowfall gave the landscape a softness, muting the edges between the dark sea, white land, and red-tinged clouds of evening.

Smelt stepped behind him, his boots squeaking on the snow that was collecting on the canvas. They were now back-to-back. Buckle looked at Howard and nodded.

"One!" Howard yelled nervously.

Buckle took one stride forward. The carved wooden handle of the dueling pistol felt warm in his hand as he held it at his chest, barrel upright. It was a good weight.

"Two!"

Buckle had never been in a shooting duel before. He was an excellent marksman, but if he had his druthers he would always fight with swords. Blackbang firearms were unpredictable—even the master-crafted dueling pistols could easily misfire.

"Three...four!"

Buckle's boots almost floated under him, his tread spongy on the taut canvas. The world felt unstable, and he felt loose in it. It was not nerves—even his rage had calmed, tempered by the opportunity to exact his revenge. Killing Smelt would throw a big wrench into Balthazar's diplomatic plans, yes, but the die had been cast. There was no going back now.

"Five...six!" Howard shouted, his voice gradually falling off behind Buckle.

When he turned to fire, Buckle knew to rotate halfway, standing sideways to Smelt, presenting his slender flank, rather than his chest, to present as small a target as possible.

"Seven!"

The wind gusted, cold, driving a handful of snowflakes into Buckle's face. The next two strides seemed as if they might take a thousand years. Even if Smelt did manage to pot him, he would get his shot off as well. Buckle would not miss. Perhaps today the crew of the *Pneumatic Zeppelin* would fire two more funeral pyres on the snowy Catalina slopes. If Buckle sent Smelt to his grave, he could die happy...and then he remembered Elizabeth.

"Eight!"

The sinews in Buckle's cold fingers stiffened as he tightened his grip on the pistol. His injured right wrist, freed from its sling, ached. He thought he heard something lightly scamper across the canvas behind him, as if a gazelle had just passed through.

Death arriving to make a collection, perhaps.

"I, uh, nine!" Howard stuttered.

What in blue blazes was wrong with Howard Hampton, messing up the count like that? Buckle thought, as he took another stride. Well, in one second it would not matter.

"Ten!"

Buckle whirled around and flung out his arm.

How he stopped himself from pulling the trigger, Buckle would never know.

─LXXXIV─

THE WHITE ANGEL

WHEN BUCKLE TURNED, HIS FINGER full on the trigger, the sinew coiled to jerk, he discovered Lady Andromeda standing directly between him and Katzenjammer Smelt. In that instant she seemed an apparition in white, an angel, her long infirmary gown and untethered hair flowing in the wind, her skin as pale as the snow under her bare feet, her eyes startlingly black, her lips bright red, her ivory white hands thrust out, long fingers quivering.

It was as if she had risen up from the *Pneumatic Zeppelin* itself.

"Curses, woman!" Smelt bellowed, attempting to aim his pistol past her. "Get out of the way!"

Buckle peered down the barrel sight. He could see Smelt lurking beyond Andromeda, but she was in the way of a good shot. He did not trust the accuracy of his blackbang pistol to aim past her by a hair's breadth. And neither did Smelt.

"I shall do no such thing!" Andromeda shouted. "Either shoot me or lower your weapons, for I shall stand for nothing less!"

Frustration dug its claws into Buckle. Smelt should be lying dead on the roof by now. "With all due respect, Lady

Andromeda, this is not your affair," Buckle said, still trying to keep Smelt as square as he could in his sights.

"You fools! Can you not see?" Andromeda despaired. "Can you not think for yourselves? We are doomed if we continue to fight one another. Fortune has made us allies, and I, for one, shall not see the workings of fortune undone. So now, Romulus and Katzenjammer, lower your pistols."

The duel was over. Buckle lowered his pistol to his thigh and saw Smelt do the same.

"Thank you, Lady Andromeda!" Howard Hampton interjected, with a sigh of relief.

"Come to me, both of you," Andromeda ordered.

Buckle marched forward to arrive at Lady Andromeda's left shoulder, just as Smelt arrived at her right. Up close, Andromeda looked terribly ill: her skin was too pale, the blood beneath coursing too faint and blue, her eyes too dark, her lips too sinisterly crimson.

"Lady Andromeda," Buckle said, "we need to get you back inside and into bed."

"I must agree," Smelt said with a concern that seemed genuine. "I am afraid you look entirely unwell."

"No!" Andromeda said with a grimace. "Not until you two end the blood feud between you. The Crankshafts, the Imperials, and the Alchemists must join as one, or be destroyed in turn when the Founders crusade begins. The time for your private little war is over. Swear to bury your hostility toward one another before me, here and now."

Buckle and Smelt locked eyes and stared. The hatred Buckle felt for the man seemed insurmountable. "But, my lady," Buckle said, "Smelt and the Imperials broke a treaty of truce between us. They attacked our stronghold in the night and bombed our houses and airships. Dozens of our clan were killed, including my sister and Balthazar's wife. Such a thing cannot be forgiven."

"Liar!" Smelt snarled, his face purpling. "My clan made no such attack. It was you who broke the truce, you who invented this lie so you could raid us. Do you think I would allow you to steal my airship, this very airship which you just wrecked, and never come to take it back from you? Your punishment is at hand, Romulus Buckle."

"I saw the crosses on your airships in the night, Smelt," Buckle said evenly. "I saw the bombs falling from your gondolas. Upon the souls of those you murdered, how dare you claim that you did not attack us."

Smelt fell into a smoldering calmness. "The Imperials have never broken a treaty or truce. Never. When we make war, we declare it first."

"Enough! Yesterday, bloody and contentious as it may be, is done," Andromeda said. "If you cannot bury the past, then none of us has any future, except as graves or slaves. End your feud now."

Buckle and Smelt glared at each other: their hatred and distrust stifled them. They could neither speak nor move.

Andromeda's teeth started chattering uncontrollably. She coughed and pressed her hands against her lips. When she pulled her white fingers away, they were speckled with bright-red blood, the same bright-red blood that now ran in a small rivulet from the corner of her mouth. She uttered a soft sigh and collapsed.

Buckle and Smelt dropped their pistols and lunged to catch Andromeda as she fainted. Buckle wrapped his arms around her slender waist as Smelt caught one arm and cradled her head.

"Lady Andromeda, we are taking you to the infirmary now," Buckle said.

"No," Andromeda replied, her voice strident, despite its weakness. The snowflakes landing on her skin did not melt as fast as they should. "Swear. Swear on your honor to end your feud, or leave me here to die."

Buckle looked at Smelt again. Their faces were much closer together now as they supported Andromeda, and Smelt looked like a man, more a man than a monster, with large pores in his nose and eyes both angry and distraught. Buckle hated him, but Andromeda's frailness forced Buckle's hand, if only until circumstances no longer made an alliance necessary. "I swear, Lady Andromeda," Buckle said. "I swear to honor an alliance with the Imperial clan."

"I shall also swear," Smelt grumbled, "that the Imperials shall prove worthy allies to the Crankshafts for the duration of the war to come."

"Very good," Andromeda said, placing her trembling hands weakly against the chests of both Buckle and Smelt. "You may now return me to my sickbed."

Without a word, Buckle and Smelt gently lifted Andromeda and carried her at their best speed back to the observer nacelle hatch. When Buckle glanced back through the thickening snowfall, he was struck by the sight of Howard Hampton, alone on the colossal roof, standing over the two unfired pistols and a splatter of red blood in the white snow.

–LXXXV–

ELIZABETH

BUCKLE STEPPED INTO HIS QUARTERS and smelled mutton stew.

Balthazar had ordered Buckle to meet him there. That suited Buckle just fine—he had a bone to pick with Balthazar.

Balthazar stood in front of the nose-dome window, looking out the cracked glass at the snowy slopes of Catalina, his hands folded behind his back, motionless, as if in a trance. He wore his heavy gray overcoat, which made him look even stockier and bigger than he was. A bowl of Salisbury's mutton stew rested on the freshly wiped Lion's Table, and beside that was Balthazar's open medicine pouch, one vial drained and empty.

Buckle slowly closed the door. He felt twisted up inside. He wanted answers to the zookeeper's whispers about Elizabeth. It hurt him terribly that Balthazar might be keeping such information from him.

For the first time in his life, he was furious with Balthazar.

"How fares our Lady Andromeda?" Balthazar asked, without looking back.

Buckle spoke slowly, trying to read the angle of Balthazar's shoulders. "Not well. I intend to look in on her again before we depart."

Balthazar paused, lowering his head slightly, then raising it again. "You are a fool, Romulus," he said, still facing away. "You should never have allowed yourself the self-indulgence of a duel with Smelt."

"I had no choice, Father."

"You always have a choice."

"But—"

"No," Balthazar interrupted. "There is a war coming, Romulus, a war for domination of our world. A war engineered by the Founders. And if they can prevent our coalition and engage each of us, one at a time, piecemeal, then none of us has any chance at all."

"As long as we still breathe, we still fight," Buckle replied. "And if we still fight, then we always have a chance."

"But a leader must fight intelligently," Balthazar replied with his usual low, calm voice.

"I see you took your medicine. Surgeon Fogg was looking for you."

"Yes," Balthazar replied. He turned to face Buckle. "Despite my disappointment with your latest actions, I am proud of you and your crew. It was a magnificent rescue and escape. Well done."

"Thank you, Father," Buckle answered. "We are a clan. A family. We are duty-bound. There are no secrets between us."

Balthazar slowly, deliberately, walked across the chamber, his boots crushing wooden splinters and glass, and stopped in front of Buckle. His gray eyes, striking in their intensity over his magnificent blond-white beard, bored deep. "You wish to speak of something with me, Romulus?" Balthazar asked.

Buckle cursed himself. How could Balthazar read him so easily? It wasn't as if he were a Martian, with the aqueous humor around his eyes glowing bright red with rage. He had his left hand inside the pocket of his winter coat, and his fingers were clamped around the smooth leather cover of the message scroll Osprey Fowler had given him. He pulled the scroll out of his pocket, opened it, and read it aloud: "Elizabeth alive. Founders prisoner. Perhaps escaped. Whereabouts unknown. Aphrodite."

Buckle lifted his eyes to Balthazar's and found sadness in them.

"Alas, so now you know," Balthazar whispered. "Now you know."

"*Now* I know?"

Balthazar turned, placing his hand on the steampiper helmet on the Lion's Table as he looked out through the nose dome. "Never trust a zookeeper to keep a secret," he said.

Buckle clamped his fingers over the scroll and strode around the table to face Balthazar. "How can you joke?" he blurted, feeling the blood rise in his face. "You knew that my sister was alive? You knew and you did not tell me?"

Balthazar's eyes turned so hard, and with such a suddenness, that Buckle, despite his anger, almost took a step backward. "I cannot be certain that she is alive," Balthazar said.

"When? When did you get the message?"

"Just before I left for the truce meeting at the Palisades Stronghold."

"But how, Father," Buckle blurted, his anger shifting to hurt confusion. "Why, why, if you knew, why in the world would you not tell me that Elizabeth was alive?"

"Because it wasn't the time," Balthazar said.

"Wasn't the time? What the hell does that mean?"

"My decisions are always made for the common good of the clan, not for what might best suit you, or me, or even Elizabeth."

"She is my sister."

"She is my daughter, whom I would give my life for, whose absence has buried me in sadness. I understand your anger with me—and your confusion at my decision not to tell you of the rumor immediately. It was not the time."

Buckle paused, swallowing hard. The leather scroll bit into his palm as he clenched it. "Why, Father? Why didn't you tell me?"

"Because she is out of reach, Romulus—for now. Because you are an excellent airship captain, but as an individual, you are impulsive and tend toward recklessness. I knew that the Founders were up to something, and that we were in danger. I did not need you shooting off on your own to try to find your sister. Forgive my silence, but you know this to be the truth."

"Perhaps it was true a year ago—before I became a captain. I wish you would have had more faith in me than this."

"If you are honest with yourself, I think you will understand why I did not tell you," Balthazar said, stepping forward and placing his hand on Buckle's shoulder. "The Founders are mobilizing for war, Romulus. The Palisades ambush was their first move. Treacherous, yes, but with the success of this rescue their machinations shall, I believe, prove to have been a monumental mistake. They have thrown us together with the Alchemists—aye, even the Imperials—in a way we could have probably never managed if left alone. Now we have spilled blood together in a common cause. And with Andromeda and Smelt safely restored to their people, I am certain we can negotiate a three-way alliance. If we can convince two or three of the other major clans to come in with us, such as the Spartaks, the Gallowglasses, or the Tinskins, then we have a fighting chance."

Buckle nodded as his fury ebbed away, leaving a deep pool of frustration. "You say that Elizabeth is out of our reach?" he asked.

RICHARD ELLIS PRESTON, JR.

"For the time being. You must trust me on that."

"And we do nothing to try to find her?"

Balthazar's eyes twinkled, the way they did when his mischievous streak came to the fore. "I did not say nothing is being done. I said that she is out of *our* reach for the moment."

"You are counting on your mysterious Aphrodite?"

"To some extent."

"But how do the Founders have her? It was the Imperials who blitzed us at Tehachapi the night Elizabeth disappeared," Buckle argued. "How did the Founders get ahold of her?"

"I do not know the connection," Balthazar said. "Or even if the rumors of her survival are true."

Buckle stepped up to the shattered nose window. "If Elizabeth is alive, I shall find her. I shall. I shall smash the City of the Founders—I shall rip the earth in half to find her." What he did not say was that he would also kill any Imperial who had a hand in her kidnapping, even if that Imperial was Katzenjammer Smelt.

"And I shall be there at your side." Balthazar said calmly. "But we shall do it my way. Promise me that you shall wait, and we shall do it my way."

Buckle stared at Balthazar. He did not want to promise. Balthazar would let other considerations take precedence and delay the search. He wanted to strike out on his own and find Elizabeth—he also realized that Balthazar knew exactly what he was thinking. "I promise," Buckle croaked. He felt as if he had just stabbed himself in the soul.

It was the first promise he had ever given to Balthazar that he was not sure he could keep.

⊣LXXXVI⊢

IT IS A WAR COMING

BUCKLE ENTERED LADY ANDROMEDA'S CRAMPED infirmary cabin with a knot in his stomach. Surgeon Fogg had bundled her up warmly and sedated her; she rested in her bunk, pale as a porcelain doll, lost in a warm drowse.

"She is bleeding internally," Fogg had said, his exhausted eyes red rimmed, before he stepped out. "I must prepare for surgery."

Buckle took a long breath through his nose and exhaled. Scorpius was there, sitting beside Andromeda with her fine white hand cradled in his thick, scarred, dark brown fingers. Smelt stood at the foot of the bed, silent, ramrod straight, his monocle dangling at his collarbone, looking for all the world like a gruff but concerned father.

"She is truly a creature all her own," Scorpius whispered with admiration. "We had left her to rest. Someone must have come in and informed her of the impending duel. Even though she was so badly injured, she still had the will to climb up to the roof to give you two a piece of her mind."

"In the long run, she may have saved us all," Buckle said. He looked at Smelt, who nodded.

"She will be fine," Scorpius whispered. "She is tougher than any one of us, I assure you."

"Of that I have absolutely no doubt," Smelt said softly.

Buckle stood up. His right arm ached so badly he feared that the sword wound had sprung open again. "We shall go. Rest assured, Surgeon Fogg is an excellent physician, General Scorpius."

"I have faith in him," Scorpius replied.

Buckle nodded and stepped out into the main keel corridor. He paused as Smelt exited beside him, and then shut the light wooden door to Andromeda's cabin with a soft *click*.

Buckle and Smelt stood in an uneasy silence. Howard Hampton arrived with the chest of dueling pistols in his hands and Kellie trotting at his feet, looking bored.

"How is the beautiful lady?" Howard asked.

"Resting well," Buckle replied.

Howard offered the box up to Buckle. "I recovered your equipment, Captain. I also took the liberty of unloading the pistols."

"Thank you, Howard," Buckle said. "Now off to your duties like a good lad, and take Kellie with you."

"Aye, Captain. Come on, girl." Howard saluted and took ahold of Kellie, who looked interested in being anywhere else but there, by the collar.

Buckle watched Howard and Kellie depart down the corridor, passing teams of crew persons on various errands of repair.

"It appears that the highly persuasive Lady Andromeda has made us unlikely allies for the moment, Captain Buckle," Smelt said.

"Yes," Buckle replied. "And I shall honor our pact. But know that I shall never, ever, even for one instant, ever trust in you, sir."

Smelt's eyes narrowed. "Although you have grievously wronged me, sir, in the illegal taking of my airship—and in that action it was you and not I who broke our truce a year ago—I must also thank you for rescuing me along with your Balthazar yesterday. And in return for my freedom, let me say this to you: I swear, upon my honor, that the Imperials had nothing to do with the attack upon your stronghold at Tehachapi."

Buckle scrutinized Smelt for a long moment. He sensed that the man was telling him the truth, but his mind was swimming in an abyss of suspicion, and what he sensed confused him. He did not trust his own gut. Surely Smelt, the trickster, was lying to him. "If not you, then who was it?" Buckle asked.

"That, I cannot say for certain," Smelt replied. "But we both know who would be interested in setting our two clans at war with each other, do we not?"

Buckle could no longer dangle about the question marks in his mind. Dusk had fallen. He still wanted to check in on Ivan before he tried to get the *Pneumatic Zeppelin* airborne again. He offered the chest of dueling pistols to Smelt.

"What is this?" Smelt asked with surprise.

"A gift. To commemorate our new alliance."

"It is far too extravagant," Smelt said, almost backing up. "I cannot accept."

"But you must," Buckle pressed.

Smelt carefully took the wooden box from Buckle. "It is a magnificent gift. But I still want my airship back."

"Then keep them safe," Buckle said, turning to walk down the corridor. "Perhaps we shall have the opportunity to use them again."

Buckle reached the door of infirmary cabin number three and rapped his knuckles across it.

"Pretty girls enter," Ivan's muffled voice came from within. "All others go away!"

Buckle swung the door open and stepped inside. The small infirmary chamber was dark despite a small buglight, where the fireflies glowed unenthusiastically inside the lantern glass.

"Hello, Ivan," Buckle said brightly, even though he did not feel bright.

"Hello, Romulus," Ivan said, his voice too raspy and weak to make Buckle comfortable. Ivan's head and shoulders were propped up by a pillow as he lay on the bunk. Pushkin poked his fuzzy head in and out of the breast pocket of his white infirmary tunic.

"I heard you got a little crisped last night," Buckle said. "But Fogg says you will be fine."

Ivan smiled, at least with the side of his face that was not covered by bandages. All that was visible of him was his right eye, his nose, and the right side of his mouth. "I'll be right as rain in a couple of days. Nothing worse than a bad sunburn here, really. Just need to rest up a bit."

"Good to hear, old salt," Buckle said as he sat on the edge of the bunk. "I would be most irritated if I had to try and find a new chief mechanic on this forsaken island."

"I hear they are a penny a dozen anyway, Cap'n." Ivan grinned and winced.

"You saved the entire ship, you know."

"What? By letting a steampiper bomb go off in the middle of the forward gasbags?"

Buckle laughed. "No. You did not let them position the bomb. Had that happened, *inside* the stockings, we would all surely be fish food now."

"Bah!" Ivan snorted. "I did nothing more than get myself blown up. If they make medals for that, I'll let them pin one on me."

"By the way, a repair team found that flea-bitten dead rat you call a hat," Buckle announced. With a flourish, he pulled Ivan's ushanka out of his pocket. The fur cap was singed and missing most of its left earflap, but he knew that would not matter so much to Ivan—he loved that damned hat.

Ivan grinned and winced again, planting the mangled ushanka on top of his head bandages. "My ushanka!" he exclaimed. "How am I looking, brother?"

"Like a true Russian mechanic."

Ivan nodded and sighed. "Yes, I am looking spiffy. And right now the enthralling Holly Churchill, standing outside the playhouse back home, is wondering why I stood her up, and planning never to speak to me ever again."

"I think she will give you a pass on this one."

Ivan's eyes turned serious. "How is the ship?"

"In one piece, more or less," Buckle said, stepping to the door. "We'll be back on our way in a matter of minutes."

"It is a war coming, isn't it, Romulus?"

Buckle paused. "Looks like it. So rest up, you crazy Bolshevik. You're going to be needed."

"Aye, Cap'n. Aye."

~LXXXVII~

TO THE END OF THE WORLD

WHEN BUCKLE CAME DOWN THE companionway into the piloting gondola, he found his bridge crew, indeed the entire airship, ready and waiting. Sabrina, Kellie, Welly, Nero, Max, De Quincey, and Wong all stood poised at their stations, along with Sergeant Scully and his blackbang rifle, posted to the gondola until the *Pneumatic Zeppelin* was safely off the ground. The great rent on the port side of the chamber was temporarily sealed with wood panels, a strikingly ugly backdrop to the elegance of the rest of the interior.

Everything was quiet as Buckle plugged in. His top hat gurgled, hissed, and steamed. "All right, let's get some air under our feet, right now," he said, leaning into the chattertube. "All hands prepare to up ship, emergency launch. I repeat, though do not make me repeat it again, all hands prepare for emergency launch."

"All hands ready, Captain," Sabrina said. "Eighty-six souls aboard."

Buckle winked at Nero. "Ballast. Release all hydrogen into the cells. Slam, bang. Up ship!"

"Aye, Captain," Nero responded, cranking his hydrogen reserve-tank wheels. "All hydrogen across the board. Slam, bang!"

The mighty, eerie hiss of every reserve hydrogen tank heaving open along the length of the ship filled the air. The *Pneumatic Zeppelin* trembled like a baby bird with new wings.

"Come on, old girl," Buckle said. "It's your sky."

The airship released a mighty shudder and groan.

"Reserve tanks empty, Captain!" Nero shouted. "All cells close to maximum capacity."

The *Pneumatic Zeppelin* surged, slowly, even on her keel. She creaked at every joint, knot, and cable as she escaped upward from the press of the earth. The swirling yellow buglights rocked gently outside the gondola, everything inside floating in the bioluminescent green glow of boil in the glass —altimeter dials, deflection pointers, water compasses, gyroscopes, thermometers, thermohygrometers, and the inclinometers with their bubbles. And then the behemoth lifted free with a great sigh of canvas, a small moon breaking away into the moonlit sky.

Buckle's heart rejoiced with the air under his feet, the sway of the deck cradling his spirit. "Good girl! Good girl!" he shouted. "Max! You and your repair teams are wizards."

"Thank you, Captain," Max responded, all business, her eyes close on her instruments. "Positive buoyancy holding steady."

"Ten feet altitude," Sabrina announced, watching her dials. "Twenty feet. Equilibrium good. Static inertia good. Thirty feet."

A voice crackled through the chattertube hood. "Emergency! Emergency! Prisoner has escaped!"

"Of course this could not have gone smoothly," Buckle said in a droll tone.

"He jumped!" the chattertube voice screamed. "Blue bloody blazes! He jumped! Starboard side!"

Scully leapt to the open starboard gunwale, leveraging his musket over the rail.

Buckle stepped to the gunwale alongside Scully and peered down at the dark, silvery-white mass of Catalina Island, now forty feet below.

"There he is!" Scully shouted, swinging his musket to take aim. The steampiper prisoner had appeared, dashing through a snowy ravine; he was still locked into his wrist manacles, but he had gotten free of his leg irons somehow.

Buckle pushed Scully's barrel aside. "Let him go, Sergeant."

Scully gave Buckle an incredulous look. Then he nodded. "Aye, Captain Buckle. Letting him go, sir."

Buckle ducked back into the gondola and replaced De Quincey at the helm wheel, wanting to feel the life of the rudder with his own hands. He felt strangely encouraged that he had let the steampiper live. There would be far too much killing for anyone's taste in the days to come.

"Eighty-five souls aboard," Sabrina announced with a wry smile in her voice.

"Ninety feet," Welly said.

Buckle could have kissed his zeppelin, his giant daughter, as she rose into the darkling night. The familiar gray clouds, forever shrouding the moon, supported the soft ceiling of the sky, while the black sea anchored the earth beneath. The *Pneumatic Zeppelin* was a happy shadow, slipping through the netherworld, heading for home.

"All ahead standard," Buckle said into the chattertube, cocking the chadburn handle forward, ringing the bell. The engineering bell rang immediately after, the sister dial cranking round to match the position of the first.

"All ahead standard, aye!" echoed the affirmation from engineering.

Buckle looked at his crew, nestled around him on the bridge, and felt more fatherly toward them than he ever had before. "We shall get home safe and sound, I am certain, my friends," he said. "But there are many trials and tribulations ahead. Of that we can be certain as well."

Everyone nodded.

"Aye. We know this," Sabrina replied. "And each and every one of us is with you for the long haul, Captain. We shall follow you to the end of the world."

"Wherever fate might cast us?" Buckle asked warmly, smiling at the strong faces around him. And what of the mysteries afoot in the underground of his mind: the looming threat of the Founders, the tangled tales of Katzenjammer Smelt, Sabrina's red hair, and where Elizabeth might be at that very moment?

"To the end of the world it is then, mates," Captain Romulus Buckle said, cranking the rudder wheel over to starboard. "To the end of the world."

THE END

ACKNOWLEDGMENTS

EVERY NOVEL IS A LABOR of love, and there are many wonderful people who have shared this journey with me. I am fortunate to be the son of Richard and Janet Preston, my stalwart patrons, whose inexhaustible love and support have always fueled my sense of who I am and what I must do. My wife and eagle-eyed reader, Shelley, whose love, positivity, and enthusiasm keeps me afloat, and our two daughters, Sabrina and Amelia, who inspire every word I write. I must also thank my sisters, Marsha and Joanna, and all of the family and friends who have lavished me with encouragement along the way.

Special thanks go out to Julia Kenner, a tremendous writer and friend, who generously opened doors for the manuscript. I must also thank Trident Media Group and my first agent, the fantastic Adrienne Lombardo, who championed this book and believed in Romulus Buckle as much as I did. Heartfelt thanks go out to my new agent, Alyssa Eisner Henkin, my brilliant caretaker, who is currently constructing ambitious plans for our future. I also owe a huge debt of gratitude to my wizardly and most patient editor Alex Carr and everyone on my 47North team, and also to my incomparable development editor, Jeff VanderMeer.

I must also express my thanks to Kellie, a little dog whose memory, in some lovely, wonderful way, inspired the writing of this steampunk series.

ABOUT THE AUTHOR

 RICHARD ELLIS PRESTON, JR. IS fascinated by the steampunk genre, which he sees as a unique storytelling landscape. *Romulus Buckle and the City of the Founders* is the first installment in his new steampunk series, The Chronicles of the Pneumatic Zeppelin. Richard has also written for film and television. He lives in California and haunts Twitter @RichardEPreston.